WITH HIS PERMISSION

11 SWEET AND FILTHY WIFE SHARING STORIES

LACEY CROSS

A HOTWIFE REUNION

HOTWIFE HOLIDAYS 1

CHAPTER 1

The garage door grinds open, vibrating the wall that separates my home office from our garage. I quickly type out a message to my best friend, Jessica, on the app we use to chat during the workday.

MIRI

Shit, gotta go. Hubby is home and it's my night to cook dinner.

She gives my message a laughing emoji.

JESSICA

See you on Saturday. Tell him takeout is on the way!

Ooh, she's brilliant. I'm totally going to do that. I give her a thumbs-up and close the program.

Jessica and I have been texting back and forth for hours today while we pretended to work. We were discussing a trip we're taking to the Oregon coast this weekend, a reunion of sorts, with a group of our closest friends from high school and their spouses. Jessica is leaving tomorrow to spend a couple of extra days there with her husband, Lucas, before our Saturday gathering.

I quickly open a spreadsheet before my husband, Joey, finds out it's been social hour all day. I want to maintain the illusion that I've been diligently working while he slaved away, crunching numbers for "the man." Tipping back in my chair to peek out the door of the office, I spy him coming down the hall towards me and exchange a smile with him. Desire ripples through me at the sight of him in his suit and his tousled brown hair. It looks like he was running his fingers through it recently, and it gives him a rakish appearance. Dang, I married a sexy man.

He comes in, sets his leather work bag down, and kisses my forehead. "Hey, baby."

"Hi, my love. How was work?" I appreciate the forehead kiss, but what I really want is a panty-melting kiss with lots of tongue.

My job affords me a ton more freedom than his does, so I try to not bug him on instant messenger all day. He gets focused and in the zone, so I save up any news for when he gets home. He's a certified public accountant with one of the biggest CPA firms in our town, mainly working with clients in the wine industry. Between the two of us, he's the one bringing home the bacon.

I have a fabulous job, but I don't make a ton of money. I got lucky by being Jessica's best friend. As soon as I saw her sitting all alone in the school cafeteria in seventh grade and reading my favorite book, I introduced myself and we've been besties ever since. Her family had recently moved to town, and she's an introvert who never would have approached me. She was always daydreaming and had her head in the clouds back then, and she turned that into a creative writing career.

One of Jessica's smutty reverse harem vampire stories exploded four years ago, and after a year of trying to juggle everything herself as an indie author, she finally begged me to work for her full time as her personal assistant. I've been doing that for about three years now, and it brought out hidden marketing talents in me. She only has to worry about writing, and I take care of most everything else for her.

She pays me enough to make me happy but also not feel bad if I goof off or have an unproductive day. She claims I pay for myself in increased sales, so she doesn't care when I work as long as I keep up with what needs done. I basically have my dream job at 33; I don't clock in, I can do whatever I want, and I listen to music all day. Life is good… or it would be if I were getting more sex.

Now that I have a flexible job, at some point Joey and I plan on trying for a baby. I'll be the primary caregiver while he's at work. We keep putting it off, though, so I'm not sure it will actually happen. The older we get, the more we appreciate being child-free, especially when we want to take spontaneous trips. But even the trips have slowed down in recent years.

He takes his time before answering how his day went and removes his suit jacket. When he unbuttons his shirt, my pussy perks up. It's been over a week since we've had sex, which isn't that uncommon anymore. Normally when I'm horny, I take care of myself with my extensive collection of sex toys, but Jessica distracted me today with chatting about high school and theorizing how different our friends will be when we see them this weekend.

Joey sighs and rolls his head as if he's trying to loosen his neck muscles. "Work was… work. But I'm glad to be home, and you're looking cute today." He grins at me and my pussy tries to remind me again that she hasn't been plowed recently.

I wonder what my chances of getting some sex are tonight? It's Wednesday, and despite the jokes about hump day, there usually isn't any humping in my household on Wednesdays unless it's me going to town with my vibrator. I agree with him, though; I'm feeling quite cute in my favorite cotton pajama pants with penguins on them and a white lace corset-style top that molds to my breasts and shows my cleavage to its full advantage. Yeah, I put this on at lunchtime on purpose, hoping to lure him into bed tonight. Since he didn't walk in and immediately bend me over the desk, my chances seem low.

My husband isn't a man of many words, so I'm not surprised that he doesn't elaborate on his workday. I always make an effort to show interest in his job, but from what I can tell, it's reeeaaaalllly boring. He never shares funny stories about the office, and I sometimes wonder what happened to the man I married. He was the goofy class clown, and now he's the dependable, married for 14 years, barely having sex, accountant.

He doesn't take his shirt off once it's unbuttoned, and disappointment runs through me. He gets up early three times a week to go to the gym before work, and I was hoping for an eyeful of his sexy man pecs. If I'm not getting a hard boning tonight, I could at least enjoy some eye candy. I haven't given up hope yet though. I might need to get some tasty food in his belly and then jump him after dinner when he's relaxed.

Almost as if he read my mind, he says, "So what's for dinner?"

Oh shit, right... dinner. Damn Jessica and her distractions.

"Oh, I thought we should do teriyaki delivery since we need to pack for the trip tomorrow night. No need to mess up the kitchen." Knowing my excuse is flimsy, I give him my cutest smile and bat my eyelashes at him.

He laughs. "Okay, and I'm sure you've already ordered it… right?"

I vigorously nod my head and widen my green eyes innocently. "Oh, yes. Why don't you change into something comfortable and it'll be here before you know it."

He goes to leave but pauses in the doorway and glances back at me. "Miri, bring that top you're wearing on the trip this weekend. I have an idea."

Ooh, what's this? I'm instantly wet and squirm in my chair once he's gone. I'd like to think his idea is me wearing it while he fucks me, but I have a sneaking suspicion he's talking about something else. Staring at the empty doorway for a few moments, I contemplate what he might ask me to do this weekend.

It's a cruel joke that women sexually peak in their 30s. By this age, we've got busy lives, and possibly kids, and a lot more responsibilities. It's not as easy to stay up all night having wild sex when you're a responsible adult who can't blow off work the next day. That's why I'm looking forward to the trip this weekend. Joey and I always have trip sex. I told him once it was a hidden clause in our marriage vows, and he chuckled and agreed. So I WILL get some vacation sex, goddammit!

I order dinner online and think about what he said. His interest in my top intrigues me because we've been talking the last couple of months about broadening our sexual horizons to spice things up. We had a frank discussion about our lack of sex, and he admitted that work is stressful and since he gets up early for the gym some days, he isn't in the mood that often during the work week. He assured me he still thought I was hot and he wanted to have sex with me. And while I intellectually understood that, I still missed the 4-5 times-per-week sex we were having in our 20s. I mean shit, right now I'd settle for once per week and consider myself lucky.

Joey's idea of spicing up our love life was not anything I expected, and he floored me with the suggestion that maybe I would like to be a hotwife and he would allow it as a way for me to satisfy my urges. I learned what a hotwife was from Jessica because she and her husband have an arrangement like that, where he chooses guys for her from a listing on an app and then she has one-night stands with them. I don't know how often they do it, but she said it's pretty fabulous.

At first I thought Joey was afraid I was going to divorce him if I didn't get more sex, and I tried to tell him I was perfectly happy with my toys, but he admitted that after I told him what Jessica and her husband were doing, he did online research and found the idea hot. And it's just like my husband to frame something as helping me out when it's really his dirty fantasy that I fuck a bunch of men.

One thing we both agreed on was that we wouldn't rush into something like that without discussing boundaries and expectations. We've taken this time to talk things out, and I told him recently that if the right opportunity presents itself, I'd like to give it a go. Of course, once I agreed to that, I've been horny as all hell for the last two weeks and masturbating practically daily. So whatever plan he has for me and this tight lace shirt this weekend, I'm down for it.

CHAPTER 2

Joey took Friday and Monday off work, and we're making the ten-hour drive from Washington State to Gold Beach, Oregon, in one day. We planned to do all the packing after work on Thursday so we could be ready to walk out the door early Friday morning. Since we're staying at a vacation rental home, we don't need to bring much and we agreed to keep it down to one bag each to avoid a car full of unnecessary supplies.

While we pack, I grumble about the drive. "I wish we could have picked somewhere closer. Ten hours is going to suck."

"You know why. Jeff lives in L.A. so this was the most central location for everyone."

I stick my tongue out at him when he's not looking. I hate it when he's logical while I'm complaining. Joey and I've been dating since we were 16, and we got married at 19. In high school we ran in a group with four other people, but only three of them could make it this weekend. Joey was disappointed to find out Zane, his best friend in high school, wasn't coming. Everyone else is bringing their spouse or significant other with them, which means four couples.

Joey and Zane had drifted apart over the years, so all the information I learned about Zane since after we left school came from Jessica.

She told me that he was unmarried and owned a bar in Montana and couldn't take the time off. I wasn't sad to discover he couldn't come. Zane and I have a complicated past, and I'd had a major crush on him originally instead of Joey. Zane had that alluring bad boy vibe, and Joey was his goofy sidekick. Like most misguided young girls, I wasn't interested in the goofball and I craved the excitement of the bad boy.

I was half in love with Zane from when I met him at age 14 until we were 16. Things got heated one night at a Halloween party where Zane and I had an intense make-out session that bordered on actual sex. I've debated over the years what defines sex, since we both orgasmed, but all we did was touch with our hands and kiss. Afterwards I thought we would end up dating or at the very least hooking up again. I expected Zane to be the first cock inside me, but after the party he ignored me for weeks. I don't know what happened since he and I never talked about it, but his rejection hurt more than I wanted to admit and I asked Joey out on a date in retaliation.

My "Fuck you, I'll date your best friend" attitude was childish, but it turned out to be the best decision of my life. Once Joey was out of a group setting and dropped the class clown routine, I found out he was smart and thoughtful. Within a few months I was over Zane, and Joey and I were officially an item. The only problem was that whenever I was around Zane, I could sense he was watching me and my body still reacted to him. He and Joey were inseparable, so there was no way to avoid him, and I never felt at ease around him.

I'm sure 18 years changes a lot of things, but I'm still secretly pleased he won't be there this weekend. I've never told Joey about my history with Zane, and as far as I know, he's not aware that Zane and I had our hands down each other's pants at the party.

Trying to get focused on the packing so it doesn't take all night, I scrunch eight pairs of panties into tiny balls and shove them towards the bottom of my travel bag. I sense I'm being watched, and when I glance up, Joey is standing across the bed in front of his open bag, amused.

"What disaster is going to befall us on this trip that requires so many panties?"

He knows me well and laughs at me every time we take a trip since

I always pack twice as much underwear as needed. I always have an excuse, and I grin at him. "It's the coast. What if there's a tsunami and we're stranded for days?"

Panties are the one piece of clothing I can't stand to wear unless they're clean. Even in an absolute emergency, I'm more likely to go commando than wear the previous day's panties.

"Uh-huh" is his only reply, and I grab a pillow from the bed and toss it at his head. He catches it easily and laughs.

I continue packing, ignoring his teasing. "We should have told everyone to go to Cannon Beach. It's closer."

"That would have been too far for Jeff."

"Yeah, but they filmed *The Goonies* there. How could anyone resist that?"

With everyone's various travel arrangements, the full group is only getting together on Saturday. The rest of the trip is our own, and I would have loved to sit on the beach and stare out at the ocean from the movie.

Joey snorts. "Who even remembers that movie?"

I narrow my eyes at him and grab another pillow, ready to chuck it at him. He's treading on dangerous territory if he disparages my favorite movie as a kid.

"I'll have you know LOTS of people loved that movie."

His eyes twinkle at me when he responds. "Yeah, old people, since it came out before we were born."

I huff at him but set the pillow down. He might have a point. Most of my friends growing up had never watched it before meeting me. I corrected the oversight quickly with everyone, and one of my first dates with Joey was a movie night in my parents' basement that included *The Goonies* and some heavy petting afterwards. The movie didn't turn us on, but we were 16 and in a secluded basement watching a movie… what else was going to happen?

"Okay, Mr. Funny Guy, get your stuff packed so you're not dragging ass in the morning when I'm ready to leave."

He just grins at me and keeps folding his clothes meticulously while I toss mine into a gigantic pile and attempt to shove it all into one bag. There is no way this will all fit, but I refuse to give up without trying. Every trip we take, I'm the one who isn't ready to leave on time, but I always pin the blame on him. Last trip we were running late because *HE* hadn't remembered to pack my make-up kit, so I had to rush back into the house to grab it.

"Hey, Miri?"

My bag is overflowing and I'm eyeing the small pile of clothing that didn't make it in, debating whether I need to break the one-bag rule. I give him a casual, "Hmm?" Do I really need a second bathing suit? We're only going to have two full days there, so am I going to visit the beach more than once? Plus, it's Oregon and not a tropical vacation; it's probably going to be cold, even in June.

"Did you remember to pack the white lace top?"

A zing of pleasure rushes through my core at his words. You bet your ass I did, but I try to sound nonchalant about it. "Oh, yeah, I think it's in there. Why do you want me to bring it?"

His "You'll see" is mysterious and gives me a jolt of excitement.

I pluck some clothes out and sort them while I think about his request. My only guess is that he plans on having me wear it in public, and I grow wet at the thought. The lace leaves nothing to the imagination, and it's not designed to have a bra underneath it. In the right lighting, someone would see the color and shape of my nipples. Why is this idea so hot?

I start to suggest we have some pre-vacation sex, but Joey lets out an enormous yawn at that exact moment so I quickly close my mouth and go back to my packing. I can be patient. He knows I'm expecting sex on the trip, so I'm confident it will happen. If I play my cards right, maybe I'll get it twice.

CHAPTER 3

By the time we make it to the vacation house, we've been on the road for over 12 hours when you count in rest stops and food breaks. Fuck, this was a long way to drive in one day. On the drive we decided to unpack when we arrived and get an early night's sleep so that we're refreshed to visit with everyone tomorrow. As we pull into the long driveway at last, it's early evening, so nothing exciting is happening tonight.

The house we rented is an adorable bungalow a few blocks from the ocean. We can't see the water from here, but we only have to walk to the end of the street and pass a couple of houses to get to the beach. It's decorated in a nautical theme, and since it's small, it only takes a few minutes to explore the house while Joey hauls in his one bag and my two. He agreed to hit the grocery store close by and heads out to do that while I unpack my bags. It doesn't take me long since I basically just dump it all in one of the dresser drawers, but I spend some time organizing our joint bathroom supplies and admiring the large walk-in shower.

When Joey calls out, "I'm home," I go out to give him a kiss and help him unload the groceries. We're having a barbecue tomorrow with everyone, so Joey grabbed chips, buns, and a bunch of soda and beer. I wrinkle my nose at the beer. I should have requested hard cider since I can't stand the taste of beer.

We're both yawning after we eat a simple dinner of hoagie roll sandwiches, but we spend some time unwinding on two Adirondack chairs on the screened-in porch. We're tired, but somehow neither of us wants to go to bed yet. Even though we can't see the ocean, we can hear it. The salty night breeze through the screen and the crash of the ocean lulls us.

Joey eventually breaks the silence. "I'm glad we came. I'm already feeling relaxed."

The chairs are close enough together that I'm able to reach over and hold his hand. I know he tries to downplay the stress from his job, and I'm glad to see he's able to shake it off quickly for this trip.

I give his hand a squeeze and entwine my fingers with his. "Yeah, this is nice."

He wants to go to bed before I do, but I join him, intending to read for a bit. I loaded up some new books on my e-reader for the trip, but I'm asleep within minutes of my head hitting the pillow.

We wake up later than we meant to, but the solid sleep felt pretty damn amazing and I'm refreshed and pumped for today. Jessica lives in Oregon so I only see her a couple of times a year, but we talk or message each other almost daily. I stayed in touch with her after we were out of school, but I haven't seen or talked to Jeff or Shelly in years and I'm excited to see them again. Jeff is a software engineer in California, and he's bringing his husband with him, whom I've never met. Shelly is an elementary school teacher and still lives in Washington, but since she's across the state from me, we didn't keep in contact like we should have. She's bringing her fiancé with her, and Jessica knows nothing about him other than that Shelly said he was wonderful.

It's easy to let the years drift when everyone has busy lives. Joey was in school for six years, and I worked full time while he was getting his B.S. in Accounting and his Masters of Business Administration. Then we moved across the state because he got the job offer with the

CPA firm he still works for. That first year was hectic while he was studying for the CPA exam and I was trying to get settled into a crappy job I hated. We always intended for me to go back to school once he got established, but it never happened and now I'm content as Jessica's assistant. If we ever have a kid, I might consider school again when they're older, or maybe not… who knows. I'm mostly happy, and that's all that really matters.

I'd been hoping for morning vacation sex, but since we got up late, we have to rush to get ready. We're meeting Jessica and her hubby at the house they rented in an hour to help get ready before everyone shows up for lunch.

Joey makes us coffee while I claim the bathroom first. I'm impressed by the spacious tiled shower with a built-in bench. The house might be small, but they didn't skimp on some of the nicer vacation amenities. Right when I finish rinsing the shampoo out of my long brown hair, the glass shower door slides open and Joey joins me. My pussy perks up and my nipples pucker. Oooh, shower sex time?

I give him a seductive smile and wink. "Well, hello there."

"If we shower together, it'll save time."

His voice has a dry tone, and I can't tell if he's joking or if he really thinks showering with me will save us time. I press my wet body against his and slip my arms around his neck, pulling him down for a deep kiss. Our tongues dance and I give a soft, "Mmmm," when I taste coffee. Since I haven't had caffeine yet, I want to gobble him all up.

I'm still soapy, and my hard nipples are sensitive as they glide across his hairy chest. Desire consumes me. God, it's been far too long since I've had his cock inside me, and I evaluate how long it will take me to come. I'm turned on, but we probably really don't have time for sex. I'm not at the boiling point where he only has to slide inside me and I'll explode. So unless I want to be a needy mess with a pussy full of cum today, I shouldn't press for more than what we're doing already.

My resolve lasts until his erection bumps against me. Shit, I'm sure Jessica won't mind if we're late. Joey presses me against the wall of the shower and I run a hand down his chest and stomach until I reach his cock. He eases back a little to give more room between us, and I stroke him slowly.

He groans, and his voice is thick with lust. "I wish we had more time."

As he nibbles on my neck, I pout. "We could be late."

I gasp when he pinches one of my nipples. "Miri, behave. Jessica and Lucas are expecting us. Do you want to tell them you were a greedy slut who couldn't wait until later?"

Oh, fuck. I love it when he calls me a slut and I've hinted he could call me filthier things, but he never does. Jessica would understand if I told her we were late because I was getting railed in the shower. But I don't know her husband that well and it would make the conversation awkward if he was around.

I sigh, "No, I suppose not."

He steps away from me, and I hog the water for a quick rinse.

I tease, "Since you refuse to fuck me, I need coffee," and blow him a kiss as I get out of the shower.

I towel off and I head into the bedroom. While picking out my favorite pair of jeans and a red silk blouse to wear tonight, I can hear Joey clearly when he starts singing a made-up song about a woman who bangs a bunch of guys in her neighborhood. Giggling, I'm light-hearted as I get dressed; looks like the goofball in him didn't totally disappear.

CHAPTER 4

The house Jessica and Lucas rented is a mansion compared to our bungalow, and through the backyard you can walk over some sand dunes directly to the ocean. Lucas is an actuary, and I'm not totally sure what that is, but it has something to do with statistics and pays well. Between his income and her writing career, they aren't hurting. They seem to take lavish trips a few times per year, and I'm always envious. I wish Joey would take vacations with me more often.

"Shelly told me they were camping instead of renting something this weekend."

I'm sitting on a bar stool at the kitchen counter, helping Jessica chop vegetables for the food trays. I'm not sure why Jessica is the social director for everyone, but I appreciate she has all the insider info. She's been chattering nonstop about everyone since we arrived.

I shrug at her. "Well, she's a teacher and vacation rentals during peak season aren't cheap, you know."

Does Jessica actually know this? I never really thought about it much, but it's possible she and her husband are more well off than I realized. I know what she brings in and it's nothing to sneeze at, but I don't know what actuaries get paid other than it's good money.

Jessica pauses the chopping on a head of cauliflower. "Oh, should I have invited them to stay here?"

I laugh. "No, there are people who actually like to camp. She could be one of them. What do we really know about any of them anymore?"

She starts chopping again. "Well, you said you're a slut who tried to get Joey to fuck you in the shower today, so I know a few things about some people."

A blush creeps over me and I peek towards the sliding glass door to the patio, where Joey and Lucas are fussing over a fancy gas grill. Since the patio door is closed, they can't hear our conversation, and I breathe a sigh of relief. They're not even looking our way, they're on the deck and acting all macho because they know how to turn on the grill, but Jessica and I are happy to perpetuate the myth that they are gods if it gets us out of grilling.

"Hey, pipe down," I hiss at Jessica. "The entire world doesn't need to know how big of a slut I am."

A cough from the kitchen entryway behind me startles me.

A deep, masculine voice speaks. "Should I come back later?"

I whip around in my chair and lock eyes with my vision of what Adonis should look like… if Adonis were tattooed with piercing blue eyes, looked like he might be part of a biker gang, and had the name Zane. Holy fuck, what is he doing here?

Jessica squeals, drops her knife on the counter, and runs over to give him a hug. "You came!"

Watching Zane's hands as he encircles Jessica and gives her a bear hug that lifts her off the floor creates a fluttery sensation in my stomach. My heart pounds in my chest, and the room is uncomfortably warm.

Zane looks at me over Jessica's shoulder. "Hello, Miri."

I know I'm flushed, but I try to keep my voice normal. "Hi, Zane. Glad you could make it."

The guys on the patio must have noticed the commotion because the glass door slides open and Joey bursts in, excited.

"Hey, I thought you weren't coming."

Zane and Joey punch each other's arm, and Zane laughs. "Your email changed my mind."

Wait, Joey emailed Zane to ask him to come and he didn't tell me? I'm flustered and confused, and my entire body tingles every time I look at Zane. The years might have changed some things, but not the way I'm reacting to him. I try to ignore the buzzing in my pussy as I look at his hands again. Now that I'm an adult and I understand sexual pleasure better, my body is even more interested in him than it was in high school. Fuuuck. I'm going to have to avoid him tonight as much as I can, and thankfully we're only getting together with everyone this one day.

I can't stop looking at his hands and imagining them caressing my body. He's larger than Joey and more muscular, and his hands are huge. I realize Joey is watching me with an unreadable expression, and I feel my cheeks flame an even brighter pink.

I swivel back around in my chair and busy myself cutting celery sticks. A moment later, the familiar woodsy scent of Joey's cologne engulfs me as he comes up behind me and kisses my neck.

He speaks softly enough that only I can hear. "It's nice the gang was all able to come, isn't it?"

"Yeah, it's nice," I echo back to him while emotions war inside me. I'm not sure I'd classify this as nice, but I don't want to be rude or have to explain why I wish Zane hadn't come.

The three men gravitate back out to the patio and Jessica and I continue the meal prep. She's bubbly and clearly thrilled that Zane is here.

"Dang, Zane is hotter than he was in high school. I think he melted my panties when he hugged me."

A moment of envy overwhelms me when I think about how she got to touch him.

I'm not really sure what to say, so I agree with her. "Yeah, and back then he could get any girl he wanted, so he probably has all the PTA moms in his town drooling over him now."

Jessica gives me a sharp glance. "Well, he couldn't have ANY girl he wanted, but most of them for sure."

Wait, did Jessica like him? I try to think back on who Jessica was dating in high school, but she had a string of boy toys wrapped around her finger and I can't pinpoint any one guy who lasted more than a couple of months. Oooh, did they hook up? Another swift jab of jealousy hits me, and I brush it aside. God, this is stupid. We're not still in high school and we're both married, except Jessica has an open marriage of sorts. Would her husband let her fuck Zane? Is this why she's so excited to see him?

An undefined emotion coils in my belly and I tell myself to calm the fuck down. Jessica can screw whoever she wants, and Zane can as well. I love Joey and I'm happy with him, no matter what sexy godlike creature walks past me.

Thinking about Joey helps soothe me. He really is the best thing that's happened in my life. I peer out the patio door and catch Joey's eye. We smile at each other, and a wave of contentment washes over me. I'll just think of Joey all night and stick close to his side.

By the time the rest of the guests arrive, lunch is ready and with the addition of four more people, the party gets lively and loud. Shelly surprises us all with her gently rounded tummy, which makes Jessica hiss at me that she should have invited them to stay because pregnant women shouldn't have to camp. I only laugh at her. It's not like Shelly is in her last trimester, and she doesn't even waddle yet. She is happy and has a beautiful pregnancy glow and sounds like she's enjoying the campsite.

Jeff and his husband are very much what one would expect from software developers who live in L.A. since they're very sophisticated and cultured. Both of them are sweet and the love between them is obvious. Jeff wasn't out in high school, but within our circle we sensed he was gay, even if he hadn't told us yet. It warms my soul to see him happy. I always wanted him to have the best in life because I could tell he sometimes struggled.

All through the meal, I keep catching Zane's eye. I flush every time and have to look away. His continued interest in me keeps my libido on a low simmer, and I want to squirm in my chair but force myself to sit still. Me squirming around would make Joey ask me what's wrong, and there is no way I want to tell him that Zane is getting me all worked up. Joey better be up to fucking me tonight because I'm going to need a rough pounding by the time we get to the rental home. There is only so much sexual tension a person can take without release.

After lunch, everyone wants to visit the ocean, so we trek out the back door and brave the sand dunes. Joey and I walk hand in hand, trailing behind the pack, and every step is laborious since my feet sink into the sand and it requires extra force to walk.

"Miri, I have an offer for you."

Oooh, his offer better include his cock in my pussy. I pause, and a tug on his hand makes him stop and turn towards me.

"If this involves you, me, and fucking behind a dune, count me in."

He laughs. "No, not exactly."

I pout at him. "Fine, what's this offer?"

He's quiet for a minute and stares out towards the ocean, and when he turns to me, his eyes are bright like he's excited. "How would you like one hour with Zane tonight?"

A trail of wetness leaks from my pussy and a thrill runs through me. I tell myself to calm down. There's no way he's offering to let me fuck Zane.

I laugh at him. "To do what?"

"Whatever you'd like" is his simple reply.

Uh, what? "Are you talking sex?"

"Yes."

Suddenly I feel like I'm in some weird-ass version of The Twilight Zone. Did my husband just offer me an hour with his best friend from high school? I'm about to tell him no when I realize there is a very definite bulge in his jeans. Holy fuck, he's hard at the thought. Knowing he's turned on makes the idea even hotter.

I try to save face and not reveal my true feelings even though my body is crying out yes. "Who says Zane even wants to have sex with me?"

Joey smiles. "He wouldn't have come if he wasn't interested. My offer was in the email I sent him."

My mouth flops open and all thoughts drain from my head. I'm not sure how long I stand there in shock, but when my brain clicks back on, all my senses go into hyper-drive. A bolt of electricity ripples through me and all the hairs on my arm stand up. I'm breathing rapidly, and my heart races.

To make sure there is no mistaking any of this, I look Joey straight in the eyes as I say, "Yes."

He squeezes my hand and tugs on it. "Then let's get this party over with so you can get your vacation sex."

CHAPTER 5

The rest of the party is a blur. It involves lots of beer, a bonfire, laughter, and some off-key singing after a few people get drunk. Someone produces my favorite hard cider, but I don't take any since I want to be sober tonight. I notice Zane isn't drinking either, and every time his smoldering gaze meets mine, lust explodes in my brain and I become tongue tied. I see Joey and Zane speaking together halfway through the gathering, and afterwards Joey tells me the plan is on, but he never actually says what the arrangement is.

When the party winds down, I hug Jessica goodbye. She can tell I'm distracted, but she doesn't question what's going on. Joey leads me to the car, and when we are both seated, he leans over and digs around in a bag on the floor behind me. He straightens up and drops my white lace top in my lap. Flabbergasted, I stare at it.

"Put that on."

"Here, in the car?" I peek out the window. It's dark, and no one else is around.

His voice is thick and I can tell he's incredibly turned on. "Yes, now."

I shrug out of my red blouse, take off my bra, and toss them both in the back seat. Joey is watching me intently, and he reaches over to play with a nipple. I pause and don't put the lace top on as pings of pleasure head straight for my clit. I almost want to tell him let's forget about the hour with Zane and he can take me back to our place and fuck me, but this is probably my once in a lifetime chance with Zane, and I'm going to take it.

When he stops pulling at my nipple, my pussy is a wet mess and my brain is fuzzy from desire.

"Put your shirt on. Zane is expecting us."

Uh… us? Is he planning to watch? I slip the shirt on, and I'm about to question him when he continues.

"I'm going to drop you off at his rental, and exactly one hour later, I'll pick you up. I expect you to come out to me. Don't make me come in and collect you."

Oh, fuck. Joey's being demanding, but this side of him is hot.

"Okay, my love."

"And if I ask, you'll tell me everything that he did to you."

I nod and realize he might not see it in the dark. "Yes."

Telling him everything that happens was something we previously discussed when talking about boundaries, and I already agreed to tell him anything I do with other men, but he obviously needed to hear it again.

Joey starts the car, and as he drives I adjust the top and settle my boobs in their correct position within the form-fitting lace. Since the town is small, it doesn't take us long to arrive at the tiny rented cottage. We park in front of the house, and Zane opens the front door as if he was watching for us out the window.

I unbuckle my seat belt and turn to Joey. "Love, are you sure you're okay with this? We can call it off right now."

He leans over and gives me a soft kiss. "I want us to try, and Zane is safe. I'll be back in an hour."

I give his hand a squeeze before opening the car door and climbing out. I guess I learned the reason for why he chose Zane. He wanted this first time to be with someone he felt we could both trust. I walk towards the house but can't help but look over my shoulder at Joey, and he's staring intently but doesn't try to stop me. I hear the car drive away as I reach Zane.

Zane steps back from the doorway. "Come in."

His voice is firm, and a shiver runs down my spine. He doesn't look like he's in a fun-loving mood, and I'm suddenly uncertain how this will go. But we only have an hour so we better not waste any time.

I walk past him and glance around the cute living room. His cottage also has a nautical theme, and I wonder if all the rentals use the same general concept when decorating rental houses close to the ocean.

Zane closes the front door with a loud click, and I hear the deadbolt turn. Hesitation filters through my brain. Why am I here? This is crazy. I don't know what he's been doing for the last 18 years. He could have been in prison for all I know.

I turn towards him right as he steps up to me and yanks me against his chest. I gasp as he swoops down and claims my mouth. His lips fuse to mine and my pussy clenches with need. He's not kissing me gently, and the passion excites me further. I throw myself into the kiss with the same intensity, and we devour each other.

All thoughts of this being crazy drain away as passion consumes me. I need to feel every inch of his skin against me, and I pull the hem of his shirt free from his jeans. He stops kissing me long enough to help, and then swiftly removes his shirt. He's got less chest hair than Joey has, and I start at his neck and nibble my way down his chest, exploring the differences between the two men. Other than Joey, Zane is the only other man who has ever had his hands on my pussy, and it feels like I've come full circle. I'm about to fulfill a fantasy from my youth.

"Miri?"

I sink to my knees and paw at the button and zipper on his jeans, suddenly desperate to see his cock.

"Miri, answer something for me."

I look up, and he stares down at me for a moment before cupping my face. He brushes his thumb along my lower lip.

"Why did you agree to this?"

I don't know what to say to him since I have so many reasons for doing this—Joey finds it hot, I've always wanted it, I was in love with him once, curiosity, wish fulfillment—but I can't say them all.

I go with the safe bet. "Curiosity."

My answer makes him smile. "Well, Ms. Curious Kitten, rumor has it you like it hard, and I'm going to give you what you want. Is that okay?"

Oooh fuck, Joey told him how I liked rough sex? A wave of love for my husband washes over me, and I nod. "Yes, fuck me hard, please."

Zane hauls me up off my knees and removes my top so fast my head spins. I'm going to laugh at Joey later and tell him I didn't need to wear it. He bends down and engulfs a nipple in his mouth and I sway against him as ripples of pleasure rush through me. It's surreal and erotic that someone other than Joey is sucking on my tit. I close my eyes and sink into the bliss as his mouth creates an inferno in my belly. He rolls the other nipple between his thumb and index finger to cause continuous spikes of delight to shoot down to my clit, and I moan loudly.

He stops sucking on my breast and tugs at the zipper on my jeans. I kick off my shoes, and when he has the jeans undone, he shoves me towards the couch. Wait, are we not going to the bedroom? I barely have the thought formed before he's bending me over the arm of the couch and dragging my jeans down.

He yanks them off and tosses them across the room with a soft thud. All I'm wearing now are blue satin panties and white ankle socks.

"Spread your legs," he commands, and I immediately comply.

When he rubs my pussy through the fabric, I moan some more. My panties are probably soaking wet, and he'll know how much I want him.

"Miri, there are a few rules for tonight that you have to obey."

"Mmm, yes."

My reply makes him snort. "You haven't even heard what they are yet."

I wiggle my ass and press against his hand, forcing him to rub harder. "Doesn't matter, it's a yes."

He sounds almost amused. "Oh no, that's not how this works. I'm going to tell you, and you'll agree or disagree."

Ugh, whatever. He knows we're on the clock, and I need his cock inside me. The sooner he stops talking, the sooner I get fucked.

"First; if I do anything you don't like or want me to stop, say red."

My brain buzzes. Did he just give me a safeword?

"Do you understand?"

I shimmy my hips, wishing he'd press his fingers into my pussy and pant out, "Yes… red… if I want to stop."

"Good girl." He slides his fingers underneath the band of my panties and slips them between my wet folds, finding my clit. I groan as he rubs circles against it.

"Next one: you aren't allowed to come without permission, and I may not let you. Joey said I could send you home to him without coming. Do you understand?"

What… the… fuck? My head spins with the thought that those two masterminded me not coming. What sort of fucked-up game is this? And yet, his fingers against my clit and the swirls of pleasure in my core tell me I would agree to anything to get his cock inside me.

He dips two fingers into my wet pussy and starts finger-fucking me roughly. "Do you understand, Miri?"

Ooooh, fuck. "Yes, I understand. No coming without permission!"

"Good girl. Now, are you ready to be fucked?"

"Yesssss," I groan out as he speeds up the slamming of his fingers inside my wet hole.

Zane removes his hands and slides my panties down. A rush of cool air hits my inflamed pussy lips, and I shiver. I hear him removing his jeans and as soon as they drop to the floor, his cock is against my pussy and he slams into me.

"Ooooh, fuck!" I cry out as he grasps my hips with both hands and starts hammering against me. His cock is bigger than Joey's, and he's stretching me out as I've never been before.

"You know what other rumor I heard, Miri?"

The couch creaks as he fucks me, and I'm having a difficult time thinking while that monster cock of his is massaging nerve endings I didn't know existed. Does he expect an answer?

"What?" I half pant, half squeal as he thrusts deep and hard.

"Someone told me you like to be called vulgar names."

I don't even know how to respond. Since Joey never said more than 'slut', I didn't think he was paying attention when I hinted for more. My mind blanks as he drills away at my pussy.

"Answer me, Miri. Do you want to be called a filthy whore?"

I groan, "Yes," when he whacks against my pussy and the intense pleasure is almost too much.

"Is that what you are?"

He draws out all the way, and I immediately miss the thrill of being stretched out. I mewl in protest.

"Tell me Miri. Tell me what you are, and I'll put my cock back in."

Fuck. I'll say anything to get his cock. "I'm a filthy whore. Please fuck me!"

He rewards me with a, "Good girl," and plunges back into me.

Zane is quiet for a bit as he bulldozes my pussy. Each thrust spirals me higher and higher, and sparks of rapture threaten to explode the closer I get to my orgasm. He never said what would happen if I don't ask to come, so I don't tell him how close I'm getting.

"Miri, rub your clit."

When I don't immediately do as he says, he growls, "NOW."

I slip my hand between my legs and brush against my clit in the perfect rhythm. My thigh muscles quiver with each stroke. I'm teetering on the precipice, and I can't take much more of this. I can tell I'm going to come at any moment.

Panting and moaning with each nudge of his cock, I know I've never been this completely full, nor have I ever been this frantic for an orgasm. It's going to be horrible if I don't have one, which is why I'm not asking if I can come.

Just as I'm about to tip over the edge, he pulls out fully.

"Noooo! Oh god, please fuck me. Please?"

Zane chuckles at my neediness. "Don't worry, I'm going to fuck you again and fill you with my cum. But I think you almost came without asking me something."

Oh fuck. I peep out a small, "Yes."

He slides back in, and I involuntarily buck from the pleasure.

His tone is harsh, but amused. "I'm about ready to cum, my little cocksleeve, so you better ask. Once I come, it's over and Joey will take you home. This is your last chance."

He sets a slow pace, which is worse than fast because it gives my brain time to process every sensation. I have a hard time gathering my thoughts as the intensity in my core builds.

"Zane, can I please, please, please come? I need to come so bad."

He speeds up his thrusting a little. "Are you a cum-hungry slut?"

"God, yes. I'm a cum-hungry slut. Please, can I come?"

Chuckling, he gives a few rough lunges against my pussy. "Did you ever think about me all these years?"

What's this? Fuuuuck. I pant out, "Yes. Please, can I come?"

"Did you imagine what my cock would feel like?"

I don't immediately answer and he sinks into me so hard I see stars. "Yes, thought of… cock… please, can I come? Please?"

Suddenly, a warmth invades my body, and I feel like I'm floating. Every push of his cock between my nether lips is amazing, and the pleasure builds upon itself. In this moment, I'd do anything he asks if it would get me an orgasm.

"One last question, Miri. If you answer it correctly, I'll let you come."

I give him a dreamy, "Hmmmm?"

"Did you…" he pauses and jackhammers against my pussy as spikes of pleasure threaten to send me over the edge. He continues on. "… Ever think about me while your husband fucked you?"

The pressure in my core mounts, and I sigh out a long, "Yeessss."

My answer makes him grab a fistful of my hair and drag my head back.

"Good… little… slut…" he pants out. "Now come for me."

As soon as he says I can come, my body convulses as if lightning strikes me. I scream out as waves of ecstasy wash over me in a never-ending tsunami of pleasure as he hammers my pussy. I vaguely hear him grunting and cry out with his release as a warm stickiness coats my cave walls. Fireworks explode behind my eyes, and I'm not sure if I come again or if this is the same orgasm, but I cry out as the waves intensify for a moment.

The room spins too much, and I close my eyes as I come down from the peak. Zane lifts me up and carries me over to sit on the couch with me in his lap. Resting against him, I keep my eyes closed as he rubs my arms and cuddles me. I might have had the best orgasm of my life and I don't know how I'm going to describe what happened to Joey.

I'm not sure how long we sit there, but eventually the brain fog clears.

"Zane, why did Joey ask you to do this?"

He chuckles and I can hear the rumble through his chest. "Because he knew we always had the hots for each other, and he said he wanted to give you a great first experience with another man."

Damn, I have an amazing husband. Maybe I can tell him how great my orgasm really was. Something Zane said confuses me.

"Wait, you always had the hots for me? You didn't like me after the Halloween party."

Zane is quiet for a minute and continues to rub my arm. I almost don't think he's going to answer.

"No, I liked you, but you brought out things in me I was afraid of."

Now I'm even more confused. "Things?"

He kisses the top of my head. "This, tonight... this was tame for me."

Zane fucked me harder than I've ever been before, and this is tame? I peep out a small, "Oh."

He continues on without me asking. "That night at the party. I almost lost control as soon as you started moaning, and I was afraid I was going to hurt you. That wouldn't have ended well for either of us."

I analyze what he said for a moment, thinking back on things I've read about sadism when helping Jessica do research for a book. If he's into roughness and pain, that could have sent me down a path I didn't want to take.

"I understand," I whisper. "Thank you for tonight."

He's quiet for another few moments. "The next day I told Joey we hooked up, and I found out he was in love with you. He was devastated, and I knew I would end up hurting both of you. It was better for all of us if I stayed away."

My head whirs, and I don't know what to think. Joey knew about me and Zane all this time and he still let me do this. Zane's explanation makes me doubly glad I ended up with Joey. Tonight was amazing, but I don't know that I would ever want rougher. Once again, love for my husband washes over me and I want to be in Joey's arms right now.

I sit up, panicked because I didn't pay attention to the time. "Wait, how much time do we have? I only had an hour."

He helps me up. "He'll be here in a few minutes. I've been watching the clock." He tips his head towards a clock on the wall and I relax. Shit, I can't believe I didn't think of setting an alarm.

I'm a little wobbly, and he helps me stand until I find my balance. He gathers my discarded clothes and brings them over to me, and I use the couch to stabilize myself as I get dressed.

He walks me to the door, but before he opens it, he gives me a deep kiss.

"Thank you for tonight, Miri. I'll never forget it."

I smile at him. "Me neither."

EPILOGUE

Joey is waiting in the car outside, and I try to walk normally even though my legs still feel like Jello-O. I slide into the passenger seat and neither of us speaks. I expect him to at least say hello, but he doesn't. We're both silent on the short drive to the rental house, and my head swirls with disjointed thoughts. Is he angry at me? Why isn't he asking what happened? Shit, did we just fuck everything up? I want him to kiss me and tell me he loves me, and a wave of vulnerability washes over me.

As soon as we get inside the house, I go to the bedroom and remove my clothing as if I'm on autopilot while I try to process my emotions. I'm standing in the middle of the bedroom and about to slip a nightgown on when Joey strolls in naked with his cock jutting straight out. I swear I can see it pulsating and I lick my lips.

Even though Zane gave me a mind-blowing orgasm, I immediately crave Joey's cock inside me. I can't even explain how much I need him right now. It's almost a physical pain. Joey pauses two feet from me, and I can't handle his silence anymore. He's clearly turned on, and I'm desperate to hear him say he loves me while he fucks me. I walk up to him, rub against him, and slowly stroke him.

I kiss him softly and move my lips to his ear and whisper. "My love, I need you inside me."

As soon as Joey hears that, he takes control. He presses me back to the bed and once I'm lying down, he covers my body with his. We kiss deeply and passionately, and I arch my body up towards him as our tongues duel. When he slides inside me, I moan and meet him thrust for thrust, ever so slowly. For as rough as Zane was, Joey is the opposite, and he fucks me tenderly and lovingly as gentle waves of rapture swirl in my core.

It's exactly what I need.

"Miri, god, I love you," he groans out.

"I love you too. I love you so much, Joey."

Hearing me say I love him spurs him on, and he becomes a little rougher. I didn't think it was possible to come again tonight, but I can tell I'm heading for another orgasm. My head is swimming, and spikes of bliss ripple along the length of my body.

The room fills with our moans and sighs, and the bed squeaks slightly as he raps against me harder.

He pants out, "Miri, you need to know something."

I'm so close to my orgasm and it's difficult to think, so I answer, "Hmmm?"

He gives a hard thrust and I yelp from the painful pleasure.

"You may have just fucked another man, but you need to know that you are MINE and you always will be."

His voice has a slight roughness to it when he says the word, "mine," and the unexpected primal response from him thrills me. Holy fuck, this is amazing.

"Say it, Miri," he growls. "Say you're mine."

I don't hesitate and cry out, "I'm yours," as my orgasm hits.

He explodes inside me and his groan mingles with my cries as we both ride the waves of pleasure.

After we come down, I snuggle into the crook of his arm and drift in a sea of happiness, thinking about how this simple trip to the ocean turned into something wonderful. He kisses the top of my head and whispers, "Mine."

I smile against this chest and whisper back, "Yours."

The End

A HOTWIFE HELPER

HOTWIFE HOLIDAYS 2

CHAPTER 1

As I tug on the tiny red dress and try to pull it down further past my ass, I wonder for the umpteenth time if agreeing to be Santa's helper at my husband's work Christmas party was a good idea. Joey works as a certified public accountant with one of the biggest accounting firms in our town. They recently scored a big new client, and the company claims they're doing something special for everyone at the holiday party.

One of Joey's coworkers agreed to play Santa, and they asked for volunteers to be Santa's helper. My dear husband signed me up without asking. When I complained, he fucked me senseless and wouldn't let me come until I agreed to do it. It wasn't all bad. After that, it became a running joke. Every time I threatened to not help, he'd fuck me again and not let me come until I changed my mind.

I blame my pussy for getting me into this. If she wasn't such a slut who loved being edged, I wouldn't have kept using it as an excuse to get him to fuck me.

Since the party isn't for children, why does Santa even need a helper? Hell, why is there even a Santa? Joey's work parties never include people under twenty-one since there is free-flowing alcohol, and everyone gets wild towards the end with ribald jokes and flirting. The company's motto is work hard, play hard for their social activities outside the office. The Christmas events are usually informal, but everyone dresses up. In past years, I've gone with a sexy number that gets my tipsy husband to drag me to bed when we get home.

Once I resigned myself to helping, I scoured online for a new sexy costume. The plan is to tease my husband and offer to polish his pole later... or maybe it's jingle his bells? Hmm, maybe.

My best friend Jessica is a writer, so I should have asked her to come up with some filthy Christmas-themed jokes. I guess I could have searched online, but what's the fun of that? I'm sure once I've had a few glasses of wine, I'll be able to come up with something that will make him laugh and want to fuck me.

Joey has been gone for the last few hours to help set up the party. He should be home any minute — or he better be, since it's almost time to leave.

I admire myself in the bedroom mirror to make sure the outfit isn't too slutty. The vibe I want tonight is classy slut, not use-me-in-a-dirty-bathroom slut. Picturing Joey getting so turned on he can't wait to get home, dragging me into the bathroom so we can rut like wild beasts against the wall sounds like my kind of fun. Still, I think classy slut is the way to go tonight.

This dress is a short one-piece, with red velvet and a white fur lining, and I'm pretty dang sexy. The top is a bustier and made for people with a smaller chest. I'm not spilling out over the top, but a generous amount of cleavage is visible.

Not that I'm complaining. It ups the chances of getting my husband worked up enough to fuck me tonight. I paired it with white fishnet thigh highs and some black fuck-me platform heels with ankle straps. These shoes might not be the best idea, since I plan to drink tonight, but my legs look too good in them to change to something more sensible.

And I can't forget the Santa hat.

Grabbing the hat from the dresser, I adjust it over my wavy brown hair and blow kisses at myself. Oh yeah, this Santa's helper is ready and willing to assist my wonderful husband with all of his needs.

Fuck, he should have offered to be Santa. I've got plenty of kinky ideas about helping Santa empty his sack.

I'll save that joke for after the party.

When I hear the garage door open, a thrill runs through me. I'm ready to get tipsy. More, I'm ready to have Joey's hands all over me.

Joey is secretive and distracted on the drive as I try to pry details out of him.

"So what's the big surprise, huh?"

He doesn't answer for a moment, and I'm assuming he isn't going to reply. Then his lips turn up and he teases me.

"You're going to have to wait and find out, just like everyone else."

"Fine," I huff and run a finger over the fur trim of my skirt. "Do you like my outfit?"

He said nothing about it when he picked me up, only giving me a long, unreadable look, which didn't boost my confidence about my chances of getting laid tonight.

"You're gorgeous like always, and a very sexy Santa's helper."

His voice is sincere, and a tingle spreads through my stomach. Okay, maybe he's forgiven for not saying something earlier.

"So... not even a little hint? Come on, you know you're dying to tell me."

That makes him chuckle. "No hint, but you'll be very *pleased* at the end of the night."

He stresses the word pleased and my pussy clenches as if she thinks it was directed towards her.

Heck, maybe it was. I think of several ways he can please me tonight. I need to get a few glasses of wine in him, and he'll be putty in my hands. If I play coy and cute, he'll think fucking me was his idea all along.

The drive is about thirty minutes, so I relax into the heated car seat and turn on some Christmas music, singing along to get in a more festive mood. Santa better be coming down more than just my chimney tonight.

CHAPTER 2

My wonderful husband disappeared shortly after we arrived, off to do something or other. My heart pounds as I watch the clock creep toward five o'clock, the official start of the party. I glance around the room again. I'm the only Santa's helper, but I see plenty of people in outfits more revealing than mine, so I'm in good company. Everyone is in high spirits and the anticipation in the air holds the promise of a night of laughter and inappropriate behavior.

Once the party starts, one of his coworkers approaches me with two glasses of wine. The guy is massive and fit, with yummy salt and pepper hair at his temples and gorgeous blue eyes. I'd estimate him in his early fifties, but he obviously works out and is blessed in the genes department.

"Joey asked me to bring you a drink. Do you want one?"

He holds out a glass and I gladly accept, taking a sip.

"Thanks. I'm not sure where Joey went..."

I hope he'll fill in the details since he saw Joey last.

"He's doing last-minute work on the presents. He asked me to entertain you. I'm Caleb, by the way."

His eyes twinkle and I notice his eyes sweep over my cleavage. My pussy revs to life and I resist the urge to sway towards him and flirt. This is exactly the type of guy I'd want a dirty encounter with at a Christmas party.

I've always had a thing for sexy older men.

"I'm Miri, but I'm guessing you knew that."

He nods and I catch him taking a peek at my top again. Not that I blame him. This bustier is incredibly flattering, and it's such brief glances, it's obvious he's trying not to stare. I press my chest forward, hoping my womanly charms will addle his brain and I can pump him for information.

"Do you know what gifts Santa is giving out?" If he knows, maybe he'll tell me.

His grin blossoms slowly. "Something naughty."

I wasn't expecting his response and I can't hold in my giggle. "Naughty gifts make the best presents." I take another sip of wine. "So... how about you show me around the party, huh?"

I don't really need him to show me around, but when he offers me his arm, I take it. The strength of his body gives me a pleasant thrill and my nipples harden.

Oh fuck, I haven't reacted to a guy like this in several months... not since my first hotwife experience with Zane, my high school crush, when we were vacationing on the Oregon coast.

Joey and I have talked about me fucking someone else again, and this time with him watching, but we haven't found the right person yet. We're not rushing; we want it to feel right for both of us. The way my body is reacting, Caleb feels very right to me, but I'm not here to fuck someone else. I need my husband so I can drive him wild.

We walk around and chat with other couples. Every time my body brushes against Caleb's, a neediness builds in my core. It's silly to be feeling this way around a virtual stranger, but he's so damn sexy.

I notice several other women eying him, but he seems oblivious and is attentive to me. My body is bursting with energy, and I'm flushed and extra giggly. After a bit, it seems like I'm on a date with him, which is odd. When I imagine this hunk taking me to a secluded corner and grinding against me, I know I'm in trouble.

Dammit, where is Joey? He needs to save me from these insane thoughts.

I finally spot him across the room, facing me, and chatting with a couple of people. His eyes follow my every move. The searing heat in his gaze makes my lips part as my heart rate speeds up. I think he's been watching me flirt with Caleb, and from his intense interest, I can tell he likes it.

I turn to Caleb and trail my hands down his arm for the benefit of my watching husband, and to get Caleb's attention.

"Hey. I see Joey and I'm going to join him. I'll talk to you later."

A huge grin spreads across his face, and his eyes twinkle. "I need to go get ready, anyway. Santa has presents to give out."

I stop and stare at him while he walks away. Wait, does he mean HE's Santa? A forbidden burst of delight burns inside of me at the thought of him in a Santa costume. Oh fuck, it's HIS sack I want to empty tonight.

Shaking my head to clear my slutty thoughts, I almost stumble on my way to my husband, but steady myself with a chair at a nearby table. Stupid shoes. Too bad they're so sexy.

When I get to Joey the other couple is walking away. He sets his empty glass of wine on a nearby table before taking my hand, pulling me into his arms, and kissing me so hard my knees go weak.

Whoa, okay. I'm liking where this is going.

I moan into his mouth and then pull back and laugh. "What's got into you?"

He doesn't answer and kisses me again until I'm on fire. His tongue invades my mouth, and I respond by sliding my hand around his neck and pulling him closer. His fingers dig into my hips as his hardness presses against my stomach.

I'm the one who breaks off the kiss. "No really, what got you all turned on?"

I'm certain it has to do with Caleb, but I want to hear him say it. He kisses me again, and I can feel my pussy spasming as our tongues dance. My head spins when he finally stops.

"Maybe it's because I watched you flirting with Caleb for the last thirty minutes, or it's possible I'm just excited to see you."

I don't add that it could be the empty glass of wine he had in his hand. I'm not sure how much he's drank, but it looks as if my flirty husband has come to play.

He traces my bottom lip with his thumb. "Baby, are you having fun tonight?"

"Yes." My breathless reply is cut off as he swoops in for another kiss.

Hot damn, this is great. His hands roam all over my body. My dress suddenly feels too tight as my panties dampen and my breasts ache. His lips brush against my neck and I moan softly.

Shit, I hope no one is looking this way. I'm about ready to drag him to a back room and go to town on his cock.

He nibbles on my neck and his breath is a warm puff on my sensitive skin when he speaks. "I really like your dress."

I want to laugh, but I hold it in. Oh yeah, I can tell he likes it.

"Yeah, it's kind of slutty, but in a good way."

He nips at my neck some more. "In the very best way."

I was only joking, but my insides quiver at his words. I gasp when he slips his hand under my short dress and cups my ass. His palm slides over my silky panties and the friction sends a shockwave through my body. God, at this rate, I'm going to be a wet mess when I help Santa with the gifts.

As if Joey is reading my mind, he pulls away from me. "This will have to wait until after the party."

I'm half disappointed but know it's for the better. He links his fingers with mine and leads me towards a side door.

"Yeah, fine. I'm telling you, you got me all worked up so I better get something out of you by the end of the night."

He glances over his shoulder at me, and his eyes smolder. "Try not to think about the fact that Santa has a massive cock."

What?

I trip over my feet at his words, and he helps me find my balance as I tease him.

"Really? And how would YOU know this?"

He laughs and tilts his head to the side with an evil grin.

"I've heard rumors."

I snort. Rumors my ass. Are people walking around the accounting firm talking about each other's cock size? I think not.

When we reach the side door, he opens it and a warm glow lights the room. Caleb, dressed up as Santa, is standing next to a table with a sack of presents on it.

Caleb is enormous. Somehow, the red costume accentuates his size.

Fuck.

I can imagine this guy having a massive cock. Joey might be right.

I glance around the room, trying to focus on anything except Caleb. The room appears to be an employee breakroom with couches lining the far wall. This is definitely a room where Santa could get lucky... maybe on one of the couches.

"Hey again," Caleb calls out.

I'm forced to look at him and he's staring at me with those gorgeous blue eyes.

"H-hi."

Ugh, I sound like an idiot. Why isn't Joey speaking?

Caleb abandons the sack of gifts and comes over to us. He's so close I can smell his cologne. A sharp glance at my husband reveals him watching us. Yeah, he's enjoying Caleb's closeness.

"You ready to be my helper?"

I imagine helping myself to Caleb's cock and I can feel a blush creep up my face. Fuck, I need to get a grip.

I blurt out, "Sure," before I say what I'm really thinking.

Joey takes my hand and squeezes it to get my attention. "Baby, I'll be out there with everyone else."

I nod and he leans towards me with his mouth close to my ear. "And don't forget to think about what I told you."

He kisses my cheek with a laugh, and I stand there in shock as he leaves. How big of a cock DOES Caleb have? God, I'm such a slut. Better still, my husband obviously adores this side of me.

Caleb goes back to the table, secures the red bag, and throws it over his shoulder, pulling my thoughts away from his cock.

"Miri, do you know why Santa always lands on the roof?"

I blink and don't reply. Uh, what?

"Because he likes it on top."

He winks at me and walks towards the door, and I stand there dumbly.

Is he flirting with me? When he realizes I'm not following, he glances at me with a smile in his eyes.

"You coming?"

My pussy buzzes and my brain kicks in finally.

I give him my best coy smile. "Not without permission."

He barks out a laugh. "Come with me and I'll tell you why Santa is always so jolly."

Oh god, I'm supposed to be the one telling the Santa jokes tonight. I catch up with him as he opens the door.

"So why is Santa jolly?"

Caleb motions for me to go through the door first and as I pass, he whispers, "Because he knows where all the naughty girls live."

The door closes behind us, and I giggle. Yeah, I fell into that one.

When a guy sees us, he climbs up onto a chair and holds a microphone. "It's time for our big announcement."

Everyone quiets down, and I glance around the room for Joey. Where is my man? I don't see him, and the announcer continues.

"We've had such an amazing year we're giving each of you a bonus check."

The room erupts in cheers and the guy waits until it calms down before continuing.

"You thought that was good? There's more. In February, we're closing the office for a week and taking all employees, and their plus one, on vacation."

The hooting and hollering from that announcement almost drown out him telling everyone that the details of the trip are in the envelopes with the bonus checks. As the guy steps down from the chair, Caleb takes it as our cue to pass out the gifts.

We walk around the room and pause at each table. Santa has me reach into his sack of presents and give one to each person. The gifts come in three different sizes. As we walk away, I see people opening them. They are boxes of expensive chocolates with an envelope, presumably giving details about the trip and bonus. Since the presents don't have names on them, I am assuming the money isn't in the envelope, especially since we're giving one to everyone at the party, including the invited guests.

When we're done passing out the gifts, Caleb turns to me and whispers. "Thank you for helping me empty my sack."

My eyes grow round. HEY, that was supposed to be my joke!

He laughs at my response and gives a little wave. "I'll see you later, Miri."

The way he says it makes it sound like he really thinks he will see me later, and I call out, "Bye," as he walks away.

In a few seconds, Joey is by my side. He moves behind me and puts his arms around me. I lean into him and feel his hardness press against me. Well, he's still turned on, so that's good, but now my jokes are ruined.

Something must have tipped him off that I'm disgruntled. "What's the matter, Baby?"

I grumble, "Santa stole all my best jokes."

Joey laughs, and hearing myself makes me smirk. Okay, it'll be fine. Joey hasn't heard the Santa's sack joke yet, so I guess all is not lost.

He kisses my head. "That's okay, Baby. You can take it out on Caleb while you fuck him in the back room."

What? I'm fucking him tonight?

I pull back so I can look at Joey. His face is flushed and his eyes shine, as if the thought turns him on. He's not joking.

"But only if you want," he adds.

My nipples tighten and a zing of pleasure zips straight to my pussy. Oh yeah, we want. We want.

"Yes... oh, yes." I nod eagerly.

He laughs again. "Good. I want to watch you empty Santa's sack."

My mouth falls open and I squeak, about to complain that now *he's* the one stealing my jokes. When he tugs on my hand, I close my mouth and follow him. No way am I going to risk him rescinding the offer.

He leads me towards the room we were in before. When he opens the door, Caleb is by the table waiting for us. He still has his Santa suit on and I want to gobble him all up. He's that damn sexy.

Oh, shit... am I going to actually fuck him as Santa? A shimmer of lust ripples through me.

God, I hope so. This is my kind of dirty.

CHAPTER 3

When the door closes, the sound of the party dies out. The click from Joey locking the door makes this suddenly real. Do I really want to do this or is this the wine talking?

Caleb leans a hip against the table, and I sweep my eyes up and down the length of him, taking stock. When I meet his eyes, I'm slightly breathless and I feel my panties get wetter.

Oh yeah. I want to find out if he really has a gigantic cock.

Joey kisses my cheek. "I'll be on the couch watching. Okay?"

Giving him a grateful smile, I murmur, "Yes, my love."

As he settles in on the couch, I take a deep breath and move to stand in front of Caleb. I have no clue what to expect, but I'm going into this willingly, so I won't play shy. My legs tremble and my heart races as I wait for him to make a move.

What if this is just a fantasy that will disappear once he removes his clothes?

Fuck, I'm being silly. I want to fuck him with or without the costume.

His gaze sweeps over me. "Hello again."

I raise my chin and offer him a sweet smile. "Hi."

"Did you enjoy the gift exchange?"

His small talk amuses me, but I guess it's better than him grabbing me and shoving me on the table... or is it?

"Actually, I did."

What I really enjoyed was watching his massive hands. He held the sack open for me, and I was thinking of them on my body. I can't imagine how much more of a thrill it would have been if I had known we'd end up here. He lifts one of those enormous hands to caress my cheek and I shiver, feeling a warmth settle in my belly.

His simple reply of "Good" lights me on fire.

His touch is electric, and I want his hands everywhere. This is not how I expected my night to go, and I have a sudden moment of uncertainty.

Wait, should I really do this? I glance at Joey sitting on the couch to make sure he's okay with this. He's watching us intently with a soft smile.

Okay, he's fine.

Knowing Joey still wants this gives me the freedom to relax. I take a deep breath and hold it as I tilt my head back to look at Caleb. Visually, he's almost my perfect man, so I will not waste this opportunity.

I'm going to fuck him.

His hand is still on my face. When he strokes his thumb across my cheekbone, I moan softly.

"Miri, do you want this?"

I swallow hard and nod. "Yes."

He chuckles. "No hesitation, huh?"

"What can I say? I'm in a festive mood tonight."

He grins. "Let's see if you're going to be an obedient little helper."

A simmer of lust punches me in the gut. I'm ready to do whatever he commands.

"Someone warned me earlier that Santa likes to be on top."

"Is that right?"

I'm having fun flirting with him and keep my tone light. "Yeah..."

Caleb arches an eyebrow. "Well, let's see if I'm up to the challenge."

I grin and shake my head. "I don't know... you seem more jolly than dominant."

"I'm jolly because I found a very naughty woman."

Before I can laugh, he pulls me into his arms and brushes his lips against mine. His kiss is soft and I melt into him. When he cups my breast, I shiver, then inhale sharply when he rubs one of my pert nipples through the velvet fabric.

He groans. I barely realize he's pushing me backwards until I feel the cold plaster of a wall. He kisses my neck and nuzzles me as he squeezes and plays with my breasts. My nipples ache and harden under his touch, and I wish I wasn't wearing the dress. I want to feel his skin against mine.

He kisses down my collarbone, licking and tasting my skin. I moan, wanting more.

"How long has it been since you've gotten off?"

My eyes snap open and I glance at Joey. "Yesterday."

Joey shifts positions when he hears my answer. I assume it's because he knows we didn't have sex yesterday, so that means I was playing with myself while he was at work. Whoops.

Caleb growls and unzips my dress in the back. He pushes down the front so he can get to my breasts. I'm wearing a strapless bra so he pulls my tits out of the top of the cups and plays with them. He sucks on a nipple and my panties get even wetter.

I can't believe I just met this guy and now his mouth is on me.

He stops sucking and asks, "What were you thinking about when you came?" before moving to give attention to my other breast.

Oh, fuck. I don't want to say in front of Joey.

I gasp as his teeth graze my sensitive nipple, but I don't answer. Caleb's tongue laps at me, then his teeth gently bite down and I whimper. It feels good, but I want more. He releases my breast, and his fingers slide between my thighs, inching ever so close to my panties.

"Tell me."

I release a shaky breath. His hands feel so good, and I want him touching me, but... Fuck it.

"I was thinking about fucking an old friend from high school."

I can't believe it. Did I just admit I was thinking about fucking Zane?

I dare to glance at Joey again, and he's stroking his cock through his jeans. Holy shit. The look on his face is one of intense desire. My attention is dragged away by one of Caleb's hands grabbing my hip. He rubs my pussy through the fabric of my panties with his other hand.

Oh yeah, I definitely need more.

I rock against his hand, wishing he'd push my panties to the side while he murmurs, "What else?"

Oh god, this is so slutty. I want to whisper, but Joey needs to hear me as well, so I can't.

"I was imagining lying on a bed while we made out and he started kissing my breasts and squeezing my nipples."

Caleb's voice is a dark rumble. "Keep going."

I moan, and my stomach muscles quiver as I continue. "Then he spread my legs and licked my pussy until I came... hard."

When one of Caleb's fingers slips under the band of my panties and slides between my wet folds, seeking my clit, I bite my bottom lip and shut my eyes tightly.

Fuck, this feels amazing.

"Tell me what happened next."

"We fucked until I came again."

He rubs circles around my clit and my legs quiver as pleasure courses through me. It's a good thing I'm up against a wall.

"You're a filthy slut, aren't you?"

I moan "yes" and he slips two fingers into my pussy.

He finger fucks me for a few moments. The bliss skyrockets me into an unexpected orgasm.

"Ohhh, fuck!" I cry out and ride his hand. When I've come down, he removes his fingers. I pant out "more" as I try to catch my breath.

"Since you're naughty, you need to be punished."

He pushes me onto my knees. My pulse pounds wildly in my ears.

Ohhh, it's time to see his cock! He pulls down the pants of the red Santa suit, revealing black form-fitting boxers that mold around the length of his sizeable package. He's hard and clearly the rumors were true. It looks impressive, and I haven't seen it in all its glory yet. His thick, muscular thighs make me think about him behind me, pounding away. He's fit and probably has the stamina and strength to go all night.

"Take my cock out."

I lick my lips and caress him through the fabric before pulling his boxers down just far enough to free his cock.

I gasp.

He's the biggest guy I've seen in the flesh. I've seen pornos where men have big cocks, but this is different. He's thick and a large vein runs along the top. The tip glistens with pre-cum. I want to lick it and see how it tastes.

Caleb reaches down and tips my chin up, making my Santa cap fall off.

"It's time for my helper to suck my cock."

Desire flutters in my stomach, and I wrap my hand around his shaft, pumping slowly. I can't help myself, so I look up and tease him.

"Are you sure it will fit?"

His nostrils flare as he stares down at me. "Oh, yes."

I pump him harder, and he grabs my wrist, holding me still. "I told you to suck my cock, so start sucking."

My pussy clenches and my mouth waters.

Shit, I love how demanding he is. It borders on feeling like I'm being used, and it's working me into a frenzy.

I stroke his cock and wet my lips before sucking on the tip. I'm really unsure if this is going to fit, but I'm game. Just the tip is large enough to give me pause. Caleb thrusts his hips forward and I relax my throat as his shaft slides halfway into my mouth.

Oh god, it's not going to fit!

He grips my hair and holds my head and pulls out fully, but it's only a moment before his cock is back at my lips.

"What a good little slut."

His words make me shudder and as he pushes into my mouth slowly, still only going halfway in since he's so large. I moan around his cock. The taste of his pre-cum mixes with his natural musk, and I want him to fuck me so bad. I pull him out of my mouth and trail kisses down his shaft.

"You like my cock?"

"Yes," I whisper.

"Beg for it."

"Oh god, please fuck me. Please?"

He groans and shoves himself back into my mouth. I suck and swirl my tongue around the head of his cock, and he growls. He grips the back of my head and becomes forceful, as if my mouth is his toy, and yet not being so rough that it's uncomfortable. He uses my mouth for quick, shallow thrusts. Since he's not forcing me to deep throat him, I'm able to relax and enjoy it. This is absolutely filthy, and I briefly wonder what Joey is thinking. I'm not sure he expected someone to face fuck me like this when he and I discussed him watching.

I run my tongue along the length of his cock and feel him jerk and tense. He holds my head tight as he fucks my mouth with firm strokes. My pussy is on fire, and I desperately need his cock inside it, but at this rate he might come in my mouth. I press my hand against the base of his cock and rub while he continues to fuck my mouth.

He pulls his cock out and I whimper.

Oh God, please, let him fuck me now.

He grips my arm and lifts me onto my feet, then turns us both so his back is against the wall. As he slips his hands under my skirt and drags my panties down, I sway towards him, feeling his cock rub against the velvet at my stomach. Anticipation pulses through me.

My panties fall to my ankles and I step one foot out of them, being careful not to tangle my heels. Leaving them on the floor makes the slutty vibe hit home.

Caleb hooks his hand around one of my legs and lifts, using his other hand to guide his shaft towards my wet slit. Holy fuck, I'm not sure the last time I fucked in this position.

I slide my hands around his neck to help steady me while I moan at the feeling of him controlling me this way.

When he places the tip against my entrance, he says, "How much do you want this?"

Shit, how do I define this? I'm dazed with lust and I can only murmur, "Please."

He pushes inside me, and his massive cock stretches me further than I've ever been before. I can't believe how wide he is.

His length hits bottom and triggers a spasm of pleasure. I almost come and cry out, "Fuuuuck."

He slides out of me and then slams back inside. As hard, rough strokes rock my body, I gasp and go completely rigid, unable to move as he hammers into me.

Caleb holds onto my hip to control my movement. "I like how you're reacting."

I'm breathing heavily and shaking, trying to regain my composure as I peep tiny moans with each thrust.

He pulls out and rams into me again. "I like how you squeeze my cock."

I moan louder and grind my hips towards him. He's hitting all the right spots, and I can't hold back any longer. I cling to him, expecting to come at any moment.

He slides out of me and then slams back in, making me scream in pleasure. He continues to slam into me and I tighten around him. I'm on the brink of coming and I'm not sure whether to fight it or welcome it. I close my eyes as the pleasure builds, layer by layer, but right before I come, he pulls out all the way and lets go of my leg. I gain my footing and wobble, almost blissed out. My mind reels.

Wait, why did he stop?

"You're a dirty girl, aren't you?"

I nod, barely coherent. "Yes, I am."

"Good. I want you to bend over the table so your husband can watch me fuck you hard."

Ohh, yes, please.

I abandon my panties and walk towards the table. I sneak a look at Joey. My heart leaps at the sight of him with his cock out, stroking and watching us. Thank god he's enjoying this.

Once I bend over the table, I spread my legs wide apart and look over my shoulder at Caleb.

"Like this?"

"Yes."

He steps close behind me, and I grip the edges of the table to steady myself. His cock stretches me wide open again. I turn my head towards my husband and rest my cheek against the table. I want to see him enjoying the show.

When Caleb speaks to Joey, I'm surprised.

"Joey, do you want to see your slut of a wife fucked hard until she comes? Do you want me to use her body and make her scream?"

Joey doesn't answer and I moan as Caleb slams into me, hard and deep. My eyes roll back in my head as I almost come undone.

Fuuuuuck.

He's relentless and keeps slamming into me. Each thrust brings me closer and closer to ecstasy.

"Is your slut ready to come, Joey?"

My husband's silent response is enough for Caleb to keep up his pace. He's pounding into me, and I know he won't stop until he gets what he wants. I'm lost in the sensations, and I barely register Joey moving to stand beside me. His breathing is ragged and he's stroking himself close to my face.

Oh god, I want to suck on him while I get fucked from behind, but we didn't talk about doing that.

Caleb's grunts become louder and faster, and I'm on the verge of coming. I'm about to explode when he pulls out.

"You said you don't come without permission. Do you need to ask me something?"

I wiggle my ass, hoping he'll fuck me again. When he doesn't fill me, I realize what he wants.

"Can I come, please?"

"Hmm... Joey, does she deserve to come?"

I glare at my husband. He better say yes. He's still stroking, and his eyes are filmed with lust.

"Yes. I want to see her come."

Caleb twists my hair around his fist and pulls my head up. "It's time for you to get fucked and come. Now get on the floor on your hands and knees."

When he releases my hair, I scramble to the floor, using the table to help me down. My husband is in front of me and when I glance up, I have to look past his cock.

Wait, is he going to come all over me? I keep my eyes trained on my husband's hand on his cock, mesmerized by his stroking.

Caleb kneels behind me, and I cry out as he drives into me with an animal fierceness. He's tireless as he pounds against me. I'm immediately on the brink of coming again. I close my eyes briefly as the sensation of his thick cock massages every nerve ending inside me.

A rustling in front of me makes me open my eyes, and Joey kneels, aiming his cock towards my lips.

Holy fuck, yes!

I open my mouth and willingly engulf the tip. A sharp lunge from behind forces his cock further into me, and I moan from how slutty I am. Shit, this is fabulous.

Caleb's loud grunts and the sound of skin slapping together fill the room. I swear he's trying to split me in two. I'm so close to my orgasm I can't bear it.

"Come for me, slut."

His words are my undoing. I'm moaning around Joey's cock while squeezing my inner muscles around Caleb's thick shaft. My orgasm explodes and I scream, bucking my hips.

"Ahhh!"

Caleb doesn't stop fucking me as Joey thrusts into my mouth. My orgasm continues as waves of bliss ripple through me. Wetness streaks down my inner thighs and I don't care how messy it is. This is fantastic and I don't want it to stop.

Caleb growls and his cock pulses before he erupts. He grasps my hips and slams me hard against his cock, holding me there as his warm cum paints my cave walls. My husband moans a split second before he fills my mouth with his seed and my mind switches off from being filled by two men at once. I didn't realize how awesome this would be.

Both men fuck my holes as they finish coming. As the aftershocks of my orgasm subside, Caleb pulls out of me. Joey continues to kneel in front of me while Caleb speaks.

"Did you enjoy watching me fuck your wife?"

I look up at Joey as he nods.

"Yes."

Caleb slaps my ass, and I squeak.

"Now Miri, say thank you."

"Thank you," I pant.

"You're welcome."

Joey helps me up. I cling to him as my legs wobble. He guides me to the couch and sits me down.

Now that I'm done fucking Santa Caleb, I focus all my attention back on Joey. I need to know he enjoyed what happened, more than just getting an orgasm. A wave of vulnerability hits me. I need him to say he still loves me.

I hear water running in the kitchenette area, and I guess it must be Caleb cleaning up. Things got messy, and this dress is shot, especially since I'm sitting on it. We might have to hide out in here until the party is over. Joey puts his arm around my shoulders, and I lean into him. His scent is intoxicating and relaxes me. I love him so much.

"So, that went well," Joey murmurs.

"Yeah..."

It went better for me than just well, so I'm not sure how to take his comment. I would have used magnificent or mind-blowing. I'm about to ask him if he really had fun when Caleb walks over to us with a grin.

"Hey, I'm going to head out. Thank you, Miri, for a wonderful time."

I give him a dreamy smile. "Thank you too. It was nice meeting you."

Shit, was that a lame response?

The guys exchange thanks. When Caleb opens the door to leave, the sounds from the party have died down. Some people must have gone home. He closes the door behind him, and I resume my position, leaning against Joey. He rubs my side, and I can't help asking him how it went.

"My love, was that good for you?"

He kisses the top of my head.

"Oh yeah. Seeing someone else fucking you while you were sucking on my cock was... something else."

I bury my head in his side and smile. If Joey is at a loss for words, that means he really did like it.

"Let's get home and get you cleaned up. My filthy wife needs a shower."

I can tell by the tone of his voice he's teasing, and he helps me stand up. We retrieve my panties and Santa hat from the floor, and Joey peeks out the door before waving me over.

"Everyone seems busy with the Karaoke machine. Let's make a run for it."

When I get close to him, he grabs my hand and pulls me along. We're breathless and laughing when we get to the car.

CHAPTER 4

The drive home is mostly silent, and I drift in a sea of contentment. Halfway through, he rests his hand on my thigh and makes circular caresses. I give him the side eye, wishing I could kiss him. It seems someone isn't done tonight.

When we arrive home and get out of the car, Joey walks around to my side and gently tugs me towards him. He wraps his arms around me and kisses me deeply.

"I think you need to be a little dirtier before you shower."

"Mmmm," I moan. "I like the way you think."

We walk into our house and he leads me to the kitchen. I'm not sure why we're in here, but I immediately yank my dress over my head and drop it on the floor. He watches as I kick my shoes before unhooking my bra and freeing my breasts. Conveniently I'm still not wearing panties, and I turn to Joey, awaiting his next move.

He grins and slips a hand between my legs to rub my pussy.

"Turn around." He removes his hand. I spin and put my hands on the countertop, spreading my legs wide. I'm dripping wet and already excited. He steps up behind me and slides his fingers into my slick folds. My body is on fire with pleasure.

"Baby, you're so wet."

I can only moan, grinding against his hand, my clit throbbing. I didn't expect a round two, but this is a great way to end the night. Joey rubs my clit and I whimper.

Shit, I need him inside me. "God, Joey, please fuck me."

"Not yet. You aren't desperate enough."

Shit, he needs to fuck me. I look over my shoulder at him.

"What makes you think that?"

He grins and rubs faster. "Because you're not begging."

I arch my back and push against him. My body feels like it's melting under his touch as he plunges two fingers into my pussy. I gasp as he hooks his finger and rubs against my cave walls.

"That's it, my dirty slut. Beg me to fuck you."

Oh, I'll beg.

"Fuck me, please! I need you!"

He slides his fingers out of me and brings them to my lips. I suck his fingers clean, and he tugs me to a standing position.

"Come. I want to fuck you in our bed."

I don't care where it is, it just needs to happen now.

I follow him into the bedroom. He wraps his arms around me, holding me close to him as kisses me deeply. Our tongues duel and the inferno in my core kicks up a notch. Wetness trails down my leg.

When he breaks off the kiss, I sit impatiently on the bed and watch him remove his clothes. I can tell by his movements that he's eager, stripping quickly and tossing his clothing aside.

Mmm, I want to run my hands all over his body, but he's clearly not in the mood to take this slowly. He pushes me onto my back and pulls me to the middle of the bed. He climbs on top of me and positions himself between my legs. His body covers mine, and he presses the length of his cock against my pussy.

I caress his chest and flex my hips to force him to rub against my wetness.

"Now will you fuck me, please?"

He doesn't answer. Instead, he reaches between us and guides his cock inside me, nice and slow. Thrills run up and down my body from the bliss and I moan loudly. I've fucked two other guys since we've been married, but no matter how great the sex is with the other men, it's just not the same as it is with Joey. This moment is what I need, the familiarity of his cock comfortable and perfect. I wrap my legs around him as he thrusts.

"You're so beautiful and hot, and you feel so good."

No words come, though I want to respond. I can't speak past the pleasure coursing through my body. I run my hands up his arms and around his neck, hang on, close my eyes, and get lost in the moment. The pleasure builds and I'm aching for release as he drills into me.

When he pauses, I whimper and rotate my hips to continue the pleasure. After a moment of him not moving, I open my eyes to find he's staring into mine.

"What's wrong, my love?"

"Nothing. I want you to look at me when you come."

"Okay," I whisper.

He moves again, slow thrusts in and out. His hips rock against me and the tension builds again. I keep my eyes glued to his, watching the pleasure overtake him. I grip his shoulders and hold on for the ride. My skin is flushed, and I moan as he continues to drive into me, pushing me closer and closer to the edge.

"Oh god, oh god..."

I release my death grip on his shoulders as I give in to the pleasure with total surrender. My back arches and my toes curl as I climax. I scream as I writhe from the powerful waves of delight. He slams home, holding me tight and driving me wild.

I squeeze his cock as my orgasm continues. He gives one final plunge and comes with a roar, filling me with his seed. He spasms against me, bucking wildly, before relaxing. His warm cum coats my cave walls. As my orgasm subsides, my body goes limp, and I release my legs from around him.

"Fuck," he pants.

After a few moments, he gets off and lies beside me while we relish the afterglow. I roll to face him, and he rests his arm over my hip.

"That was amazing."

He chuckles. "Yeah. I wasn't kidding about you needing to be a little dirtier."

I snort. "Oh yeah, I'm filthy."

He kisses my nose. "I wouldn't want you any other way."

I run my fingers through his hair and put my head against his chest, breathing in his manly scent.

"My love, does this make you happy? I don't need to fuck other guys. You're enough for me." Not that I'm objecting, but I feel ought to check in.

Joey pulls me close to him. "Of course, baby. I want you to be satisfied and fulfilled. And I loved watching you tonight."

"I love you," I murmur as I nuzzle into his chest and close my eyes. My multiple orgasms tonight are catching up with me. Before I fall asleep I'll get up to shower, but I want to savor our closeness for a bit longer.

"Baby?"

"Hmmm?"

He presses his lips to the top of my head before continuing.

"The vacation in February. They're taking us to Cabo..."

"Ohhh, nice!"

Wow, I've never been to Cabo. I'll have to do research on it later.

"And while we're there..."

I kiss his chest and wait for a moment before prompting him.

"Yeah?"

"I could ask Caleb if he wants to play with you on the trip."

My pussy perks up and I'm immediately wide awake. I tip my head so he can see my expression as I grin eagerly.

"I'd like that."

We exchange a soft kiss before I snuggle against him. An all-expense paid trip to Cabo was already amazing. Now I have something even more to look forward to. This upcoming trip might end up better than our visit to the Oregon coast. Maybe Cabo is like Las Vegas and what happens in Cabo stays in Cabo....?

We'll find out!

The End

A HOTWIFE'S FILTHY WISH

HOTWIFE HOLIDAYS 3

For Wordcat. As I was writing this, I realized my first erotica short story was published exactly two years ago. Your suggestion that I should try writing something changed my life. Thank you.

CHAPTER 1

Breathing in deeply, I try to relax as I settle into the lounge chair by the resort pool in Cabo San Lucas. The scent of chlorine masks the smell of the ocean just steps from the edge of the resort. I've always liked the smell of chlorine, so it's not unpleasant. My husband, Joey, stretches out in the chair next to me, and it's nice to see him unwinding from his stressful job as an accountant.

He's been teasing me and working me up for this trip to Cabo for weeks because he arranged for me to have some sexy fun with another guy while we're here. I bought a gorgeous purple lingerie set for the trip, and I've yet to use it. The plan is to wear it one of these nights to thrill him.

A couple of months ago at his work's Christmas party, I played the part of Santa's helper to pass out gifts and ended up fucking the guy from his work who was dressed up like Santa.

Caleb made one sexy Santa, and as his helper, I helped myself to his cock during the party while Joey watched. Eventually Joey couldn't resist temptation, and he came over to fuck my mouth. Being spit roasted between the man I love and a massive cock in my pussy was an experience I won't forget.

As a Christmas present to all the employees, his work planned an all-expense paid trip to Cabo for a week in February. Joey has it all arranged that I'll get an evening with Caleb while we're here, but Joey's being mysterious about when it will happen.

We've been in Cabo for two days, and I've yet to get Caleb's cock in me. Whenever I pester Joey about it, all he says is, "Soon." Yeah, well *soon* my dear husband is going to have a sexually crazed wife on his hands. Wait, who am I kidding? He already has a sexually crazed wife. I love vacation sex, and knowing I get to fuck Caleb again makes me even hornier.

The resort where his company booked our rooms is gorgeous. We're staying for six nights, and each day the company has an event planned for everyone. Yesterday, we went sailing along the coast on a sunset cruise. Tonight, there's a banquet at the resort, along with a speech from the president of the company and then a presentation. The office voted for various humorous awards to give out to their coworkers, so it's supposed to be a lighthearted couple of hours. Joey is looking forward to it more than I am, but so far, the resort is treating us like royalty, so the food is bound to be delicious. I'm interested in going just for that.

I've seen Caleb several times so far on the trip, but we've only said hello and briefly chatted. He didn't bring anyone, which makes me feel better. I'm not interested in fucking a guy who has a girlfriend unless it's an open relationship. This isn't the first time I've seen him since the Christmas party. Joey invited him over to our house a few weeks later, and he fucked me on the coffee table.

Knowing that Joey arranged a play date with Caleb in Cabo has turned me into a nympho. Joey and I have already had sex four times since we got here. Even though we were exhausted from traveling, I jumped him as soon as we got into the hotel room, and with the way my pussy is buzzing just from lying here in the sun, I'm planning on fucking him before the banquet tonight.

Besides Caleb, another coworker — a guy named Ben — keeps drawing my attention. He's a super sexy older guy with streaks of gray in his hair and mature laugh lines on his face. I've caught his eye twice, and the twinkle in them makes me think he's fun loving.

The company allowed everyone to bring one person with them,

and when I saw Ben with a woman who looked to be in her early 20s, I joked with Joey that his coworker likes them young. He laughed and said that Ben's single and that was his daughter. It pleased me to know he's single. I mean, not that I'm planning on fucking him or anything, but it gives me free license to imagine a threesome with him and Caleb whenever I see one of them. I'm horny and having fun with my slutty fantasies so far on this trip.

I shift positions on the lounge chair to avoid squirming. It's warm under the sun, but it's more than just the outside temperature heating me up. The pool's sparking blue water is gorgeous, and the palm trees lining the pool area are beautiful. We came to the pool to relax, but how am I supposed to unwind when I'm surrounded by smoking-hot men in swim shorts or Speedos?

Joey's squeeze to my hand brings me back to the present.

"Baby, do you want to swim some more, or should we head back to the room until dinner?"

A flame of desire kindles between my thighs. Oh yeah, the room sounds like a perfect plan. I give him my best sultry smile.

"I think there's some pressing business we need to attend to in our room."

He mock groans. "Didn't you get enough of me this morning?"

The memory of our earlier quickie is still fresh in my mind, and my pussy throbs. I purr, "I could never get enough of you. I've been thinking of your cock all day, and I need you inside me."

We just won't mention I've also been thinking of every cock that walks past.

Joey chuckles. "You're such a little slut sometimes."

I stand up and tug on his hand. "You love it when I'm a slut for *you*."

When he gets up, he pulls me into his arms for a deep kiss. "Yeah, you're my slut, and don't you forget it."

Lust blossoms in my stomach. I love it when he gets possessive.

I nod. "Only yours."

We link hands and make our way to the hotel lobby. I swear to God Joey is taking his time. I try to walk faster, but he keeps a firm grip on my hand and makes me slow down. When he stops to chat with a couple of people, I want to pout, but I have to play nice. Plus, it's not like I haven't gotten plenty of sex so far. I suppose I can wait a few more minutes.

By the time we get to our room, lust is burning in my brain and all I can think about is fucking him. As soon as the door shuts, I pounce. I shove him onto the bed, and he falls onto his back, laughing. "Whoa, okay...I guess you can have my cock if you insist."

I grin wickedly. "Oh, I insist all right. Get it out."

Making quick work of my bikini bottoms, I shimmy them down my hips and then remove my bikini top. Joey pulls his shorts down, but he's not moving fast enough for me. When he gets them down to his knees, I yank them off the rest of the way and flick them over my shoulder. They hit the wall before falling to the floor.

Joey's cock is already hard, so he must have been thinking about this on our way upstairs. I lick my lips and crawl toward him, rubbing my body against his. "Do you want me on top?"

"Hell yes!" He grabs my hips as I straddle him and lower myself onto his shaft. This is going to be fast, just like our quickie this morning, but I'm too horny to care about prolonging the pleasure. As I sink down on him, I rub my clit and moan. This is just what the doctor ordered.

"Fuck, you're so wet," he growls, grabbing my ass and pulling me harder down on him.

Resting one hand on his chest, I continue to rub my clit as I bob up and down on his lap. I moan loudly as he thrusts his hips upwards, loving the way he fills me. Delight runs up and down my body as I rock on his shaft. Since I'm feeling in control today, I chant, "Come for me," as I ride him faster and faster.

He thrashes under me as if he's trying to hold back, and once his eyes roll to the back of his head, I know I've won. When he groans in release, I come with him. Fireworks explode along the corner of my vision as my pussy clenches around his cock. I fuck him through the waves of pleasure as he unloads inside me for the second time today.

When my orgasm subsides, I lean my forehead against his neck and try to catch my breath.

"Oh god, you're going to be the death of me," he pants.

I giggle. "Yeah, but what a way to go."

Within moments, I'm next to him and we're snuggled together. I'm so relaxed I might just melt into the bed. I idly scan the room, and I study the plush chair facing the corner of the bed.

I tap him on his belly and giggle as I gesture in the chair's direction. "Don't you think that chair would be the perfect spot to sit while you watch Caleb fuck me?"

"Huh, maybe."

He's non-committal, as if he hadn't ever considered it. Maybe, my ass. I can tell he's having fun keeping me on tenterhooks about his plans. That's probably exactly where he's going to sit while I get railed by Caleb's massive cock.

I don't press him any further, and when he and I both yawn, I let my thoughts float away. A nap before the banquet is sounding good.

CHAPTER 2

Dinner was delicious, just as I expected. The awards ceremony is over, but the party's still going. It's turned into an impromptu comedy hour while Joey's coworkers take the microphone and tell funny work stories. People are laughing and having a good time, but I don't understand some jokes since I don't know the technical side of Joey's job as an accountant. But the atmosphere is pleasant, so I'm not racing to get out of here.

I wore a sapphire-blue silk dress that leaves my shoulders bare and ends above the knees. Joey's hand has been resting on my thigh for the last five minutes, and he's been slowly inching it upwards. When he slides it more towards my inner thigh, it tickles, and I try to clench my knees together so I don't laugh.

Leaning towards him, I whisper in his ear. "You're being a naughty boy."

He turns towards me with a grin but keeps on inching his hand up my leg. My panties grow wet, and I want to shift so he can rub my pussy, but his coworkers might notice that. Ben, the hot older coworker, takes the microphone, and I'm momentarily distracted from Joey's fingers. Damn, Ben really is hot. Tonight's dress code is semiformal, and the way his shirt hugs his shoulders, I bet he's muscular and fit under his clothes.

Joey tries to get my attention. "Hey, Miri?"

I'm still admiring Ben and preoccupied. "Hmmm?"

Joey's voice is low, and he's close enough to my ear that no one else at the table could hear him. "If I gave you one wish to do whatever you wanted tonight, what would it be?"

What's this? Joey finally has my full attention. "One wish?"

He nods. "What is your heart's filthiest desire?"

The crowd laughs, and I look again at Ben telling his joke. Oh yeah, I know what my wish would be. I turn and kiss Joey softly before speaking.

"If I had one wish and could do whatever I wanted, I'd want to fuck Caleb and Ben tonight."

Joey's eyes widen like he's surprised. "Ben?"

I don't want him to know exactly how hot I find Ben, so I shrug. "Yeah, I mean he's got that sexy older guy vibe, and he seems nice."

Yeah, he seems like he'd be nice to fuck and probably knows a thing or two about pleasuring a woman, given his age.

I think of something else. "Oh, and..." A blush creeps up my face. This next part is hard to admit.

"Yes?"

I try to not be embarrassed. This is my husband, for Christ's sake. I should be able to tell him about my dirtiest fantasies.

"I'd want them to treat me like a sex doll, like I'm just a hole they're using."

Oh, God. I said it. My filthiest desire. Um, shit, I hope no one else heard that. I glance around the table, and none of the other couples are paying attention to us.

"Huh." Joey takes my hand and kisses the back of it. "Guess I better go see if Caleb minds having company tonight."

What? I don't have time to question him, because he drops my hand and heads towards the back of the room. My entire body buzzes, and I can't concentrate on anything being said. All I can think about is how Joey is off asking Caleb if he's willing to share me.

Tonight! The jerk didn't tell me we had plans with Caleb tonight. He was obviously going to just spring it on me.

Ben passes the microphone to someone else, and I don't pay attention to the next person who takes it. When Caleb slides into Joey's vacant seat, heat rushes between my legs and I'm flustered.

His voice is deep. "I hear you want to fuck two guys."

My mouth forms an 'O', and I take a moment to speak. "Um, is that okay?"

He laughs. "Oh yeah, sounds like fun."

Shit, is anyone listening to this? I peer around the table and everyone is focused on the speaker. Thank God.

His hand brushes against my knee, and I almost jump while another splash of wetness hits my panties. Jesus, now he's teasing me too. Caleb caresses my leg while pretending to pay attention to the last couple of speakers. He gets tantalizingly close to the edge of my panties and then moves his hand away again. I'm a vibrating bundle of energy, and my need for him blots out everything else.

When the party breaks up, I'm so keyed up I'm about ready to throw myself on Caleb's cock. Joey and Ben walk up to us before I do something stupid in front of all their coworkers.

Joey's gaze sweeps over me speculatively before he grins. "Hey, let's get out of here."

I shiver from arousal and rise from my seat. "Yes, please."

Joey takes my hand. Caleb and Ben tail behind us as we leave the room.

"Where are we going?" I ask him quietly.

His voice is low, matching my volume. "Our room. I hear it's got a chair that gives a good view of people fucking on the bed."

Ohhh, hell yeah. My pussy clenches, and I want to skip to the elevator.

CHAPTER 3

In the elevator, I drop Joey's hand, and the doors are barely closed before Caleb presses me against the wall and ravishes my mouth. Well, hello there. Between kisses, he groans, "I want to fuck you right here."

I get a nice zing of lust at his words. It's been less than two months since his cock was inside me, but it feels like an eternity. I've been thinking about this trip and hoping nothing would mess up my chance to fuck him again.

Sliding my arms around Caleb's neck, I meet his passion with my own. Joey and Ben lean against the opposite wall so they can watch the Caleb and Miri Elevator Show. I bet it's a good show.

Caleb continues to kiss me as he slides his hand between my legs. When he brushes his fingers against the silk of my panties, the friction against the smooth fabric makes my pussy tingle. I buck my hips, needing more. My reaction encourages him to push past the elastic band and slide two fingers inside me. I moan into Caleb's mouth as he massages the perfect spot against my cave wall.

Caleb breaks off the kiss and murmurs in my ear. "Do you want us to fuck you?" His hot breath tickles the sensitive skin under my earlobe, and I bite my lip to hold in more moans.

When I don't answer, he asks again. "Do you, Miri? Do you want Ben's cock…and my cock…both inside you…using you?"

His words make my legs quiver. I nod and whimper. I'm so fucking turned on right now, he could take me here in the elevator if he wanted. All three of them could take turns using my holes, and I'd just beg for more.

Caleb steps back and flips me around, shoving my breasts against the cool steel of the elevator wall. *Ohhh, this is good.* He doesn't ask for permission or give me time to say no, which is *exactly* what I want tonight.

He pulls my panties down to my knees and then pins my shoulder against the wall as he slides his fingers inside me again. He finger fucks me roughly, and I gasp as I lean into his touch. Pings of delight ripple through me as he works my cunt. I wasn't expecting him to be all over me in the elevator, but this is fabulous.

He removes his hands from my shoulder and pussy, grabs my ass, and pulls my hips back, forcing me to bend over. I have to place my palms flat against the wall to steady myself as he grinds his hardness against my ass. God, I need his cock inside me. The fabric of his trousers is thin enough that I can feel the ridge of his cock, but all he's doing is smearing my wetness over the front of him and making me even more desperate.

The elevator slows to a stop, and he lets go of my hips. I assume we're at our floor, but he quickly stands in front of me, blocking the view from the hallway as the door slides open. Shit, maybe not? I stand up and adjust my dress back in order when someone from the hallway speaks.

"Oh, sorry, we're going down. Not up."

Ohhh, fuck. Yeah, this isn't our floor. My panties are still at my knees, and I flush from the embarrassment as I peek over Caleb's shoulder. An elderly couple smiles at us. Oh no, did they see anything?

Joey laughs. "No worries. You have a good night," and the door slides closed again.

Caleb turns around and smiles. "That was a close one."

I laugh nervously. "Yeah, it was. They almost got a surprise."

His eyes darken, and he kisses me again. Our tongues twine

together and I mold myself against his body until the elevator reaches our floor.

We stumble out, and I almost feel as if I'm drunk as the four of us briskly stride towards the hotel room. Thank God the hallway is empty. We're walking like people on a mission.

Once inside our room, Joey takes over. "I want you guys to fuck her on the bed. I'll watch from the chair."

He motions towards the chair I was laughing about earlier. It really is in the perfect position to watch the action on the bed. He sits down and starts loosening his dress shirt as I kick off my high heels and yank my dress over my head. Having a threesome while Joey watches is going to be fucking amazing. My pussy desperately wants Caleb's cock inside her, so I'm not wasting time.

Caleb and Ben both start undressing as well, and I pause before removing my bra and panties so I can watch them. I already know what Caleb looks like naked, but I'm dying to see if Ben is as sexy under his clothes as I imagined he would be.

Ben's bulge is impressive, and when his pants hit the floor, his cock looks even larger. He's wearing boxer briefs, and they clearly outline his cock. I'm not sure I've ever seen a cock that size. Um, will it even fit?

My brain blips out for a moment when I realize I'm about to get fucked by two massive cocks. Caleb is very large, and now Ben is even bigger than Caleb. Holy fuck.

Joey whistles at Ben's cock. "Damn, you're going to ruin her with that thing."

I can tell by the gleeful tone of his voice that he really wants to watch me get ruined. How did I get so fucking lucky? My husband sees a dude with an enormous cock, and he's all excited for me to get pounded with it? I seriously have the best husband on the planet.

Caleb and Ben laugh at his words, and Ben says, "I aim to please."

Joey leans back in his chair and uses one hand to stroke his cock through his pants while gesturing towards me with his other hand. "Have at it. I want to hear my toy scream when she comes."

Ohhh fuck, that's hot. When I told Joey earlier that I wanted to be treated like a sex doll, I didn't think he would do or say anything to push me towards feeling that way. But him acting like I'm his toy to share and telling two guys to fuck me puts me in the frame of mind I craved.

Yep, it's time for this toy to get used.

As I reach behind me to unhook my bra, Joey and Caleb remove the rest of their clothes. My bra falls to the floor with barely a whisper as I step out of my panties.

It's odd to be naked in front of two guys I barely know, but I try not to focus on that. I'm a sexy goddess who is about to get her filthiest wish fulfilled. Goddesses don't have time to feel vulnerable and awkward when the action is about to start.

Putting an extra swing into my hips, I stroll over to Caleb and tip my head up towards him. He kisses me passionately and runs his hands over my body. The warmth of his palms sends a pleasant tingle to my pussy. Mmm, I always love how large his hands are and how he knows when to take charge with them. He threads his fingers through my hair, and I gasp as he tugs, forcing my head to tip back.

"Are you ready to get fucked mindless?" The slight growl in his voice gives me goosebumps.

"Yes, please. I need it."

Caleb chuckles and looks at Ben. "What do you think? Should we give her what she wants?"

Ben nods. "Let's do it. I heard she's begging to feel used."

Mmm, yes I am.

Ben continues. "Not that I blame her, since her husband is a bit of a softie. I bet he only fucks romantically, nice and slow."

Um… My breath catches from shock, and my eyes widen. My heart races as I glance towards Joey. What the hell is going on here?

Caleb laughs harshly. "I bet that's true."

Joey speeds up the rubbing of his cock through his pants and groans before he laughs along with them. "Oh, fuck off you two. Shut up and get on with it."

Ben grins and moves to stand next to Caleb. "I think we need to do a hole inspection first. See if we even want to fuck her."

Caleb nods. "Good idea."

I'm not exactly sure what a hole inspection includes, but the fire in my stomach tells me I don't care as long as I get something in one of those holes soon.

Caleb grips my shoulder and spins me until I'm facing the bed. Ben grabs my wrists as Caleb pushes my shoulder down to the mattress. Raw, wild need pulses through my pussy. I love being manhandled like this.

I bend over, and Caleb pulls my legs apart, forcing me to widen my stance. My face smashes against the comforter while Ben keeps hold of my wrists. Did they fucking choreograph this? Hell, maybe they've done this together more than once.

Ben says, "You check her pussy. I'm checking her ass."

Ohhhh, fuck.

"Wait," Joey calls out. "Use lube, so you can inspect it easier."

I hear the dresser opening before it slides closed again, and I tense in anticipation of what is about to happen.

"Good thinking," Ben replies, letting go of my wrists.

When my hands are free, I move them close to my face and grip the comforter. The squeeze of the lube bottle is loud, and drops of cold liquid rain onto my ass cheeks. Um, I think he missed the spot he was aiming for. I keep silent though since sex dolls don't talk.

Fingers explore along the length of my pussy lips. I assume it's Caleb, and a glance over my shoulder confirms it. He gathers moisture from my pussy and rubs circles around my clit. Holy fuck. I thought the guys were going to come in here and start fucking me immediately, but this is dirtier.

I straighten my head and stare unseeingly at the wall as Caleb continues his exploration of my pussy. His swirling fingers spread me wide as his thumb sinks into my ready wetness. Ben massages the lube into the crack of my ass, and I welcome his touch.

"Miri, spread your legs wider for me."

I obey, moving my feet even further apart. They are both standing close enough that I can feel the heat of their bodies, and Caleb's hard cock brushes against my thigh.

Caleb's "Good girl" makes me want to please them even more.

I tilt my head back and close my eyes, letting the sensations become my only focus. When Ben's lubed-up finger works its way into my ass,

I groan involuntarily. He presses deeper as I squirm, and I suck in air, trying to hold in any further sounds. The quieter I am, the nastier this is.

Ben whistles softly. "That's a nice tight ass. I bet it'll feel good around my big fat cock."

"Yeah, I'm sure it will," Caleb murmurs. "You can stretch her ass out. I'm all about this wet pussy."

Uh...he thinks he's fucking me in the ass with that third leg he's sporting? A forbidden longing zings straight to my core, and I almost come all over Caleb's fingers. I squeeze my eyes shut, and I'm panting as I fight for control.

Holy fuck. Will he fuck my ass while Caleb is in my pussy? My entire body zings alive at the thought of being double stuffed.

Jesus, why didn't I think of this earlier? All day, I've been fantasizing about getting fucked by two men and somehow didn't consider it happening at the same time. To have the chance to do it with my husband watching is overwhelming, but this is an experience I'd want to share with him.

Ben laughs. "She has two tight holes to fill. Why not?"

Caleb's cock brushes against me again as both guys work their fingers inside me. Pleasure builds in my core, and I bite my lip and clutch the comforter tightly as my legs begin to shake.

CHAPTER 4

With sudden clarity, I know I really *do* want that monster inside my ass. This is the filthy wish I didn't know I lusted after. I won't be satisfied tonight unless I'm stuffed and stretched more than I've ever been.

"This hole is ready," Caleb announces, and his cock throbs against my thigh.

Ben slaps my ass. "I'm almost done getting this one ready. I need it to be loose and relaxed."

Ben continues to massage the lube around my asshole, and I whimper when he adds a second finger to the first one and presses them into my ass. They're treating me like I'm just holes to use, and it's exactly what I wanted. This is fucking amazing. Joey deserves a goddamn medal for arranging this.

Caleb runs the tip of his cock up and down the back of my leg. "I can't wait any longer. I need to fuck something."

I whimper as Ben removes his fingers and Caleb climbs onto the bed and lies down on his back.

"Climb up onto me and ride me like the cock-addicted slut you are."

This is the third time I've had sex with Caleb, and it's making the dirty talk even better because I've seen the softer side of him. I know he's not a jackass who means what he's saying.

And he's right; I am a cock-addicted slut. I'll do anything he wants tonight.

I nod eagerly, shift up onto the bed, and straddle him. He grips his cock to hold it steady, and I pause right before pressing down. I look over my shoulder at Joey and smile at him. "Is this a good view, my love?"

His cock is out of his pants, and he's stroking it slowly. He's nice and hard, and I bet he's leaking pre-cum. Mmmm…I know exactly how he tastes, and I wish he was in my mouth. The haze of lust in his eyes tells me he's been enjoying everything.

He has to clear his throat before he can talk. "Yes, it's a lovely view, but sex dolls can't speak. They just take cock."

My lips part slightly in surprise as Caleb holds onto my hips and thrusts up.

"Ohhh." I accidentally let a moan slip out as I sink onto his shaft. His wonderfully thick cock burrows its way to my core, and the pleasure almost short circuits my brain. Even though I've fucked him before, his size still surprises me. He's so thick it feels like he's splitting me apart. I rock my hips, enjoying how he massages every inch of my cave walls. He reaches up to play with my nipples, and spikes of bliss head straight to my clit. Mmmm, this is perfect.

He digs his fingers into my hips, dragging me up and down his shaft, and little sighs and peeps of pleasure escape me as I speed up my movements. I'm rushing towards an orgasm, and I don't want to stop.

"Kiss me," he demands, and I lean forward and plaster my lips against his.

I'm a woman possessed as my tongue tangles with his. He wraps his arms around me, and the blistering kiss sets my soul on fire. I'm so focused on the building desire in my core that I don't pay attention to anything else until I feel the tip of Ben's cock against my asshole.

I squeal into Caleb's mouth and grind harder against his shaft. Oh god, this is why they have me in this position. Caleb is lying on the bed at the perfect angle for Joey to see both their cocks sliding into me from his chair.

"Take it slow," Joey warns. "She isn't used to having such a gigantic cock in her ass. I don't want my toy hurt."

My head spins, and I have the insane urge to laugh and moan at the same time. Joey taking care of me in a filthy way is exactly like something he would do. Such a romantic.

Caleb continues to kiss me as Ben applies more lube to my ass. Even with the added slickness, I know it's going to hurt when he presses in, but the initial discomfort never lasts long.

"Get ready." Ben gives the warning a few moments before the pressure against my opening increases.

I try to relax, knowing it will hurt less, but it doesn't stop the pain.

"Fuuuuuck," I cry out as he pushes inside slowly.

Oh god, he's so fucking huge. I thought Caleb was splitting me in two, but this is beyond anything I could have imagined. Pain shoots through me, twisted with intense pleasure. It's a delicious thrill as he stretches my ass.

Caleb continues to piston his hips up, thrusting into my pussy while Ben sinks deeper inside me. I whimper as pings of bliss explode in my mind.

I hope Joey can see everything. Thinking back on what happened at the work Christmas party, I can't help but wish Joey would come fuck my mouth like he did then. I could have all my holes filled for real. Shit, I want that.

I'm distracted from my thoughts when Ben pauses. I can tell he's in my ass as far as he can go because he pulls out and presses back in. The pain is gone, and it's replaced by a rapture I've never felt before.

As both guys fuck me, I lose my mind and can't keep quiet any longer. I'm writhing and moaning continuously as they use both my holes.

"Fuck, this feels soooo good," Caleb murmurs, as he squeezes my breasts and tugs on my nipples.

Ben's voice is strained when he agrees. "Yeah, I could use this piece of ass all night long."

Caleb grunts and thrusts faster. "I think Joey's toy likes being used."

"God yes," I moan, as every press from Ben makes me take Caleb's cock further inside me. "Use me."

Caleb laughs harshly. "We're not stopping until we're done with you."

I grind against Caleb's cock and speed up my rhythm, thinking of nothing else except the growing bliss. The bed creaks from our combined movements, and my tiny mewling joins in with wet slapping sounds and the moans and groans from the guys. It's all too much, and my body shakes as I rush towards my orgasm.

Both cocks massaging my insides create a ripple of pleasure through me. My cries of "Oh god" turn into whimpers and moans as Ben pushes me down closer to Caleb so he can put his foot on the bed and drill into my ass.

I bite down on Caleb's shoulder as I explode with pleasure. My pussy clenches down hard, and I scream as I come. Energy courses all the way from my fingers to my toes as the guys fuck me through my orgasm.

I collapse on top of Caleb, but the guys don't stop using me. My pussy flutters with aftershocks of pleasure. The bliss is too much, and my brain switches off. I become a mindless fucktoy that they both continue to use, and time holds no meaning.

Ben comes first. He roars and fills my ass with his hot cum a few seconds before Caleb blows his load into my pussy. They fuck their cum back into me for a few strokes before pulling out.

Ben groans, "God, that was amazing," as I roll off of Caleb onto my back.

I close my eyes and drift while one of them goes into the bathroom. I'm surprised when hands hook around my thighs and tug me to the end of the bed. What's going on?

Someone pushes my legs open, and I look down at Caleb kneeling between them. He puts my knees on his shoulders while he leans in to lick me. He spreads my labia, pushing his tongue into my dripping slit as he cleans up from the mess he made in my pussy.

"Ohhh," I moan, and my hips move with his rhythm.

I twist the comforter in my hands as each swipe of his tongue pings me with gentle pleasure. I've never had anyone clean me up like this before, and it's the right kind of dirty.

Just when I'm about to come again, Ben speaks up from the bathroom doorway. "It's my turn."

Caleb and Ben switch places, and Ben's mouth latches onto my clit. He sucks and swirls his tongue around my swollen nub, and I moan loudly, which makes him pause his licking.

I tilt my hips, desperate for his tongue. "Oh god, don't stop!"

Ben slides his hands up the outside of my thighs and cups my ass. He squeezes my cheeks as he attacks my clit again. I buck towards his face and peep out tiny moans as the ecstasy builds.

"You sound so damn sexy," he murmurs with passion.

His tongue drives me crazy, and I can't focus on anything but the pleasure. I press my pussy against his face, desperate for another orgasm.

I almost don't notice when Caleb kneels on the bed next to my face. His cock is hard again, and he's stroking it as he moves it towards my mouth. Ohhh fuck, this is filthy. Caleb presses the head against my lips, and I open as wide as I can so he can slide in. I suck greedily on the tip, enjoying the combined flavor of our juices.

"Fuck, she tastes so good," Ben says as he slides his fingers into my pussy and fucks me with them while he continues to suck on my clit.

I moan around Caleb's cock and wrap my hand around his shaft so I can stroke him while he fucks my mouth.

Ben stops licking me and announces, "Fuck it."

He holds my legs and stands up. I barely have time to wonder what he's doing before my feet are on his shoulders and he's sliding his cock into my pussy. Since he's thicker than Caleb, his cock stretches my pussy even further than it was earlier. I'm immediately on the edge of my orgasm.

Caleb pumps into my mouth slowly while Ben sets a punishing pace. My body responds to each movement, and I whimper and moan with each deep thrust. I can't take much more of this, and I'm going to come any second.

"Be a good girl and come for me," Ben commands with an extra hard thrust that shoots me over the edge.

My body convulses with pleasure, and Caleb's cock muffles my scream. My orgasm seems never-ending as Ben hammers into me. He doesn't let up until he groans and shudders as he blows a second massive load deep into my pussy.

Ben coming lights a fire in Caleb, and his thrusts become shorter and quicker. Within moments, a burst of cum hits the back of my throat as several more spurts coat my tongue. I try to swallow and clean him up the best I can, but saliva and cum run out of my mouth when he pulls out.

He leans over and kisses me softly, sucking his cum off my tongue. Jesus, Caleb is one dirty mofo. It's awesome.

I wonder if Joey would ever let me fuck Caleb again. The same guy three times seems a bit more than a casual fuck, but I can't help but want it. Sure, Ben's also got a great cock, but something about Caleb's ability to fuck me hard and yet be sweet makes him a perfect fuck buddy.

A warm fuzziness steals over me as Caleb pulls me up onto the bed so I'm not hanging off it. My eyes drift closed. I'm on a higher plane of existence, one where nothing matters but the amazing afterglow of having two massive cocks double penetrating me and using me.

The guys talk quietly, and I don't follow the conversation. I listen to the sound of clothes rustling, and I assume they're getting dressed. The bed dips next to my head, and I open my eyes when a hand strokes my cheek.

Caleb is fully clothed and looking at me with a soft smile. "Thank you for another wonderful night. Joey is one lucky man."

Joey's "I am" pleases me.

"Thank you, Caleb..." I don't know how close Ben is, so I raise my voice, "And you too, Ben. This was wonderful."

Ben laughs. "Believe me, the pleasure was all mine."

I smile in his general direction and close my eyes again and doze while Caleb and Ben leave. Within minutes, the room is silent.

CHAPTER 5

Joey climbs on the bed next to me and kisses me gently. "You're such a beautiful mess."

I peek at him and search his eyes to make sure he really means it. The love shining from him warms me. He cuddles close, but I can't fully relax because I expect him to pounce on me any moment. The last two times I fucked someone else, he was all over me as soon as we were alone. He rubs my arm and tries nothing further. Huh, maybe he came while watching me get double stuffed.

Wetness drips out of me, and since he's not seeming like he wants to fuck me, I tease him. "I *am* a mess. I need a shower."

"You do. I'll go start the water for you."

He kisses my nose and climbs off the bed. When I hear the shower running, I get up and dig out a cotton nightgown from the dresser. I finger the new purple lace lingerie set before closing the drawer. I'll wear that for him tomorrow.

"Your shower awaits, my lady."

Joey's standing in the bathroom's doorway, and I stand on my tiptoes to brush my lips against his as I pass.

"Why thank you, my kind sir."

I leave the bathroom door open. When I step into the shower, the water is the perfect temperature. My wonderful husband knows exactly what I like.

I stand under the spray for a bit, doing nothing but letting the water cascade over me. My pussy and ass aren't sore yet, but I can tell they will be by morning. A person can't get pounded in both holes by two huge cocks and not expect a little tenderness.

Squeezing body wash out of its travel container, I lather up a washcloth and run it over my body, washing off the cum on my inner thighs and butt. Movement outside of the frosted glass shower door tells me Joey is in the bathroom.

He's naked, and he leans against the counter while he watches me. A simmer of desire coils in my stomach. I really need him to fuck me to show me what happened tonight doesn't change anything between us.

"Want to join me?" I use my cutest sing-song tone in the hopes to entice him.

His voice is lust-thickened when he says, "No, I'm just enjoying the show."

Heh, he definitely enjoys watching me. When I'm rinsing off, I spend extra time with my hand between my legs, pretending I'm doing a very thorough cleaning. I purposely face him so he can see where my hand is.

After a minute of touching myself, his voice is stern. "I think you're clean enough."

I hold in a giggle. "I think you're right."

Turning off the shower, I step out, and he immediately wraps a towel around me and dries me off. All I have to do is stand there as he bends down and starts at my feet and works his way up. I widen my legs as he gets closer to my pussy so he's able to rub the cotton against me. I give a soft moan as he spends extra time between my legs, and when the towel drops away, he uses his fingers to rub along my folds instead.

I run my fingers through his hair, and he leans in to kiss along the soft curls of my landing strip. Maybe I was wrong about him not wanting more tonight, or it's possible I got him worked up while he was watching me shower. My pussy is loving the attention, so it doesn't matter why.

He uses his hands to pull open my pussy lips, and he presses his face against me so he can massage my clit with his tongue.

"Ohhh, god," I moan and tilt my hips towards his face to give him better access.

The room spins a little, and my knees go weak as he licks and sucks the sensitive bundle of nerves. I'm not in any danger of falling, but I'm feeling unsteady as pleasure runs up and down the length of my body.

He slips a finger inside me, and I buck against him and cry out from the pleasure. While I'm not one to normally stop my husband from giving me a thrilling tongue bath, I really need him to fill me up with his cum. Ending the night with a pussy full of his seed is my favorite part of being a hotwife. No matter how slutty I am, I want Joey to be the last guy to come inside me.

I tug on his hair, forcing him to look up at me. "Love, I need you to fuck me. Please?"

He stands and holds my hand as we move to the bed. Before we lie down, he pulls me against him for a deep kiss. His hard cock pokes against my stomach, so I reach between us and stroke him while our tongues swirl together.

I'm so in love with him. My heart feels like it's ready to burst. I'm having a wonderful time being a hotwife, and it's so fucking hot to see how turned on he gets watching me with other men, but I'd give it all up if he asked me to. All the enormous cocks in the world can't compare to this moment with him right here, right now. His cock is the only one that really matters to me.

He gives a sharp intake of breath when I slide my hand lower and run my fingers over his balls before moving back to the tip. He's already leaking pre-cum, and I swirl my fingers around the head of his cock.

He groans. "No more teasing. I need you."

I let go of his cock and give him a sassy, "As you wish, sir," before climbing onto the bed. I'm too tired to be on top again, so I lie down in the middle on my back. He joins me, and I open my legs to welcome him.

He settles between my thighs and rubs the head of his cock along my slit. Fuuuck, now he's the one teasing me. He takes his time and gets the tip of his cock nice and wet before pushing into me.

As he stretches me for the last time tonight, the pings of delight are stronger than what I felt earlier. This is how I know he's the one for me. It's just sex with the other men, but no matter how slutty I get with Joey, we're always making love.

"God, I love you," he groans as he begins to thrust.

I hold on to his shoulders and wrap my legs around him. He's being gentle, and I appreciate the care he's taking with me.

I feel so incredibly full and happy. "I love you too."

Keeping my eyes glued to his, I watch desire flicker over his face. His pleasure brings me closer to the edge, but I don't want to come yet. I'm waiting to come when he fills me.

"Please, faster," I beg.

"Yes, baby," he growls and picks up the pace.

He quickens his thrusts while still not fucking me hard. I'm so close to coming, and I can't wait any longer. I unwrap my legs from his waist and spread them wide as I put my feet down, pushing my hips up to meet him and force him deeper. He hits the perfect spot, and my eyes glaze as waves of pleasure crash over me.

"Ohhh, god!" I cry out as my climax builds and I splinter into a thousand pieces. I'm free-falling through space when he growls and unloads his warm cum deep inside me. He thrusts in a few more times, making sure I get every drop.

We're both flushed and panting when he climbs off me. Holy fuck, that was a perfect ending to the night. I float in a daze for a few moments, and when I come back to my senses, Joey is in his own little world as he lies on his back, staring at the ceiling.

Oh yeah, I think I fucked my dear husband senseless.

Curling against him, I wrap a leg around him and snuggle into the crook of his arm. I trace figure-eights on his chest, and I can tell the moment he can think again because he brings his hand up to rub my back.

I keep my tone light and flirty. "So, did you enjoy watching me get stuffed by two guys?"

He gives a strangled laugh. "Yeah, that was good."

Thinking about how wonderful having all my holes used reminds me of my thought in the middle of it all.

"You know, you could have used my mouth while the guys were inside me."

His hand stills for a moment. "You seemed a little busy."

Giving his shoulder a little kiss, I purr at him. "I would have gladly sucked your cock."

He rubs my back again but is quiet for a moment, as if he's thinking. "Guess I'll know that for next time."

A zing runs through me. Next time? Nah, he's just fucking with me.

I tease him back. "Yep, guess you'll have to do it next time."

He pulls me close and kisses the top of my head. I'm exhausted, but my brain churns at the thought of him in my mouth while two other guys fuck me. It's really too bad there isn't another work event planned. I smile softly at myself and force myself to relax.

Okay, yeah, I'm totally a slut. I guess I'll just have to think of another excuse to get double stuffed in the future.

The End

THE FREEUSE CAMPING SLUT

HOTWIFE HOLIDAYS 4

CHAPTER 1

When Joey told me to pack my white lace top for our Fourth of July camping trip, I knew he had something thrilling planned for me. I'm excited as I place it carefully in my duffel bag. The top in question is a reminder of our first foray into the hotwife lifestyle. I wore it on a trip to the Oregon coast last summer, where Joey shared me with his best friend from high school. The memory still makes me wet.

After that trip to Oregon, we continued to explore new territories in the bedroom. Namely, inviting other men to fuck me. I've had multiple cocks inside me that didn't belong to my husband, and Joey and I both are having fun.

Joey can't keep his hands off me as I stuff another tank top into my duffel bag. He presses up against my back as his fingers trace the lace trim of my bra, slipping over the fabric to graze my nipples. They instantly harden, and a throb of desire pulses between my legs.

"Mmm...Miri, I can't wait to see you in that top again," he murmurs in my ear before nibbling on my lobe.

"What do you have planned for this weekend?" I ask, leaning back into his embrace. His hands slide down to cup my ass, squeezing roughly.

"You'll have to wait and see," he chuckles, grinding his hard cock against me. I whimper, aching to get him inside me, but he pulls away before I can beg for it. The hunger for him is sweet torture.

We finish packing in a sexual haze. Whenever he gets close to me, he goes out of his way to brush up against me. Every touch of his is charged with promise. My panties are soaked by the time we're done. I don't know what Joey has in store for me this weekend, but I'm sure it involves something slutty in front of another guy. Maybe he's going to make me walk around in the barely there top and show off my tits to everyone.

Joey takes his bag out to the living room to set it by the door for easy loading into the car in the morning. I follow him out there and sidle up to him, wrapping my arms around his waist. "So," I purr. "I think you should give me some hints about this weekend."

He grins, pulling me flush against him. I can feel the hard ridge of his cock pressing into my belly, and I rock against it, trying to get him to fuck me before we go to sleep.

"Patience. You'll find out soon enough."

I pout and run my hands up his chest and play with the hair at the nape of his neck. "You're not playing fair."

"When have I ever played fair?" His hands slide under my shirt, fingers dancing over my skin. "You'll get what's coming to you, don't worry."

"And what exactly is coming to me?" I ask breathlessly.

Joey grins, eyes dark with promise. "More than you can imagine, starting right now."

Now? Before I can question him, he walks me backwards towards the sofa. He peels my shorts and panties down to my knees in one swift motion, and I moan as he spins me around and bends me over the armrest. Oh fuck, yes. I didn't even have to beg for his cock.

"Spread your legs," he growls.

I obey him instantly, and I drop my shorts and panties to the floor so I can move one leg out of them. I spread my legs, trembling with need. His cock nudges at my entrance, sliding in with a hard thrust that steals my breath. I moan, rocking back to meet his strokes. He drills into me, making sure every inch of his cock is inside me. My legs quiver from delight, and I grip the couch cushions so I don't get knocked around too much.

Ever since I've become a hotwife, our sex life has been reinvigorated. Tonight is the perfect example. Last year, before our trip to Oregon, we hadn't fucked for weeks. Tonight, he can't keep his hands off me. It's like he's a different man.

He hammers into me, his hands gripping my hips, and I moan as I barrel towards my orgasm. I'm so wet that each time he bottoms out, a slapping sound fills the air. My thighs shake as the ecstasy intensifies. I'm chanting, "Fuck me, fuck me," and right before my orgasm hits, he gives a final hard whack, groans loudly, and fills me with his cum.

Wait, what? He slowly fucks his cum back up inside me for a few strokes before stopping as his cock throbs inside me. My head is woozy from the lack of orgasm, and my body cries out in displeasure. We can't be done.

"Did you just…?" I ask, confused.

"I'm finished," he says, smacking my ass as he withdraws from my pussy. "We should go to bed."

Oh fuck, I'm not coming? We've been experimenting with power play dynamics lately, but this is the first time he's fucked me without finishing me. What's going on?

"See you in bed," he says, and walks away.

I slump on the sofa, trembling and unsatisfied. Being under Joey's control is both torture and bliss. He always takes me to the brink and holds me there, wielding my pleasure like a weapon. I hate it and I love it all at once.

I briefly consider taking care of business myself, but deep down, I enjoy being edged and I'd rather go to bed aching. It will make whatever happens on the trip that much sweeter.

I stay in the living room until my head clears. When I crawl into bed, I'm still buzzing with need, my pussy aching to be filled. Joey is already asleep, but when I cuddle beside him, he drapes one arm over my waist in a possessive hold.

Tomorrow we're heading out on our camping trip. I have no idea what to expect, but if tonight was any indication, Joey has some surprises planned. Just the thought makes me squirm, rubbing my thighs together. I'm not sure how I'll survive an entire weekend under Joey's control. But that's the thrill. Letting go and giving myself over to the games we play.

Joey stirs beside me, pulling me closer in his sleep. I relax into his embrace, elation and apprehension twisting in my belly. I toss and turn for what seems like hours, visions of Joey and his wicked grin flashing behind my eyelids. The ache between my legs refuses to fade, my clit throbbing with every beat of my heart.

When I finally drift off, my dreams are filled with faceless men. Their hands and mouths explore my body, bringing me to the brink again and again, only to leave me empty and wanting. I wake with a gasp more than once, my pussy dripping wet and pulsing.

Beside me, Joey sleeps like the dead, the bastard. I consider waking him for revenge, but one of us needs enough sleep to drive tomorrow. My frustration only makes me needier.

CHAPTER 2

I'm not refreshed when the alarm blares, startling me from my erotic dreams. I blink awake to find Joey gazing down at me, a smug smile on his lips.

"Rise and shine, baby. We've got a big day ahead of us."

His words send a bolt of arousal straight to my core. I stretch with a groan, the sheets tangled around my naked body.

"You suck," I mutter with no real venom.

Joey just laughs, pulling me in for a deep, claiming kiss. "No, I don't. You love every second of this."

Damn him, he's right. And it's a good thing he's driving today. I'm going to sleep the entire way to the campsite.

I doze in the passenger seat while Joey drives. The gentle hum of the SUV's engine lulls me into a deep sleep, and I drift away, wrapped in the sun's warmth.

When the car stops, I crack my eyes open and look at the clock on the dashboard. I've been asleep for two hours. We're at the rest stop closest to the exit for the campgrounds. The forested area around us is tranquil, filled with a sense of peace that seems to seep into my very being.

"So pretty," I say as I step out of the SUV and stretch my legs. The sunlight filters through the trees, casting dappled shadows on the surrounding area.

"Want to hear what I have planned for the weekend?" Joey replies with a grin as he gets out of the SUV to stretch as well. He walks around to my side and slides his arms around me.

He doesn't wait for me to respond. "I talked to my friends, and if you want, you can have a freeuse night with all of them tonight."

My mouth drops open in shock, and my chest tightens. "Freeuse, like they use me?"

His simple reply of "Yes" creates soft tingles in my core. My heart skips a beat, and I feel both a surge of excitement and hesitation at his words.

"I…I don't know, Joey. Aren't some of them married or have girlfriends?"

"No, I only invited my single friends."

He brushes his lips against mine, and I lean into his arms, accepting his kiss while my thoughts race. God, I want what he's offering, but what if something goes wrong? How well do I know these guys?

I tense up, and he rubs my back in circles, as he does when he's trying to help me destress. "Miri, they all know your safeword. I trust them. You can have a good time tonight."

I take a deep breath, noticing a mix of emotions—fear, longing, curiosity. I never considered anything like this. Freeuse for all the guys tonight? Fuck, that's hot.

As the initial shock fades, I'm more and more intrigued by the prospect of surrendering to these men. A dirty thrill courses through me, making my skin flush with longing. My pussy aches as I daydream about a bunch of men fucking me.

"All right. Let's make this weekend one to remember."

Joey's eyes light up. "You're amazing, Miri. Trust me, you won't regret it." He gives me a passionate kiss that leaves me breathless.

CHAPTER 3

We take a few minutes walking around the rest stop before getting back into the SUV. As we continue driving towards the campsite, my body buzzes, and the more I imagine the men lining up to use me, the wetter my panties become. The thought of being used by multiple men, each with their own unique touch and taste, sends shivers down my spine. I bet some of them will even watch while the others fuck me. Oh God, maybe it'll become a circle jerk in the end.

"Are you sure they all want to do this?" I ask Joey, double-checking that I'm not getting all worked up for a bunch of guys who don't really want to fuck me.

He grins. "Definitely. They can't wait to get their hands on you."

My stomach flips at his words as a yearning courses through me. I'm teetering on the edge of an exhilarating unknown, ready to dive into the depths of pleasure and surrender. I glance over at Joey, and his smile seems equally eager for the adventure ahead.

Suddenly, all my fears seem trivial compared to the amazing opportunity that Joey is letting me explore. How in the hell did I get so lucky to marry him? How many guys would let their wife fuck all his friends while camping?

I keep my tone light and teasing. "Then bring on the fuckery!"

Joey laughs and reaches over to squeeze my hand reassuringly before putting it back on the wheel.

The rest of the drive is a blur as my mind races with thoughts of how this will work. Are they going to just bend me over the picnic table while everyone is eating? Drag me off to the woods? My body hums with anticipation. I imagine the touch of powerful hands on my skin, rough kisses leaving me breathless, and the hunger in their eyes as they take whatever they want from me.

As we park the SUV at the campsite and step out into the serene forest, a rush of exuberance runs through me. This is it. I'm ready to be shared.

Joey's friends are gathered around a firepit, and I quickly count six guys. I've met them all before, but I only know a couple of them well. Their faces light up when they see me. Joey smiles at his friends and gives them a discreet thumbs up. Wait, what did the thumbs up mean?

"Ready?" Joey asks me, his eyes filled with enthusiasm.

Nodding is all I can do as my heart races. Joey and I move to the back of the SUV to unload our bags, and I notice Darren walking towards us. He's one of the friends who I've only met briefly before. I always thought he was sexy as all fuck, his dark hair and piercing blue eyes making him an irresistible presence. A predatory smile graces his lips as he approaches me.

"Hello, Miri." His voice is low and filled with hunger. "Nice to see you again."

"Hi, Darren," I stammer, my cheeks flushing at the intensity of his gaze. His eyes roam over my body, taking in every curve and leaving no doubt about his desires for me.

Joey grabs supplies from the trunk, and I see the guys exchange a knowing glance.

Darren focuses his attention back on me. "Don't you need to help your husband unload?"

I almost laugh and tell him he could help as well—or better yet, I could help him unload something inside me instead. But really, what does he think I'm doing back here? I wasn't planning on just watching. I give him the side-eye as I turn to get a bag. But before I can grab it,

Darren reaches out and puts pressure on my shoulder, forcing me to bend over.

Ohhh, fuck. I really should have seen this coming.

I grip the edge of the cargo space as my jeans-covered ass is presented invitingly to him. My heartbeat quickens, and a jolt of eagerness thrills me. He's not going to fuck me right here, is he? Anyone could walk by. We're in a secluded camping spot, but I've been here before and there are trails throughout this area.

He reaches around to my front and unbuttons and unzips my jeans. My entire body ignites with desire. No, I think he's really going for it.

"You're going to be my dirty little slut tonight," he whispers, and I shudder in response. He didn't ask, but I still nod, unable to speak as desire threatens to consume me. This is what I get for being worked up last night without release. I'm ready to beg for the first cock that gets close to me.

He yanks my jeans down just far enough to expose my panty-clad ass. "Look at you," Darren murmurs, his fingers toying with the edge of my already-soaked panties. "So eager for this."

He tugs at the fabric, the sensation causing me to moan. "You enjoy being called a slut, don't you? Admit it."

"Yes," I confess breathlessly, my cheeks flushing with both embarrassment and arousal.

I hear the clink of a belt buckle before he continues. "Good. Because that's exactly what you are tonight, and I'm going to make sure you don't forget it."

He shoves my panties aside and plunges his thick cock inside me, making me gasp. Holy fuck, this is surreal. We haven't even been at the campground for five minutes, and I already have another guy's cock in me.

"God, you're so tight," he groans, grasping my hips tightly and thrusting into me with wild abandon. Joey continues to unload the car, pulling bags from around me and seemingly unfazed by our actions. The fact he's not watching and is acting like this is an everyday occurrence only fuels my hunger to be used further.

"Fuck me, Darren. Make me your filthy slut." I can't stop myself from begging, overcome by the sensations coursing through my body.

"Damn right I will." He slams into me even harder. The sound of our bodies colliding fills the air, accompanied by my moans of ecstasy. In this moment, I can't imagine anything more perfect than being taken and used like this.

He continues to fuck me roughly, his voice strained with effort. "There's something you need to remember tonight, Miri. You don't get to decide what happens. We're the ones using you." He punctuates each word with a deep thrust. "Over, and over, and over."

My moans grow louder. I'm trembling from the force of his thrusts, and he pounds into me with renewed intensity. My head swirls, and I get the insane thought that even though I'm being used, I've never felt so alive or so free.

Darren's voice is tight with urgency. "You better be close. I'm about to blow my load inside you, and you won't get to come after that."

"Almost. Just a little more..." I moan, the rapture building inside me.

"Such a dirty little slut," he grunts.

Biting my lip, I moan as he smacks my ass and sends a shockwave of pleasure through me. I clench my inner walls around him and lose myself as I tip over the edge.

"Ohhh, fuck," I scream out, not caring if anyone hears, as pure joy ripples from my fingers to my toes. He rams into me, and his cock throbs as he explodes.

He continues fucking me, knocking me against the SUV as he unloads ropes of sticky cum. My brain is numb, and I can barely hang on while he finishes using me.

When he finally slows down, my heart pounds, and I try to catch my breath as he leans over me.

"Good girl," Darren murmurs, his breath hot against my neck as he gently withdraws from me. His touch lingers briefly before he steps back, leaving me feeling suddenly exposed and vulnerable.

I look around as Darren drags his pants up and heads back to the other guys without another word. Joey comes up to me and rubs my back while Darren's cum and my juices run down my inner thigh. I don't think I brought enough clean clothes for this.

I struggle to stand up and Joey helps keep me steady while I pull my panties and jeans back into place. His eyes glow with lust as he wraps me up in his arms, his hardness brushing against me through his jeans.

His voice is husky. "How are you feeling?"

"Amazing," I reply honestly, leaning into his embrace. "That was…wow."

"Good, I want you to enjoy yourself." He places a tender kiss on my forehead.

When he doesn't make a move to fuck me, I'm confused. "My love?"

"Yes?" He rubs circles on my back, and I want to melt into him and beg him to fuck me. He needs pleasure as well. Why is he not pounding into my pussy this very second?

"Who is this weekend for?"

He murmurs into my hair. "It's for both of us."

I hug him more tightly, breathing deeply and letting his masculine scent soothe me. My husband's a little more twisted than I realized, but if this is what he wants…I'm game.

CHAPTER 4

After we unload the car, the men help Joey set up our tent while I sit at the picnic table, feeling like a queen. If I'm going to be the freeuse slut tonight, I'm not going to lift a finger. They can set up the tent and feed me. I've got other duties—I'm their hole to use.

I snicker to myself. Yeah, I've got limits, dammit! I'm just here for a good time.

While I'm waiting, I grab my phone and earbuds out of my bag. When I plug them in, the world falls away as the music soothes me. The weight of my adult responsibilities falls from my shoulders, and I feel like I can finally relax. I'm in a state of bliss as I lean back against the table, enjoying the sunshine and the cool breeze drifting through the forest.

I don't even notice the guys approach me until Joey puts his hands on my shoulders, startling me. I jump, nearly dropping my phone on the ground. "Jesus!"

He grins down at me and says something I can't hear over the music. I remove the earbuds. "I'm sorry, what?"

"I asked if you were having a good time." His eyes sparkle with mirth and something else I can't quite place.

"So far," I say with a grin. "Darren's a really good fuck."

Joey chuckles. "I'll take your word for it, though I hear Miles has a bigger cock."

I blush at his words, surprised he's giving sexual information about his friend. "That's good info to know."

Joey rubs his thumb over the pulse point in my neck. "The guys are almost done putting up the tent. After that, we're going to grill some food and have a bonfire."

"So, should I start getting ready, then?" I'm eager to find out what's coming my way tonight.

"We'll give you some time to relax and freshen up. Don't take too long. They can't wait to get their hands on you."

He gives my neck a nip before sauntering away, and I'm left feeling turned on and a little lightheaded. Damn, I think I'm going to enjoy this camping trip.

I take a change of clothes with me—including the white lace top Joey told me to bring—and scout out the central bathrooms. Peeking into the showers, I note they look well maintained. I'm going to need to clean up at some point tonight, but for now, I'm enjoying being dirty with another guy's cum in me. It gives me that delicious, slutty feeling I crave.

When I get back to our campsite, the guys are all poking at the coals in the firepit. This seems like a start of a joke. How many men does it take to light a fire? One, plus one more...yeah, I can't think of a good punchline...unless it's something about how it takes six guys to light MY fire.

I'm snickering to myself, and Joey looks up from the fire when I approach. His eyes roam over me, lingering on the white lace top. My nipples harden, and I know they are visible through the lace. It takes six guys to light my fire...or just one very sexy husband.

He grins. "Looks like someone's ready for a good time."

Arousal pulses through me at his words as I step closer to the fire.

I'm dressed in nothing but the top, skimpy tight shorts, and my socks and shoes. The next person to fuck me will find out I'm not wearing panties. My hair is wild and messy from the trip and from being bent over the tailgate of the car. I'm like a wood nymph who's ready to be ravished by hungry men.

I'm still trying to wrap my head around the idea that Joey wants to watch me getting used by a bunch of his friends. He seems totally at ease and happy, so he obviously does. Hell, I might be more uncertain than he is.

He leans in to kiss me, and his tongue plunders my mouth as he moves his hand up to tweak my nipple. My legs buckle, but he holds me steady. His eyes blaze with heat, and he murmurs, "It's going to be a fun night."

"Yes," I pant as I struggle to keep standing, my legs wobbling.

"But first, we eat." He smacks my ass as he steps away, and I stagger from the impact.

I stand there for a moment, watching as he returns to the grill and flips the hamburgers and hot dogs. The other men are busy watching Joey or looking at me. I've seen these guys a handful of times, but how well do I really know them? Does that even matter? They're here to use me, and Joey is getting his kicks from this as well. I just have to remember that.

My mouth waters at the smell of dinner cooking. I'm also craving a taste of cock. I'm not sure which I need more...maybe cock.

Wandering over to the cooler, I grab a bottle of water and turn to see Miles sitting at the picnic table, staring at me like I'm a scrumptious snack he plans to devour. *Come and get it, big boy.* I almost wish I didn't know he has an enormous cock. Now I'm desperate to see it. I wonder if he's already hard?

My breath catches, and I force myself to look away from him. To distract myself, I return to the firepit, and Joey hands me a plate with a hamburger patty on it. They spread the burger fixings out on the picnic table, so I have to get close to Miles to put condiments on my bun. It's hard not to picture Miles putting his special sauce all over me. I know there's a joke in there somewhere, but my brain is having trouble concentrating. As I squeeze the ketchup out, I can sense Miles's eyes still on me, and my entire body vibrates from sexual tension.

When he stands up and moves behind me, I fight the urge to rub my thighs together in anticipation. Please God, let him fuck me right here, right now. Miles wraps his arms around my waist, holding me flush against his chest. He grinds his hardness against my ass, and I moan softly. *Oh fuck, yes.*

He snakes his hand down the front of my shorts to my pussy as he kisses the back of my neck. I want to melt back into him, and I moan from joy when he rubs his finger against my clit. I get lost in the moment and almost drop my burger. Shit, I need to pay attention. I catch Joey grinning at me, and I smile back. This really is messed up, but I'm loving it.

Miles removes his hand and bends me over the table. I barely have time to set my plate next to me before my face is practically in a bowl of chips. They look tasty. Would I get a laugh if I licked one up and started eating it?

My shorts being dragged down my legs distracts me from the chips. A moment later, Miles plunges his cock inside me, and I cry out as he fills me up. Fuuuuck, Joey was right, Miles is huge.

He keeps me pinned to the table with one hand as he pounds into me and groans, "Your pussy feels amazing."

I want to tell him that his cock is the amazing thing, but the way it's stretching me out fries my brain, and I can't speak. Miles with the wonder schlong. Who knew? Okay, well, apparently Joey did.

Miles skims his free hand up my stomach, squeezing my breast, and I arch my back to give him better access. He rubs my nipple between his fingers as his other hand wraps around my waist and rests on my stomach.

Oh fuck, this is so hot. My heart races, and my senses are on high alert. Every plunge is more intense, and being in clear view of everyone makes me dizzy. I didn't think I had an exhibitionist streak in me, but knowing anyone can walk past and see us is turning me on more.

I rock my ass back to meet his thrusts as rapture builds in my core.

I'm hanging on to the picnic table for dear life, writhing in ecstasy. His thick cock makes me forget about our audience.

My pussy clenches around his cock as the orgasm builds. Miles moans, "Fuck, you're so fucking tight. I can't wait to come inside you."

My head is swimming as he drives into me. The pleasure is too much, and I scream as my orgasm rips through me. The bliss is overwhelming, and my legs shake uncontrollably as he continues to fuck me through it. He gives one last hard thrust before he erupts inside me with a loud groan.

When he pulls out, a gush of warm cum trails down my leg as I slump forward. Yeah, this guy just fucked me senseless.

He tugs my shorts back up around my waist and slaps my ass. "Good slut."

Whaaa? I watch Miles walk towards the firepit, and Joey smiles at him before approaching me. A raging beast of need is in his eyes as he helps me stand. I want to drop to my knees and suck his cock right here in front of everyone. The more guys I fuck, the more I want to give Joey pleasure.

His eyes shine in the dim lighting. "How are you?"

"Mm...good," I pant. "Really good."

He gives me a tight embrace. "I'm glad. We're going to have a blast tonight, but right now, you need to eat. You need your strength."

Shit, he's right. I really do need to eat. Only two guys have fucked me so far. The night is young. I take my burger with me to a chair by the firepit and absentmindedly eat while enjoying the feeling of my full pussy. How many loads of cum am I going to take tonight? What sort of woman enjoys being used and having multiple guys' cum in her like this? God, I really am a whore. It's wonderful.

While the guys chat about sports scores and work stuff, my mind churns over my sluttiness and what I'm expecting tonight. When I catch Joey's eye again, he's happy and animated. Hell, he looks like he's having the time of his life. My mind clears as I focus on him. It doesn't matter what type of woman does what I'm doing, because I have Joey's full blessing. He wants me to embrace my inner slut, and he's set up tonight for me to do it safely.

A sense of power engulfs me and my body zings alive with the awareness that all these men want me. They agreed to this camping trip because they want to fuck me. I've never felt more desired in my life, and suddenly every glance at me is foreplay. I become hyperaware of everything; the soft breeze, the crackle of the fire, the cum dripping from my pussy. I'm a sexual goddess, and I'm ready to embrace every cock I can get.

But first, I want a shower.

CHAPTER 5

I don't tell anyone where I'm going, and the weight of their stares is erotic as I grab my bag with my shampoo and towel. The showers are deserted as I strip and get in the lukewarm water. I wash my hair and soap my body up quickly. Yeah, I don't want to be in here any longer than necessary. I've got more men to fuck.

When I step out of the shower, another one of my husband's friends is waiting for me. He's sitting on a wooden bench across the room. I freeze as the water drips off of me, and my nipples harden in the cool air. Shit, this is the women's shower room. I didn't expect one of the guys to show up. I hope he put an out-of-order sign outside or something.

Of all my husband's friends, Ryan is the one I know the least. He's always the silent one at gatherings. It makes him seem mysterious, and the intensity of his gaze makes me shiver. I open my mouth to say hello to him, but he speaks first.

His voice is low pitched and commanding. "Kneel."

Oh shit. My eyes widen and, without even thinking about it, I sink to my knees on the cement floor. He studies me for a moment and then gives a half grin. "Do you like being a whore for all these men?"

"I...yes."

His mouth quirks up into a full smile. "You're such a slut, you don't even try to deny it."

He unzips his jeans, and my heart beats faster as I watch him. His long, thick cock is fully hard when he pulls it out. I lick my lips, hoping he'll tell me to suck it. When he starts stroking himself, I find my voice.

"I wouldn't be here if I didn't enjoy being a whore."

And it's true. The more Joey and I journey into this hotwife lifestyle, the more I appreciate the freedom of being shared. Tonight is the culmination of all my experiences, and seeing how happy Joey looked at the campfire sealed the deal for me. He wants me to be a freeuse slut.

Ryan continues to stroke his cock slowly. "It's hot watching you let a guy use your body however he wants."

His words set off a fire in my belly and slickness from my pussy coats my inner thighs. Someone could walk in here at any moment and catch us. I almost want it to happen.

"Crawl to me like a good girl, and I'll give you a treat," Ryan orders.

I don't hesitate and make my way across the cold cement. I keep my eyes trained on his cock, and I swear I can see it pulsating. The roughness under my knees is uncomfortable, and doing his bidding fulfills a need I didn't even know I had. I want him to control me and tell me exactly what to do. When I reach him, I sit back on my heels.

"Now suck on it."

He doesn't have to tell me twice. He spreads his knees, and I move between them. I lick the tip and then suck it into my mouth, moaning softly as I taste his pre-cum. He presses my head down, and his cock slides deeper into my mouth. My eyes drift closed as I enjoy the submission of obeying him. His hands tangle in my wet hair, and he forces me to move up and down his shaft.

"Such a good little cocksucker. Joey didn't tell me you were so talented with your mouth. He only said your pussy feels amazing."

Oh fuck, Joey told them sexual things about me? I guess it makes sense if he's offering his wife up to be fucked, but knowing he talked about my pussy is hella dirty.

Ryan hauls me off his cock, and I whimper as the saliva dripping from my mouth makes a mess on my chin. "Stroke it. I want to come on your face."

I immediately wrap my fingers around his shaft and slowly jack him off while looking him in the eye. He's handsome, and his square jaw covered in stubble makes him look dangerous. My pussy throbs and I almost wish he was going to fuck me, but it's not often my hotwife experiences end with a facial. I'm curious how dirty this will feel afterwards.

As the euphoria in his expression intensifies, Ryan moans and starts to fuck my hand. He's close, and with every stroke, I imagine him exploding.

"Look at you," Ryan pants, bumping harder into my grip. "You want me to come on you. I can see it in your eyes."

"Yes," I breathe out, opening my mouth and sticking out my tongue. As soon as I close my eyes, he comes with a loud groan. His cum explodes from his cock, spraying onto my face in ropes and splashing against my lips and tongue.

My pussy throbs with need, but this is so fucking hot I'm not going to complain about the lack of cock inside me. When he's done, I lick my lips and use my fingers to clean up my face, sucking his cum from each digit. I finally open my eyes and look up at him.

His face softens, and he strokes my hair. "You're such a good whore. Joey is lucky."

I want to tell him that Joey and I both are lucky, but I stay quiet. If he wants to think Joey has the most spectacular wife in the world, who am I to argue?

He leans down and kisses my forehead before tucking his cock back in his jeans. "I'll see you back at the campsite."

I grin at him. "Yeah, I'm going to need to clean up again. I'll see you in a few."

He helps me stand up, and when he leaves, I examine my knees. They're a little red but totally fine. I want to rinse off again, but I better make it fast before he tells the guys what I did. Someone else will get the bright idea to make me crawl on the cement.

I hop in the shower again, just long enough to clean my face and wet my hair. By the time I'm out of the shower and clothed, I'm ready to take on every cock at the campgrounds. I can lie on the picnic table while a train of men uses me.

Fuck, I need an orgasm.

As I walk back to Joey, all the guys watch me approach. Joey immediately stands up and strides over to me. His gaze burns into mine, and I can tell he knows what happened with Ryan—and he approves.

He takes my bag from me and hands it off to Miles before wrapping me up in a tight hug. "Are you still good?"

"Mmm, yes. Come to find out, you married the biggest whore ever."

He laughs before kissing me deeply. As my tongue twines with his, my pussy protests that I still don't have a cock in me. When someone steps up behind me, Joey breaks off the kiss. His smile is the last thing I see as a blindfold covers my eyes. It's a long scrap of fabric, and the person ties it behind my head. Ohhh, fuck yes.

Joey holds on to my hand. His voice is gruff. "Walk with me."

I can't see where I'm going, but Joey leads me forward and I can tell he's opening a tent door. He releases my hand. "Duck down."

He helps me through the tent door, and when my foot encounters something, I kneel and find out it's an air mattress.

My heart pounds loudly in my ears as the men chat outside the tent. Joey moves his hands to the hem of my shirt and, in one swift motion, pulls it over my head, exposing my breasts to the cool air. He throws the shirt aside before sliding his hands over my sensitive nipples.

"Now for the shorts," he says as I lie back so he can strip them off me after he removes my shoes.

He spreads my legs, and I gasp when he rubs my pussy. "Fuck, baby, you're already dripping wet."

I rock against his hand as he caresses my clit. I'm assuming the men are going to take turns with me, but maybe Joey wants to be first. When he stops touching me, I mewl in disappointment. Shit, I guess not.

"I'm going to be close by, baby. Enjoy yourself tonight."

I murmur, "Yes, my love," and I can tell he gets up and leaves the tent. I tremble with desire as I wait for someone to join me, and I imagine every man getting his turn with me. It's going to be a long night. I better get a damn orgasm out of this.

I don't wait long before someone comes in. There's a rustling of clothing and then whoever it is joins me on the air mattress. The man slides a finger into my pussy, and I gasp as he strokes it in and out of me. Mmmm, so good.

I spread my legs further apart and buck my hips. The man groans into my ear, "Such a good slut."

Oooh, who is that? Shit, I don't recognize the voice from the one line.

When he stops rubbing me, I whimper at the loss of contact, but then he positions himself between my legs. He brushes the head of his cock against my clit, and then slides it up and down my wetness. I moan and tilt my hips in time with his cock, enjoying the sensation and hoping I can angle myself at the perfect moment to get him to slip inside me. Oh fuck, this is so hot.

My breathing grows heavy, and my body thrums with yearning. The man brushes the tip of his cock against my clit and rubs it in slow circles. He's teasing me, and I'm in a mental fog from the stimulation. I need him right now.

"Fuck me, please," I gasp, hoping my pleas don't make him stop and say I don't get to choose tonight.

The man doesn't respond, and I almost start begging again when he sinks inside me in one swift move. My body tenses, and I cry out in joy as he starts fucking me. He's not rough or savage, and it's perfect. He drives into me with slow, steady strokes that make my pussy clench around him. The ecstasy builds in my core, and I can't hold out any longer.

"Oh god, I'm gonna come," I gasp as my thighs quiver and shocks of delight rush through me as I climax. My back arches off the mattress as the man continues to fuck me through my orgasm.

"Fuck," he groans. "I can't stop."

That's good, because I don't want him to stop. As the orgasm fades away, I rock my hips against him and moan, "Fill me with your cum, please."

I still don't know who it is, and I don't care. My words seem to unleash his wild side. He pumps into me harder and faster, and I can hear the wet sounds of him slapping against my pussy. My brain is fuzzy, and the world disappears around us as we ride out the storm of pleasure.

He comes with a groan, his warm seed filling me up. Imagining all that cum inside me puts me deeper in the mindset of wanting to be a fucktoy for all the men. I can't tell one cock apart from the other, and they could just enter the tent and use me one by one.

Finally, he collapses with a loud sigh. I embrace him and smile as our breathing slows down. He only rests a few seconds before he gets up.

As he leaves the tent, I stretch out and smile, waiting for the next guy to use me.

I can't see anything past the blindfold, but it's heightened my other senses, and I hear the next guy's footsteps before he comes into the tent. He crawls over me and straddles my body. The tip of his cock nudges against my mouth, and I swirl my tongue over the head. It throbs in response, thrilling me. Shit, I wasn't expecting someone to use my mouth while I'm lying here with a waiting pussy.

The guy moans and grinds himself against my face, his cock sliding past my lips. My core throbs with need, and I wish he would just fuck me instead of teasing me like this. He withdraws from my mouth and repositions himself between my legs. Now this is more like it.

When he runs the head up and down my slit, I wiggle against him in desperation. Damn it, this guy is going to drive me crazy if he doesn't fuck me right now. Even when I think he's about to slide inside me, he plays 'just the tip' with my pussy.

I'm moaning and giving little coos whenever he almost sticks it all the way in. When he finally sinks in fully, my breath hitches, and I give a long groan as he fills me. He's not thick or long, but he's hitting all my sweet spots. My inner walls quiver as he thrusts vigorously. Another orgasm builds, and I forgive him for being such a tease. This was worth the wait.

He's not as gentle as the guy before him, and he fucks me enthusiastically. When he forces my knees towards my chest, I wrap my arms around my thighs to hold myself open for him. I can imagine what he's seeing and being such a complete slut for an unknown guy almost makes me come.

Wait...this could be anyone. It might not even be Joey's friend. They could be standing out there and inviting anyone to come in and use me. Deep down, I know Joey isn't doing that, but fantasizing that this guy is someone I don't know tips me over the edge. I scream as pleasure rockets through me in convulsive waves.

My orgasm triggers him to fuck me harder, and my body jolts with each thrust. He's breathing heavily and moaning with each plunge, and when he comes, he roars like he's won a competition. HIs eruption is violent, and he's gasping when he's done depositing his cum inside me.

Fuck, how many men have come inside me today? I'm so mentally out of it, I don't even know anymore. When the guy climbs off me, I let go of my thighs and stretch my legs out. I'm so busy trying to gather my thoughts and count the men, I don't hear the next guy come in until he touches my feet.

He slides his hands along my soles, and I almost giggle because it tickles. When he lifts my feet up, my heart flips with anticipation. Yeah, he's not going to fuck me like the other two did. I try to imagine what he looks like as his firm hands grip my ankles. Fuck, I'm in the tent with an unknown man, and he's going to use me however he wants.

I hear a rustling of clothing before I feel his cock running along the bottoms of my feet. My brain freezes as he holds my feet together and wedges his cock between them. Which friend has a foot fetish? Or is he just doing this because he can? Nothing anyone has done to me today makes me feel like a freeuse slut as much as this guy fucking my feet does.

I play with my nipples and my clit throbs in tandem with his thrusts as he uses my feet. I know I can't have an orgasm like this, but this is so naughty that I don't care. It's even better that I can't see what he's doing to me. The idea of being blindfolded and at the mercy of whoever comes in to use me however they want makes me whimper with desire.

The man growls, and his pre-cum coats my arches and toes as he fucks me harder. My feet tingle from the friction, but it just makes it more erotic. A moment later he gasps and his cock explodes, shooting cum onto my feet.

He massages his cum into my skin while I lay there slightly shocked. Shit, someone really did just fuck my feet and didn't touch me anywhere else. He zips up his pants as he leaves the tent.

When I hear someone else enter, I wonder what this guy will do to me. The world becomes hazy as the guy rolls me onto my stomach, drags me up on my knees and fucks me from behind. I'm just a dirty plaything for all these men, and I want them to do anything and everything to me. When I come from the guy plowing into me and whacking against my ass, it turns into a never-ending orgasm. Each brush against my skin sends shockwaves through me until my brain shuts down from sensory overload. I become just a hole for them to use while I drift in ecstasy.

I don't know how many men come in and use me, and it doesn't matter. I revel in every nasty thing they do to me. The pleasure is beyond anything I've experienced before, and I lose count of the times I come.

Eventually, I realize I've been alone for a bit. When someone enters the tent, they zip it closed and remove their clothes. When a body lies close to me on the mattress, I can tell it's Joey. His familiar, comforting scent envelops me as he slides his hand under the blindfold and removes it. It's dark, but I can see his face from the glow of the campfire through the tent wall.

My heart catches in my throat as I search his eyes, desperate to know that he still loves me. He kisses me gently as his hands roam over my body. My hair is matted against my head and my skin is coated with sweat. There's dried cum all over me, but he doesn't seem to mind. He plays with the wet folds of my pussy and smiles into the kiss as his fingers probe through the stickiness from the other guys.

"That's so much cum," he murmurs against my mouth.

He brings his fingers to my lips, and I eagerly suck them clean while he watches. "My gorgeous wife."

I clasp my arms around his neck and kiss him back. When our tongues touch, he turns wild. He rolls on top of me and grinds against me. He eases a hand between us and caresses my clit. I moan into his mouth as he presses his cock into me while continuing to finger my bundle of nerves. I'm so sensitive, I quiver from his touch, and he slows the speed of his finger on my clit.

My heart rate kicks up as he kisses down my neck while his fingers continue to work magic on me. I'm desperate for him to come. I don't even need another orgasm, I just need him to be the last one to fill me tonight.

I wrap my legs around him and rock against him, moaning, "Joey, please."

He nips at my earlobe, his breath warm on my cheek. "Do you need my cum, baby?"

"I do," I gasp as the pleasure builds.

"Good, because you're going to get it all."

I want to see him when he comes, and our eyes lock onto each other. His eyes are glazed with lust, but he's keeping eye contact with me. When he flutters his finger against my clit, I cry out and an orgasm rushes through me. My body convulses and my pussy clenches around him. He gives a low growl as he watches me come undone under his touch.

When the tremors subside, he smiles. "My turn."

He speeds up his thrusts while I watch his face contort with pleasure a moment before he explodes. He groans as he comes, filling me with his warm cum. Knowing his seed is mixing with all the other men's is dirty but feels right.

He jerks several times, unloading everything he's got before collapsing on top of me.

"Are you okay?" He nuzzles into my neck as we pant and come down from the high.

I take a moment to answer, analyzing my emotions to make sure I mean what I say. I smile softly. "Yeah, I'm very okay. I love you so much."

He murmurs against my ear. "You're my everything. The freeuse night is over, so just relax, baby."

I'm glad he told me, and I'm able to get lost in the comfort of being in his arms. I'm not sure how often I would want an experience this intense, but having Joey organize it and knowing he wanted it made all the difference. But this is my favorite part of the night. No matter what other men I fuck in the future, Joey is the love of my life.

I want every night with other men to end with me in Joey's arms.

The End

SHARING HIS ADVENTUROUS WIFE

PREFACE

Thanks for picking up my longest Jessica story in this series. I received a few requests to write Jessica's first hotwife experience, and this story ended up being a lot longer than planned. If you move on to the rest of the Itty-Bitty Vixen series, they are shorter and quicker to the sharing. But hopefully this one is hot enough that the slow burn of her first time is well liked. This also is the last Jessica book written in the series, despite being the first in her journey.

Enjoy!

Lacey

CHAPTER 1

The sound of kids running around and laughing wakes me up. I blink at the harsh light filtering through the air vent on the roof of our tent. It's already stifling in here, and the day has barely begun. I'm so *not* the camping type, and this isn't my preferred way to wake up. Give me a big soft bed in a fancy hotel with a spa to pamper me, please.

Why did I come on this trip again? I smirk when my pussy buzzes. Oh, yeah, my wonderful husband claims he has plans and this will be fun. Ms. Kitty believes him, so it better be worth it.

Recently I found a bunch of slutty hotwife porn in my husband's browser history, and he admitted he gets off on the idea of me fucking other guys. Even though Lucas is worth never having another guy's cock inside of me, I have always wrestled with the idea of monogamy. I'd never cheat on him, but before we said "I do," I gave deep thought to our marriage vows. I didn't think I'd ever meet someone who could rein in my slutty side or be able to satisfy my high sex drive, but I found the perfect guy for me.

My marriage is pretty awesome.

And finding out my husband was masturbating while imagining me with other guys? That was fucking hot.

After he admitted to his filthy desires, we banged like rabbits on every surface in the house for days while I kept a running fantasy in my head. I kept thinking I was fucking different guys while Lucas watched.

Yeah, that was a *wonderful* week.

Eventually, we had a heart-to-heart chat about what he really wanted. He asked if I would consider being a hotwife. Ms. Kitty started fluttering and tingling, like she was getting ready to train for a marathon of cocks, but my brain was more cautious than my slutty pussy. I told Lucas I'd consider it, but I wanted to take it slow.

Which, I guess, is why we're here. He's got something planned, but I don't know about this. I don't *need* to be a hotwife. What if it ruins our marriage? Sure, the idea sounds amazing, but how good can it really be? It's not like Lucas sucks in bed. I'm incredibly satisfied. He knows exactly what I like, and there's none of that awkward first-date-sex bullshit.

Where is Lucas anyway?

I sit up and stretch. My sleeping bag falls, exposing my naked breasts to the warm air. There is one positive about camping: it puts Lucas in a kinky mood. We zipped our sleeping bags together last night, and he fucked me so thoroughly he had to put his hand over my mouth to muffle my screams. I woke up wet, and thinking about how hard I came makes me want to find Lucas and ride him before I shower. We'll get nice and dirty before we get clean.

The sound of the zipper on the tent flap breaks through my slutty daydream, and I pull the edge of the sleeping bag up to cover my breasts out of caution. When the door opens, the familiar sight of my hubby makes me let go of the edge of the bedding so he can get an eyeful. I only have to flash my boobs at him, and he's putty in my hands.

Hey, wait. His hair is wet, and he's carrying a towel. Well shit, there goes my plan. He's already showered.

He blows me a kiss. "Good morning, baby. I think it's safe for you to hit the showers. Most of the kids and parents left. I only saw a bunch of guys."

His words and a lusty twinkle in his eyes perks Ms. Kitty up. Um… he's not thinking I'm going to do anything with another guy, is he?

I keep my voice light and teasing. "Since there are separate bathrooms for the men and the women, I doubt I'll be showering with a bunch of guys."

Mmm. I don't hate the idea. All those soapy hands running up and down my body, making sure they get every crack and cranny clean? Okay, focus Jessica. Your life isn't one of the reverse harem books you write.

My stomach hardens at the thought of the latest story I'm writing, and I try to push aside my concern. I've got a half-edited draft waiting for me at home, but Lucas and I need this break. My book and my readers will have to be patient.

It's actually amazing to me. People wait for my books. A couple of years ago, I got brave and published a vampire reverse harem series, and it took off. It's still difficult to wrap my head around the fact that people want to read the dirty stories that rattled around in my head all my life. I'm making enough money writing that I hired my best friend, Miri, to work as my personal assistant. Miri told me to enjoy a long weekend because there's nothing that has to be done right this second. So I went, and that's what I'm going to do.

So, yeah… chill the fuck out, brain. We're here to relax and fuck our sexy husband.

A low hum of desire rumbles through me as I watch Lucas put down his shower supplies. He's tall enough he can't stand up inside the tent, and he's moving around in a crouch.

I definitely don't have that problem. I like to claim I'm five feet, one inch tall, but that's if I stretch my spine. I'm really only five feet tall, but only me and my doctor know the truth. Not that the one inch matters, but I was teased growing up for being so tiny, so I always lie about my height. Spiked high heels give me a nice lift, and I enjoy being short. I have fun pretending to be helpless when I can't reach the top shelf in the kitchen. Lucas *has to* come in and get things down for me, and then I always give him a proper reward.

Yeah, I've got sex on the brain this morning. I clearly need an orgasm. It's got to be a rule for vacation, right? Orgasms every day!

Lucas keeps glancing at me, and I can tell his devious brain is churning over something. God, I hope it's sexual. Starting the day relaxed after another orgasm is perfect.

Once he's done puttering around, he lowers himself to the ground and crawls over me. He pushes me onto my back and gives me a deep kiss. Mmm, now this is more like it.

I wrap my arms around his neck and pull him to me. My nipples harden as he coaxes my lips open and slides his tongue inside, twining it with mine. I try to grind against him, but the puffy sleeping bag is too thick. Dammit, this isn't going to work.

With his hands on either side of my head, Lucas pulls away from the kiss and looks down at me, murmuring, "You're so fucking sexy."

I'm sure my long blonde hair is a mess, and I've got morning breath, but if he thinks I'm sexy, who am I to argue?

I smile at him and rub my legs together. "Why don't you take your clothes off and we can continue where we left off last night?"

He brings a hand up to my breast and plays with the nipple, tweaking it gently and making me gasp. When he doesn't immediately respond, I assume I've won. Hell yeah, Ms. Kitty is going to get another workout.

His eyes deepen with lust as he continues to pull on the stiff peak. "Oh, I've got a better idea."

Pleasure shoots from my breast downwards and I moan. "Mmm, yes?"

My eyes drift closed as I enjoy the delicious sensations his nimble fingers create deep in my core. I'm down with whatever plan he's cooked up, as long as he keeps his hands on me. He moves down to suck on the opposite nipple and the pleasure sets my mind adrift.

He mumbles around my tit. "Baby, I've got a challenge for you."

What's this? I crack my eyes open and run my fingers through his hair, tugging gently so he raises his head from my breast.

"Challenge? Whaddya mean?"

I'm still mentally fuzzy and not paying attention to anything but his hand on my other breast. I'm desperate to get his cock inside me, so I'll do whatever he asks as long as we can fuck afterwards.

"It's your first official hotwife challenge."

I stop running my fingers through his hair and stare at him. "Official what?"

What is he talking about? What's a hotwife challenge? We've only talked about dipping our toes into this area. I'm not sure I'm up for a challenge of any sort.

My body heats, and I grow even wetter when his lips twitch deviously. He says, "The shower rooms have a row of windows with blinds. I want you to open the blinds and leave the shower curtain open while you're in there."

That's it? That's the challenge? Easy enough. What are the chances someone is going to walk by?

I pretend to think about it. "Hmm.... What's my reward for doing this?"

He laughs. "That depends on you. We'll discuss the reward when you get back."

I arch an eyebrow at him and give it one second of consideration. "Okay. I'll do it."

No problem. I can take a quick shower and when I choose my reward, I'll tell him I want his cock.

I push him off of me and climb out of the sleeping bag, wiggling my naked ass in his direction as I dig through my duffle bag for clothes. It's not far away, so I toss on some tiny jean shorts and a t-shirt before grabbing my shower supplies.

I wink at him as I leave. "See you soon for my reward!"

He laughs. "Have fun, baby."

The park is quiet as I walk to the central bathrooms. I think he's right. Most of the families are off on their day adventure. The women's bathroom is deserted, and I put my stuff down on a wooden bench before opening the blinds in front of the shower stall.

Oh shit, people *can* see straight in here. Calm down. I mean, really, what are the chances? If it happens, which I doubt, it'll most likely be a woman coming to take a shower, anyway.

As I take my clothes off, I peek outside the window and scan the park. My pussy clenches as I imagine a stranger walking past. It's been years since anyone but Lucas or spa professionals have seen me naked.

This is more erotic than I expected.

The shower requires quarters if I want warm water. Since I don't plan on being here long, I don't need to give it many. As I step under the warm spray, a twinge of vulnerability makes me consider closing the curtain, but I brush it aside. No, this is the challenge, and I want Lucas's cock.

I keep it open and quickly soap myself up while eyeing the window. Every second that goes by without someone walking past turns me on even more. I give my shaved pussy more attention than is necessary, slipping a finger between my folds to rub my clit. Pings of bliss ripple through me and I bite back a moan. Why is this turning me on?

A thought stills my hand. Oh, holy fuck, I want a guy to see me naked.

My entire body lights up and I release my moan this time. I'm petite, blonde, and I have big breasts. I know I'm sexy, and the thought of someone other than my husband seeing me and possibly enjoying the view is so fucking hot.

Lucas might know me better than I know myself.

I lean against the shower wall and work my fingers on my clit. I imagine Lucas sending a guy into the shower to fuck me, and my legs quiver as I race towards my orgasm. Little gasps of pleasure escape my lips. Just when I'm about to close my eyes and let the bliss overtake me, movement outside the window catches my attention.

A guy and a woman walk past, chatting. The woman doesn't look this way, but the guy does. His eyes meet mine and I freeze with my hand between my legs. He gives me a wide smile. Before I can react, they walk out of view.

Ohhhh, my god.

I work my hand furiously against my clit, oblivious to anything but my pleasure. In moments, I'm on the edge. When my orgasm hits, it's so hard I cry out. I buck my hips as waves of delight rush through me and my mind blanks.

I'm panting as I come down, and a sudden blast of cold water shocks me back to my senses.

Fuck!

I squeal and step out of the shower before feeding in another quarter so I can rinse off. I want to make sure Ms. Kitty is clean again.

My brain is mush from the intense orgasm, and I rush through drying off and stalk towards my tent and my husband. I don't know what reward he's going to offer me. I almost feel like I already got rewarded, but I'm curious to see what he says.

He's sitting cross-legged on our bed, waiting for me with a shit-eating grin on his face. A glance at his crotch reveals he's hard. I drop my stuff and launch myself at him. He laughs and lies down so I'm on top of him as I ravish his mouth. I grind against his hardness, and Ms. Kitty makes it abundantly clear she wants more than my fingers this time.

Between deep kisses, I ask my question. "So what's my reward?"

He chuckles and pulls me down for another toe-curling kiss before answering. "You'll see later."

I fumble with his pants, desperate to get his cock out. His answer frustrates me, but also turns me on even more.

Yeah, this trip got a lot more interesting.

CHAPTER 2

Something tickles my nose and wakes me up. My eyes are still closed and I brush it away from me in my groggy state. When it comes back again, I crack my eyes open. Lucas is lying on his side next to me. He's holding a feather he found in the grass while we were setting up our tent. My first instinct it to tell him to stop touching my nose with a filthy feather, but his adorable grin melts my heart.

I stretch and yawn. "Did we sleep long?"

After masturbating in the shower, I came back to the tent and rode Lucas until we were both exhausted and had to nap.

"Not too long, but I still want to take that nature hike. We need to go before it gets any later."

Bleh. Doesn't he understand I'm a city girl and don't go hiking? He claims this is a walk along a scenic path through the woods and isn't really a hike. He also promised I'd see pretty flowers, and I'm a sucker for flowers, so I guess it'll be fun.

I unzip the sleeping bag and kick it down. "Okay, let's do this."

As I crawl to the end of the tent and dig around in my bag for clothes to wear, Lucas paws through the bag next to him.

"Jessica, I want you to wear this."

Huh?

I glance at him, and he's holding a blue flowered sundress of mine in his hands. I didn't pack the dress. I might be a city girl, but I know enough about the woods to know it's completely wrong for camping. The fabric is soft and billowy, and the spaghetti straps require a strapless bra. It's also extremely short and only goes to mid-thigh.

I squint my eyes at him. "You want me to wear that on a nature hike?"

"Yep." He tosses it at me and I catch it. "It's your next hotwife challenge."

Ohhh. Hey, I liked the first challenge. This one doesn't seem too difficult, though. It's not as bad as showering with the blinds open.

Well, except I didn't bring a bra to wear with the dress, but I suppose I can go braless. My breasts are large — especially for my tiny frame — but they're firm, so I don't always need to support them. I'm sure this will change as I get older, but I'm not there yet.

"Okay, sure. I'll wear it."

I pull the dress over my head and bend over, digging into my bag for clean underwear.

"No panties."

My head pops up and I look at Lucas. "What? No panties?"

Doesn't he see how short this dress is? A soft breeze might blow it up and I'll flash everyone looking in my direction.

"Yep, it's part of the challenge."

I shift uncomfortably.

Do I want to do this challenge? What are the chances we're going to see that many people on the trails? My pussy buzzes as I think about how I assumed I wouldn't see anyone in the shower, and yet I did. Ms. Kitty is a traitorous slut. She wants the entire campground to see my bare cooch. Okay, I kind of like the dirtiness of this challenge, but I don't want to sound too enthusiastic.

I give an exaggerated sigh. "Fine. No underwear."

As we step out of the tent, the breeze flutters the edge of my dress. I immediately feel naked. Oh shit, this might not be a good idea. I debate telling Lucas I changed my mind while he digs sandwiches out of the cooler for us. When we sit at the wooden picnic table, the dress barely covers my shaved pussy. Not good. I stand to tug the dress down as far as I can before sitting on it again.

Lucas smiles at me and takes a bite of his sandwich. I want to gripe about how dumb this idea is, but my hard nipples and a tingle from my core keep me quiet. I'm getting turned on, which I'm guessing is the point. Lucas better want more sexy times today. If this keeps up, I'm going to be all over him when we get back. Or maybe before.

We make small talk about the campsite and the weather while we eat. When we're finished with lunch, he takes my hand while we head towards the trail head. Thank God it's not a super breezy day. I have to keep my free hand near my thighs in case I need to rescue a sudden flyaway dress.

We pass a few couples in the campsite. Knowing the only thing stopping them from seeing me naked is the thin fabric sets Ms. Kitty buzzing. At the start of the trail, Lucas pauses and reads the sign about the two-mile walk. I'm keeping my eye out for people heading our way from down the trail, so I don't notice someone coming behind us until rocks and branches crunch under their feet.

A quick glance over my shoulder reveals a cute brown-haired guy that I'd guess is in his late 30s. He's alone, and wearing long pants and hiking boots, so I assume he's planning on walking the trail.

"Oh hey," he calls out and looks at Lucas.

Lucas turns and laughs. "Well, hi again!"

Uh, they know each other? Lucas must have interpreted my questioning glance.

"Jessica, this is Mike. I met him earlier when taking a shower. Mike, this is my gorgeous wife I was telling you about."

He was talking about me in the shower room? My pussy clenches and my inner thighs suddenly feel damp.

Mike laughs. "You weren't exaggerating. She *is* gorgeous."

Lust ripples through me, and my nipples pucker even more. I fight the urge to rub my thighs together. This is an odd introduction, but it's also erotic.

"Hi, Mike. It's nice to meet you."

I think I sound awkward as all fuck, but his eyes twinkle when he looks at me, so he must not notice.

"It's nice to meet you. Lucas was singing your praises this morning, but I like to put a face to the name."

When his eyes drop briefly to my chest, my body warms up. He definitely checked me out, but he's not being a perv about it. I enjoy being admired as long as the people do it respectfully. I'm not getting creepy vibes from Mike, so his peek turns me on even more.

He shifts his attention to the sign that Lucas is reading, and I study the two men together. They're both attractive, but I think Lucas is cuter. I married one sexy man.

Lucas turns to Mike. "Hey, want to walk with us?"

When Mike says, "Sure," Lucas winks at me. Uh-oh. What does my husband have planned? He only winks when he's up to something.

"Let's get going. We're burning daylight. Jessica, I want you to walk in front of us."

Um… yeah… It suddenly becomes clear what he's doing. He wants me to struggle to keep my dress down, knowing they're behind me. I will *not* give him the satisfaction of saying no.

"Sure," I purr at him and set off down the trail.

I don't even wait for them. If I'm in front, they have to go at my pace. The sound of their feet on the dirt path tells me they're behind me, and I slow my pace slightly and roll my hips as I walk to give them a sexy view of my ass.

Lucas and Mike chat about Oregon and various hiking trails as we walk. Every once in a while, a warm breeze blows over us and I have to rescue my dress. It's not too bad since the trees block the wind, but it really doesn't take much to make my dress flutter up.

"Jessica, pick some flowers to take back with us."

I was so busy thinking about them watching my ass, I didn't notice the pretty wildflowers along the trail. I glance back at the men and both are smiling at me.

Oh sure, Lucas wants me to struggle to bend over, but I'll show him. I crouch down instead of bending at the waist. My pussy lips slide apart in this position and I realize it's saving my modesty, but it feels even dirtier.

Fuck.

I quickly pick a couple of flowers and straighten up. I'm flushed and a throb from Ms. Kitty tells me she's getting impatient. Yeah, I know… we want Lucas's cock again.

We occasionally pass other people, but no one tries to talk to us other than a brief, "hello," or "have a good day." As we walk along, Lucas keeps telling me to pick flowers, and I keep crouching down to do it.

Each time I get more and more turned on. My lips are open slightly and I'm breathing heavily the longer the walk takes. By the time it loops back around, my brain is fuzzy and all I can think about is getting Lucas's cock inside me.

I see the sign that signals the end of the trail. I'm almost to freedom and Lucas's cock!

"Jessica, I want that flower over there."

Lucas gestures towards a flower, probably the last one I can pick before we leave the trail, and I'm suddenly brave.

Bending at the waist to pick this one, my dress rides up past my ass. If the men are looking at me, my shaved, wet pussy is on display. I take my time before standing, straightening my dress, and twitching my ass in their direction without looking at them.

I keep walking and I hear them talking, but it's low enough I can't make out what they are saying. They are following me and that's all that matters.

When we stop at the sign, Mike takes my hand and kisses the back of it. His voice is husky, and there is admiration in his gaze. I can tell he's turned on. "Thank you for a very interesting walk, Jessica. I'm glad I ran into you guys."

I smile sweetly at him. "Thanks for joining us."

He shares goodbyes with Lucas, and once he leaves, I turn to my husband. I'm vibrating with need.

"Lucas, I want…"

He puts his finger to my lips. "You just showed your bare pussy to a guy, and he liked what he saw."

Ms. Kitty clenches. "Really?"

"Yes." He runs his hand through my hair and caresses my cheekbone with his thumb. "He seemed interested in seeing more."

His words send a shiver down my spine. "How do you know?"

"He told me I could invite him on this type of nature walk whenever I wanted."

My heart skips a beat. "He did?"

He nods.

I lick my lips and eye my husband. While I enjoyed turning them both on, Lucas is the one I care about, and the one whose cock I need inside me right now.

I take his hand. "You have five minutes to get me back to the tent and get your cock in me before I explode."

He laughs. "Then we better hurry."

We're not exactly running back to our campsite, but we're speed walking fast enough that we catch a few eyes. I don't know what they think, and I don't care.

We tumble into the tent, and I barely get the zipper door closed before he's all over me. He doesn't bother removing any of his clothes. Since I'm not wearing panties, there's nothing in the way of him pulling his cock out and fucking me.

We're on top of the sleeping bag, and he ravishes my mouth as his cock slides inside me.

"God, yessss." I cry out and rock against him.

Wrapping my legs and arms around him, I meet him thrust for thrust. I'm still in my hiking boots, and I'm probably getting dirt everywhere, but I don't care.

We're like crazed animals as we claw at each other. He fucks me harder than he has in a long time. Each whack against Ms. Kitty shoots lightning through my core, and I'm moaning with each plunge.

When Lucas speeds up, I can tell he's about to come. As our gazes lock, we both peak. I cry out as waves of pleasure hit me, and he groans as he unloads ropes of sticky cum deep inside me. Watching him get lost in the pleasure intensifies my orgasm and it seems like the waves will never end.

When he slows down and stops, I slump down into the sleeping bag. "Oh God, you're going to kill me by the end of this trip."

He rolls to his side, pulls me close, and nuzzles my neck. When he speaks, his breath tickles me. "Maybe we shouldn't go on another hike. That was too strenuous."

"Mmm hmm." I'm floating in a fuzzy post-orgasmic haze. "Something more relaxing."

"Yeah," he agrees with me. "But tomorrow we're going swimming. We can't come here and not visit the beautiful lake."

I squint up at him. He's got a devious glint in his eye.

Uh-oh. What does he have planned for me at the lake?

CHAPTER 3

I swear it's the crack of dawn when Lucas wakes me. He shoves a granola bar and a banana at me.

"Baby, eat some breakfast. I want to hit the lake early, before it gets crowded."

Struggling to sit up, I fumble with the wrapper on the bar. I blink at him, confused. "Wait, what time is it?"

My brain is not ready to wake up.

He shrugs. "Does it matter? The sun is up."

Hmm, is it? The window isn't open, but the campgrounds are quiet and it's not that bright in the tent.

Camping sort of sucks. If I wasn't getting so much sex, I'd say I was never going camping again, but I'm having fun since he's keeping me needy and at a low simmer all the time. He could persuade me to do this occasionally if it includes a weekend of sexual abandon.

Yawning, I finish my granola bar and banana before I get dressed. It's going to be a warm day, so I put on my tiny, ass-hugging shorts and a white tank top. I debate on a bra, but opt to skip it. Maybe it's his turn to be distracted. I'll use the power of my tits to mesmerize him. We're not hiking, so my sandals are good enough for a walk around the campgrounds.

We separate for a few minutes to finish our morning routine. When we reunite, my teeth are minty fresh and my long, blonde hair is in a braid. I'll shower later after our walk, and the braid will keep my hair from being too crazy if it gets windy. I'm ready to face the day. Or at least as ready as I'll be.

Lucas has a beach bag slung over his shoulder and I eye it as I approach him. "What's in the bag?"

"Nothing you need to worry about."

He kisses me. I stand on my tippy toes so I can wrap my arms around his neck and plaster my body to his. I know he's only kissing to distract me, but I welcome it anyway. A soft tingle runs through me. Uh-oh, Ms. Kitty is waking up.

Lucas breaks off the kiss. I hold on to his neck and try to tempt him into more. I purr, "We don't need to visit the lake, do we? We could go back to bed and have more fun."

He chuckles and shakes his head. "Nope, we're going to the lake. I didn't come all this way to not see it."

I want to tell him a two-hour drive isn't far, but I hold my tongue. Fine, back to Plan A: torturing him with my bouncing boobies all day. That might be more fun, anyway.

We walk past several tents and barely anyone is awake. It's a short walk down a dirt path to the lake, and when we get there, it's deserted and peaceful. It's one of the major attractions at the campground for families. I've heard it's busy mid-day when everyone is swimming.

There's a dock that runs out to the deeper part of the lake for people to jump off. No way in hell is that happening this morning. We walk past the dock, and Lucas drops the beach bag at the edge of the dry sand.

I'm only planning to wade into the water, so I kick off my sandals and dip my toes in. Okay, yeah, that's a little too cool for me. I'd need a hot day before I'd go swimming — preferably in a pool at a hotel.

When Lucas walks into the shallows, I follow him. The water laps softly against my ankles as I splash around playfully, avoiding any slippery rocks. My writer's mind expects a sea monster to grab my legs and pull me under to trap me in the seaweed. Luckily, the water is clear, so I can tell nothing is swimming at me. After a few moments, I relax and enjoy the serenity.

Lucas closes his eyes and breathes deeply before opening them and smiling at me. "Let's stay here awhile. I love being by the water."

"Me too." The tranquility of the morning settles over me. I lean against him and sigh. This isn't bad at all.

He wraps his arms around me and gives me a quick smooch. "I'm glad you're having fun."

"Mm hmm." I melt against him, enjoying his strength and warmth. No need to tell him I'm only having fun because of all the sex.

He kisses me again, but this time he takes his time with it. A glow of desire builds, and I press closer against him. Our tongues twine together as each stroke shoots electricity through me.

Mmm, now this is more like it. He slides his hands under my tank top, and I tremble when he skims the sensitive skin on my side. He knows how to drive me wild.

As he continues to explore with his hands, I moan when he caresses the soft skin next to my breasts. My nipples harden and I ache for him to play with them. But we're in public and someone could walk past any moment. Shit, we really should behave, but what's the fun in that?

When he pulls back, I mewl in protest. Dammit, it was getting good.

"Baby, it's time for your next hotwife challenge."

All my nerve endings tingle. "Oooh, yes?"

What could he have planned here? Ms. Kitty is fully awake and the slickness between my legs has me scanning the wooded area next to us. Whatever he's got planned for me is bound to turn me on even more. I bet I could find a secluded spot and ravish him. We don't need to go back to the tent to fuck.

His eyes twinkle when he grins. "I want you to go for a swim."

That gets my attention, and I bark out a laugh. "Oh, hell no. The water is cold, and I didn't bring a bathing suit."

He studies me for a second, and his voice is firm. "You're going skinny dipping."

My mouth opens slightly. I'm about to protest when he slides his hands back under my shirt again and cups my breasts. When he tugs on my nipples, I gasp and bite my lip to keep from crying out. Fiery sparks rush through me from his touch. I'm already wet, so he's adding fuel to the fire.

His voice turns silky smooth. "Come on baby, this will be fun."

Ugh, it's impossible to think when he's tweaking my nipples. His hands feel so damn good. If he kept doing this all day, I'd agree to anything.

I finally give in and nod my head. I'll take a quick dip and call it good. No one is here yet. It'll be fine.

We get out of the water and I take a quick glance around to verify we really are alone. I pull off my tank top and drop my shorts and panties.

Fuck, this is so wrong, but as soon as I'm naked, an illicit thrill makes me feel alive. This is naughty and I sort of love it.

I drop my clothes on top of the beach bag, and Lucas follows me back to the water. Wait, what is he doing? Oh shit, I didn't even notice his shorts were his swim shorts. He pulls his shirt off, tosses it back towards our stuff, and enters the water with me.

Fuuuuck, this is way too cold. "How long do I have to stay in the water?"

"Until I've decided you've won the challenge."

I'm *so* going to pay him back for this someday. I wade in further and suck in a breath as the water rises to my waist.

Someone calls from the shore. "Hey guys!"

Oh fuck, it's Mike! I dip into the water up to my neck and hold in several swear words as the coldness envelopes me.

Lucas laughs, and he sounds delighted. "Hey Mike, do you want to join us?"

Hmm… what are the chances Mike shows up at the lake while I'm skinny dipping? This is suspicious.

"Nah," Mike calls out. "I'll watch from the shore. It's too cold for a swim."

Yeah, no shit. I shiver, but it's from more than the water temperature. Mike saying he's going to watch gives an added zing to this experience. It also proves that anyone could walk down here at any moment and catch us.

Lucas grins at him. "I guess we'll have to give you something to watch."

I don't know what my dear husband has planned, but he's going to have to get fully wet to do it. I take off and swim further into the lake towards the dock. Lucas follows me and when I reach the end of the dock, I hold on to the edge as Lucas catches up.

He swims up behind me and presses my breasts against the wood. The contact with the rough panels almost makes me moan, but knowing my luck, any sound I make would echo over the water.

Mike walks towards the dock and stands on the shore, observing us. Hell, he really does plan on watching.

Lucas's hand slides between my legs, and he rubs my pussy. "I could fuck you right here, and you'd let me, wouldn't you?"

As his finger slides against my clit, I can't hold back my moan. "Yessss."

He whispers in my ear. "I want to fuck you. Ask me to fuck you while he's watching."

Does Lucas have an exhibitionist streak in him? Fuck, this is hot. I moan and pant. "Please fuck me."

I should tell him to stop. We shouldn't be doing this in public — and definitely not while Mike is here — but I can't help myself. I want Lucas's cock, right here, right now.

He thrusts a finger inside me, and I grind on it while I beg. "Please, Lucas? Please fuck me. I need you."

He's nimble and his fingers move fast inside me. We're both breathing heavily and my head is spinning. "Oh god, I can't think. Fuck me, please."

He kisses the side of my neck, and I stop caring that Mike is watching. I need my husband's cock inside me and I'll do anything to get it. I widen my legs and grip the wood firmly, daring him to fill me.

He continues to finger fuck me, and I go wild from the pleasure. Arching my back, I push against him to force his fingers in deeper. I keep my eyes glued on Mike, and he's staring at us with a smile on his face. I'm not sure he knows what we're doing. I'm guessing he can tell Lucas is up to something since Lucas's mouth is still on my neck. Each tiny bite and lick makes me coo in delight.

Lucas pulls his fingers free and moves his hips forward until the tip of his cock presses against my wetness. My mind is a buzzing mess of static. He pauses there to tease my pussy, and I'm dying to feel him inside me. He gives a low growl in his throat as he gently thrusts against me, but doesn't enter me. Holy fuck, he's going to make me insane with lust.

He's barely poking his hardness against me, and I throw my head back and moan loudly. Oh god, this feels incredible, but I need him to fuck me.

Lucas pulls back. "I want you to beg."

Oh god, what more does he want? I can feel my pussy clenching and I whimper. "Please fuck me. I need your cock."

He stops moving, leaving his cock nestled between my folds, but still not inside me. I try to rotate my hips to create friction.

"Baby, you keep doing that and I'm going to come without fucking you. Do you want that?"

My brain fizzles at his words. Shit, no, no, no. I stop all movement.

He continues. "Say you're a dirty slut who loves knowing someone is watching us."

A wave of shame hits me, but he's right. I'm loving this. My pussy throbs from the forbidden pleasure as I blurt out, "Yes, I'm a filthy slut who's getting turned on by Mike watching. Now please fuck me… Please!"

Lucas chuckles and releases me. "You won the challenge. Now we can leave."

Whaaaat? I'm dizzy and confused, my entire body throbbing in protest. "You're not going to fuck me?"

"Not yet. That's later."

He swims towards the shore.

I stare after him for a few heartbeats before following. Mike walks over to the edge of the water to greet Lucas as he gets out. Lucas's shorts are wet and clinging to his body, exposing his visible hardness underneath them. I can't believe he didn't slip his cock inside me. This game of his is torture for both of us.

Shit. Now I'm stuck in the water since I'm naked. Damn those two. I'm in the shallow area and I stay submerged past my breasts.

Without Lucas fingering me and distracting me, I'm reminded of how cold the water is. Once we get back to the tent, I'm going to bundle up in my sleeping bag and Lucas will have to rub me all over to warm me up. I'll convince him that Ms. Kitty is freezing and needs lots of attention.

Lucas calls to me from the shore. "I'm adding to the challenge. Get out of the water while we watch."

I almost protest, but worry that Lucas will change the rules yet again. Oh god, do I want to do this? My stomach muscles tighten as my heart rate speeds up. I close my eyes for a moment and imagine rising like a goddess with the water streaming off me.

Okay, I can do this.

When I open my eyes, Lucas is holding a towel for me. Well, I guess I know what was in the beach bag. This proves he planned this all along.

As if I didn't know.

I draw in a long breath and stand up straight. The slight breeze against my wet skin creates goosebumps, and my nipples harden into sharp peaks. The hot and heavy gaze of both men gives me a shiver of pleasure as I straighten my shoulders and slink towards them.

Wet heat flares between my legs, as I keep my eyes locked on to Lucas. Even though I'm not looking at Mike, I can feel the lust pouring from him the closer I get.

I'll show them. I ignore the open towel and put my back to the guys as I bend over to get my clothes. They've seen this view before, so now they get another peek.

Turning to face them, I shimmy my panties and shorts up my wet legs. It's a bit of a struggle, so my breasts sway as I work to get the shorts buttoned. When I drag my tank top over my head, it sticks to my skin. Since it's white, the pink of my nipples shows through the fabric.

Both guys are silent, spellbound, and my bravery has me practically vibrating with need.

I slide my sandy feet into my sandals and toss my head defiantly. "I need a shower. Lucas, you coming?"

I don't wait for him and head off, twitching my ass in their direction. I hear Lucas say a quick goodbye to Mike as he runs to catch up with me.

"Bye Mike, see you at eight!"

What's happening at eight? Pleasurable anticipation hits my core and I'm so distracted, I almost trip. I right myself just in time and look over my shoulder at Lucas as he slows down to walk with me.

"We're seeing Mike tonight?"

He gives me a slow grin. "Yes. Another challenge."

My mind glazes over as I try to imagine what that could be. Mike has already seen me fully naked.

How far is this going to go?

CHAPTER 4

The walk to our tent is quiet and I savor the feeling of being alone with Lucas. I can barely contain my excitement. As soon as we duck inside the tent, I turn to face him. His eyes are hooded and dark, and his lips form a half-smile.

He sits down, cross-legged, on our sleeping bags and pulls me into his lap. I fit my ass against his hardness and wiggle, pretending I need to get comfortable. I'm going to take a shower soon, but he deserves a little teasing first for what he did to me at the lake.

His hand travels slowly down my arm until he cups a breast. I gasp softly as my nipples tighten and my pussy pulses with pleasure.

His fingers squeeze my tit, and he kisses my neck, murmuring against my skin. "I was so close to fucking you in the lake."

My breath hitches in response, and Lucas slides his hand from my breast, down my flat belly, dipping beneath the waistband of my shorts. His palm is warm against my bare skin, and I drop my head back as pleasure ripples through me.

So much for me teasing him. He's doing a good job of working me up more than I already was. I want to know what's happening tonight before desire fogs my brain and I forget to ask. "Why is Mike coming to visit?"

Lucas unbuttons my shorts so he can reach more skin. He's intent on what he's doing, but he kisses my nose before he answers. "I invited him for s'mores."

Uh-huh, right. There's no way I believe he's coming for s'mores. "That's all? Nothing else?"

He chuckles and slides his hand further down my shorts, brushing his fingers over my wet panties and rubbing me through the fabric.

"Ohhh god," I moan.

I'm so distracted, I don't notice he didn't answer. Ms. Kitty is buzzing, and I'm desperate for him to fuck me. I need him.

"Are you ready to beg for my cock again?" His voice is husky and his fingers slide my panties aside so he can rub my clit.

I nod and then shake my head no. I'm so aroused, I can't think straight. What did he ask? Oh yeah, I need to beg for his cock.

My voice is barely above a whisper. "God, Lucas. Please fuck me."

He chuckles softly. "No, that's for later."

Whaaat? He told me to beg, and now he's not going to fuck me? I want to argue with him, but I'm too turned on to think straight. Fuck, he's driving me crazy.

I cup my hands around his face and pull him down for a kiss. Our tongues duel for dominance as I ride his fingers.

As soon as our mouths part, I ask, "Did you tell Mike about the challenge?"

"Yes." He kisses me again, and I try to take control of the kiss, but he keeps pulling away.

I whine in frustration. "Why aren't you fucking me?"

He lifts his head and smiles at me. "Because you have to wait for tonight."

Oh, hell no. He's teased me long enough that I don't want to wait. I can get his cock now, and I'll still want it again later. I grip his hair and kiss him passionately.

He groans and pulls away, laughing. "You're so impatient."

I lean up and nip at his bottom lip. "I love your cock, and I'm always hungry for it."

He tries to change the topic. "Well, we're going to shower — " I look up at him, hopeful, and he cuts himself off. "No, get that look off your face. We're showering alone."

Dammit.

He continues. "Then I need to go buy some more firewood. You're going to stay here and think about what I might ask you to do tonight for the challenge."

He slides his hand out of my shorts. Yeah, this isn't going how I hoped.

"Fine," I huff at him and climb off his lap. His laugh is infectious, and it coaxes a smile from me. As much as I claim to dislike being edged, a part of me also loves it.

I knew Lucas had plans for this weekend, but this seems beyond having a vague idea of what he wants to do. It really seems like everything he's doing is calculated, and it's leading me towards, I don't know?

Fucking Mike?

Shit, do I want it? As I carry my shower supplies with me to the bathroom, a wave of lust rolls through me, and Ms. Kitty flutters in response. Yeah, who am I kidding? I want to fuck Mike. I don't want to assume this is where the weekend is leading, because I told Lucas I wanted to go slow with the hotwife plans. But a weekend of escalating challenges is slow enough, and I'm ready to take the next step.

This camping trip is exactly why I love Lucas so much. How many husbands plan an entire weekend set around thrilling their wife with little adventures aimed towards turning her into a crazed nympho?

I'm so fucking lucky.

Lucas takes longer than necessary to buy wood at the tiny store on the campgrounds. I suspect he's off planning something for tonight.

I'm showered, dressed, and sitting at the picnic table, lost in a daydream of Mike fucking me while Lucas watches. When I hear voices getting closer, I lift my head and squint into the bright sunlight.

A man and woman are walking past our campsite. I recognize them from the day before. It's the guy who smiled at me while I was showering with the blinds open.

He winks at me. I suck in my breath from shock and feel myself blush. A second later, my nipples harden and I shift my position so I can press my pussy against the wooden bench.

The woman gives me a tiny wave and a knowing smile as they continue past, but neither of them greet me. Ohhhh fuck, did he tell her he saw me in the shower? If so, she seems to approve. I hope she got a nice hard pounding after she found out.

My daydream switches to thinking about those two going at it in their tent before I shake my head to clear it. Fuck, Lucas needs to get back. I'm getting turned on by every little thing.

When Lucas walks back from the store carrying a bundle of wood, I hop up from the bench and rush to him. "Where have you been?"

My voice is deeper than normal. I know I sound turned on and excited. I'm sure he can tell as well.

He gives me a speculative look. "I had other business to attend to. Something fun for tonight."

Tonight. I've gotta wait for tonight.

He sets the wood down by the campfire and walks back to me. I try one last time to seduce him into the sleeping bag. I walk my fingers up his arm and rub his neck. Using my most seductive tone, I purr at him, "So now we go make sweet, sweet love for hours, right?"

When I run my other hand over his chest, he stops me by wrapping his arms around me and holding me tight. "Baby, you have to wait. We have a hot date tonight."

I raise my eyebrows at him. He's finally admitting this is more than a meetup with Mike for s'mores? "Who said this was a date tonight? I thought we were going to stuff ourselves sick with marshmallows and chocolate."

He laughs and his eyes sparkle. "Trust me."

"Hmmm, maybe," I tease.

He kisses me, and I melt against him. After a few moments, his hands move to my hips and he pulls me to him. His cock is hard, and he rubs against me as he asks, "What do you think is going to happen tonight?"

My imagination is running wild, and I'm giddy with anticipation. "I think we're going to play a game."

"A game?"

I tip my head up and give him a slow grin. "Yeah, a sexy game."

"What kind of game would that be?"

"A hot one." I can be mysterious as much as he can.

He grins and kisses my nose. "You're such a bad girl."

"Yep." I laugh and push him away from me. "That's why you love me."

If he won't fuck me right now, I need to find something to occupy my mind. Otherwise, I'm sure to work myself into a frenzy. I blow him a kiss and climb into the tent to grab my e-reader. I'll read a clean romance and hopefully cool down a bit.

Nope. My clean romance didn't get my mind off tonight, and I tried to guess what Lucas is going to suggest. I finally settled on strip poker. I'm not sure how he expects us to do it while the people at the campgrounds are still awake, but I think Lucas is going to get me naked somehow.

When I go outside, I lounge in one of the camping chairs we brought with us. Lucas keeps himself occupied by sharpening the end of three sticks into points. Oh fuck, maybe we really are having s'mores.

The rest of the day drags. By the time Mike's supposed to arrive, my panties are wet and I'm jumping at every footstep I hear. Mike is five minutes late — not like I was watching the clock on my phone or anything. When he finally arrives, the sun is setting and Lucas has the campfire blazing.

The guys greet each other like they are the best of pals, confirming my suspicion they were making plans on the sly. Whatever. They can have their secrets. I'm sure I'll find out soon enough.

Lucas breaks me out of my sexy daydream. "Jessica, baby?"

"Yes, love?"

"Can you get the chocolate bars from the cooler?"

"Sure." I stand up to head past him towards the cooler. He grabs my wrist and pulls me close to him.

"You're so beautiful," he murmurs in my ear and then tilts my chin up so he can kiss me. "After you get the chocolate, I want you to put on the sundress you wore on the hike yesterday. Don't wear any panties."

My heart skips a beat at the thought of having so little clothes on again. Oh yeah, this is totally going to be strip poker. He's making sure I end up naked. I nod my agreement, unable to speak, as he kisses me again. When he walks away from me, I hurry to the cooler. I practically toss the chocolates on the picnic table and hightail it into the tent to change.

I strip quickly and slip the sundress over my head. I breathe a sigh of relief when I don't feel uncomfortable wearing the dress with nothing underneath. Hell, it almost feels normal.

When I get back to the guys, Lucas has arranged our camping chairs in a half circle around the campfire, and facing away from the main campground. I still don't see any pack of cards out. Huh. What is he up to?

Lucas gestures towards the middle chair. "Sit down, my goddess."

I give him a soft smile. Okay, I don't mind this so far. After all, I am his goddess, right?

Mike sits in the chair on my left. His eyes are dark with desire as he greets me. "Nice to see you again, Jessica."

I echo his sentiment and peek at him as I settle in, making sure I sit on my dress since I'm not wearing panties. Whenever I saw him before, I was always buzzing and mentally fuzzy from lust, so this is the first time I'm able to study him. He's wearing cargo shorts, a short-sleeved t-shirt, and sandals. His legs are muscular and toned, like he hikes regularly. He's not a huge guy, but he's got a sleek and powerful build. I can tell he either works out often or has a job with considerable manual labor.

When Lucas passes out the s'mores supplies, Mike's fingers catch my attention and fascinate me. His fingers are long, slender, and almost delicate. I could easily imagine him playing an instrument with them, or rubbing my clit…

Shit. Focus, Jessica.

"So…" I look expectantly at Lucas. "What are we doing?"

His mouth twists, and his eyes shine in the firelight. "Time for the challenge."

Even though I was expecting this, I still get a thrill and my pussy grows even more wet. I set the s'mores supplies on the side table attached to the camping chair and ask, "What do I have to do?"

I'm hoping I don't sound too eager. Heck, I might say no to whatever it is just to mess with him. Fair's fair, right?

He leans forward with an intense expression on his face. "I want you to spread your legs and rub your clit."

Uh… what? "Right here, right now? People might see."

"Yes?" He sweeps his arms in the direction of the campground behind me. "Who is going to see you?"

I realize he put me in this chair on purpose. Damn, he's devious. I glance over my shoulder. Nobody's close by, and it's getting darker and harder to see very far. Someone would have to be close to know what was going on.

I close my eyes and take several deep breaths. This is crazy, but I'm going to do it. I guess Mike is going to get another glimpse of Ms. Kitty.

I pull the front of my dress to my waist and spread my knees, revealing my smooth mound. The air is warm and dry, and the part of my sundress I'm sitting on is getting damp. I drop my hand between my legs and slide my fingers between my folds.

"Open your eyes," Lucas orders.

I obey and open my eyes wide as I continue to stroke myself.

Mike's eyes are glued to me — or more specifically, my pussy. Fuck, that's hot. Knowing both guys are watching me be a filthy slut quickly spirals me towards an orgasm. My thighs tremble as I rub myself faster and faster. I can feel my juices flowing down my inner thigh.

I glance at Lucas to make sure he's okay with this. He's watching my fingers intently.

"Can I come?" I ask him.

"No," he answers immediately. "Not yet."

I whimper loudly. "Please, let me come?"

Lucas's voice is gruff. "No. Keep rubbing. You can't come."

I try to stifle my moans as I plunge two fingers inside me and rock my hips up to meet them. What does Mike think about all of this? I steal a glance at him.

Mike's cock is visible, hard underneath his shorts. Mmm, yummy. I wish he'd pull his cock out so I could see it. I wet my lips while I think about sucking him in front of Lucas. Yeah, I'm such a dirty girl.

"I think she's close," Mike says in a husky voice.

"God, I am! Please, can I come?" I beg.

"No," Lucas replies firmly. "Keep rubbing."

He's sounding like a broken record. I cry out softly and move my fingers from my pussy to circle around my sensitive clit. I'm beyond being able to stay quiet, and little peeps and moans slip out. The pleasure builds, threatening to overwhelm me.

"Fuuuck." I moan loud enough for Lucas to hear me. I'm almost beyond caring whether he'll give me permission. I want Mike to see me come. Fuck, at this point I'd let a whole football team watch me orgasm. I just need it. Now.

"Jessica." Lucas's sharp voice breaks through my lust. "Stop touching."

Noooo. I don't want to stop. He was supposed to tell me to keep going. I lock gazes with Lucas and continue rubbing myself. My thigh muscles quiver and I'm going to explode any second.

Lucas's voice holds a harsh warning this time. "Jessica, stop or you won't like the consequences."

Ugh. I debate it for one second, then pull my hand from between my legs. Shit… fuck… my brain is a pile of mush.

Lucas stands up and holds his hand out to me. "Come here, baby."

I stand up shakily, uncertain what is going on. I can't think of anything but getting a cock inside me — either guy's cock would do.

Lucas leads me behind the tent and out of sight from Mike. He pulls me into his arms and gives me a toe-curlingly deep kiss. I lose myself in him as our tongues twirl together. When he breaks off the kiss, I mewl in protest. God, he's being so mean.

"Jessica, baby, do you want to fuck Mike tonight? I'd like it, but the choice is yours."

My entire body buzzes. He just handed me the golden ticket, and I wasn't expecting it. I assumed he was going to edge me once we got started.

Lucas's eyes bore into mine and a flush runs from my toes to my head. My nipples harden and wetness trickles down my inner thigh. He's waiting for my answer.

I link my fingers with his and give them a soft squeeze. "Yes, my love. I want to fuck Mike."

He lets out a deep breath like he was nervous about my answer, and then grins at me. "Then let's do this."

My pulse quickens as desire coils in my stomach. It's time for me to really become a hotwife.

I'm ready.

CHAPTER 5

The night air is cool. I shiver and Lucas pulls me closer. I snuggle in, and he rubs his thumb along my cheek.

"Baby, you can change your mind, even in the middle. Say the word and I'll stop it. Okay?"

I nod, and a rush of love for him zips through me. I'm glad we're doing this together.

He doesn't move right away, and I glance at him curiously. "What's wrong?"

"Oh, I just..." He looks hesitant. "I was thinking I'd stay outside the tent while you fuck him."

Huh. "You don't want to watch?"

He shakes his head. "Not tonight, baby. I want to listen and imagine what you're doing."

In my fantasy, he was always watching. As long as he's close by, I can adjust. I rub my cheek against his chest. Lucas smells like soap — a little musky and a little spicy — and it soothes me. "Okay, my love."

Lucas kisses me again, coaxing my lips open and swirling his tongue with mine. I get lost in the moment and my brain is fuzzy when he breaks the kiss off.

His eyes blaze with intensity. "Wait in the tent for Mike."

Nodding slowly, I enter the tent and kneel on my sleeping bag, my ass resting on my feet. I'm already wet from almost coming, and my entire body buzzes with anticipation. My breathing shallows, and I can feel the heat radiating off me. I'm turned on and practically dripping with excitement. All the minor challenges leading up to this moment did exactly what they should do — I'm needy and desperate to bang someone other than my husband.

Now that I've agreed to fuck Mike, I'm not sure what the protocol is. Do I take off my dress? Do I keep it on? What will another cock feel like? It's been years since I've fucked anyone but Lucas. A million thoughts run through my mind and my heart rate spikes at the thought of being totally naked in front of someone other than Lucas.

A few moments later, Mike appears at the tent entrance alone and Lucas calls out, "Jessica, I'm going to be right outside."

I can see his silhouette through the tent wall as he moves a chair outside the door flap. I feel safer knowing he's right there.

"Okay, love." I turn my attention to Mike and the crazy, slutty thing I'm about to do.

Mike gives me a sexy grin as he ducks into the tent. His eyes roam my body hungrily, taking in every inch of me. Ms. Kitty pulses in response and the ache between my legs grows more insistent.

Mike is too tall to stand up, so he drops on his knees in front of me. His gaze is possessive, as if he knows I'm his to play with. I can feel heat rising in my cheeks in response.

Mike clears his throat before speaking, and his voice is husky. "You want to do this?"

I nod, unable to find any words as excitement and nerves churn inside me. Oh, yeah, there is no doubt about it. If he doesn't get his cock inside me soon, I'm going to beg.

He moves closer to me and brushes the hair out of my face before kissing me passionately. Mmm, now this is more like it. I kiss him back with abandon as I run my hands underneath his shirt. He's more muscular than Lucas and I explore wherever my hands can reach from his belt line to his shoulders. His chest has a light covering of hair and I'm curious what my nipples brushing against him would feel like. Will it feel different from Lucas?

Right when I expect him to deepen the kiss and really go for it, he pulls back. "Lucas agreed to let you be my slut tonight. I want to see my slut naked."

My skin prickles with desire and I fight the urge to say 'Yes, sir,' as I pull the dress over my head. I drop it to the floor next to me and push my chest out, drawing attention to my breasts. Thanks to my dear husband, I'm naked since the dress was the only thing I had on.

Mike lets out a low whistle as his eyes scan every inch of me, lingering for a few seconds on my breasts. My nipples harden, and I want him to touch me everywhere.

Mike takes my hand and tugs, so I rise on my knees. Ms. Kitty does a happy dance as he presses against me and I feel his thick hardness through his shorts. His cock is what I'm here for. Is he bigger than Lucas? Will he reach places inside me that Lucas's cock doesn't? The unknown of fucking someone new is thrilling, and I'm extra sensitive to every brush against my skin.

He bends so his lips are millimeters away from mine. My heart races as he kisses me deeply, sliding his tongue into my mouth, exploring every inch. He tastes like cinnamon and smells like smokiness and spice. Everything about him is new, and all my senses are alive. He runs his hands down to cup my ass and pulls me closer against him.

Electricity sparks between us. I moan when he breaks off the kiss and nibbles his way down my neck. "You're so damn sexy, Jessica."

His words send shivers down my spine, and wetness coats my inner thighs as he pushes me onto my back. I don't hold in my sighs of pleasure as his hands explore my body. Every time he hits a ticklish spot, I gasp. Lucas is close enough to hear every sound, and I really hope he's enjoying this as much as I am.

As Mike moves down to kiss my stomach, he murmurs, "I can't wait to fuck you," against the sensitive skin at my navel, and my head spins. Somehow I always imagined my first time with another guy would be rough and wild, but so far Mike is doing everything he can to work me into a frenzy.

He continues lower, placing featherlight kisses all along the path until he reaches my shaved pussy.

"Spread your legs for me," he demands softly, and I open my legs so he can move between them.

I really wasn't expecting him to go down on me, but I'm so turned on, he could do whatever he wanted and I wouldn't care. He spreads my nether lips open with his hands, and his tongue is magical. I arch into him and clutch his shoulders as waves of pleasure course through me.

I'm not being quiet, and each swirl of his tongue makes me cry out in ecstasy. Fuck, this is amazing. I was dumb for hesitating when Lucas suggested I fuck other guys.

He slides two fingers inside me and starts fingerfucking me slowly. I grip the sleeping bag beneath me as I spiral towards my orgasm. He removes his hand and pushes my legs open wider as he plunges his tongue into my pussy.

"Fuuuck," I cry out, bucking my hips towards his mouth. When he speeds up his sucking and licking, the pleasure is too much for me to handle. I scream out as my climax crashes into me. Spikes of electricity ripple from my fingers to my toes as he continues to lick me.

When I come down from my high, Mike smiles up at me with a satisfied expression. He kisses his way back up my body, and I shiver as the cool air hits the wetness left by his lips.

He removes his shirt and shorts before covering my body and kissing me deeply. Our tongues swirl together as I taste myself on him. I moan against his mouth and try to grind against him. Even though I just came, I still want his cock.

Knowing that Lucas is listening makes this experience amazing. God, I hope he's stroking to this. Thinking about him being turned on by what a slut I am turns me on even more. I wouldn't want to do any of this without him.

Mike pulls away from me, and I mewl in protest until I realize he's repositioning himself. He teases my entrance for a moment with the head of his cock and I swear he's playing 'Just The Tip' with my pussy. Each short thrust makes me needier. I try to time my movements with his to force him inside me, but can't. This is making me crazier. I need it all.

With one powerful push, he sinks into me as I buck against him and cry out, "Ohhh, god."

His cock is thicker than I expect, and he stretches me as he burrows deep. I gasp at the sensation of him filling me up, inch by inch. He's gentle yet forceful, each thrust stronger than the last, until I'm almost clawing at him, desperate.

"Oh god, fuck me harder. Please?"

My words spur him on and he whacks against my pussy vigorously. Holy fuck. I wrap my legs around him and cling to his neck as the pleasure almost overwhelms me.

"Do you like my cock?" He's panting as he thrusts into me, and I can only chant, "Yes, yes, yes," as he drives me wild and fucks me with abandon.

My heart pounds in my chest, and the pleasure builds in layers as I'm reeling towards ecstasy. Mike picks up the pace, slamming his hips against mine.

Lucas fucks me hard sometimes, but it doesn't feel the same with Mike. Everything Lucas does has love behind it, but Mike and I have the mutual goal of only seeking pleasure. It makes fucking Mike dirtier and I want to be the sluttiest version of myself with him.

Stars pop on the edge of my vision as I rock against him, meeting him thrust for thrust. Tension coils low in my belly as I strain against him. After all the edging and teasing today, I need something more or I won't come.

Moving my hands to my breasts, I massage them and roll my nipples between my fingers as he hammers into me. My squeals of delight turn into long moans the closer I get.

He growls and fucks me harder. I'm so desperate, I move one hand to my pussy. Oh, god, I need to come. I rub my clit in fast circles until I can't take it anymore.

I throw my head back and scream as my second orgasm rips through me. My body convulses and my thighs quiver. He's like a machine, fucking me hard and fast through my orgasm. I'm panting and can't catch my breath.

He pulls my legs up, grips me under my knees and jackhammers into me from a new angle. Oh, holy fuck. Every nerve ending is on fire, and my brain switches off while he pummels into me relentlessly. I hear moans and words coming out of my mouth, but I don't know what I'm saying. Nothing matters other than the pleasure.

He tenses right before he comes and groans as he explodes. His cock pulses as he coats my cave walls with ropes of sticky cum. He slows down his thrusts as he fucks it back up into me, and time loses all meaning.

My brain is mush when he finally collapses beside me on the sleeping bag. We lay there for a few moments in silence, letting our breathing slow down until we can move again.

"Wow," I whisper when my brain works again.

He gives a soft laugh. "Wow is right."

I lie there blissfully, dazed and in ecstasy, while Mike caresses my fingers and absentmindedly twists my wedding ring. He appears to be just as wooly headed as I am.

I glance down at our intertwined fingers, focusing my gaze on my wedding ring. How is Lucas doing? Is he wondering what is going on right now? Is he aching for me?

Ms. Kitty gives a soft hum, and I almost smile. Yes, Lucas is the missing piece. I'm relaxed and tired from fucking Mike, but I'm longing for Lucas's embrace. He needs to hold me and let me know nothing has changed. I have to be sure that he enjoyed this, and I want him to fuck me with all the pent-up desire he's been holding in while he listened through the wall.

Mike stirs and brings my hand up to his mouth to kiss the back of it. "Thank you for a lovely evening, Jessica."

I grin at him. "You're welcome."

Lucas and I are leaving tomorrow, and I'm sure we'll never cross paths with Mike again, which is perfectly fine. I'm grateful for everything Mike did this weekend to help make my first hotwife experience enjoyable. I'll never forget him and I'm betting he'll think back on this weekend from time to time. Hopefully, he'll stroke while doing so.

I watch Mike get dressed. When he's finished, we both smile and exchange soft goodbyes as he leaves the tent. He and Lucas talk for a moment, and I hear my wonderful husband thanking Mike for giving me a pleasurable evening. Yeah, Lucas is a good guy.

When Lucas enters the tent, his eyes are glazed with lust and yearning. He quickly zips up the door flap and yanks his clothes off. His cock juts straight out and I swear I can see it pulsate. I lick my lips with anticipation as he drops to the ground and crawls towards me.

Every movement he makes tells me I'm about to get fucked hard, and I welcome it.

CHAPTER 6

"Spread your legs," Lucas demands hoarsely.

I don't hesitate and part my legs, assuming he's going to crawl between them and fuck me. When he stops to turn a lantern on, it gives me pause. Oh shit, what is he doing?

The campfire is down to glowing embers. Inside the tent it's shadowy, and details aren't crisp. Him turning the light on puts me on full display. Wetness slides down the crack of my ass and an illicit delight rushes through me. This is some other guy's cum leaking out of me.

Lucas continues to crawl towards me and pauses with his face right above my pussy, and he examines a soaked Ms. Kitty. I lean up on my elbows to watch him. I'm still not sure what he is doing.

When he runs his fingers up and down my slit, gathering the wetness and rubbing my clit in circles, my toes curl from the pleasure. I rock my hips against his hand, but his eyes never leave my pussy, like he's fascinated at how messy I am.

He pushes two fingers inside me slowly, and I moan, "Oh god, yes."

As soon as his fingers are in as far as they can go, he starts finger fucking me roughly. The bliss is intense and I arch my back to meet his thrusts. It's difficult to keep my eyes open, but I need to see his enjoyment. Tonight wasn't only about my pleasure. If we ever do this again, I have to know he wants it as much as I do.

He abruptly stops the movement of his hand and pulls his fingers out, examining how they glisten. Dang, my husband really is a bit of a perv if he's so fascinated by another guy's cum. When he gives one of his fingers a small lick, a flush ripples over me and my eyes widen.

His tongue darts out of his mouth, as if he's savoring the flavor, and then he grins at me. "Tastes like you."

Oh god, he's such a goof. I sit up and reach for him. "Lucas, if you don't get your cock inside — "

He doesn't let me finish as he launches himself at me and pushes me onto my back. He silences my squeal of delight by pressing his lips to mine and ravaging my mouth. My hands fly to his shoulders and I cling to him while he slams his cock into me. I moan, wanting more, as an intense pleasure twists through me.

"Oh god," I groan between kisses.

Lucas is a wild beast. He hasn't fucked me like this in years. I wrap my legs around him and try to pull him deeper as the bliss builds. I'm clawing at his back as he relentlessly fucks me.

His pace increases, and I can feel him throbbing inside me. My body shakes with each thrust as I race towards another climax. I need to come for him as much as I'm desperate for him to fill me up.

I'm chanting, "Fuck me," as we buck and thrash together. I'm mindless with need and consumed by pleasure.

He reaches a hand down to tease my clit as he growls and thrusts deep inside me. Heat streaks through me and I'm riding an almost painful edge as the tension coils in my core. The sounds of our shared passion fill the tent as my whimpers of delight join his moans of pleasure.

I ride his cock and his fingers until I can't take it anymore.

He pants, "Come for me, baby," and I come apart.

The orgasm is so powerful that it takes my breath away. My entire body goes rigid as I scream, "Yesssss!"

I squeeze my muscles around his cock and I'm wracked with shudders of pleasure. He pounds into me repeatedly until he explodes. His body jerks and I cling to him as his cock pulses deep inside me, flooding me with his warm cum.

He slows his thrusts until he stops fully. I'm dazed and can't speak. He's fucked me senseless.

Lucas rolls onto his back, taking me with him so I'm on top. I melt into him, enjoying the closeness. We're both damp from the workout. I can't resist kissing his chest and flicking my tongue out to taste him. Mmmm, I love his salty-sweet flavor after a vigorous lovemaking session.

We lay there in silence, savoring the afterglow. I'm sated and exhausted, but unwilling to move. I'm in my happy place and right where I want to be.

Lucas finally stirs and kisses the top of my head. I look up and his eyes search mine. I can tell he's assessing if everything is okay.

It takes a moment to find words again. I was fucked so thoroughly I'm a little loopy, and I giggle softly. "How was that?"

God, please say it was great.

His mouth curls into a smile. "It was amazing."

My heart leaps as I snuggle against him harder. "Good."

Neither of us seems inclined to say more, so I turn my mind off and drift in a haze of satisfaction. I relax, savoring the connection with him, until his breathing evens out and I can tell he's dozing.

Giving in to the exhaustion, I fall asleep on him.

I wake up on my back with Lucas cuddled against me and his hand on my breast, slowly caressing circles around my nipple. Ms. Kitty purrs with pleasure before a twinge of soreness reminds me we need a day of rest.

"Morning," he whispers when he can tell I'm awake, and kisses my neck.

"Mmm, morning."

I bump against him, forcing him off of me so I can roll on my side and face him. He puts his arm around me and caresses my shoulder while I trace heart patterns on his chest.

His voice is still gruff from waking. "I love you, Jessica."

I lift my mouth and kiss him softly. "I love you, too."

I search his eyes and I can tell nothing has changed with him. His gaze is full of love and a deep contentment settles over me. Damn, I have the best husband in the world.

"So…" His voice holds a teasing tone. "Pleasant trip?"

I give him a delighted giggle and kiss him soundly. "Best trip ever!"

"Enough, so you'd want to do it again?"

His tone is still joking, but I can tell the question is serious. I pause and pretend to think about it for a moment before raising an eyebrow at him. "Maybe not the camping part. But we can do the other stuff at home, right?"

This is his chance to get me to be a hotwife more often. Is he going to take it?

He smiles slowly. "I think I can arrange something at home for you to enjoy."

A tingle of pleasure runs down my spine. I bury my face in his chest so he can't see the huge grin that spreads across my face, and murmur, "Sounds good."

Oh hell, yes! I am going to get more cock, and I won't even have to go camping again. My mind spins as a new world of possibility opens up for our marriage.

There's much to think about, but I push it all aside so I can enjoy this moment. I know Lucas and I have more to discuss, and I need to process what happened last night fully, but for now, this is enough.

I cuddle close to him and sigh happily. I'm more in love with my husband than ever.

The End

SHARING HER TREATS

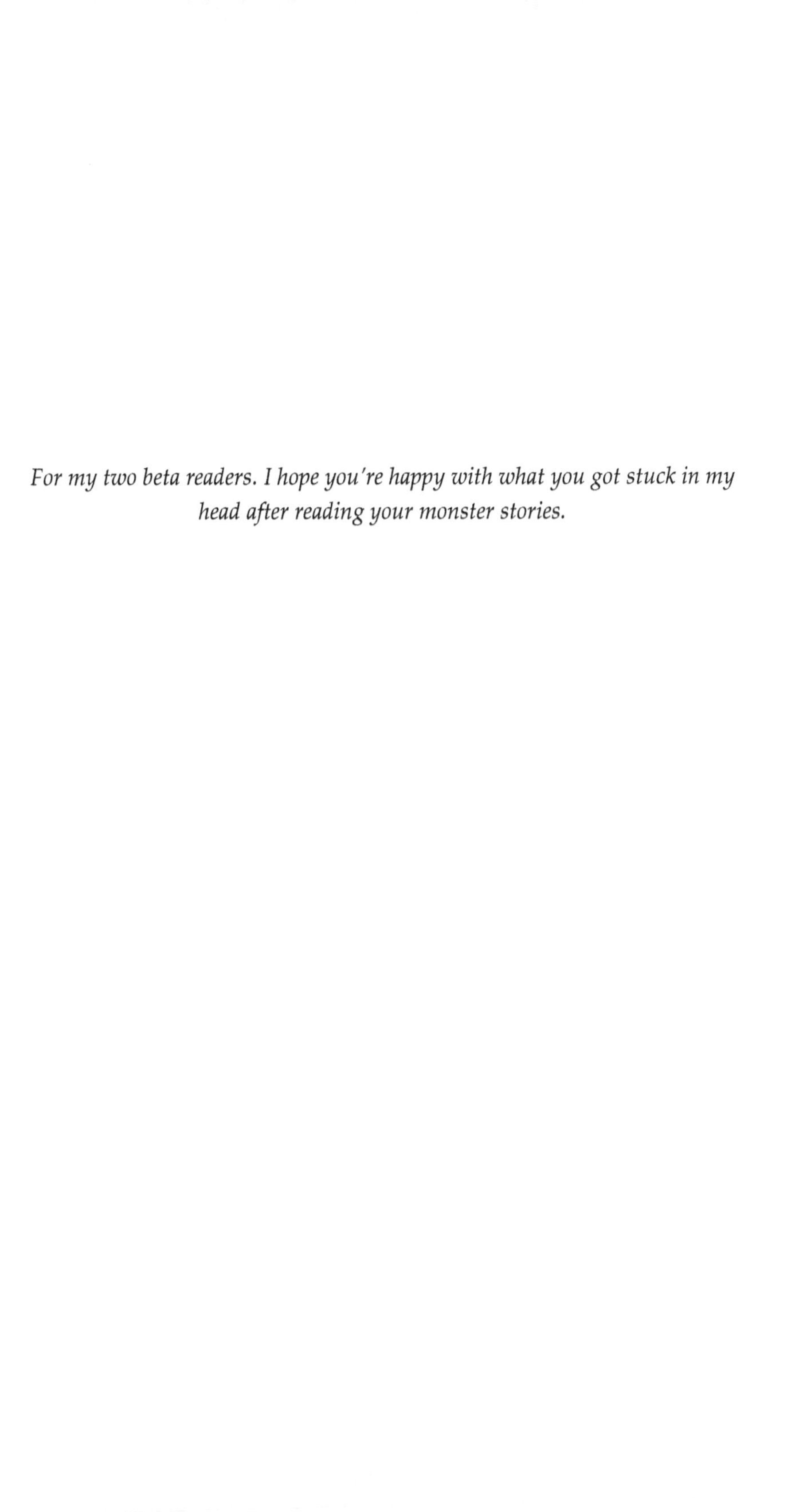

For my two beta readers. I hope you're happy with what you got stuck in my head after reading your monster stories.

CHAPTER 1

It takes my brain a few moments to figure out what the annoying beep is. Groaning, I roll over and blindly fumble around the nightstand until I encounter the rubbery edges on my phone case. I crack my eyes open, swipe my alarm off, and blink at the illuminated numbers.

Ugh. I hate mornings.

The other side of the bed is empty and cold. My husband, Lucas, leaves for work by the time I wake up, which is probably for the best. I'm a grumpy bear before my morning coffee.

I force myself out of bed and stumble into the kitchen. Yawning, I notice Lucas sent me a text message.

He better not have forgotten to put the trashcan on the curb again. If I have to put shoes on, he's going to experience the full fury of my inner beast.

LUCAS

You never told me what costume you're wearing tonight.

Oh right, it's Halloween. Yeah, I need coffee for this conversation. Tapping my fingers on the counter, I stare at my drip coffee maker. Could it go slower? I'll be forty by the time my drink is ready.

Fuck it. I type out my reply to Lucas.

JESSICA

Ugh, do we have to go? My draft is due to my editor Monday.

I'm a full-time indie author and my life is pretty crazy awesome. Since I was young, I've been writing stories on whatever scraps of paper I could find. I'd spend hours daydreaming elaborate conversations between imaginary people. I loved writing, but my parents didn't think writing was a viable career, so I struggled through a business degree.

The only good thing to come out of my college years was meeting Lucas. He was a nerdy math major who was the first guy to see the "me" beyond the petite frame, generous breasts, and blonde hair. He claims he won the lotto with me, but in reality, we both won. Before him, my dating life was a string of boys. Oh, they were fun to toy with, but not worth sticking with long term.

We married right out of college. I worked boring desk jobs and wrote smutty fanfiction on breaks and in the evenings. Four years ago, I got brave enough to self-publish an erotic vampire reverse harem novel, and it blew up. I've been riding the high since, but even though I work from home, I sometimes struggle to stay on track. It's too easy to waste my day on social media or instant messaging my best friend, Miri.

Being an author is awesome, but it's not the best part of my life. No, that's Lucas. He's the most amazing man on the planet, and being in a relationship where your partner lets you be the real you is everything.

I always struggled with the idea of monogamy. One man for the rest of my life? It didn't sound appealing until I met Lucas. I wanted it all: a man at home, others when I wanted, and maybe some extra action on the side. But just because I wanted it didn't mean it was going to happen. My parents taught me that marriage means you found the last person you're ever going to fuck. In the end, I decided Lucas was worth it. I set aside my concerns about not being satisfied with one guy and said "I do" while still daydreaming of my own reverse harem.

I didn't tell Lucas about my filthy fantasies of sleeping with other men, using my writing to explore those desires. My husband is a visual creature and prefers porn to erotica, so he didn't read my stories. He didn't realize I wrote about women fucking multiple men.

A couple of years ago, I noticed our computer browser's history was full of wife sharing porno. I watched a few for research — yeah… research — and I jumped Lucas in a frenzy when he got home from work. After a round of sweaty sex and a fabulous orgasm, I questioned him about his porn preference. He admitted to having fantasies of other men fucking me.

I never imagined I would marry a man who enjoyed sharing me. Hell, I didn't even know it was an option. What followed was a wild year of sexual exploration that has settled into a comfortable, yet exciting, routine where Lucas selects men for me to fuck. My dear husband has a kink about listening to me with the other guys and imagining what is happening, so he's never in the room with us. He finds the men, invites them over, and I fuck them in our spare room. It's hot as hell to be plowed by another guy, knowing that Lucas is listening from the other side of the wall and stroking.

Dammit. Not today. Lucas won tickets to a Halloween haunted house in a work raffle, and he expects me to go with him. This is *so* not on my to-do list. I usually enjoy holidays, but I'm not feeling it this year. I didn't even buy candy to give out. My phone dings, bringing me back to my immediate problem.

LUCAS

Yes, you promised. Now go figure out what you're going to wear.

Bleh. I stick my tongue out at the phone and want to have a tantrum, but I have to be an adult since I agreed to go.

JESSICA

Fine. I'll decide after I get caffeine in me.

Lucas replies with a kissing emoji. I pout as I pour my coffee.
Dammit, why did you have to win the stupid raffle? Angst simmers in

my stomach as my muscles tighten. The looming Monday deadline stresses me out, and wasting time at a haunted house doesn't help.

I drain my first cup of coffee and pour a second before taking the mug with me into our walk-in closet. Now to find a dumb costume I can recycle from past years. I dig around. Fifteen minutes later, I have three options laid out on the bed and I'm sending Miri a text. I'll let her choose.

JESSICA

> OK. I need your help with my costume. I can be a slutty nun, slutty cop, or slutty bunny.

It doesn't take long for her reply.

MIRI

> You should probably be a slutty something tonight.

Her message ends with an emoji of a face with its tongue sticking out. I gaze upwards and count to four slowly. I'm going to need more coffee to deal with her and Lucas today.

JESSICA

> Come on, pick for me. He's dragging me to this stupid-ass haunted house. Make my life easier.

Earlier in the week, I told her about the tickets that Lucas won. She thought it sounded fun, and I offered to let her go in my place. When she joked about fondling Lucas's ass in a dark room, I rescinded the offer. I'm assuming she was kidding, but she and her husband recently opened their marriage and she fucked a guy we went to high school with, so I wasn't sure.

MIRI

> OK, spoilsport. Be a slutty Jessica bunny and twitch your tail at that sexy husband of yours. Make him wish you were at home.

I narrow my eyes and tense my shoulders when she says Lucas is sexy. I realize what happened and roll them, snickering at myself. Shit, I need to lighten up. She's not trying to get with Lucas, and he is quite delicious. He was geeky in college, but he filled out and gained confidence. I've noticed women eying him when we're out shopping.

JESSICA

Thanks, bunny it is!

Well, that's settled. Now on to important matters. Slumping my shoulders, I expel a huge, dramatic sigh as I carry my mug to the office to fix the plot hole I found in my story.

CHAPTER 2

Around lunch time, Lucas texted me and told me he's leaving work a few hours early and he wants me ready to leave when he gets home. Once I focused I flew through my editing, so I treated myself to a long shower and gave extra attention to grooming Ms. Kitty. If I twitch my tail enough, I'm positive I'll get a vigorous fucking once we're home.

The costume is simple. It's a relic of my college years, when I thought being a Playboy Bunny was glamorous. It's a black satin one-piece body suit with no shoulder straps that plunges so deep in the front my breasts spill over the top. The outfit zips up the back and has an attached white fluffy tail and matching rabbit ears. If I'm being honest, it's a fancy bathing suit.

I slip on a pair of black spiked heels. Yeah, it's a dumb choice for shoes, but whatever. I'm going with it.

Should I have reminded Miri what the costume looked like? We've been friends since middle school, so she saw it years ago.

Nah. I bet she would have still said to be a slutty bunny. Lucas is lucky I'm wearing a costume and not my flannel pajamas. It would've served him right if I met him at the door in my comfy PJs and announced I was going as an indie author.

Once I got more in the holiday spirit, I took the time to style my long, blonde hair in loose curls because it's Lucas's favorite. I carefully apply my makeup, and when I examine myself in the mirror, I feel sexy as all fuck. The high heels give the illusion of long legs on my five-foot-nothing frame. At thirty-three, my hips are fuller than they were in college, but the costume still fits. If anything, it might possibly look better, now that I have more to fill it. This is a delightful self-confidence boost and I'm ready to wow Lucas... and get fucked.

My phone rings when it's almost time for Lucas to get home and the lock screen says it's him.

I give a hesitant, "Hello?"

The traffic noises in the background tell me he's somewhere outside. "Hey, I stopped to get gas and I'm five minutes away. Are you ready?"

My pulse quickens with desire. Now that I'm in my slutty costume with a shaved Ms. Kitty, I really just want to stay home and fuck like rabbits. I never told Lucas what I was wearing. Will he even remember it?

I keep my voice light and flirty. "Yep, your sexy bunny is ready for you."

"Is that the costume with the black bodysuit and white tail?"

Giggling, I purr, "Maybe. You'll see when you get here."

"Hmm... No. Take a picture of yourself and send it to me. No excuses. Do it."

His command thrills me. Since I'm standing by the mirror in the bedroom, I tell him to hold on and snap a side-view photo. This way, he can appreciate my shapely ass and the bunny tail.

I send it to him. "It's on its way. You can admire my tail."

He's silent for a few seconds before he gives a husky reply. "That is very nice."

My body warms at his tone and Ms. Kitty is already wet, contemplating all the wicked things we could do later. The car chimes as he climbs in and slams the door shut. The background noise is gone, and I can hear him clearly.

"So, do you want to have a little fun tonight?"

My pussy buzzes and a flutter of pleasure runs down my legs. I know my dear husband. When he suggests "fun", it usually ends up with his cock inside me in a semi-public location. Does he want to fuck me around the back of the haunted house?

I try to sound sexy to entice him. "I'm always interested in a good time. What do you have in mind?"

I can hear the smile in his voice when he answers. "His name is Chris."

Whoa, what's this? He wants me to fuck someone named Chris. Is Chris going to be there tonight? Is this a work buddy of his?

I clench my thighs together in anticipation. The last shred of annoyance at having to go to the haunted house vanishes. "Do we know a Chris?"

He snorts. "Not yet. But you could become intimately acquainted with him tonight."

I should joke with him and tell him no, but it's pointless. He knows me too well. I have no reason to play coy.

"I think me and Ms. Kitty are *very* eager to meet Chris."

He laughs when I stress the word "very".

"OK, baby. Consider it done. I'll be there in a few minutes. I'm going to message Chris the picture of the sexy bunny he's fucking."

He signs off with, "Love you. See you in a few," and I barely have time to tell him I love him back before he ends the call. My brain whirls and I stare at my phone. Tonight just got interesting. The growing wetness between my thighs proves I'm definitely intrigued by becoming acquainted with this Chris person.

Ms. Kitty offers her approval and my pussy clenches as I daydream about being fucked by a stranger. Lucas always listens in and gets worked up, and then afterwards he unloads his pent up sexual tension on me and reminds me I'm his. I wasn't sure sex was on the menu tonight and now I'm getting two cocks. God, I really am living the dream.

CHAPTER 3

Lucas doesn't need much time at home since he wore his costume to work. He's dressed as a 70s hippie, and I enjoy the view of his ass in the corduroys as I follow him out to the car.

Once we're buckled in, I press him for details. "So… Is Chris a work friend, or did you meet him on the app?"

Lucas finds men for me to fuck on an app and invites them over to our house. It's been less than a handful of times I've fucked someone anywhere else, and he keeps the app a secret so I can't sneak a peek at the pool of candidates. Spoilsport.

My sweet husband is driving, and gives me a side-eye flicker as he keeps his attention on the road. "Neither."

Ugh, is he *trying* to be annoying? "Okay, so how do you know Chris?"

"Aren't you the curious bunny tonight?"

I vacillate between thoughts of punching his arm or blowing him a kiss for being so damn annoyingly cute.

I deepen my voice and try to sound threatening. "You're going to have a cranky bunny on your hands if you don't tell me how you know him."

The corners of his mouth pull up. "Let's say he's a friend of a friend, and I heard he enjoys playing with married women."

Mmm, yeah, that's an acceptable answer. I shift in the seat and wish Lucas was rubbing between my legs. I stare out the window and study the passing fields. Wherever he's taking me is a fair distance out of town, but it's not dark yet since he got off work early.

In the end, it doesn't matter how he found Chris. I trust Lucas and I'm rarely disappointed. In fact, the only time in the last year he chose badly was when he invited over a guy who showed up in assless chaps. Chappy, as I dubbed the dude, was an eager one-minute man. After Chappy apologized and left, Lucas fucked me for hours to make up for it.

The drive takes around thirty minutes and when we pull into a dirt parking lot, I'm surprised by how few cars there are for Halloween.

"Where is everyone?"

"Oh." He shrugs with feigned casualness. "The haunted house doesn't open for another hour. We're getting a semi-private tour."

My brain blips out for a moment and I consider what this might mean. Ms. Kitty adds her two cents.

Lucas stops the car and angles his body towards me. "Baby, once we're in there, if we're separated, I want you to go with it."

My eyes grow round and my pulse beats faster. "Something is happening IN the house?"

Lucas leans forward and I instinctually meet him halfway.

He brushes his lips against mine. "Nothing is going to happen you don't want. Chris knows your safe word and I'll be within hearing distance."

All my nerve endings zing. I never included a haunted house in my fantasies, but I'm totally on board with the plan.

I throw myself across the seat to give him an enthusiastic kiss. "Okay, love. Let's do this. I'm ready to get boned by a skeleton!"

He barks out a laugh as we climb out of the car. I faintly hear him mutter, "He's not a skeleton."

I don't want to know what Chris's costume is, so I don't ask for clarification. This idea of anonymous, filthy haunted house sex is the fantasy I never knew I wanted. I'm so wet my costume is going to be a mess by the end of the night. It's a good thing it'll be dark when we leave.

I slide my palm into Lucas's and we head towards a wooded path. There's a house faintly visible through the trees. I was daydreaming when Lucas told me about the haunted house, but I remember him saying it's run by an escape room company and they turn it into a haunted house for two weeks every October.

Lucas squeezes my hand and glances at me. "Are you ready?"

Desire burns a pit in my stomach, and I lick my lips. "Hell yes. Bring on the monster fucking."

CHAPTER 4

The path through the trees is lit by hanging lanterns. The gravel crunches under our feet and walking in heels is difficult. I have to watch the ground to make sure I don't trip. Yep, I'm an idiot. I mentally curse myself until we enter a clearing.

The house isn't one of those cheesy haunted mansions you see at carnivals. It appears to be a genuine abandoned house. Broken windows line the front with scraps of old wood slapped over the openings. Any unbroken windows are dirty, and the yard is a jungle of knee-high weeds. It has a slanted porch with damaged railings that has seen better days. The warped siding was once blue, but now it's mostly stripped of paint and chipped. This is not what I was expecting. What the fuck sort of janky business is this?

We're greeted outside by a woman in her early twenties dressed in a fairy costume with an apron tied around her waist. The semi-normal Halloween costume eases some of my concerns.

Her "Hello!" is perky, and she eyes our costumes. "A hippie and a bunny. You must be here for Chris."

I glance sharply at her as Lucas replies, "Yep."

Lucas hands her our tickets, and she slides them into a pocket of her apron with a wide smile. "You can head in. Chris said he would find you inside."

Lucas thanks the fairy, and we walk towards the house. Apprehension looms over me with each unsteady step. What are we doing here? This doesn't seem like fun times. He holds my hand to help me across the porch and I hold my complaints, trying to keep an open mind.

The door is wide open, the inside dark. My heart beats double time, and I want to turn around. I'm doubting Chris is worth this. I hate scary things. A funhouse would have been so much better.

As soon as we pass the threshold, we're immediately hit with a waft of stale air. A wall blocks the path straight in front of us and a crooked sign hangs on the wall with a double-sided arrow that states, "Pick a direction."

Lucas grins at me. "You choose."

Sure, give me the choice between two evils, so when something bad happens, it's my fault.

I shake off the thought as unworthy. Lucas is many things, but he's never set me up for anything unpleasant. I tip my head and take all of two seconds before tugging him to the left. I read somewhere that if given an option, most people choose right. Ever since then, I made it a point to go left. If fucked up shit was going to go down in a haunted house, something told me it would be to the right.

I haven't been to many haunted houses, but this one isn't like any of them. I was expecting amusement park spooky music and ghosts booing and swinging out at me, but none of that happens and it's creeping me out. They wouldn't charge if nothing happens, so I get more anxious by the second. My writers' imagination is having a field day and I'm hating every step.

We walk through a short, dirty hallway with cobwebs lining the ceiling.

Ewww, they're real.

Sticky webs line the top of the walls, and I press closer to Lucas's side. Movement out of the corner of my eye has me peering at the webbing. Shit, I think there's something up there. I swear I see something black and small moving fast behind the white wisps.

Oh, hell no!

We need to leave. A shiver runs down my spine and the hairs on the back of my neck stand up while I fight the urge to scratch all over. If a spider dropped on me, it could easily slide right down my cleavage. Yeah… this isn't sexy scary and was a bad idea. Bad, bad idea. Terrible. The worst ever.

Somehow I keep moving. The end of the hall opens up to a creepy-ass nursery. The walls are half-covered with ripped and faded wallpaper, and the room is full of broken furniture. A rocking chair in the corner moves on its own. The sound of a baby crying fills the space. I grip Lucas's hand tighter and stumble into him. It's faint and the echoes give it an eerie tone. I take deep breaths.

Chill out, Jessica. It's a recording. None of this is real.

Lucas holds my arm and I about jump straight in the air when the crib shakes. The baby blanket on the mattress balloons as if there's now a baby underneath it.

"This is scary," I moan-whisper to Lucas and keep a death grip on his hand.

His presence is the only thing keeping me from screaming and running out of here. The ghostly cry continues, louder and stronger, and the crib shakes furiously until the mattress bounces and the legs clatter against the floorboards. Um, yeah, it might be time to nope the fuck out of here.

When the rocking chair speeds up, I yank Lucas towards the door on the opposite wall. He gives no resistance as we scurry out of the fucked-up nursery. My anxiety eases slightly once we're in another short hallway. There are three doors at the end in a T pattern, so we'll have to choose our direction again. I'm *soooo* making Lucas pick this time, so I can blame him if something goes wrong.

We pause at the end and look into the room straight ahead. It's an old timey kitchen, which reassures me for a moment. Then I look up. Knives hang from the ceiling, dangling above the path leading to the doorway on the other side. Okay, that's an enormous hell no. Yep, I'm done here.

Turning to Lucas, I open my mouth to tell him we're leaving, when something from the right-hand doorway grips my arm and yanks me into the room. The door slams shut. I scream, and a warm hand covers my mouth, muffling my cries.

A werewolf holds me captive while I tremble and blink to clear my vision. I stop screaming as tiny details come into focus. It's really a dude in a costume — not that I think werewolves are real. He's wearing ripped jeans and combat boots, but from the waist up, he's furry with a full mask that obscures his face. The costume is good quality, and if I saw him in the woods, I'd run for it. I mean, hell, I'm about ready to run for it right now.

My stomach muscles tighten and blood rushes in my ears. The hand against my mouth is very much human, but a fake wolf's paw covers the backside and attaches with elastic around his palm. If his arms were at his side, he'd look as if he had furry hands with claws.

A mental image of me fucking a werewolf pops into my head and my heart hammers again, but excitement ripples through me as well. Ms. Kitty buzzes a little and I feel the heat of a blush on my face. Huh, okay. I'm not hating this idea.

When he removes his hand, he steps back and examines me quietly. Shit, am I supposed to say something?

My throat is dry, and I swallow so I can speak. "You're Chris?"

This better be Chris. Otherwise, I'm going to scream Bloody Mary again.

The werewolf nods. His voice is gruff. "Now is your chance to run away."

Run away? The decision hangs in the air for a moment.

Now that I've got my bearings and I know this is Chris, that tempting, delicious, forbidden lust burns through me and my nipples harden. God, is it fucked up that I'm getting turned on by this?

Shame and desire war inside my brain. I want him to fuck me savagely until I can't think. A delicious shudder ripples through me at the thought of us rutting like wild beasts. Oh yeah, I want this. I suppress a grin. Somehow Lucas knew and arranged it.

Stepping closer to him, I give him a sultry smile. "Do your worst."

Okay, maybe I shouldn't have said that. Lust zings straight to my pussy and I get a slutty, naughty thrill. I'm getting off on this way more than I would have thought.

The werewolf nods but doesn't speak as he steps closer. He twists me around and shoves me against the nearest wall, smashing my breasts against the rough plaster.

I gasp, "Oh," as he yanks down the zipper of my costume.

Shit, I guess we're starting. I had a few scenarios in my head of how tonight might play out, and being used by a werewolf wasn't one I considered. I mean, it's awesome, but still…

A thud on the floor startles me and I glance down. The werewolf mask's empty eyes stare at me. Uh oh. In every horror movie I've watched, if you see the evil guy's face, you're a goner. This better not be a horror erotica movie.

Despite how fucked up this is, the hint of danger is turning me into a needy mess. Wet heat flares between my legs and I imagine myself on my knees, sucking his cock. A terrible hunger crawls into my brain and I want to beg him to use me however he wants.

Chris yanks the top of my costume down, exposing my breasts to the cool air. He tugs the fabric over my curvy hips until it drops to the floor. I step one foot out so I don't get tangled in it and trip. Removing that one piece leaves me naked, since I'm not wearing panties or a bra. Ms. Kitty gets even wetter at the harsh treatment as wild, raw need flutters in my core.

When he grinds against my ass and my nipples scrape the plaster, I moan from the intense pleasure-pain. He's nice and hard through his jeans, and a switch flips in my brain. Everything is now erotic instead of scary. I'm loving every minute of this.

I moan as he kisses the back of my neck and rasps, "Has a werewolf ever bred you?"

My brain freezes for a split second.

Holy fuck.

I'm not in a horror movie. This is one of my motherfucking novels. Or nearly so. It would have been vampire breeding if I wrote it, but you can bet your ass I'm going to write a filthy werewolf story after this.

I moan loudly. "No, I haven't."

He brings his hands around to my breasts and tugs on my nipples.

He continues to rub against my ass and the friction of his jeans increases my need to have a cock inside me.

No one said I had to pretend to fight, and I'd rather play easy to get. "Mmmm, I'm ready for breeding."

My novels always have kick-ass women who embrace the weird shit that happens to them, so if this is my novel, my protagonist would plead for a hard breeding.

He stops playing with my tits and forces my legs apart with his knee. I adjust my position to give him better access as he glides his hand down the curve of my ass cheek, caressing me. He slides his fingers against my pussy and grazes my wet folds. It's enough to drive me crazy.

He's teasing me and doesn't press his finger in. "I'm not sure my bunny is ready to be bred yet. I think she needs to be stroked some more."

Lucas is probably laughing his ass off at this dirty talk… or maybe not. He's probably stroking his cock and imagining all of this.

"Whatever you want." I groan as he presses a finger into my wetness and seeks my clit.

"Yes," he growls. "It is whatever I want."

He rubs circles on my clit, and a shock of pleasure consumes me. "Oh, fuck."

A gush of wetness coats his hand, and I arch against him as he continues to tease my swollen bundle of nerves. His warm breath on my neck thrills me, and I'm transported when he growls and bites my shoulder. He doesn't do it hard enough to break the skin, but it's going to leave a mark.

This is more like it.

I embrace the fantasy. I close my eyes and imagine he's still wearing the mask. I'm bent over a log in a forest, not imagining an actual werewolf, but the idea of a guy in a costume breeding me in the woods hits a kink I didn't know I had.

He continues to fondle me with one hand. My breathing speeds up at the sound of his zipper. When his bare cock presses between the cleft of my buttcheeks, I moan as my pussy throbs with pleasure. He shoves me closer to the wall. I have to turn my head and put the side of my face against the cold plaster. My moans get louder as he slides the tip of his cock up and down my wet folds, not pressing in… not giving me what I crave.

A forbidden hunger makes me whimper. "Oh god, fuck me… Please."

His voice rumbles in my ear. "Oh no, my bunny isn't warmed up enough yet."

The way he keeps saying "My bunny" has a possessive naughtiness to it. I'm Lucas's bunny, but the more Chris repeats it, the more I want to be his as he fucks and breeds me.

He plays "just the tip" with my pussy. A ripple of bliss swirls in my core every time I think he's finally going to plunge all the way in. I mewl in displeasure. Fuck, I need his cock NOW.

After several agonizing short thrusts, when he pulls out again, I cry out. "No, please, you can feel how wet your bunny is."

He growls. "We'll see."

He yanks me away from the wall and drags me over to an old dressing table with a cracked oval mirror. Chris forces my head to the surface and I catch a quick glimpse of him in the mirror before my face presses against the dusty table top.

Wow, he's cute. He has pleasant features with dark, wavy hair. With the brief look, I don't think I could pick him out of a crowd if I saw him again, but he's not going to get tossed out of anyone's bed for eating cookies and getting crumbs on the sheets.

He doesn't ask me to, but I spread my legs as wide as I can. Since we're now across the room, I don't know how well Lucas can hear us. I'm going to need to moan louder for his enjoyment. The way my head is facing, I can see a four-poster bed with ratty blankets on it and I'm glad he didn't drag me there. Yeah, no one wants to fuck on that bed. Being bent over this dirty table is much better.

This entire encounter is filthy, figuratively and literally, and I'm so on board with it. Miri won't believe the night I'm having. Hell, maybe this would've been her if I had given her my ticket.

A sharp slap on my ass snaps me to attention. "Shit."

The sting lingers as he presses his cock between my ass cheeks, placing pressure against a hole I wasn't expecting him to use. Um, this dude doesn't have lube. Fear lances my gut, but at the same time my pussy clenches in delight. This is exactly why I can't trust Ms. Kitty. She's all down with me getting ass fucked with no lube.

I'm about to protest when he shifts his position and drives straight into my pussy, drilling straight to my core.

"Ohhhhh my god." I groan from an intense spike of pleasure.

His cock is massive, much bigger than Lucas, and I feel deliciously ripped apart. My head reels as he withdraws and slams into me again, setting a punishing pace.

"You like being bred by a werewolf?" he asks in a deep roar.

"Yes," I gasp. "Fuck me harder."

I don't know why this absurd dirty talk is doing it for me, but every time he mentions breeding, I want to reply with disgusting things I've never said before… things I've never even thought about. I want to beg him to fill me with his seed, and put a baby in me. Tell him to fill my fertile womb.

I close my eyes and groan at my vulgar thoughts, and a warmth steals over me. A growing acceptance of my inner slut being unleashed sinks me into submission. He can do whatever he wants to me.

He laughs darkly, as if he can sense I've given up control. "I plan to breed you until you're a wet puddle and my seed is dripping out of you."

He takes a fistful of my hair and yanks my head back, growling as he slams into me repeatedly. I grip the sides of the vanity for leverage and my breasts scrape the surface, sending pings of bliss straight to my clit. His enormous cock feels spectacular as he stretches me wide. Jesus Christ, this is crazy and hot.

My arms shake from holding on as he rams forward, plunging himself inside me over and over again. My moans grow louder as every thrust brings me closer to the edge. I usually rub my clit to help me come, but this guy's girth massages every inch of my cave walls and I'm going to come without any added help.

I need to see how raunchy this looks, so I open my eyes and stare into the broken mirror. His head is thrown back, and he's holding onto my hips with one hand and my hair with the other as he jackhammers into me. He didn't take off the chestpiece of his costume and his hands still have the fur covering. It's a half werewolf, half human fucking me. Holy fuck, this is depraved.

My brain melts at the obscene visual and it catapults me over the edge. "Ohhhh, god!"

My back arches at the peak of my orgasm. Ripples of rapture shoot from my fingers to my toes, focusing on the nerve endings stretched around his massive tool. Waves of pleasure wash over me as he pants and fucks me harder.

I'm chanting "Fuck me" as the ecstasy spirals through me. What few thoughts I have outside the sensations blowing my mind are all about Lucas, standing in the hallway with his cock in his hand. He should have been in the room watching. This might be a once-in-a-lifetime fuck.

The bliss builds again, and just when I'm about to come for a second time, Chris shouts in pure male pleasure and explodes, coating me with his seed. He spasms against me, fucking his cum back into me for several seconds as I quiver underneath him.

When he's finished pumping, he releases my hips with a loud grunt. A stream of hot cum pours out of my pussy and coats my thighs as he pulls out. His huge cock twitches as it empties itself and leaves a trail down my legs. My legs tremble from the tickling sensation and I have the urge to taste him. I realize I'd have to let go of the vanity to do that and I'd probably collapse to the floor, so I put it from my mind.

He slumps over me, putting his palms flat on the surface to hold his weight, and presses his head against my shoulder. We stay still for several moments until his heavy breathing slows. I watch him in the mirror as I process. I'm a mess and in desperate need of a shower since he's been fucking me against dirty surfaces.

When his eyes meet mine in the mirror, they're dark with satisfaction and full of wonderment.

"Thank you, Jessica."

"You're welcome." I'm uncertain what else to say. I should probably thank him as well.

As he straightens up, his gaze drops to my thighs, smeared with his warm, sticky cum. I fight the urge to rub my thighs together, and he holds onto my upper arm to steady me as I stand. His arms wrap around me from behind, cupping my breasts with each hand. He skims his thumb across my nipples in an intimate gesture that sends tingles through me. He places a soft kiss on top of my hair, and I'm surprised by the intimate gesture.

"Your husband is waiting for you."

I give him a hazy smile. "I need to get dressed."

His soft chuckle reminds me he's only a guy in a costume, no matter how much he rocked my world and possibly gave me a new kink. He drops his hands from my breasts and gets my costume from the floor. I shimmy into it. Chris zips up the back and plays with the bunny tail. I really need to thank him, but anything I could say seems inadequate.

I can't simply walk out, so I have to try. "Thank you, Chris. This was… fucking magnificent."

Instead of responding, he flashes me a wide smile and a dimple appears in his cheek.

Oh hell, that's adorable.

And memorable. I'd probably be able to pick him out of a crowd now that I've gotten a better look at him. Lucas never picks the same guy twice, so is the only time I'll ever see him.

Dammit. This is one time I wish Lucas would change his rule.

My body is cooling down, and I shiver as his cum dries on my thighs. I peer around the room, wishing there was something I could clean with. When I see Chris again, he's slipped his werewolf mask on.

"Have a good night, Jessica." It's muffled, almost a growl, like he's back into werewolf mode, and he heads into the hallway before I can reply.

Lucas steps into the room and approaches me cautiously. My heart catches in my throat and I want to rush to him. I'm a mass of confusion at how hot that was, and I'm silent as Lucas draws me towards him, encircling me with his arms. He cups my face and his thumb caresses my lips before he kisses me tenderly.

"Are you okay?"

I nod, not trusting myself to speak.

He presses a gentle kiss on my forehead before pulling away. "Listening to him talk about breeding you was hot."

A quick glance at the bulge in his jeans confirms his words. Oh yeah, he liked it.

I can't help myself and I stroke his hardness through the fabric. "Lucas, you really should have been watching."

He groans. "Let's go home. I want to fuck you."

God, I love this man.

I tease him. "Yes please. I want your magnificent cock breeding my pussy and filling me with your seed."

His eyes glitter and he gives a delighted laugh. "I'll do whatever I want to you."

Mmmm, now this is why I married him.

CHAPTER 5

As soon as the front door closes behind us, Lucas shoves me against the wall and kisses me deeply, grinding his cock against my stomach. Looks like the car ride didn't cool his ardor. He slides his arms around me and unzips my bodysuit, pulling it down to expose my breasts. His hands move to cup them and my nipples tighten in response. My ping of lust wakes up Ms. Kitty, who clearly informs me she's ready for more action.

"Fuck," he growls as his mouth moves to my neck, nibbling and sucking on my skin. "I love your tits."

He takes one of my nipples into his mouth and sucks hard, making me gasp. I hope he doesn't want something long and drawn out, because I need him inside me. Soon. Sooner.

He pulls away, leaving me wanting more. Desire rips through me as he crushes his mouth to mine and kisses me while undressing himself. He separates enough to rip his shirt off before returning to my lips. Once he sheds the rest of his clothes, he grabs my hand and forces me towards the kitchen.

I fumble for a few steps before kicking my high heels off. My bodysuit is still halfway on, with my breasts bare. Lucas notices and pushes me against the edge of the table as he drags the costume down my hips.

"Spread your legs," he commands, and I immediately open them.

My inner thighs are crusted with another man's cum, but Lucas doesn't care. The table edge digs into me as he pushes two fingers inside my pussy. I'm dripping all over his hand as he pumps them in and out, and I sigh at how incredible it feels.

"Jessica…?"

"Mmmm, yes?" I wish it was his cock sliding into me instead of his fingers, but this is a start. Ms. Kitty approves.

"Ask me to fuck you. I want to hear you say it."

Squirming, I moan louder and embrace the sluttiness of what we're doing. "Oh god, please fuck me. I need your cock inside me. Please."

Removing his fingers from my pussy, he shoves me onto the kitchen table until I'm lying on my back. I'm dizzy with need as I spread my legs. Hell yeah, It's time for his cock. Let the fun begin.

Again.

My relief is short-lived as he slips his fingers back inside me. Why won't he give me his cock? He stands over me, one hand on my knee, holding them apart while he finger fucks me.

"Fuuuuck!" I writhe against his hand as the pleasure builds in my core. "Just fuck me, please!"

Lucas laughs and shakes his head as he moves the kitchen chair over so he can sit between my legs. He pulls me towards him and cups my pussy with both hands and spreads my lips, exposing my clit. His tongue glides over the sensitive nub, making me squeal.

"Are you sure?" His hot breath on my clit drives me wild and I squeal again. My hips buck, and he uses his free hand to guide them. He slides his fingers inside me to gather moisture, then rubs them together and places the wet tips against my asshole. I whimper at his touch and he raises his head to grin wickedly at me.

"Or maybe you want this tonight?"

I'm reminded of Chris, and how I half wanted him to fuck my ass, and my ready protest when I thought he was going to do it. But this is Lucas, not Chris, and I love him dearly. Lucas can do whatever he wants as long as I get his cock inside one of my holes.

Lucas spits on his finger and uses the lubrication from my pussy and his saliva to slide his finger gently into my ass. There's a moment of discomfort, but I relax and revel in the sensation. When he pushes it deeper, I cry out from pleasure. A second finger follows, stretching me wide and filling me. He pumps them in and out slowly, making sure I feel every inch.

"Is this what my slutty wife wants tonight?"

"Yes, this… yes." I whimper as he fingers my ass.

He pulls them out completely, and I mewl in disappointment. Why did he stop?

"You forgot something." I raise my head and see his wicked grin. "It's my choice, and I want your pussy."

He stands, and I groan as he pushes his thick cock all the way inside my pussy until he bottoms out.

"Oh, fuck…" Swirls of bliss make me groan and writhe as I try to buck against him.

"You like this cock?"

"Oh god, yes. I love it. I can't get enough of it."

Whenever I fuck other men, he needs to hear how much I love his cock… and I really do. Other men may fuck me, but Lucas owns me, body and soul.

He pulls almost all the way out before slamming deep inside me, the motion bringing me to the brink of orgasm. The best thing about what Lucas and I do is no matter how slutty I am, he still loves me and wants me. I get to experience my most depraved fantasies and come home to be reclaimed by the man who accepts every facet of me.

Everything I've done tonight rolls through my mind — being pretend bred by a guy I don't know, my husband's fingers in my ass, and now I'm begging for his cock — and my brain shuts off.

The room fills with the sounds of wet slapping as he hammers into me, and uncontrolled words tumble out of my mouth. "Oh, god, yes! Give it to me. I want to come all over your cock."

I need to watch his face as he cums inside me. It's so fucking hot. I'm so turned on I can barely breathe.

He growls, "You're such a dirty slut," as he slams into me.

"Yes, yes, I am." He whacks against my pussy harder.

"Do you want to come for me?"

"Yes," I pant. "Please, let me come."

He bucks his hips and moves a hand to hold my hip tightly, keeping me from rolling off the table. With his other hand, he rubs my clit. I can't believe how good he makes me feel. He's always there for me, always willing to take care of my needs and make sure I'm satisfied. I groan as he fucks me and applies pressure to my swollen bean. Energy builds in my core and my thigh muscles tighten.

"Oh god, I'm going to come," I cry out.

"Tell me you want my cum."

The room spins and I try to focus. "I want your cum, please."

He thrusts harder, and his finger against my clit speeds up. I finally tip over the edge, and scream his name and arch my back as rapture courses through me. I struggle to keep my eyes open and locked onto his as I ride the waves of bliss. He gives a final hard whack and moans passionately as he climaxes. His eyes glaze with lust as he jerks against me, unloading his seed.

I'm in a daze as the ripples of pleasure become faint shivers of delight. He stays inside me until he softens before he pulls me into a sitting position and wraps his arms around me.

"That was amazing," he whispers and kisses my forehead.

We hold each other close, basking in the afterglow of our orgasms. I might be embarrassed tomorrow when I think back to the crazy, over-the-top shit we said tonight in the heat of the moment, but hopefully it will help me write my werewolf breeding story.

As my mental fuzziness fades, I look down at his chest. He's covered with streaks of grime that he got from me.

I laugh and kiss him. "Maybe next time you'll give me the chance to clean up before you fuck me?"

"Hmm… maybe."

Maybe my ass. There's no way he'll *ever* let me shower before reclaiming me. My wonderful husband loves it when I'm a dirty slut.

The End

SHARING HIS EAGER HOTWIFE

PREFACE

These two shorts were originally written and posted on a blogging platform. They're not there anymore. The publication they were in changed the title on the second story, but I decided to use the original one because I like it better. Since the stories were written as stand-alone shorts, some details had to be repeated each story.

Enjoy!

Lacey

CHAPTER 1
HUSBAND CHOOSES A MASSIVE GUY TO FUCK HIS NEEDY HOTWIFE

"What do you think about this one?"

My husband, Lucas, is sitting at the other end of the couch and he tips his phone at me. On the screen is a smoking hot shirtless guy wearing a cowboy hat, and I fight the urge to lick my lips. Lucas has been searching on an app for casual hook-ups for the past 15 minutes, trying to select the perfect guy for me to fuck tonight. Since he keeps tempting me with pictures of sexy men and telling me what I could do with them, I'm a turned on, wet mess. Thinking about the guy in the picture, I immediately imagine running my hands over his chest and kissing down his abs. Moisture leaks from my pussy at the thought–yeah, my panties are going to be shot after this.

I like to play a game where I pretend I'm not impressed with the guy, so I keep my tone neutral. "Uh, a cowboy? Nah, not interested."

I'm pretty sure Lucas knows the game because the more indifferent I sound, the more he tries to tempt me. I nonchalantly pluck cat hair off my yoga pants and struggle to hold back a smile when he gives his reasoning.

"But Jessica, you could ride your own cowboy." He glances at me and wiggles his eyebrows in a stupid but loveable way. "And we both know how much you like being on top."

I blow him a kiss. "Yes, but I rode you last night. I want something different."

"Hmm...." He goes back to searching on the app and I consider sliding a hand down my pants to stroke my clit. It's so fucking hot when he chooses the guy he wants me to fuck. The longer it takes, the more turned on I'm getting. When my pussy clenches and buzzes with need, I decide to go for it. I need to release some of this tension, and Ms. Kitty needs a finger inside her at the very least.

Only the tips of my fingers are under the elastic waistband of my pants when he exclaims, "Found him!"

I lean towards him, trying to peek at his phone. "Oh?"

He draws his phone away from my inquisitive eyes. "Oh, yes. You'll see tonight."

Oh fuck, he's not going to show me! A wave of lust washes over me and my entire body tingles. It's going to be a long wait until tonight.

***

When the doorbell rings, I'm sitting on the edge of the king-sized bed in our spare room wearing sheer, ruffled babydoll lingerie that shows everything. It's light pink with black polka dots, and molds around my breasts. My dusty-pink nipples stand out through the fabric, and the matching panties don't hide the fact I'm fully waxed below. The full-length mirror on the wall across from the bed validates that I look as sexy as I feel. My blonde, wavy hair is in a braid and I toy with the end while I wait eagerly.

Lucas and I came up with several rules for our playtimes. He invites the men over to our house so that he can meet them first and assess whether he's going to allow them to fuck me. Our home office is one room over and he waits in there, listening, while I get fucked. This way he's close if something goes wrong and I'm secure knowing he's watching out for me, even if he's not in the room.

But honestly, we've yet to meet a bad guy. I'm a firm believer that most people in this world are decent, and these guys just want to fuck a hotwife. They're looking for sexual release and I'm more than willing to give it to them.

Since the bedroom door is open I can hear their voices in the living room but not what they are saying. Their laughter echoes down the hall and gets louder as Lucas and whoever he's bringing with him head in my direction. My breath catches in anticipation and I rub my thighs together. Lucas walks in first and a massive, muscular, tattooed guy lumbers behind him. My eyes widen and I'm speechless for a moment. This guy is a giant. Did Lucas hook me up with a body-builder?

I'm on the petite side and this guy might cleave me in two with a powerful thrust. My brain blips out while I picture him behind me, pounding away at my pussy. My pulse speeds up and I feel like my insides are vibrating while my body flushes from neediness.

I come back to my senses when Lucas makes the introduction.

"Jessica, this is Hank."

I have to hold in my giggle. He's Hank the Tank. Realizing I need to say something before it becomes awkward, I smile sweetly at Hank.

"It's nice to meet you."

Hank is standing halfway behind Lucas, so I can't see his full crotch area. I'm curious what he's packing because I know it's a myth that big guys have large cocks. I don't think it'll matter what size he is. My body is responding to his bulk and the knowledge he could pick me up and toss me around easily. There are so many sexual positions I could do with this guy. He could be my jungle gym and fuck me while holding me midair without needing to brace me against the wall.

God, my husband is so awesome. I enjoy being held down and feeling helpless during sex, so he probably saw this dude's picture and knew I'd love his strength.

Lucas grins at me. "Right, so I'll leave you guys alone. Have fun!"

As Lucas leaves, I notice he's sporting an erection. He better not stroke to the point of coming while listening to us. I want him ready for me afterwards. The best thing about fucking other men is the amazing sex Lucas and I have after they leave. I always get a minimum of two orgasms — one from each guy — and my pussy is hoping for three tonight.

The bedroom door closes, and as Hank approaches me, I stand up. He's easily over six feet tall to my five-feet-nothing, and I contemplate climbing up on the bed to kiss him. Hank takes care of our height difference problem by bending over to brush his lips against mine. When he deepens the kiss, my pussy hums and I realize Hank hasn't said a word to me. I know he can talk because he was laughing with Lucas. Is he the strong and silent type in the bedroom?

His mouth tastes minty as we twirl our tongues, and a bolt of desire runs through me. Since I've been wet and needy all day, I need his cock inside me now. Hank takes his time with the kiss and when he makes no move to touch me, I take one of his enormous hands and put it on my breast. He teases the nipple through the sheer fabric and I moan and sway towards him as pleasure flutters in my core.

Again, he seems in no rush as he cups both my breasts and rolls my nipples between his thumbs and index fingers. It's not like I've done hundreds of one-night stands, but so far in my hotwife experiences it's not common for the guy to want to savor the experience. The guys Lucas has chosen for me all seem to want to bang furiously, almost as if they're afraid something is going to stop them before they come. I'm always halfway to my orgasm before they even get to the house, so a quickie easily tips me over the edge. But this guy is different.

Hank kisses down my neck, flicking his tongue against my skin, and I want to suggest we lie down on the bed before his back hurts from being bent over, but his mouth and tiny bit of stubble on his cheeks and chin make my head whirl. My pussy aches and I try to clear my head enough to take control and move this forward. Ms. Kitty will not wait all night and Lucas is probably wondering what the hell is going on because we're so quiet. I'm not giving him my usual vocal entertainment.

I finally can't take it any longer, and put a hand on Hank's firm chest. I almost get distracted and want to explore with my hands, but that won't get his cock in me any faster. My attempts to shove him away from me are pointless. He's unmovable, so I switch tactics.

"Hank," I purr at him, "I want you to fuck me."

God, please, just shove your cock in me before I beg. He doesn't respond but sweeps me up into his arms. I gasp and throw my arms around his neck, and my body tingles. Holy fuck, I was right. He could toss me around if he wanted. He climbs onto the bed with me and I assume he's going to try cuddling and kissing some more because this muscular dude seems to be a teddy bear... a silent teddy bear.

When he rolls me onto my stomach and props himself up on an elbow, I'm perplexed. What's going on here? His lack of talking is arousing me further. I don't know what he's thinking or what he plans to do. I moan out when he caresses my ass cheeks through my panties, and I wiggle my bum at him to encourage him to continue.

Instead, he peels my panties down to my knees. To help him remove them, I bend my legs and he easily drags them off. They are a wisp of fabric so I don't hear them fall to the floor and I can't tell what he did with them, but it doesn't matter. Ms. Kitty knows she's closer to getting stuffed, and wetness leaks out of me.

He shifts his position on the bed and I glance over my shoulder to see he's on his knees. He tugs on my legs to pull them open, and I help him by spreading them. If he wants access to my pussy, I'm going to help him in any way I can.

He rubs my ass briefly again, and when his thick fingers slip between my velvety folds and brush against my clit, I groan loudly. "Oh, god. Please fuck me. Please?"

I can tell I'm a minute away from begging, but when he rubs circles around my clit, all thoughts drain from my head. I'm a bundle of repressed energy waiting to explode, and bolts of lightning shoot through my core.

He speeds up his caressing and I cry out, "Ooooh, god," loud enough that I know Lucas can hear it through the walls. Having my husband listening in always makes me want to put on a good show.

When Hank dips a finger in my pussy, I buck against his hand and try to rise on my knees to give myself leverage to fuck his finger myself. A firm hand on my ass makes it so I can't move. The brief moment of helplessness as I fight against the pressure and realize he can pin me down with one hand makes me hit the boiling point.

I whimper, growing louder by the end of my begging. "God, I need your cock. Please fuck me? You see how wet I am? I need your cock. Please... PLEASE?"

The bed dips as he moves between my legs. When he fits the head of his cock against my pussy, I remember I never saw his package. He presses in slowly, and it only takes a moment for me to realize his cock is as massive as his body.

"Oooooh, fuck," I cry out as my cave walls stretch and mold around him. My body zings with intense pleasure. This guy's cock might be the biggest I've ever had, and I've had some pretty massive ones recently.

I keep expecting him to haul me up on my knees, but he covers my body with his and presses me down into the bed. I guess this is how he's going to fuck me. When he bottoms out, I groan, but it turns into a squeal of delight when he pulls out fully and immediately drills straight to my core again.

I start chanting, "Oh… my… god," in a rising crescendo as he fucks me with small thrusts, hammering against a sensitive spot deep inside my pussy.

The bed springs squeak rhythmically and he's breathing heavily, but I can tell he's in shape and this isn't strenuous for him in the slightest. The room spins and I close my eyes as the ecstasy builds.

When the muscles in my body tense, I can tell I'm going to explode at any moment. All I can think about is the pleasure, and I hear myself crying out, "Fuck me," repeatedly as a tidal wave of rapture builds.

When Hank changes the tempo and switches to long strokes, it tips me over the edge.

"Ooooh, god!" I practically scream as my orgasm smacks me in the face.

I shudder and quake under him, and my pussy massages his cock as I ride the waves of the intense orgasm. Every nerve ending in my body sings and I don't know how long it all lasts because every thrust of his keeps my climax going. When he speeds up and grinds against my pussy, I can tell he's about to come.

When he finally explodes, he cries out, and his warm cum coats my walls. I shiver with aftershocks of pleasure and he fucks his cum inside me for a few more strokes. He rolls to the side and stretches out on the bed next to me. I smile at him, still dazed from the bliss, and he tenderly strokes the side of my face.

"Thank you, Jessica."

His voice is deep, and my grin widens. Finally hearing him speak thrills me. His cum drips out of me, and I revel in the feeling. This isn't the only load of cum I'm getting tonight, and the thought of Lucas draining his balls in me revs my pussy back to life.

God, I love my life.

The End

CHAPTER 2

HUSBAND CHOOSES THE PERFECT GUY TO GIVE HIS HOTWIFE A HARD POUNDING

Note: This was originally published on a blog with the title, "Husband Chooses the Perfect Guy to Give his Hotwife What She Craves."

My husband, Lucas, has a twinkle in his hazel eyes when I walk in the door from my weekend at a luxury spa resort. "I've got a surprise for you, Jessica."

Abandoning the handle of my wheeled suitcase, I wrap my arms around him and kiss him deeply. As our tongues swirl together, I detect a hint of chocolate—mmm, yummy. The entire flight home I thought about fucking him, and I'm wet and horny. He told me to expect a hard pounding when I walked in the door and it's been three days since we've fucked. I don't want to wait any longer.

When I press against his growing erection, I can't help but smile. I'm not the only impatient one. Stroking him through the fabric of his jeans, I moan while I imagine him sliding inside me. I spent the weekend on self care so I'm relaxed, fully waxed, and ready for action.

He chuckles and breaks off the kiss. "Aren't you curious about the surprise?"

Taking a step backwards, I lift the edge of my pink T-shirt over my head and ponytail, exposing my white lace bra, and drop it on the hardwood floor. "You can tell me while you're fucking me."

Unhooking my bra, I slide it down my arms and it joins the shirt on the floor. As my full, perky breasts bounce free, I groan with relief and massage the firm globes with my hands, toying with my nipples. I'm turning myself on even more and he better not make me wait long.

Lucas looks amused as I kick my sneakers off and drag my leggings and underwear down. I'm not sure what's so funny. He obviously hasn't realized I mean business. I WILL have his cock inside me. He better plan on giving me the pounding he promised.

"Well?" I toss my head in challenge once I'm fully naked. The ends of my blonde hair brush against my shoulders, causing a delicious shiver to run through me.

His lust-filled gaze sweeps down to the shaved Ms. Kitty, and he licks his lips. My pulse races and my pussy throbs as if all the blood was rushing straight to it. Whenever one of us is gone for a few days, it's always like this. They say distance makes the heart grow fonder, and in our marriage, it seems to be true. I want to fuck his brains out right here, right now.

Lucas holds out a hand to me, and I slide my palm into his. He gives me a sly grin. "You know that hard pounding I promised you?"

I raise my eyebrows at him. "Yeah…"

A tingle runs up my arm when he kisses the back of my hand, and his eyes crinkle with a smile. "I never said it was going to be from me."

Oooooh, what's this? My nipples harden while my pussy clenches. "There's a guy here right now?"

He laughs out a, "Yes," and tugs my hand. "He's waiting for you in the spare room. You ready for him?"

Lucas enjoys choosing guys for me to fuck, but this is something new. He's never had someone on standby when I got home. Moisture trickles down my thigh as he leads me down the hall. Whenever we have someone over to fuck me, my husband always stays in our home office. He can listen through the adjoining wall, stroke himself, and also be close for safety.

This situation piques my curiosity. What type of guy did my husband choose for me this time? Lucas enters the spare room first, and steps to the side so I can see the guy. He's standing by the window and smiles when he sees me. He's fairly unremarkable—average build, brown hair that needs a trim—not the typical guy Lucas chooses. I'm surprised by his casual clothes. He's wearing basketball shorts, a T-shirt, and he's barefoot. How long has he been here?

"Jessica, this is Owen."

My sharp, questioning glance must have been obvious, because Lucas continues. "Owen came highly recommended."

I hold in a snort. Who's he getting recommendations from? Was he on a website for people seeking bulls to fuck their hotwife?

Owen clears his throat and his voice is deeper than I expected. "Wow, you're gorgeous."

I realize I'm greeting this guy naked, and his compliment thrills me. I decide to let go of any misgivings. Lucas had a reason for asking this guy over and I trust my husband. Plus, if he turns out to be a dud, Lucas will finish me off.

I smile softly at Owen. "It's nice to meet you."

Lucas kisses my cheek. "I'll be next door. Have fun."

As he leaves, he smacks my ass and I squeak while a bolt of pleasure zips through me. He shuts the door behind him and I'm uncertain what to do next.

Owen walks over to me and holds out both his hands, palms up. I didn't notice it before, but his hands are enormous. I'm petite, and as I slide my hands in his, they engulf mine. A tingle of delight makes my breath catch as I imagine those massive paws on my tits. Suddenly I'm desperate for his cock. My pussy buzzes, and I almost giggle. Ms. Kitty is eager to get started as well.

He tugs me against him, wrapping an arm around my waist and using the free hand to cup my face as he kisses me. At first it's just a soft brush of the lips, but when he applies pressure, I open my mouth and welcome his tongue with light flicks of my own. As the kiss deepens and we press together, his thin shorts hide nothing and I notice that, even if his appearance is pretty average, his erect cock isn't.

He slowly pushes me towards the bed as I slide my hands under his shirt, caressing his chest and running my fingers through his chest hair. I'm delighted and want to touch him all over to see if he's got this much hair anywhere else. It's not like he's a beast, but Lucas is practically hairless so I'm intrigued. He pauses for a moment to take off his shirt, tosses it to the floor, and claims my mouth again. He's a wonderful kisser and I'm getting wetter by the minute. God, this is so damn hot and Lucas is so fucking amazing for arranging this. He's giving up the chance to fuck me right now, knowing it's going to drive me wild and we'll most likely have amazing sex later. But this still means he's waiting in sexual agony, stroking himself and listening to my moans.

"Did your husband tell you anything about me?"

I stop kissing him and search his face. What didn't Lucas tell me? "No...."

He smirks at me, states, "Good," and forces me backwards onto the mattress, catching me right before I'd fall and lowering me carefully. He crawls up next to me while I adjust my position to the center of the bed. His gaze sweeps up and down my full length, and I fight the urge to squirm.

He kisses me briefly and whispers in his soothing deep tone, "Close your eyes."

I obey and my breath catches as he explores my body with his mouth and his hands, as if he's trying to memorize every curve. He kisses down my chest, avoiding my nipples, and flicks his tongue in little circles as if he's tasting me as he works his way to my belly button and back up. When he latches into one of my nipples, I moan and arch against him as swirls of ecstasy ignite my core. He continues to suck on the tip, playing with the opposite breast with his other hand. Twin spikes of pleasure zing straight to my clit. Fuuuck, I need something inside me, preferably his cock, but even his fingers would do at this point.

Everything feels wonderful and keeping my eyes closed heightens the pleasure. I don't know what to expect, and I'm still not sure what's extra special about him. Even though his cock seemed large through his shorts, I've been with larger men. No matter the size, I still want him and he needs to shove it in me.

When he runs his hand down my legs and tugs up on them, I bend my knees, putting my feet flat on the bed. He caresses my calves and inner thighs, getting close to my pussy but never touching it. The longer he avoids the apex of my legs, the needier I become and wetness runs down my crack. If he doesn't give me what I want soon, he's going to make me beg.

When he finally brushes his fingers along my pussy lips, I moan and spread my knees wider. He's not pressing in and only using a light, teasing caress along my shaved skin.

The tickling sensation finally makes me groan, "Oh god, please fuck me."

A thick digit glides along my folds and presses in, brushing against my clit gently. I moan and thrash my head from the intense pleasure, but I need more.

I cry out in desperation, "Please, please, please, will you fuck me? I need your cock so bad."

He pulls his hand away, and I moan in protest. The gentle rubbing was driving me crazy, but having nothing against me is worse. I keep my eyes closed while he shifts on the bed, and I can tell he's removing his shorts. Oh, thank God. This means he's finally going to fuck me.

Positioning himself between my bent knees, he slowly presses his cock into me and I can't hold back my loud moan. He's thicker than I expected and my tightness molds around him. He gives me time to adjust to his size and when he's fully ensheathed into my warm, wet pussy, he pauses and leans forward to kiss me some more. I buck up against him, forcing the head of his cock to rub deep inside and causing electricity to spread from my core.

"Jessica, tell me what you want," he demands between kisses.

I'm feeling slutty and desperate, so I don't hesitate. "Fuck me hard and fast. I need it rough."

Owen nibbles down my neck and back to my breast. He sucks on a nipple for a moment and then takes it between his teeth and tugs on it, giving me an amazing, painful pleasure. "Oh, god," I moan and try to shift against his cock, desperate for gratification.

He releases my nipple from his teeth and chuckles. "Your husband said you liked it rough."

Mmm, Lucas enjoys orchestrating what happens with the men and it doesn't surprise me he gave Owen pointers. "Yes," I pant out, hoping this means he'll give me what I want.

"Good." Owen says and withdraws his cock from me as I peep out in distress.

Jesus Christ, this guy needs to fuck me. I can't handle this exquisite torture.

A strong lunge straight to my core has me crying out, and my eyes fly open as Owen hammers against my pussy. "Ooooh, fuck," I moan loudly as I meet his every thrust. His thickness caresses every nerve ending I have inside me, and my back arches as I try to get him as deep as I can.

I'm spiraling towards my orgasm and he doesn't slow his pace. He keeps whacking against my pussy and my moans increase in loudness the closer I get to coming. When I chant, "Fuck me," he really lights into my pussy, and drills into me roughly.

When he pushes one of my knees towards my chest, the new angle tips me over the edge. "Oooooh, fuck!" I scream out, and he still doesn't stop fucking me. The orgasm lasts forever, and the room spins so much I have to close my eyes.

As I come down from my peak, I assume he's going to come soon as well, and I try to relax as tiny aftershocks of pleasure ripple through me.

"Do you," he pants between thrusts, "want to know… why your husband… chose me?"

Oooh, I do! "Yes," I groan as he rams me particularly hard. The zing of pleasure makes me wonder if I could come again.

He stops and removes his cock. Wait, what's going on?

"Get up on all fours."

Oooh, hell yes. I scramble onto my hands and knees, and he positions himself behind me. He grasps my hip with one hand and uses his other to guide his cock into my sopping wet hole. As he slides in, I sigh in delight. Him behind me is so fucking amazing.

Once he's inside, he slides his hands to my waist to make me grind against him as he jackhammers into me. Oh, fuck. I close my eyes again and clutch the comforter, trying to help stabilize myself.

"He chose me… because… I take a really long time… to come."

Ohhh, damn. Love for my husband floods through me, and I come all over Owen's cock a second time. He fucks me furiously and I cry out nonsense as the rapture ripples from my head to my toes. My second orgasm doesn't slow him down and he jackhammers into my pussy, giving me the roughest fuck of my life. The pleasure mounts again and I realize I'm going to come a third time right before I tip over the edge again.

"Ooooh, fuck," I scream out. The orgasm is so intense, I lower my forehead to rest against my arms as my entire body trembles from the force of my climax.

I'm not sure how long Owen continues to fuck me, but at some point I come again. Afterwards he slows his thrusts down until he's stroking slowly. My brain is so fuzzy, and the pleasure is so intense, I'm almost surprised when he finally comes with a roar. My pussy is a quivering mess and I milk his cock, making sure he's unloaded all his cum before he pulls out.

As soon as he moves away from my ass, I collapse onto my stomach and he stretches out next to me.

"Fuck, that felt good," he pants. "Thank you, Jessica."

I mumble, "Thank you too," as my pussy throbs. I might just fall asleep right here.

The bed jostles as he gets up and I faintly hear him get dressed. I'm floating in a wonderful daze when Lucas comes in. The guys talk briefly, and Owen thanks him for a great night. They both leave the room and my eyes are closed when Lucas returns. He spreads my legs, and I try to help him but I'm out of energy.

This is the part of the night I look forward to the most. After I fuck another guy, Lucas is desperate to have me and his need to fill me with his cum is the best thing ever. I sigh in ecstasy as Lucas enters me tenderly and rests on top of me, pressing me into the bed. He makes love to me softly and the gentle waves of pleasure wash over me.

When I come again, I can only give a soft moan as stars explode behind my eyes. I'm dazed and spinning when Lucas comes with a loud groan. As his hot cum paints my cave walls, my entire body glows with love for him. I can tell Ms. Kitty is going to be sore tomorrow, and I smile as I feel the deep ache.

Lucas promised me a hard pounding, and damn, he sure delivered.

The End

SHARED HOTWIFE AT
THE CON

CHAPTER 1

I'm hyper-focused on my monitor as I type away at a werewolf breeding erotic romance, so I don't notice my husband, Lucas, walk into our home office until he drops a manila envelope in front of me. Pressing my lips together, I hold in my annoyance at having something tossed at me while I'm in the middle of the important breeding scene where the woman is about to get knotted by three shifters. I've been so busy today I didn't even take the time to get dressed after my shower and just threw on a nightgown and called it good. I tug at the neckline and roll my shoulders to loosen the muscles as I pick up the envelope and turn it over. There's no writing on either side.

"What's this?"

He shrugs casually but I can tell he's suppressing a grin, so whatever's in the envelope must be exciting to him.

"That, my wonderful wife, is our travel itinerary for a trip we're taking next month."

Whoa, Lucas planned a trip to surprise me? Has he ever done that? It's like Christmas and my birthday all wrapped up in one. About twice a year, I spend a long weekend at a luxury spa resort. He never goes with me, and I prefer it that way since it's the time I focus on myself, but I'd hinted last week that I'd like to take more vacations with him.

I hadn't expected him to take action so quickly and a surge of adrenaline makes my hands shake as I open the envelope and pull out a stack of printouts. Two tickets fall in my lap and I pick them up and study them. They're for a comic con in San Diego, California next month. Um, when I asked for a vacation I pictured sandy beaches or an adult lifestyle resort. Attending comic cons isn't really my thing.

Flipping through the printed-out papers confirms it's all related to the upcoming trip: hotel, flight information, and details about the con. Shit, I guess I'm going to a con. I try sounding enthusiastic and I study the hotel information. At least it looks like a nice hotel.

"So, we're going to California. Is something fantastic happening at the con?"

He laughs, as if I made a joke. "We've been talking about going for years, and I decided to surprise you. You wanted to take more vacations."

Oh shit, he has been talking about going to one, but I didn't know it included travel. We live in Oregon, close to Portland, so there has to be a local one, right? I was noncommittal every time he talked about it since I didn't want to kill his dreams, but I assumed it would be a day trip and not a big deal. The passes to the con are for all four days. Five nights plus a few hours on a plane is a big deal. Yeah, that's so not in my plans.

He moves behind me and massages my shoulders while I scan the papers. I don't know how to respond.

"Baby, the best thing is that I pre-planned this with Miri. She's been keeping your schedule clear for the trip."

Miri has been my best friend since middle school, and she's also my personal assistant who handles pretty much everything to do with my indie publishing except the actual writing. I didn't even question why she was giving me specific deadlines and telling me when things needed to be done. But now it's obvious she was ensuring I'd be finished with my book and not stressing about the trip.

I'm not sure whether to murder her for not giving me the heads-up that Lucas was planning this, or thank her for keeping my blissful ignorance going as long as she could. Lucas is thrilled and expecting me to jump for joy, but I'm still in shock and I'm not sure how I want to react.

"And Jessica, I was thinking… It's been a while since our trip to the Temptations Resort. If someone caught your eye in San Diego, we could have a little fun."

A shiver of longing runs through me straight to Ms. Kitty — the pet name for my pussy — and she wakes up. A kick of desire reminds me of what happened when we went to Temptations. It's a lifestyle resort, and there were plenty of men to play with. Ms. Kitty got quite the workout.

Lucas's hands continue to work the knots out of my neck and shoulders, and I groan. He's always been marvelous with his hands. The offer of playing with someone while in San Diego, plus the neck massage, melts any further resistance. Since he misinterpreted what type of vacation I wanted, I better have him spell out what his offer on the trip includes.

"So what exactly are you thinking when you say 'have some fun'?"

He runs his hands down my spine and tugs on my pajamas until I lean forward so he can slip his hands underneath the nightshirt. He skims along my skin as he moves the fabric up towards my shoulder and a tremor of awareness runs through me from the brush of his fingers.

"Put your hands in the air."

Oh, okay. I'm not totally sure where this is going, but I'm liking the direction. I lift my hands towards the ceiling and he pulls my nightshirt off over my head, leaving me with only my panties on. Since I wasn't planning on leaving the house today, I'm not wearing a bra. My nipples pucker, partly from the cold air and partly from dirty thoughts of what he might do to me. I could sit on the edge of the desk while he hammered away and whispered filthy things in my ear. Mmm, yeah…

He swivels my office chair to face him and he drops to his knees, spreading my legs so he can kneel between them. A low pleasant hum warms my blood. I'm good with him on his knees. He cups my breasts and I moan as he rubs my nipples between his index fingers and thumbs.

"My idea…" He pauses and leans forward to lick a nipple, and I draw in my breath as a spike of bliss swirls in my core.

He continues, "I'm thinking that I would check the app for a guy who you could play with one night. Does that sound good?"

He draws one of my nipples between his lips and sucks on it while I moan and run my fingers through his hair.

"Yeah, I could be agreeable to that."

Oh, fuck yeah. The best thing about being married to Lucas is that not only do I get tons of sex with him whenever we go on vacation, but he also gets horny whenever other guys check me out. It always ends up with some other guy's cock inside me while Lucas listens through a wall and strokes himself.

It's easy to find guys on vacation willing to fuck a hotwife, and it helps that I'm petite with large breasts and naturally blonde hair. I've always attracted attention based on my looks, and I find it amusing that the attention is increasing as I age. At 33, I have tons more guys drooling over me than when I was in my early 20s and in college.

When I was younger, I underestimated the allure of a woman who knows what she wants and has sexual experience. I assumed that by the time I was married and in my 30s, I'd be settled into a boring life and men would spend their time ogling younger women. But nope, the dating pool is actually larger now because younger men and older men both eye me. Yeah, this is an awesome age.

Lucas pushes against my shoulder, tips the office chair back, and hooks his hands around my knees to pull me closer to him and the edge of the chair. He kisses down my stomach and spreads my legs further apart. My blue panties are basic cotton and nothing special, and they already have a small wet patch. I'll let him think it was all him and had nothing to do with the sexy scene I was writing. He fingers my pussy through the fabric and desire swirls in my core.

When he hooks his fingers into the sides of my panties, I lift my ass off the chair so that he can pull them down. He spreads my legs wider and gives Ms. Kitty little kisses. He uses his thumbs to spread apart my nether lips, and I moan in anticipation.

"Oh god," I whimper as his tongue snakes out and slips inside me.

My hips buck up for more and he moves his mouth to my clit to suck and lick my swollen bean. This is heaven. If he keeps doing this, I'll agree to anything he wants.

"Mmmm, yes. Like that."

Lucas is fabulous at oral, and after so many years with me, he knows exactly how to make me come fast. When he sticks his tongue into my pussy as far as he can, I spasm around it and moan like a greedy slut while.

Grabbing fistfuls of his hair, I press his face further into my center and he moves his mouth back up to my clit to give it more attention. My vision is fuzzy from ecstasy when I peek down at him. His eyes glow hotly as he locks his gaze with mine and presses his fingers into my exposed wetness. I let go of his hair and squirm against his fingers.

"Tell me why you love me." I whisper.

He lowers his eyes to examine my wide-open legs. The heat in my core rises another degree as he stares at a wet Ms. Kitty. He's the only man I feel this free with, and the intimacy of the moment makes my breath hitch.

"You're my everything. I've never loved anyone but you. Not even close."

I moan at his words as my eyes drift shut, and he leans forward and licks my sensitive clit as he slides his fingers in and out of me. He continues to finger fuck me slowly, and when he makes a hook with his finger to massage my cave wall, I shudder uncontrollably at the impending climax.

He can tell I'm close, so he pumps faster and harder. When the orgasm hits, I scream as my body vibrates with euphoria.

"Ohhhh, god!"

I clench around his fingers as I ride out the waves of bliss, lost in mindless pleasure. When I come down from the peak, I drop back into the chair and sigh while Lucas strokes his hand against my pussy.

"You're still soaking. Just how I like you."

He kisses my thigh, and I open my eyes and glance lovingly at him. When he grins, his face shines with my juices and his eyes twinkle wickedly.

He announces, "My turn now," and stands, holding out his hand to me. "Baby, we're not done yet."

Ohhh, maybe I'll get another orgasm. I clasp his hand and he helps me up. Once I've found my balance, I step towards the door, expecting to go to the bedroom, but he stops me.

"No, baby. I want you to bend over your desk."

Pleasure pulses in my veins as I put my elbows on the surface of my desk and wiggle my ass at him. He steps up behind me and caresses an ass cheek while I give him a low hum of appreciation in the back of my throat. He's wearing sweatpants, and it only takes him a few seconds to pull out his cock and rub it up and down my slick folds.

Even though I already had an orgasm, I'm desperate for that first thrust. I sway my hips, trying to entice him.

"Mmm, that feels so good. I need you inside me."

He taps his cock against me, not pushing it in.

"Ask me to fuck you."

My head spins as I grip the edge of my desk and shimmy my hips, massaging the tip of his cock with my velvety wetness. My body is on fire, and I tense up for the first plunge.

"Oh god, please fuck me."

He removes his cock and I mewl in displeasure. What is he doing? A sharp smack on my ass makes me cry out.

"Shit! Please?"

He grabs my hips and gives a sexy growl.

"Yes, I think I will."

With one lunge, Lucas drives straight to my core and I have to stand on my tiptoes as he shoves me forward against the desk.

"Fuuuck!"

He immediately bulldozes into my pussy, clearly not intending to make me come again unless I can do it fast. Whenever he fucks me like this, it's as if I'm a toy and only here for his amusement. It hits a filthy kink of mine, and my brain short circuits as he uses me. This isn't my gentle, loving husband. This is the rough side that occasionally comes out, and I love it.

He knocks against me and each thrust causes ripples of pleasure to wash over me. I'm moaning and panting as he holds onto my hips and fucks me vigorously. The chorus of our moans fill the air, and every time he bottoms out, his balls whack against my clit and create a wet slap. All I can do is grip the edge of the desk for leverage and hold on as he rides me.

Oh, holy fuck. I'm dizzy from the rapture, and I hear myself chanting for him to fuck me harder. He groans as he speeds up.

"Do you like this, baby?"

My muscles tighten, and I'm half out of my mind from the continuous assault of delight.

"Yes. God… Yes!"

He slams into me with a fury and I give in to my orgasm when he hits a pleasurable spot repeatedly. I scream as my second white-hot climax rips through me. He fucks me through my orgasm, and as my cave walls shudder and milk his cock, he comes with a grunt and fills me. His warm stickiness coats me as he pistons in and out, pumping every last drop into me.

When he finally slows down and pulls out, I'm relaxing on my desk, fuzzy and floating in a warm place. I could fall asleep right here, but Lucas doesn't let me. I give a tiny protest as he helps me stand up. Ugh, I don't want to move. He holds me steady while I get my bearings.

When the lust fog clears, I understand he's taking care of me and can't leave me on the desk. I probably don't really want to sleep right there, but it felt nice for a moment.

I murmur, "Thanks," and blow him a kiss.

Since I don't plan on putting my nightshirt back on, I use it to wipe some of our joint wetness off his cock before he adjusts himself back into his sweatpants. His cum drips down the inside of my thighs, and I don't bother cleaning it up. This mess is going to require a shower, but I don't care about that now. I'll nab some clean clothes and take a shower before bed.

I slide my hand into his. "Come on, Lucas, let's find food and talk about the trip."

After that good of a fucking, he gets whatever he wants. He'll never know I didn't want to go on the trip. Besides, he promised me a playdate.

CHAPTER 2

The luxury hotel where Lucas reserved a room isn't far from the convention center and we check in the night before the con starts. Even though the flight to San Diego wasn't long, we're both tired from working part of the week and from the added stress of travel, so we crash early.

Since this comic con is for Lucas, I decided to skip the first day and looked up what amenities the hotel spa offered and booked a package for the works. I'm going to stay at the hotel and he's going to meet up with a couple of guys he knows for the gaming night after the opening ceremonies.

This is the first break from writing I've taken in months and I need to unwind. He thinks it's crazy that I'd prefer to spend the day at the spa than watching the gaming tournaments, but the spa is what I need to stay sane. Whenever I take my long weekends at a wellness spa, I get pampered and come home feeling like a new woman. I'm hoping one day at the spa here has the same effect.

He worries over me while we get dressed. "Will you be okay by yourself all day? I don't know when I'll be back."

I laugh. "Yes, hon. I'm looking forward to relaxing."

Knowing he doesn't want to ditch me fills me with warmth, but this is what I adore about being married to him. We both can enjoy separate activities without being joined at the hip.

After a late breakfast, I kiss Lucas goodbye and take the elevator down to the lobby for my spa day. I have back-to-back appointments and I spend several hours getting a massage, a facial, and a mani-pedi. Ms. Kitty gets professionally groomed as well. She needs to be a pretty kitty if we find a playmate.

Dinner is takeout from a local sushi bar, and since I'm not expecting Lucas back for hours, I put on a silk nightgown and relax on the couch to stream the latest Thor movie — Love and Thunder — while I eat my yummy dinner. I need to watch Thor for inspiration to get in the mood for the con tomorrow. It's research… I swear.

A month ago, Lucas invited a guy to the house to fuck me and the guy reminded me of Loki. Ever since then, it's been a running joke that I'm going to fuck a Thor lookalike on this trip. When the movie finishes, I lie on the couch and daydream about a hunky guy plowing me against the wall just out of eyesight from everyone at the con. Will there even be a quiet corner to fuck someone?

Lucas should get back to the hotel so I can ride him and imagine he's my own Thor. Ms. Kitty buzzes with approval and I move a hand to fondle her through my panties. My phone beeps with a text from Lucas, and I stop rubbing myself to check the message.

LUCAS

I'm getting some beers with friends. Are you OK?

JESSICA

Yep, have fun. Don't do anything I would do.

I end the message with a kissy face emoji, and I sigh as I set my phone on the coffee table. Well, shit. No sexy husband to ride. He's usually no good to me after a few hours drinking with his friends. Ms. Kitty complains that I'm ignoring her, and I slide my hand underneath my panties and head straight for my clit. I sigh with yearning as I caress lazy circles around my bundle of nerves. I'm not sure if I plan on going for the big O yet, or If I'm going to just give myself a pleasant edge.

My phone beeps again, and this time Lucas sends me a picture of a couple laughing at the bar. They're posed towards the camera, so I can tell Lucas didn't take the picture on the sly. Both are cosplaying and the woman looks like the cute brunette with the glasses from the Thor movie, and the guy with her looks like Thor did at the beginning of the movie in jeans, t-shirt, and a sleeveless red leather jacket. The picture includes a message.

LUCAS

I found your Thor.

My entire body lights up and a shock of delight ripples down my spine. Wait, there's no way that guy is for me. Plus, he has a woman with him. The way the guy's arm is around the woman in the picture says they're together. I laugh at how quickly I flushed. Lucas enjoys teasing me when he sees guys he knows I'd have fun fucking. I message Lucas back.

JESSICA

That's not nice. Ms. Kitty thought you were serious for a moment and now she's angry at you.

LUCAS

I'm almost sorry.

JESSICA

You can make it up to us tomorrow. I'm going to bed. I'll probably be asleep when your tipsy ass gets back here.

LUCAS

Okay, baby. I'll see you soon. Love you.

JESSICA

Love you.

Hmm, do I want to go to bed or should I keep touching myself and get really horny? I slip my hand back into my panties and caress my clit... as if I really was going to do anything else. That's crazy talk.

My thoughts turn dark and naughty as I imagine a muscular guy sliding inside me. Yeah, that's what I need. My toes curl as I spread my legs wider and use my other hand to finger fuck myself. The desire to orgasm hits me and I moan loudly. Yeah, okay, there's no stopping this.

I rub my clit faster and continue to daydream about a long-haired hunk spearing into me relentlessly. It doesn't take long until I'm close to coming. When I push another digit into my pussy, the added thickness shoots me over the edge. I cry out as pleasure radiates from my core, but the orgasm is shorter than I want. I come down quickly and the euphoria dies off.

My fingers didn't do the job as well as Lucas's cock would have. Should I try for another one? A big yawn breaks my train of thought. Yeah, maybe not. The hotel claims it has top-of-the-line mattresses, and the one in my room is calling to me.

Wiping my hands on my panties, I drag myself off the couch and get ready for bed. I'm sound asleep by the time Lucas gets back and I stir only slightly when he gets into bed.

"Love you, hun," I murmur.

He kisses my shoulder. "I love you too, baby."

I'm asleep again before he turns off the bedside lamp.

The next morning, I'm examining myself in the bedroom mirror while I wait for Lucas to be ready to leave the hotel. I didn't really want to cosplay, and I just wanted to wear the sexiest black leather outfit I own. But when I told Lucas the plan, he was adamant that I needed to bring fishnet stockings so I could be Black Canary. I can't argue with the results. I'm sexy as all fuck in black leather and fishnets.

When Lucas leaves the bathroom, he's dressed like Green Arrow and I give an appreciative whistle. Neither of our costumes are super authentic, but at least we're trying. Plus, I can spend all day imagining what my roleplaying Green Arrow hubby is going to do to me tonight.

He promised to make things up to me today and we've been too busy this morning.

He gives me a kiss on the cheek. "Are you ready to go?"

I double check I put everything we need in my black backpack and slide it over my shoulders. I have to get on my tiptoes to give him a peck, and I bounce on the heels of my combat boots.

"Yep, let's do this."

Lucas orders us a ride-share car and as we leave the hotel, several people in the lobby glance in our direction. I overhear a kid asking his mother if we're superheroes. I don't hear her response, but I hope she said yes. Lucas told me that Black Canary's superpower is the canary cry where her scream creates ultrasonic vibrations that can hurt people and break objects. She's also good in hand-to-hand combat, an expert motorcyclist, and a covert operative and investigator. I straighten my five-foot nothing frame and swagger to give the illusion of confidence. I'm cosplaying as a badass, and I might be small, but I'm mighty.

It takes a while to get to the convention center due to traffic and the sheer horde of cosplayers swarming the streets. The line to get our badges is crazy long, but they keep us moving at a steady pace. While we're waiting, Lucas tells me about a fight that broke out yesterday at the con that included yelling and someone punching another guy. I hope everyone is okay, but with this many people in one location, I'm not surprised that tempers would flare. I'm already cranky at all the people who are standing in the middle of the hallways.

We're soon through the line and join the main crush of people moving through the convention center. The best thing about the con is all the awesome cosplaying, and it's fun to look at everyone. The creativity of the costumes pings the writing side of my brain and I've already got several storylines brewing in the back of my head. I'll need a new pen name if I did anything but paranormal romance, but who knows, maybe it's time to branch out. Horny Hotwife at the Con has a nice ring to it.

Cell reception is spotty, so I decide to stick with Lucas so I don't have to find him later. I've been turned on all morning and I see several handsome men that I wouldn't mind riding, but there's so much to do that I'm distracted from my horniness. The plan is to find a souvenir for Miri and something cute and cuddly for myself — If it has glitter on it, even better. I'm not really sure what I want, but I figure I'll know it when I see it. The artwork distracts me. Some of it is amazing, and I'd love to support other indie artists. I tug on Lucas's hand.

"Hey, where's the sales floor? I have a backpack that needs filling."

Lucas laughs and he starts telling me something about a panel he wants to attend that starts soon, but as he talks, a guy who looks like Thor catches my eye. I'm preoccupied and I don't hear the rest of what Lucas says. Wait, is that the same guy who was in his picture last night? If it is, today he's wearing full battle armor and carrying a fake Stormbreaker weapon. Ms. Kitty hums to life as I study him. He's muscular and just all-over massive. I daydream about kneeling in front of him and sucking on his cock. I'd like to see how many licks it takes to get to the center of that lollipop.

"Earth to Jessica."

Lucas waves his hand in front of my face, and I give him a huge grin.

"Uh… See that dude over there by the wall?" I gesture towards Thor. "Is that the guy from the bar?"

Lucas's eyes follow my hand. "Oh hey. Yeah, that's James."

Now that I've seen James in the flesh, I am so down with the idea of his cock inside me, but wouldn't Lucas have made plans if James was single and interested? I try to act casual, as if I'm not desperate for the guy's cock.

"Was the woman in the picture his girlfriend? She's not with him right now."

"Nah, she's dating another guy. I'm not sure how those two know each other, but she was making out with the other guy later."

I peer at James with even more interest. Why didn't Lucas hook me up with him? You'd think with how we've been joking for weeks about finding me a Thor, he would have made it happen.

"If you're done drooling over James, we need to get in line."

Ugh, fine. Lucas takes my hand and I prepare to wait. I know this is the main thing he's here for, but I'd rather check out the eye candy and shop.

While we wait in line, Lucas chats with people about our costume and where we're from. I spend the time trying not to stare at any one person for too long, and daydreaming plots for stories I will probably never write. The longer it takes, the more X-rated my stories become. Shit, we should have gotten up early and fucked like rabbits so I didn't spend the day horny looking at hot guys in costumes.

I catch a few of the guys checking me out and I see appreciation in their eyes at how I'm dressed, but everyone is polite and no one is leering or making me uncomfortable. We're eventually let into a large conference room with rows of chairs, but I'm more interested in crowd watching than anything else. Some costumes are incredibly elaborate, and there are more than a few people strolling around in shoes that are going to kill their feet within an hour. I'm thankful for my combat boots, since it seems like today is going to be a lot of standing around.

Right before the lights dim, I spot James across the room. God, he's so yummy. If I could get him alone, he's the type of guy I would totally fuck in a bathroom. I recently hooked up with a dude in a haunted house, so the bathroom at a con seems tame compared to what filthy things I did on Halloween.

I catch Lucas's eye, and he nods towards James.

"Are you going to spend all day imagining fucking James?"

"Hey, it's not my fault that we haven't had sex on the trip. You're the one who got drunk last night and left me all alone in the hotel with nothing else to do but touch myself and think about getting railed by a sexy, muscular guy."

I hadn't told him what I had done last night, and he perks up when I say I was touching myself.

He thinks for a second. "I don't know. I'm feeling a lack of appreciation for the hard work I put in last night."

The tone of his voice tells me he's teasing.

"Yeah, I'm sure laughing and drinking with your friends was oh so hard."

Lucas leans over, kisses below my ear, and whispers, "Yeah, but baby, I was also arranging for James to come to the hotel room tonight and fuck you."

Lust zips through my body, and my nipples harden as my pussy buzzes. I gape at Lucas.

"Really?"

I can't keep the excitement out of my voice, and I want to squeal and bounce. Jesus Christ, I really have married the most amazing man ever.

"Yes, really. But you have to pay attention to me today if you want to play with James tonight."

Oh hell yeah, I'll give Lucas so much attention, he'll be begging me to fuck James later just to get a break. I turn towards him, giving him my full attention and I take his hand, squeezing it.

"Okay, my love. I only have eyes for you today."

He laughs and his, "Uh-huh," tells me he doesn't fully believe me. So yeah, I might glance at other people, but Ms. Kitty and I are only interested in two people tonight. I want a hard pounding from James, and then I want my incredible husband to fuck me and tell me he loves me.

CHAPTER 3

Once Lucas tells me I'll be fucking the Thor lookalike tonight, I'm in a sexual daze and unable to concentrate on much. It doesn't help that Lucas is using every opportunity to fondle my ass, or standing close behind me when we're at a vendor booth so he can brush against me. I try pushing my ass back to get more contact, but all I'm doing is making myself hornier. By late afternoon I'm ready to shove Lucas against a wall and have my way with him in front of everyone. God, he's such a tease.

I saw James several times throughout the day. It's a big convention, but he seemed to orbit the same areas we were in. It's possible he's just so damn sexy and a massive guy so he stands out above the crowd. One time he was posing for pictures and holding Stormbreaker in a battle pose. He should have gone with a previous version of Thor so he'd have his hammer, Mjöllnir. He missed a genuine opportunity with that one, because now how can anyone joke about him hammering them, or wanting to touch his massive hammer? And what is Stormbreaker anyway? A battle axe? I don't even know, since I may have possibly been paying too close attention to the eye candy in the movie last night. I'm surprised I remember the names.

I take plenty of pictures to show Miri, always asking permission first, but most people seem to enjoy being photographed in their costumes. One of my favorites is a woman in a cow print bikini with a bell around her neck. The Wi-Fi sucks at the convention, so I can't send them to Miri immediately. I'll surprise her with them later. She'll love the cow bell.

Since I want to get Miri a souvenir for being wonderful and helping Lucas keep the trip a secret, we hunt the vendors for the perfect, funny, present. I spot a vendor selling high-end fantasy dildos. Oh yeah, Miri needs a dragon dildo… the biggest they sell. Dragging Lucas over to the vendor, I can see he's trying to pretend he's not interested until I start examining the enormous ones.

"Uh, Jessica?"

I'm busy trying to choose between a red or a blue one and give him a distracted, "Hmmm?"

"Is this for Miri or for you?"

I pause and blink at him. "Good point. I'll get both."

As I pay for the dildos and tuck them safely in my backpack, Lucas mutters, "I didn't mean you should buy them both."

I ignore him, lost in thought. Do I want to keep the red or the blue one for myself? Eh, I don't have to decide today. I'll figure it out when I get home.

Hooking my arm through his, I grin at him. "If you treat me nicely, I might let you use it on me."

He perks up and kisses my cheek. "Once you're screaming my name tonight, you'll beg me to stuff you with it."

Wet heat flares between my legs and anticipation flickers through me. Jesus, this afternoon can't end fast enough. A glance at my phone tells me I still have a couple of hours to go. Fuck.

By the time we get back to the hotel, I'm ready to shove Lucas on the bed, straddle him, and grind against his hardness. I'm not sure I even need James at this point. My husband's cock will do the trick within a few minutes.

Lucas sits on the bed and types a message on his phone while I unlace my boots and drop them to the floor with a loud thud. Tossing my leather jacket on the back of a chair, I quickly strip. Lucas doesn't know what's in store for him, but as soon as I'm naked, he's mine. As I peel the fishnets down my legs, Lucas distracts me.

"Hey, James will be here in 30 minutes. I'm going to go downstairs and get some snacks. Do you want to take a shower?"

Desire swirls in my stomach as my nipples harden. Well hell, I suppose I can wait 30 minutes.

"Yeah, I'll take a quick one."

I bring the sexy lingerie I plan to wear tonight into the bathroom with me and turn the shower on so the water can heat. What I really need is a good fuck. It's difficult to think of anything else. I wasn't always this randy, but once we started our hotwife arrangement, my sex drive easily doubled. Just thinking about Lucas fucking me after James is done with me gives me shivers and I press my thighs together. We both love this arrangement and I don't see us stopping.

Being a hotwife is awesome, and I didn't know how fulfilling it would be. I always assumed if you had an open marriage, both partners got to play with other people. I wouldn't have guessed there were men out there who wanted their wife to fuck other guys without them having equal opportunity with other women. Lucas says he's perfectly content with this arrangement and this is very much about my pleasure. What we do works for us because Lucas is in control of the situation. I'm not out fucking random men and we're very much doing this together, even if Lucas isn't in the room. It might be a weird relationship to some people, but we're happy.

My shower takes longer than I planned since I was ruminating. I'm dressed and almost ready, but I'm still in the bathroom when James knocks on our hotel door. All my senses ping alive and I feel myself growing wet, despite having just dried off. I hear the men's voices through the door, but I can't make out what they're saying.

After I blow dry my hair, I smooth my silk negligee over my stomach to quell the sudden butterflies fluttering around in there. With how turned on I am, there's no way this won't have a happy ending, so I shouldn't be nervous. As I step out of the bathroom, the men are telling jokes and laughing, and it eases some of my concerns.

The suite is one large room, and they're sitting on the couches along one wall. Oh damn, James isn't wearing his costume. It looked uncomfortable long-term, so I guess that's for the best. He's wearing jeans and a blue t-shirt with Captain America's shield on it. I almost laugh at that, but his bulging biceps sidetrack me. Oh, hell yes. He looks too big for the hotel couch. Please God, let him have a cock that matches his size.

"Jessica, this is James."

Oh, heh. I guess we haven't met, despite me fantasizing about him all day.

I smile and give him a soft, "Hi."

The twinkle in James's eye when he says, "Hi," in return does dangerous things to my inhibitions. He could bend me over any surface and have me begging within seconds. I didn't bother wearing underwear, and with how wet I am, his cock would slide right in.

Lucas rises from the couch and comes over to kiss me. As his lips claim mine, I wonder if this is for show. I'm assuming he's going to be in the bathroom listening, since there isn't any other door he can hide behind. He's stroking my tongue with his, and I'm mentally fuzzy when he stops.

"Baby, tonight is going to be different."

"Different, how?"

I'm addlebrained with lust, and I don't care what happens as long as I get fucked. Lucas's eyes are dark with desire while he caresses my cheek with his thumb.

"I'm going to sit on the couch and watch."

Whoa, what? A shiver of arousal heads straight for my clit and I almost moan at the thought of Lucas in the room. He's never watched before, and sometimes I wished he would. This is a delightful surprise.

"You're sure?" I ask, moving my hand between us and rubbing along the hardness in his trousers as I search his face. He's clearly turned on, and he groans, "Yes," as I fondle the length of him through the fabric. He presses against me for a moment and then steps back out of reach.

"Have fun, baby."

Lucas takes a spot on the couch in clear view of the bed and it hits me how different this is, knowing he's going to watch. I've been wanting to fuck James all day and now that the moment is here, I'm uncertain how to get the ball rolling because Lucas is in the room. I swing my arms and try to not look nervous.

My pulse quickens as James approaches me, and I realize how enormous he is compared to my petite frame. His thigh muscles strain the fabric of his jeans, and his narrow waist gives him a V shape since his shoulders are broad. I lick my lips as I focus again on the defined muscles in his arms… Mmm yeah, those arms.

He's going to have to make the first move, and I wait as he slides his arms around my waist, pulling me towards him. The clean scent of fresh pine clings to him, and I can tell he showered before coming. A forbidden longing burns in my core as he brushes his lips against mine. He's thorough, but tender, as if he's giving me time to say no. It helps ease the rest of my nervousness, and I'm able to enjoy the sensations he's creating within me. The need for his cock grows stronger every second.

When he deepens the kiss, his tongue tangles with mine — hot and playful — and I want more. My head whirls, and I moan as I throw myself into his embrace, almost forgetting Lucas is watching in my attempt to devour James's mouth.

James breaks off the kiss, and his voice is husky with need. "You smell nice, like coconuts."

I wasn't expecting him to notice my body wash, and I giggle. "Thank you, you smell good too."

James leans in and nibbles on my neck and my knees feel weak when he touches me this way.

His voice rumbles in my ear. "You're so beautiful."

I'm warm and tingling from his nearness. He's doing a fabulous job with seduction so far, and I run my fingers through his long, dirty-blonde hair. He takes hold of one of my wrists and moves my hand down to the hardness in his pants. Oh shit, this is hot. The wetness in my core increases and desire courses through me as his cock throbs against my hand. I can tell his cock is huge, and my pussy clenches and my breathing quickens as I wonder how much longer it'll be until he slides that monster inside me.

The noise of Lucas shifting on the couch makes me glance in his direction. He's still in his costume, and his cock is out of his pants. He's slowly stroking as he watches us. The soft smile on his face is all I need to see. My love for Lucas envelops me, and all my concerns about him being in the room fade. I'm ready to give Lucas the show of his life so he'll want to watch more often.

James rocks his hips, forcing me to smooth my palm over his hard length. He moans quietly as he bites at my earlobe. The inside of my thighs are slick with moisture and there isn't an ounce of patience left in me. I need him inside me right now, and I'm going to do whatever it takes to hurry this along.

Squeezing his cock, I apply pressure and yank on him.

"Fuck!" he groans. "That feels amazing."

A sense of power builds inside me. Maybe I should take control and be the badass I assumed Black Canary was... small, mighty, and in charge.

I release his cock and step back, purring, "James, why don't you take those clothes off and lie on the bed?"

He lifts one eyebrow, and I don't have time to wonder what that means because he pulls his shirt off over his head and his well-defined abs distract me. Oh, hello. Yes, I will lick those soon. Ms. Kitty buzzes in appreciation of the view as James quickly removes the rest of his clothes, dropping them into a pile on the floor.

Once he's naked, he approaches me and my breath catches when he lifts the bottom of my negligee and strips it off me without warning.

"Beautiful," he growls and cups my breasts, rolling the nipples under his thumbs.

My heart races and I want to squeeze my thighs together in eagerness. Wait, I'm the one in charge, right? He walks me backwards to the bed and when the mattress touches my calves, I accept I misjudged the situation. He's taking control. A thrill courses through me at the thought of Lucas watching this. I bet he'll enjoy seeing me manhandled. This is what he always imagined was happening, and now he's witnessing it.

James presses on my shoulder and I sit on the edge of the bed. He moves to the side, so I twist my body, realizing he's giving Lucas a clear view of the action. James's cock is thick and the veins stand out along his shaft. It's slightly curved upwards towards his stomach, and saliva gathers in my mouth as I imagine sucking on it. He's so big and my hands are small, so it might require both of them to encircle it. Previously, I might have questioned if he would fit inside me, but after being with several large men, I know better. He'll stretch me out gloriously, but he'll fit. God, I love that first thrust, and his cock is going to be one to remember.

When he grasps the base of his shaft and moves a hand to the back of my head, I part my lips eagerly. This better only be a tasty snack before the main course. I wrap my mouth around his fat cockhead and suck. Okay, I'm not sure he's going to fit in my mouth. I've had bigger guys than this, but I didn't give them a blowjob. Fuck it, let's try.

James doesn't force anything, and I relax my jaw and ease him further inside. He barely fits, and he slides into my throat all the way to the hilt before pulling out. My eyes dart to Lucas and he's focused on the cock at my lips, so I grip the base of James's shaft with both hands and caress it while swirling my tongue around the fat tip. The heat of his body against mine gives me a pleasurable tingle, and dampness pools between my legs.

"You're incredible."

His voice is low as he slides into my mouth and fucks it slowly, allowing me plenty of air between strokes. His hips move faster and his moans are music to my ears. The longer he fucks my mouth, the more dazed from lust I become. I feel myself sink into the slutty mindset I crave. This is one of the amazing benefits of what Lucas and I do. I'm able to fully let go and become a fucktoy for these men, getting gratification while also driving Lucas wild.

When James pulls his cock out of my mouth and steps back out of reach, I mewl in displeasure. Damn him, I wasn't done with my treat.

"Get up on the bed on all fours. I want to see how tight your pussy is."

Yes... that. I scramble up on the bed, positioning myself so that Lucas will get a side view of James fucking me. Lucas is still stroking himself slowly while watching us, so I know he's having fun. James grasps my hips and pulls me closer to the edge and I lower my head, presenting him with a wet invitation. He rubs his length along my slit, and I moan as ecstasy swirls in my core.

"Is this what you want?"

He pokes me with just the tip of his cock, and I cry out. "Yes, please fuck me!"

I expected him to make me beg more, so when he slams straight into me, I moan again, louder, as I grind against him from the unexpected spike of bliss. Fuck, he's huge. I'm filled beyond belief, and it's wonderful. My fingers claw at the comforter, trying to stabilize myself as he drills into me. The sensation is overwhelming, and my mind fogs as his shaft massages my cave walls. The tip of his cock knocks against a sensitive place deep inside with every thrust and sends a jolt of pleasure through my body.

"So wet and tight," he grunts.

James's dirty talk taps into my desire to be used like a toy, and I welcome the mindless rapture as I arch my back. A low sound of passion escapes my throat as he drives himself deeper, hitting the magical spot over and over again. He's ramming against me so hard that the bed creaks and the headboard thumps the wall. I give a silent prayer that no one is in the room next to us, but I'm too far gone to really care. The sounds coming from James are erotic as hell, and my pussy squeezes around his cock as I grip handfuls of bedding beneath me and cling on for dear life. I'm reeling as I edge closer to my orgasm.

I'm almost in shock when he pulls out before either of us come.

I attempt to protest, but it's a mumbled, "Wha..."

"Get on your back."

I obey immediately, and peek over at Lucas to make sure he's enjoying himself. He's a rapt audience and his eyes are glued to the show while he plays with his cock. I blow a kiss towards Lucas and he smiles as James climbs onto the bed and parts my raised knees.

I turn my attention back to James, and he grazes his thick cock against my clit. I rotate my hips, hoping he'll push inside me. He examines me with hungry eyes, and there's an animalistic glint to them that makes me want to beg him to fuck me as hard as he wants. I want to see what he'd do if unleashed, but I'm not able to speak coherently and can only moan as he torments me. Fuuuuck, I'm going insane.

When he finally sinks into me, it's a torturous, slow grind. His thick shaft pushes in, Inch by Inch, until he bottoms out. I whimper in pleasure as he rocks his pelvis, fucking my tightness. My face contorts as the joy increases. I can't take much more of this. His thickness massages every nerve ending I have, and it's impossible to concentrate. I've lost all rational thought in the desire to come. The tension builds inside me and I moan in delight with his next powerful thrust.

"You look like you're about to explode."

James sounds amused. His words make me undulate against him, so close to the brink, but I can't come while he's fucking me slowly.

"Yes... God, yes. Fuck me harder.... faster. I need to come!"

He speeds up, slamming into me vigorously. I stop trying to hold on to the bedding, and I grip his shoulders while wrapping my legs around him. Each hard whack against my pussy shoots fiery sparks down my spine.

"Ohhhh, god. I'm going to come."

Hot waves build in my center and I cry out as I peak. Pure ecstasy rushes from my fingertips to my toes and I writhe against him as he hammers into my quivering pussy. I'm dizzy as he uses me for his fulfillment, and I close my eyes and thrash under him while he fucks me through my orgasm. He slides his hands under my ass so he can hold me steady while he pounds away repeatedly. The sensation of being fucked with such force keeps the ripples of bliss going and my orgasm seems like it's never going to end.

He stiffens and moans as he roars with satisfaction. I gaze at him and watch in amazement as his eyes roll into the back of his head from pleasure. His cock pulses as his hot seed floods into me, filling me completely. My body trembles uncontrollably, still shuddering from the intense climax, even after he pulls free from me. A tiny part of me wishes he hadn't pulled out because that means my time with him is ending, but Lucas still needs to fuck me.

I'm panting with satisfaction when he climbs off the bed. He disappears into the bathroom with his clothes and I melt into the mattress, savoring the relaxation from the incredible orgasm.

Lucas chuckles. "Don't get too comfortable on that bed."

I mumble, "Mmm hmm, I won't," and he laughs again.

I float in contentment while Lucas and James talk. Before James leaves, he thanks me for the fun and I stir awake enough to say goodbye to him. Lucas brings over a bottle of water and insists I take a sip. It perks me up and I stretch out on my side while he sits on the bed with me and plays with my hair. This is nice, but his cock is a hard bulge in his pants and I want him to get his pleasure.

"Baby, you ready for more?"

He's still stroking my hair, and I lean into his hand. His fierce facial expression says he's desperate to come and he won't be gentle. I'm probably going to be sore in the morning. But this is how it goes every time he shares me, and we both crave the connection of him fucking me after the other men.

I beam at him. "I'm ready."

CHAPTER 4

He removes his costume, taking the time to fold it carefully, and clambers onto the bed as I raise my knees and part them for him. He kneels and nestles his cock against my pussy, but doesn't press in. Instead he strokes his shaft along my wetness, taunting me and working me up again. My eyelids flutter closed as the bliss builds. He better not edge me tonight. I want to come again.

"Did you enjoy James fucking you?"

I keep my eyes closed and nod. "Mmm, yes. So good."

Desires swirls in my core as he rocks against me, still not pressing in, but the pressure against my clit is wonderful. He leans over me and brushes his lips on my cheek. When he moves to my mouth, he kisses me thoroughly, probing the depths with his tongue while my pussy buzzes and demands his cock. I caress his arms and shoulders, trying to reach what I can, as an inferno of need builds inside me. I know his body almost as well as my own, and his muscles twitch beneath my hands as I search out the sensitive spots along his neck and sides. The ache from Ms. Kitty reaches new heights when he props himself up on one arm and moves his free hand over my breast, playing with a nipple.

His voice is soft. "I'm going to fuck you hard enough to make you scream."

His whisper contrasts with the harsh words, and I groan.

"Yes."

He rises to his knees and hooks his arms around my thighs, pressing my thighs up towards my chest.

"Hang on, baby."

Oh, shit. I wasn't expecting him to bend me like a pretzel tonight. The position opens me and he fits the head of his cock against my slit. He gives me a few seconds to get ready for the invasion before he slams home.

"Shit!"

My breath catches as he pounds into me. He's not tender and romantic, and if anyone saw us, they wouldn't understand that every movement is filled with love. He drills into me, whacking against my tender flesh, letting me know that I'm his to use however he chooses. I cry out from the impact but it only adds fuel to his fire. He pummels my cunt mercilessly until I'm moaning continuously in pleasure. I want us to orgasm together, but I can't take much more of this without coming.

He grasps my thighs and grinds his cock inside me as we both thump against one another. Fuck, his cock feels incredible. Spikes of rapture radiate from my core. Our bodies collide repeatedly, and he's in a frenzy. My muscles tighten like a bowstring, and I expect to skyrocket over the edge at any second.

He pushes my knees further forward until they are close to my ears. He knows exactly how flexible I am, and I cross my ankles behind my head. I move a hand down to my clit and furiously flick my bean while he kneels and pounds into me. My pussy is a mess from James's cum and my previous orgasm, and Lucas fucks me so hard that a chorus of wet slapping sounds mingles with our panting and moans. This is wonderfully vulgar, even though there's nothing wrong with what we're doing. We both enjoy it.

"I'm going to fuck you raw," he growls as his balls slap against my ass and I sigh in delight.

"Yes... yes! Fucking yes!"

Whenever he shares me, he fucks me harder than he does other nights, especially if the guy has an enormous cock. The bed rocks back and forth with every swift bang, and my mind blanks from ecstasy. He grips my nipples between his fingers and pulls hard on them before slapping each breast. I yelp in surprise and almost come. Ohhhh, fuck. The pleasurable pain is intense, and when he smacks them again, I can't stop my orgasm.

Throwing my head back, I scream out his name and erupt. My body jerks violently from extreme bliss, and he pistons his hips so hard and fast my head spins from the onslaught of pleasure. I watch him through a haze of lust as he grinds his cock inside me. My moans become whimpers as he continues to use me.

"Who owns you?" he growls.

When I moan and don't answer, he spanks my ass.

"Hey!"

Ms. Kitty tries to sputter alive from the slap, but two mind-blowing orgasms might be enough for her tonight. Yeah, she's a pain slut, but we all have our limits.

"Tell me who owns you."

A sheen of sweat glistens on Lucas's chest and his pained expression says he's trying to not come.

I lock eyes with him. "You. You own me."

He stiffens and cries out, "Yes," as he explodes, burying himself balls-deep inside me. His cock throbs as he shudders and releases hot spurts of his cum. When he slows his thrusts, I unwind my legs from behind my head and he helps me lower them into a comfortable position as he pulls out. He climbs over me so he can stretch out on the bed.

He wraps me up in his arms, completely encasing me. I lean against his chest, needing the skin contact as we both come down from our high. When he chuckles, I tip my head up and he's smiling down at me with love shining in his eyes, but also possessiveness. Mmm, yeah, this is one of the great things about being a hotwife. Lucas gets territorial after someone fucks me good, and I enjoy the attention for a few days as he doesn't like to be apart from me for very long.

He rubs circles on my back as our heart rates slow down. The utter relaxation makes me feel boneless and I want to just stay in bed and not move, but I'm going to need a shower before bed. Knowing Lucas he'll take a shower with me to soap me up, paying special attention to my tender bits. This is part of his aftercare when I've been ridden hard, and it's another reason I know I married the perfect guy for me.

He kisses my forehead and his voice rumbles through his chest.

"Are you glad you came on the trip?"

Wait, does he know I didn't really want to go? I try to keep my voice light.

"Hey, who said I didn't want to?"

He laughs softly. "Jessica, after all these years, you think I couldn't tell?"

I snuggle closer and nuzzle his neck. Okay, so maybe he's not clueless after all.

"Mmm, well, it's been a lovely trip so far. Who do you plan for me to fuck tomorrow?"

His bark of laughter is louder this time. "Oh no, you need a few more days to be reminded you're mine."

"What? Dammit, I thought you were going to find me a cosplaying Star Lord next."

He tilts my chin towards him and kisses me passionately.

"No, baby. Not this time. That's how I'm getting you to attend the next comic con."

A tingle runs through me at his words. Well, shit... I guess I'm going to become a fan of attending comic cons now.

The End

SHARING HIS GIFT TWICE

CHAPTER 1

After submitting my latest reverse harem vampire manuscript, I needed a break, at least a week of relaxation, with no deadlines, no nagging editors, nothing that wasn't about me. My initial plan was to treat myself to my favorite wellness spa for a start, but it was fully booked for Valentine's Day. Figures. Instead, I've been nude sunbathing in my backyard. The warmth on my skin is a balm to my senses, and I feel my creative energy recharging.

I'm content and drowsy as Lucas returns from work, striding onto the deck. The grogginess fades as my pulse quickens with anticipation. Yay, he's home. His voice rings out clearly.

"Hi baby. You're a sexy sight to come home to."

I squint against the bright sun and stare at him, feeling my cheeks flush as his words linger in the air. Ms. Kitty buzzes from his appreciative smile.

Yes, yes, I know. It may be silly, but I call my shaved pussy Ms. Kitty. She's been responsible for enough of my wildest misadventures. I figure she's earned her own name. Of course, it comes in handy to blame her when we're late to something because I seduced Lucas into bed. "No, it's not my fault, it was all Ms. Kitty. I swear!"

Our acquaintances think we have a demanding cat. Our close friends? They just smile.

Lucas is dressed in his typical work clothes: slacks and a button-down dress shirt. He undoes the cuffs of his sleeves. My stomach gives a soft growl from hunger, reminding me I forgot lunch. We always end up in bed on Valentine's Day, whether early or late, but I need food before he fucks me.

I question him. "Did you bring dinner home with you?"

He stops in his tracks, surprised. "Uh, no... I didn't know I was supposed to."

Oh, this man. Amirite? I mean, a smart husband would have thought about bringing home food on Valentine's Day, but we've been busy and time creeped up on us. I didn't even know it was Valentine's until this morning and I saw the date on my phone. The days blur together when you work from home.

A small part of me is hurt that he's treating this like any normal day. Just because I forgot doesn't mean it's okay for him to forget as well. But I'm determined to not spoil the night.

I want my Valentine's Day sex, dammit.

"Oh, I didn't say anything." I roll onto my side and prop myself up on an elbow. I want to drive him crazy, so without taking my eyes from his, I run my fingertips along the curves of my hip and stomach, lightly grazing the skin with soft swirls. My fingertips linger on my hip, and I give him my best sultry voice. "You were supposed to read my mind. I'm on vacation, remember? People on vacation don't cook."

He says nothing, but I can feel his eyes on me, burning with desire. I didn't *exactly* plan to be naked when he got home, but I know how to make the most of a situation. I've played this game for years now.

Rising from the lounge chair, I let my long, blonde hair cascade down my back before standing and stretching languidly. He doesn't reply, but he's staring at me with a lusty gaze. Despite only being five feet tall without heels, I've been blessed with curves in all the right places, especially my chest. My breasts are my not-so-secret weapon when it comes to Lucas. If I can't get him to make an order for delivery within minutes, then I'll be surprised. Very surprised.

I seductively blow him a kiss. "Don't you worry, I'll take care of it.

Ms. Kitty had her heart set on teriyaki chicken, but I'm sure she'll love something else. She'll get over the disappointment eventually... probably tomorrow."

He yanks out his phone, his fingers already heading to the familiar app. "Does Ms. Kitty want the usual?"

I grin wickedly, inching closer to him. "Yes, order her favorite. I'm going to get dressed."

I brush my lips softly against his before spinning away. He usually makes me work harder than this to get what I want. He must be in a good mood.

I slip into a pair of form-fitting cotton shorts and a tank top that hugs my breasts. My bare feet glide across the tile as I enter the kitchen to find Lucas pouring me a glass of white wine. I take the crystal glass from him and our fingers brush for a few seconds.

When I perch on a bar stool, our eyes meet in a knowing glance. Lucas smiles, a hint of mischief playing on his lips. We don't have wine with dinner every night. I want to joke with him he doesn't need me drunk to get me into bed tonight; I'm as close to a sure thing as he'll ever get. He probably wants to make tonight seem special since it's Valentine's Day and he obviously forgot.

I giggle at him. "You know what I like. Teriyaki and wine."

He winks at me before draining his first glass and promptly refilling it. Hey, he better slow down or else he won't be any good for me later. I'm about to say something, but he distracts me.

"Baby, today is extra special."

Yeah, no shit, it's Valentine's Day. I keep my thoughts to myself and I give him my best flirty smile.

"Every Valentine's Day is special."

He chuckles. "That's not the only reason. I also took the next two days off work."

"Oh?"

What's this? I perk up, and Ms. Kitty throbs with delight. I love it when he has days off and I don't need to be writing. Maybe we won't even get out of bed for two days. We can order food and alternate watching movies and fucking like rabbits. It will be an extended Valentine's Day celebration.

Lucas sets his glass on the counter. "I've been thinking about taking some time off. It's been a stressful year. I deserve to relax."

I nod. He does. He's an actuary, and he makes good money, but most nights he complains about feeling mentally drained when he gets home from work. Two whole days in bed with me should refresh him. I'll send him back to work with a shit-eating grin plastered on his face. I'll call it pussy relaxation therapy.

Wait, I guess I better make sure he doesn't have any grand plans before I chain him to the bed. "What are you going to do with your time off?"

"That depends on you." He moves around the counter, and I slowly turn on the chair to face him. My open legs are an invitation and Lucas stands between them. He towers over me, and I can feel the heat radiating from his body. He leans down and takes my chin in his hand, brushing his lips against mine and whispers, "I met someone at the gym. I want you to fuck him."

His voice sends a shiver down my spine. Now this is interesting. I pull back to see his facial expressions. "Who is it?"

He twirls some of my hair around his finger and plays with the silky strands. "His name is Brian."

It's rare for him to pick up someone he meets. Usually he finds guys who want to fuck me on some online forum. I like to joke it's a rent-a-bull website. No money is exchanged; these guys all agree to fuck me after Lucas shares a picture with them.

"And what, dear husband, makes Brian someone you think I'd want to fuck?"

This is the game we play. I try to sound uninterested, while Ms. Kitty does hula hoops at the thought of being stuffed by a stranger. Usually the guy has something special about him that makes Lucas choose him: a huge package, tons of stamina, great at licking pussy, something.

He kisses me again and licks his way up my neck. "Brian is hot, has a nice cock, and is super friendly. I met him in the gym locker room the other day and we started talking. I bragged about you and showed him a picture."

I interrupt him. "Which picture?"

His gaze glows with desire. "The one of you wearing the sexy Halloween bunny costume."

Oh yeah, that's a good one. "He liked the pic?"

Yeah, I'm totally fishing for compliments.

"He adored it, and then I told him about what happened in the haunted house."

My eyebrows rise while my body flushes from desire. "You told a stranger at the gym that I fucked a dude in a haunted house?"

God, I'm so aroused. I love it when he tells people how slutty I am.

He nods. "Yeah. He thought it was great and told me I'm lucky to have such an adventurous wife."

I take a sip of my wine. Uh-huh, he *is* lucky, but so am I. I'm damn grateful to have a husband who enjoys sharing me with other men without wanting to fuck around himself.

He takes another sip of his wine. "Anyway, after I told Brian about what happened at the comic con—"

I cut in again with a laugh. "Oh god, you told him I was a slut at the con also?"

My panties grow damp, knowing Lucas is spreading it around I'm a filthy whore and willing to open my legs for anyone he chooses. Lucas tells people on purpose because he knows how much it turns me on.

He sets his wineglass down and kisses me deeply. I moan against his mouth. Oh yeah, he's soooo getting some tonight.

Lucas murmurs between kisses. "After I told him about the con..."

He trails his mouth down to my neck. A tingle of delight ripples through me as he sucks and bites gently before he continues. "He offered his services if I was ever looking for someone local."

He must have really hit it off with Brian. I've fucked plenty of guys with big cocks, but it would be just like Lucas to give a friend a shot at me without being massive. Lucas is kind like that. Brian better give me a good orgasm, though.

"Mmm, so when am I fucking him?"

Lucas rubs my bottom lip with his thumb. "Well, the thing is, Brian likes to work in pairs."

My eyes widen.

Um, two guys? No, I've got to be wrong. I shake my head to clear my confusion and laugh. "Shit, I almost thought you meant he was bringing a friend. You want to be in the room?"

The way we do it, Lucas hides in the office. He listens through the adjoining wall while I fuck in the spare room.

Lucas grins in response. "No, you had it right the first time. He's bringing a friend, and I'm going to be listening in, like usual."

My brain freezes for a moment. When it kicks back on, a splash of wetness leaks into my panties and my nipples harden painfully. "You've arranged for TWO guys to fuck me?"

I keep thinking Lucas can't possibly surprise me, but he's taken the cake with this one. I never considered he'd want two guys to fuck me in one night.

He slides his hand into mine and squeezes it. "Yes, Brian and Damien. Only if you want it, baby. They are free tonight. Do you want two men as a Valentine's Day present?"

"Hell yes!" I answer quickly, and he chuckles.

"All right. Guess I should send out a text. Can you get the door when our food arrives?"

Shit, the food. My appetite evaporated when he mentioned two people were going to fuck me. Who needs food now? Oh wait, I need stamina.

"Sure, I got it."

He presses a kiss against my forehead. "Thanks, baby. I'm going to change my clothes and send the message."

My eyes glaze over as Lucas leaves the kitchen. What am I going to do with two guys? Hell, I'm going to have three cocks inside me tonight, since Lucas always fucks me afterwards.

Mmm... three cocks. Ms. Kitty buzzes her approval and I wiggle in my chair, trying to ease the growing ache. This Valentine's Day is shaping up to be a good one.

I bet I get at least three orgasms tonight. That's all I'm saying.

CHAPTER 2

The guys agree to come over in two hours, after we have dinner and I've showered and gotten ready. Since I'm not hungry, I pick at my dinner, moving the food around on my plate. At least I'm able to get enough down so Lucas doesn't complain.

We're both lost in thought while we eat, and it's good he didn't want to chat much. I'm way too busy daydreaming about two guys fucking me.

Are they going to tag team me? Like will one blow his load in my pussy and then let the other one have a go at me?

Ohhh.

Am I going to suck on one while the other fucks me?

The possibilities are endless.

Once I've eaten all I can, I push the plate away. "Love, I'm going to go take my shower. I can't eat another bite."

He winks at me in response. "Alright, baby. I'll take care of things here while you clean up."

Too excited to help, I blow him kisses and say, "Thanks, love," before heading to the bathroom. I let the shower water heat as I strip off my clothes. I pile my hair on top of my head in a loose bun; I don't have time to blow dry it this evening.

My mind wanders as I stand beneath the steaming hot shower. I rub the soapy loofah over my body and enjoy the vanilla scent of my body wash. Ms. Kitty was recently waxed, so I'm silky smooth in all the right places.

After my shower, I contemplate the contents of my lingerie drawer. If Lucas had given me more warning, I might have bought something new tonight. Fucking two strangers on Valentine's Day deserves a shopping trip. He didn't, giving me this delicious surprise, so I have to settle for something I already own. I tap my finger on my chin. Hmm... which item in my drawer says, "I'm a dirty slut who wants to take two men at once"?

I settle on a sheer lace lingerie teddy in red. The best thing about it? It's crotchless. They can bend me over and fuck me without removing it or ruining it. Plus, red seems appropriate for Valentine's Day.

Once I'm all put together, Lucas orders me to stay put in the spare room until he brings the guys in. He wants to have a little chat with Damien before the fun starts. This isn't my first rodeo, so I don't complain. It's how Lucas handles our casual flings.

Since there's two of them planning to fuck me, I feel extra slutty tonight. Hell, maybe I should be naked instead.

Nah.

I want to wear something feminine and festive. I stretch out on the bed and admire my reflection in the full-length mirror across the room. I'm like a sexy gift waiting for them to unwrap.

The doorbell rings. Since the spare room door isn't closed, I can hear murmured male voices down the hall. I'm a bundle of sexual energy while I wait. The guys must be single if they are free on Valentine's Day—wait, when did Lucas plan this? He didn't go to the gym this morning.

I don't have time to think about it because the guys head in this direction. Shit, it's go time. I peek into the mirror one last time to make sure I still look good.

Yep.

I smile seductively at them as they pause in the doorway, taking me in.

Damien and Brian are younger than I expect, maybe in their mid-twenties. They're tall and handsome with fit, muscular bodies. Oh fuck, it's been a while since I've had a young stud. Do I have the stamina to satisfy two younger guys? My pussy flutters at the thought of being used all night long by these two.

Yeah, we're willing to try.

"Hi guys," I deepen my voice to sound sexy and give them a little wave. "Come in."

Neither of them says anything as they jostle into the room. Do I make them tongue tied? Lucas is behind them and he stays in the doorway.

"Jessica, you okay?"

I nod. "Yes, I'm fine. I'll see you soon."

He closes the door. I wait a moment until I hear the soft click of the office door next to the spare room, giving him enough time to get settled into his usual chair.

Since neither guy has spoken yet, it seems I need to break the ice. "So, are you two ready to fuck me?"

Consider that ice broken.

They both laugh.

Brian replies, "Yeah, let's get this party started."

Mmmm, yes, let's.

Damien adds, "Sounds good to me too."

The guys strip quickly, and I'm glad I opted for the crotchless teddy. These eager guys might flip me over and use me. Shit, this is hotter than I expected. Two guys coming over here to fuck me and leave seems like the sluttiest thing I've ever done.

Their cocks bob slightly with every movement as they strip. I'm temporarily shocked at how enormous they are. I have a perfect view, and I can tell Ms. Kitty is going to get an incredible ride. My body hums with anticipation and my nipples tighten beneath the lace bodice. I'm too excited to wait and bring a hand up to tease one of my nipples.

Brian is undressed first and leans on the bed to kiss me. I respond to his gentle touch and the pressure of his mouth against mine by moaning. He leaves a trail of kisses along my neck and tenderly bites my earlobe. It's a good thing I'm lying down. My knees wouldn't hold me up right now.

When Damien takes a seat on the bed and starts rubbing my feet, I let out a blissful moan.

Fuck, I didn't know tonight came with a foot massage.

"Look at her tiny feet!" Damien comments.

What? Brian and I both glance down. My foot is so much smaller than Damien's hand. I'm not sure what they expected, as I'm quite petite, but maybe they hadn't noticed until now.

Brian laughs. "Shit, if that's how small her feet are, is she going to handle your cock?"

Me and Ms. Kitty perk up.

Damien's got a big cock compared to Brian? I'd looked, but maybe I needed to look again. Obviously, I missed something.

Oh. My. A tingle zings from between my legs and my pussy throbs. Oh yeah, we're so ready to get stuffed by an enormous cock.

The guys run their rough hands all over my body, caressing and kneading me. They're thorough, finding the small of my back, my thighs, my breasts, the sides of my neck. I close my eyes and let the sensations wash over me. My breathing quickens, and I am intensely aware of how hot and hungry they are for me.

Damien fondles my backside, and his voice is husky. "Fuck, Jessica, you look gorgeous in that lingerie. You have such beautiful breasts and an amazing ass."

Heck yeah! Tonight comes with compliments along with the foot massage? Score! I moan, "Thank you," as Damien runs a hand between my legs and rubs my pussy through the lace.

Brian whispers in my ear. "You know, we could do this while you're on your hands and knees."

Mmmm. I love being fucked from behind. He kisses my neck again and I murmur, "Whatever you want."

That makes Brian laugh. "Oh yeah, it is whatever we want tonight. Your husband said you were our little slut to use, and you enjoy being called filthy things."

I moan and bite my lip. "Yes."

Damien continues to rub my pussy while Brian explores my backside. I'm aching for a cock inside me, but their hands on me feel too good to make me want to hurry them along.

I lift my head to kiss Brian again and he groans into my mouth. "I can't wait to fuck you."

Ms. Kitty throbs. Shit, I don't know how long I'll last before I explode. Three orgasms is seeming likely.

Damien nudges me onto my back and then spreads my legs. The room spins a little as he slides a finger inside me. Why are they being so gentle? I gasp and arch my back off the bed when he massages my cave wall as pleasure radiates from my core.

"You're so wet, baby."

Oh, fuck. He used the pet name Lucas uses for me. I'm sure he didn't realize it since it's a common-enough pet name, but it still mentally fucks me up—well, that and the four hands all over me.

Brian plays with my nipples while Damien pushes a second finger into me. Ms. Kitty is a wet mess and I moan in bliss.

I don't know what to do with my hands, so I clutch at the comforter and try to hold on to some self-control. It's going to be hard not to scream when they fuck me tonight. Actually, Lucas would probably love to hear that.

Damien's fingers swirl around my entrance, making me gasp and shiver. "I think she's ready for us to fuck her."

I can feel my pussy throb with need. You can bet your ass I'm ready.

"I think she is too," Brian says. Damien pulls his fingers out of me, and I whimper. Damn it, I need a cock!

Brian kisses my neck and whispers in my ear, "I hope you're ready for his big cock."

"Yes, please." My voice is a murmur.

Mmm, I can't wait. Brian moves his mouth down to my breast. He runs his tongue over the lace on my nipple while I moan softly.

"Damien, I think this teddy is in our way. What do you think?"

Brian nips at my nipple. Damien responds. "Yeah, let's remove it."

Even though I'm comfortable in my skin, I'm still a little nervous about being naked in front of two people. Damien slides the teddy off my body, then they each grip one of my ankles, pulling my legs apart.

Oh, fuck. A wave of self-consciousness washes over me and I feel the urge to cover myself or turn off the lights.

Both men stare at me, and Damien's gaze lingers on my pussy. A trickle of moisture between my legs confirms what I already knew—I'm turned on. I become hyperaware of their every movement. It feels like they're drinking in my body with their eyes.

"You're gorgeous," Damien murmurs.

Brian says, "She's going to be a good little slut for us."

Damien laughs. "A slut who is going to get split open with two big cocks. She's so tiny, we're going to have to really jam in there to fit."

Fuck, that's filthy. I wish I could talk dirty back to them, but I'm tongue tied from lust, and I can't think.

Damien's finger strokes my pussy again, then he moves closer. I try to relax, but it's difficult. I'm wound up tight and ready to pop. My pussy throbs as Damien slides a finger inside me.

"You're so tight," he says as he finger fucks me, and delight pings my brain.

Brian moves to suck on the opposite nipple from earlier. His hot breath flutters across my sensitive skin and I groan.

"Mmm, so tasty," He murmurs. "We're going to stretch you out until we're balls deep in your little cunt. Do you want that?"

I whimper. "Yes, god... please."

"Such a good little slut." Brian latches onto my nipple and sucking hard enough that I gasp.

I love dirty talk. I already felt like a slut, but this drives me further into the mindset of being a slut. I'm about ready to let them do whatever they want to me.

Lucas better be able to hear this.

Damien rubs my clit again, and I moan. "Oh fuck, that feels so good."

He pushes another finger inside me, and finger fucks me roughly until I'm on the edge of exploding. I'm going to come all over his fingers if he keeps this up.

"Fuck, I need to be inside you, baby," Brian moans.

I get an illicit thrill whenever he calls me 'baby.' This is so fucking amazing.

I groan in protest when Damien pulls his fingers out of me. He rubs my clit with one hand while he lifts my leg up and presses the head of his cock against my wet entrance. They've been touching me and fondling for so long, I'm shocked that one of them is finally going to fuck me.

Jesus, it's about time.

"Are you ready?"

I groan and nod.

Damien grins and thrusts forward. Oh god, I can feel the tip of his cock stretching me open. It's so much bigger than Lucas's cock.

"Fuck," Damien moans. "We really might split her in half. She's such an itty bitty thing."

He's not wrong. My pussy feels stretched wide, and it hurts a little — a glorious hurt. I try to think about Lucas and relax my muscles. I've taken big cocks before, so I know it's going to feel wonderful once I adjust and he's buried balls deep inside me.

Brian kisses me again, and my tongue dances with his. My heart thuds in my chest in time with Brian's kisses and I swear I can hear it beating.

"You're so fucking sexy," he growls.

It feels naughty to be kissing a stranger while another stranger is shoving their massive cock inside me.

Brian keeps murmuring dirty things to me. "Your husband is going to love hearing us fuck you tonight. We're going to make you scream."

I groan, "Yes... yes," as Damien rocks his hips, sliding deeper inside me. I toss my head from side to side and writhe as he pushes in until he bottoms out. Jesus, it's such a delicious pain.

"Ohhhh, fuck," I cry out when he pulls out and slams back into me.

The headboard thumps against the wall with each thrust. I whimper and grip the comforter as he fucks me in quick strokes. Bliss radiates through me, and I can't think or do anything but hold on while he uses me. Moaning loudly, I put my feet flat on the bed and meet Damien's thrusts.

The room smells like sex mixed with my vanilla body wash and a hint of spicy cologne. The unfamiliar scent emphasizes how dirty this is. I may never see these two again. It's a wham-bam-thank-you-ma'am fuck. God, I love Lucas so much for arranging this.

Brian sucks on my tits again and the intense pleasure spirals me higher and higher. I'm mindless and insatiable. If I had known two guys would be this amazing, I would have begged for it months ago.

"Fuck, you're so wet and tight," Damien groans. "Your husband didn't tell us how tiny you are."

Damien whacks against me sharply and I cry out from the pleasurable pain. Quiet? I'm not being quiet now, so I know Lucas can hear, and I hope his cock is out. I imagine his hands moving up and down his length as he listens to my moans.

"Mmm, I bet she's never had two cocks at once."

Groaning loudly, I shake my head. "No, never."

I really want that. I want to suck on one of them while the other fucks me.

Damien pulls out completely and then slams back into me. "Are you ready to come?"

"God, yes."

He withdraws again and then slams home. I'm moaning continuously as he fucks me faster. I try to keep up with his rhythm, moving with him to match the intensity of his thrusts. I'm spiraling close to my orgasm as my pussy clenches around his cock.

"Fuck, I'm going to come," Damien moans. "I'm going to fill your little cunt with my cum."

Shit, I need to come before he does! He hammers into me frantically and his final slam skyrockets me into my orgasm.

"Ohhhhhh, fuck," I scream as a burst of pleasure shoots through my body.

Damien growls and jets of hot cum coat my inner walls. His cock pulsates and he moans. Ripples of delight continue to crash into me as Damien fucks me through my orgasm.

I don't notice when Brian stops sucking on my tits, so I'm surprised when he whispers in my ear. "You're such a good little slut. I can't wait to see how you look when we're done with you."

He kisses my neck and I shiver when he says, "Now it's my turn."

My brain is mush when the guys flip me over and pull me up onto my hands and knees. One of them rubs my ass and murmurs, "Such a pretty ass. Too bad Lucas said we can't fuck it."

Whaaa? Not that I want those monstrous cocks in my ass, but I didn't realize Lucas gave the guys instructions on what they couldn't do. I have such a wonderful husband.

Brian holds onto my waist. I arch my back and cry out as he slides his cock into me.

"Fuck, you're right. She's tight," Brian growls. "But she's gonna take every inch of this."

Brian grabs my hips and hammers into me. Sharp thrills run up and down my body. Fuck, this is amazing. I'm probably going to be sore tomorrow, but it's worth it.

"Mmm, you're so fucking hot," Brian moans. "I could fuck you all night long."

Damien moves in front of me on the bed and wags his cock at me. Fuck, he really is huge. That thing was inside me? Wait, how is he already hard again?

He holds his cock steady and aims for my lips. Um, he's expecting that to fit?

Brian gives a sharp thrust, forcing me forward. My gasp opens my mouth. Damien takes that as an invitation.

Ohh, fuck.

I have to open my mouth as wide as I can and stretch just to get the tip of him past my lips.

Yeah, there is no way I'm giving this dude a deep throat blowjob.

I study what I can see of his cock as I swirl my tongue around the head and suck on it. Prominent veins run up the length of his shaft. I taste myself on him, mixed with a manly essence that is all him. His breath hitches, so I can tell he's enjoying the suction of my mouth and the soft motion of my tongue.

Each time Brian thrusts into my pussy, it pushes me forward a bit onto Damien's cock. I have to hold myself steady while Damien slides his cock in and out of my lips, never fully withdrawing, while I suck like the greedy slut I am.

Damien reaches down and grabs my hair. "Fuck, your mouth feels so good."

I try to tell him I love sucking cock, but my words are muffled by his thick shaft in my mouth.

"You're such a good little slut," Brian pants. "You're going to make us both come really hard."

My moan is garbled. All I can do is hold on to the comforter while they use both my holes. My pussy is stretched wide and sensitive, and I can't think beyond the sensations coursing through me.

Damien groans, "Fuck, I'm going to come again."

He pulls out of my mouth, causing saliva to drip down my chin, and starts jerking his cock above my head.

"Tip your head up and stick out your tongue," he commands.

I close my eyes and do what he asks. Dammit, I really wanted to watch him come again, but with how enthusiastically Brian is fucking me, I'd probably end up with an eyeful of cum.

Damien groans and droplets of his warm cum splatter on my cheek and nose. One spurt actually lands on my tongue, and I swirl the salty goodness around my mouth before swallowing.

Yummy.

Once he's done showering me with his cum, Damien presses my shoulders down to the bed. I lower my head. What the heck is he doing?

The new position sets Brian off and he furiously pounds into me. Oh shit, he was just helping his buddy.

The erotic slapping of skin is louder than I expect as Brian's balls whack against my clit in this position. It's a sensation overload. My toes curl as my body shakes.

Oooh, god, I'm going to come! My brain is reeling, and liquid fire scorches through my veins as the tension inside me explodes.

I scream as convulsive waves grip me. My mind splinters as I get lost in my climax. Pleasure ripples through me in a tumbling wave as Brian's fingers dig into my hips and he comes with a roar.

He keeps slamming into me, filling me with his warm cum, while I shiver from the aftershocks of my intense orgasm.

When he finally pulls out, I collapse onto the bed, face down and ass up. Both guys are quiet for a few moments, and I drift in a blissful haze.

"Um, is she okay?"

Hands touch my cheek and I crack open one eye and try to smile at them. My mouth is half buried into the comforter, but I'm loud enough to be heard. "I'm fine."

I want to say, "Don't mind me, you just fucked me senseless," but that's too much work.

Damien strokes my hair and tells Brian, "I think you should go find Lucas."

The door opens and I assume Brian leaves. Damien keeps touching my hair and his voice is soft. "Are you really okay? We weren't too rough? Lucas said you wanted rough."

He sounds concerned, so I force myself to be more coherent and lift my head. "Oh god, that was amazing. I'm more than fine."

I can tell I've eased his concerns when he laughs softly. "Jessica, you're something else. I'm never going to forget this."

Yeah, I'm not sure I'm ever going to forget his cock, but I keep that to myself.

Lucas and Brian come back into the room. When I look at Lucas, I can see the tension ease from his face.

"Hi love!" I'm floating on cloud nine and giddy from my orgasm, almost to the point of sounding loopy.

Lucas chuckles. "She's fine guys. You just did a good job."

I hear fabric rustling, like Brian and Damien are getting dressed, but my focus is solely on Lucas. I crave being near him, assuring myself that our connection remains strong. Lucas sits on the bed and gathers me into his arms, kissing me passionately.

When he pulls away from the kiss, he laughs, using his hand to wipe drops of cum from my face. His hard cock presses against me as he whispers in my ear, "I'm going to say goodbye to them, then come back and make you mine."

I'm happy as I nod at him.

He kisses my nose and I settle back onto the bed. The men converse as my thoughts drift. I've seen some huge cocks, but Damien's was definitely the most impressive I'd experienced so far. I always think some guy is the biggest ever, as if I forgot the size of all the previous cocks, but this time I really think it is. If I had seen it in advance, I might have called off the whole night. That thing is intimidating.

Ms. Kitty gives a soft pulse in protest, and I chuckle to myself. Wait, who am I kidding? Ms. Kitty would have been begging to scale that flagpole.

I sigh in contentment and relax some more. Lucas needs to hurry back before I drift off completely.

CHAPTER 3

I'm lying on my side with my eyes shut when Lucas returns.

"Baby, you awake?"

I slowly open my eyes and smile at him. "Yes, I was thinking about you."

"You're stunning." He kisses my forehead.

I giggle in response. "Uh, thanks, but I'm kind of a mess right now."

He climbs onto the bed behind me and nuzzles my neck. "You smell like sex—it's hot."

My face lights up in a grin and I roll onto my back. "Well, I got used pretty good."

His hand cups my cheek and he looks into my eyes. "That's because you're a sexy little slut."

I giggle. "I'm *your* sexy little slut."

He kisses me and I run my fingers through his hair. We hold each other for a few moments, reveling in the warmth of our embrace, but soon the need for more becomes too great to ignore.

"Lucas," I whisper.

He kisses my cheek before pulling away and settling himself above me. He pushes his shorts down and our hips meet as his length presses against my entrance. His voice is deep and husky when he speaks. "Yes?"

"I want you to make love to me. Please, fuck me."

He kisses me tenderly as he slides into me. His thrusts are gentle yet intense, sending delightful pings through my entire body.

I grab his ass and urge him on. "More, please!"

He increases the speed and power behind each thrust, and I wrap my legs around him as he becomes the primal version of my husband.

"Did those cocks feel good?" he groans in my ear.

"Yes," I gasp out.

"Tell me how they felt."

"Big... hard... heavenly."

He thrusts faster, and my muscles around him tighten. I hold on to him, pulling him deeper as he pistons vigorously. I cry out as a soothing wave of pleasure washes over me. This orgasm isn't as intense as the prior ones, but the gentle bliss is a perfect ending for the night.

Lucas comes a moment later and groans with release. His body tenses and convulses as he pours himself deep into my pussy. He moves in and out a few more times before easing out completely and melting into my embrace. My pussy flutters from aftershocks of my orgasm and I almost giggle.

Oh yeah. Ms. Kitty is going to need a day of rest after this.

I'm not sure how long we stay cocooned together, but eventually Lucas shifts to lie beside me.

"Wow," I whisper.

He kisses my shoulder and sighs in contentment. "That was incredible."

I smile and snuggle up to him. "I love you so much. You've given me the best Valentine's Day ever."

"You're very welcome, baby," he murmurs.

My eyes droop, but a thought pops into my head and wakes me up. I steal a glance at him, and his eyes are shut.

"Hey, Lucas?"

I nudge him gently until his eyes flutter open. "Hmmm?"

He's looking sleepy and adorable. I could squeeze him in my arms and smother him with kisses.

Right. I was asking him a question.

I poke his stomach. "When did you plan all of this?"

He smiles as I question him and kisses my shoulder again. "A few weeks ago. I didn't tell you in case you couldn't finish your book. You might have been too busy daydreaming about being fucked by two guys with enormous cocks."

I erupt in laughter. Oh, shit. He's probably right. "Yeah, that was a good call."

He snuggles closer to me, laying his head on my breast as I run my fingers through his hair. I'm so damn happy. I don't think life can get any better than this.

The End

THE HOTWIFE KEY PARTY: JESSICA

CHAPTER 1

The morning sun filters through the curtains, waking me from a deep sleep. I stretch out my arms and legs, my bare skin sliding against the cotton sheets. My pussy, or Ms. Kitty, as I like to call her, purrs between my thighs, already slick and ready for someone's cock.

Lucas's side of the bed is empty and cold, the scent of his cologne lingering on his pillow. He's probably in his office, working on one of our "projects." I smile, wondering what lucky bull he's organizing to fuck me today. This is what Lucas and I do. I'm his hotwife and he finds guys over an app for me to fuck. We'd previously planned that today he'd choose a guy for me to fuck, and I'm ready for action.

My pussy buzzes at the thought of the unknown cock I'm getting, and I slide my hand down to rub my clit. Shit, I'm horny. I need to get fucked, and soon.

I roll out of bed and pad to our home office, naked, hoping to find Lucas for an early morning quickie. No such luck. The house is empty, silent. Bleh.

Since there's no cock to be had, I need a shower and caffeine. Maybe when Lucas gets back, I can seduce him—or at the very least demand he service me. I'm not opposed to taking charge occasionally. I take a quick shower and slip on a robe. After I make a cup of coffee, I take it to my home office to work on my latest reverse harem vampire novel. I might as well write a little while I wait. Lucas and I live a very nice lifestyle between my income as a writer and what he makes as an actuary. I'm successful enough to hire my best friend, Miri, as my personal assistant. She has the day off, so there's no message from her waiting for me—boo. I was hoping for an excuse to slack off and chat. I'm ahead of schedule on this book, so I'm not too dedicated to writing this morning.

My mind keeps wandering to the man Lucas might pick out for me. Lucas has a type he usually goes for. My kinky husband finally admitted to me several months ago that he enjoys imagining a huge cock splitting me open. I figured that, but it was cute when he got all flustered and told me about his kink. I'm fit, five-foot nothing, with big breasts and long blonde hair. His fantasy of tiny-me with some monstrous cock is great. Am I going to stop him from finding guys with big cocks to fuck me? Nah...

I abandon trying to write and slip my hand between my legs, rubbing slow circles on my clit as I daydream about a guy with a gigantic cock sliding it inside me. I'm dripping wet from my fantasy. Yeah, I'm way too distracted to write. I hope I don't have to wait too long before Lucas finds someone for me to fuck.

When I hear the garage door open, I pull my hand from between my legs. I can at least pretend I was being productive. Lucas comes into the office with a grin on his face.

"I've got a present for you, baby," he says, eyes glittering with lust. "Go get dressed in something sexy and meet me in the spare room in ten minutes."

My heart leaps. Whenever Lucas invites someone over to fuck me, it happens in the spare room. This means he found someone. Oh, hell yeah. Miss Kitty is going to get what she needs. Finally.

"Yes, my love," I stand and kiss Lucas hard before practically skipping to the bedroom. The day is looking up already.

He didn't specify what I should wear beyond it being sexy, so I pick out a red lace babydoll lingerie set. It's low cut and molds to my breasts like it was custom made for me. It has matching panties that are like dental floss. I consider not wearing them, but put them on anyway. The guy can unwrap his present. I attack my hair with a brush, giving it a tousled look that says I'm ready to be fucked.

Getting ready takes longer than 10 minutes, and when I get to the spare room, Lucas is waiting, leaning against the wall, arms crossed over his chest. He's watching the bed with a smug little smile. I follow his gaze and swallow a gasp.

There's a gorgeous half-naked blonde man on the bed. He takes an enormous cock out of his shorts and starts stroking his shaft as soon as he sees me. My mouth waters at the sight. It's been a long time since I've walked in to a guy being practically naked and ready for me quite like this. Ms. Kitty buzzes with happiness.

"Jessica, meet Trey," Lucas says. "I told him all about you and your appetite for cock. He's very eager to help *satisfy* you."

Lucas raises and lowers his eyebrows in an adorably stupid way when he says the word 'satisfy.' A rush of love for him almost takes my breath away. He chose a guy to fuck me, and now he's so on board with the plan, he's joking with me about it in front of the guy. I found myself a rare husband.

Trey continues to rub himself and silently observes the banter. When I turn to him, I put an extra swing into my hips as I saunter over to the bed.

I keep a seductive lilt to my voice. "Is that so?"

Climbing onto the bed, I brush a hand over Trey's muscular chest. His warm skin ripples from my light touch. "Did Lucas tell you I like it hard and fast?"

Trey grins, revealing a dimple in one cheek. "He might have mentioned that." His hand closes over my wrist, forcing me to stop my movements. "I think we'll get along just fine."

My pussy tingles in anticipation. This is exactly what I've been needing. Lucas moves to the door, drawing my attention. He winks at me. "Have fun, you two."

I blow him a kiss as he closes the bedroom door. Two heartbeats later, Trey yanks me down on top of him and crushes his mouth to mine. He kisses me hard and deep while his hands roam all over, squeezing my tits, slapping my ass, and sliding under my lingerie to plunge two thick fingers into my pussy.

I moan against his mouth from the pleasure and grind down onto his hand. It looks like Ms. Kitty is going to get fucked well today. I'm desperate to get his cock filling me, stretching me, and pounding me into oblivion.

Trey breaks off the kiss, panting. "I want your mouth on my cock. Now."

Mmm, I like a man who can take control. I move and willingly position myself between his muscular thighs. His thick cock is right in my face and moves slightly, like it's waving at me. I kiss the tip and he groans.

"Suck my cock, slut," he orders, and wraps my hair in his hand.

Fucking men other than my husband and loving it as much as I do makes me feel like a complete whore—in the best way. When a guy calls me a slut, it gives me a naughty zing. Couple that with Trey's rough treatment, and I'm ready to do whatever he wants.

Hurrying to obey, I lap at the bulbous head, tasting his pre-cum and smelling the faint tang of his masculine musk. Trey presses my head down, forcing his cock in deep. I relax my throat, taking him all the way in.

"Fuck, you really are a wonderful cock-sucking whore, aren't you?" He uses my hair like a handle, thrusting his cock in and out of my mouth. I almost gag, but he eases up. My pussy grows wetter at the rough treatment as he uses me.

"Too bad your husband isn't here watching how well you're taking my thick cock."

He slips out of my mouth long enough for me to gasp out, "Oh god," before shoving himself back in. I would have loved for Lucas to watch me being a complete slut, but he likes to listen and imagine it. If that keeps him happy and lets me fuck other guys, I will not complain.

Trey's cock pulsates and his balls tighten like he's about to blow his load, but he pulls my head off his cock right before he does. Oooh, maybe now I'll get a rough pounding.

He gets off the bed and demands, "On your hands and knees, slut."

Shit, I love that Lucas found a dominant man for me today. I scramble to obey, getting into position. My lingerie is up over my hips, and my panties can't hide my wet pussy. I'm almost completely exposed, and love it.

"What a view." Trey smacks my ass hard enough to sting, and I moan loudly. He spanks me again, and again, until I'm whimpering and pushing back for more. Wetness leaks down my inner thigh and I'm ready for him to fuck me.

"You want this cock, don't you?" Trey tugs my panties down to my knees and rubs the head of his cock between my folds. "Beg for it."

I hate it and love it when guys make me beg. It's difficult to think with a head foggy from lust, but I try my best.

"Please!" The word comes out as a whine. "Please, fuck me! I need your cock so bad!"

Trey slides in with one hard thrust. I cry out at the sudden fullness as my pussy stretches around his girth. It's perfect.

He sets a brutal pace, slamming into me over and over. Holy fuck! Sharp pings of delight ripple through my body as the bed shakes under the force of his thrusts. I'm lost in a haze of pleasure and pain, and all my awareness narrows down to his cock pounding into me. I'm so turned on, I know I'm going to come quickly.

Trey grunts, "You love this, don't you? Being fucked like a whore while your husband listens?"

"Yes!" The word is almost a sob. "I love it. I love being a slut!"

Pleasure ripples through me, and my toes curl as I race towards my orgasm.

"Then let's give your husband something to listen to. Come for me. Now."

He gives a sharp thrust, and his command pushes me over the edge. My orgasm crashes over me, waves of ecstasy radiating out to my fingers and toes. I scream, "Oh, fuck!" as I convulse around Trey's cock. He follows soon after, burying himself to the hilt and emptying into me with a groan.

When he's done filling me with his cum, we collapse onto the bed in a tangle of limbs, panting for breath. My brain blips out and I'm not sure how long I lay there before Trey stirs. He touches my back and I peel my eyes open and look at him.

He's sitting up and smiling down at me. "Thank you, Jessica."

I give him my best lopsided grin. "You're welcome."

I don't have the energy to move yet, so I stay there while Lucas opens the bedroom door. The guys chat while I drift in my post-orgasmic haze. Lucas escorts Trey to the front door and returns to me.

I roll over as he enters the room. His eyes are full of desire as he stalks towards the bed. I can see the bulge in his jeans, and my pussy perks up, ready for more action.

"Did you enjoy listening to the show, baby?" I ask coyly.

Lucas growls as he climbs onto the bed on top of me. He grabs me, kissing me fiercely. I moan into his mouth as his hands roam over my body. He's rougher than normal, squeezing my tits through the lace of my lingerie, like he's reclaiming what's his.

"You're mine," he groans against my lips, pinning my wrists above my head. "My enchanting little vixen."

I whimper, "Yes…yours. Only yours."

Lucas releases my wrists and kneels to unzip his jeans, freeing his throbbing cock. I press my body up against his, aching to have it inside me. Lucas rubs the head of his cock against my dripping entrance.

"Please!" I mewl out shamelessly. "I need you so bad!"

"Tell me what you need. Beg for it like you did with Trey."

I'm beyond caring about what I say. "I need your cock! Please fuck me! Pound my slutty cunt and fill me with your cum!"

Lucas moans and slams into me, making me whimper. He fucks me hard and fast, almost like a crazed man, and I'm not sure he cares whether or not I come. I'm incoherent with pleasure, babbling and moaning like the cock-hungry slut I am.

When Lucas explodes inside me with a roar, it triggers another earth-shattering orgasm for me. I cry out as I ride the waves of bliss.

He continues to fuck me through my orgasm, and when he can tell I'm coming down from my peak, he withdraws and collapses on the bed next to me. I groan and roll onto my side, facing him. I'm a sweaty mess.

Lucas kisses me tenderly. "I love you, baby"

"I love you too," I murmur, snuggling into his embrace.

I lie in Lucas's arms, basking in the afterglow of incredible sex. My body feels loose and liquid, every muscle relaxed. Miss Kitty is sore in the best way, still tingling from her pounding.

Lucas strokes my hair, his touch gentle and loving. "How was it, baby? Did you enjoy yourself?"

I smile, tilting my head up to kiss him again. "You know I did. It was amazing, like always."

"Good." Lucas's eyes gleam with satisfaction. "I'm glad Trey could give you what you needed."

I caress Lucas's cheek, gazing into his eyes. "He was great, but you're the best. No one fucks me like you do."

Lucas chuckles, tugging me closer. "Flattery will get you everywhere."

We both know what I said isn't true. I've slept with enough guys that have taken me to places Lucas never has, but it's always just fucking. Nothing comes close to how complete I feel with Lucas afterwards.

He rubs my back slowly and I think he's about ready to fall asleep, so I'm not expecting it when he speaks.

"I have a surprise for you."

Giving his neck little kisses, I murmur, "Oh?"

"I've arranged a trip for us next weekend. It's a sex party."

What's this? I lean back so I can look him in the eyes. "What type of sex party?"

He grins and kisses my nose. "One where my gorgeous wife is going to get fucked by multiple men while I wait for her to be done so I can then enjoy her luscious body."

A tingle of pleasure rushes through me, and Ms. Kitty throbs. Yeah, we're interested in a sex party.

I try to sound like I'm not excited. "Hmm, I don't know. Sounds boring."

"You're going to love it." He growls and attacks my neck with kisses while I squeal from delight.

I laugh, "Okay, okay, maybe I'll have fun."

He murmurs, "I already cleared your schedule with Miri. You're free to fuck all the guys you want," while nibbling and biting my throat.

His mouth tickles me, causing a fit of giggles. "Yes, yes, I'll fuck them all!"

He pulls me on top of him, and I melt against him as he turns serious. "This party is special. I want you to enjoy yourself."

"Hey, as long as one of the guys has an enormous cock. I'm sure I'll enjoy it." I give him a deep kiss and lay my head against his chest. We've never gone to a sex party before and the sound of it intrigues me. I'll try to weasel more information out of him later.

CHAPTER 2

Lucas is being a jerk. It's been four days since he told me about the party, but he won't give me any details. He just keeps fucking me all over the house. He showed me the engraved invitation to the party earlier. It reminded me of a wedding invitation. Based on the golden cardstock alone, you could tell the party was going to be swanky. It was deceptive in its simplicity with just the announcement we were invited to the party and a website on the back. But sadly, the invitation didn't tell me anything about the actual party.

Now he's got me naked on the bed again, and I'm determined to get information out of him since we leave for the trip in two days.

Lucas nuzzles Ms. Kitty with his nose, inhaling deeply through his nostrils. "Mmm, you smell delicious."

He holds my pussy lips open and swirls his tongue around my clit. My head spins and I tremble under his touch as I gasp, "Tell me about this party. You've been teasing me for days."

"So impatient," he laughs, the vibrations tickling my clit. "Good girls who wait get rewards, you know." He licks the length of my folds, and I groan from the pleasure.

My back arches off the bed. "Please, Lucas. I want to know. I've been a very good girl."

"I suppose you have." He slides two fingers into my pussy, massaging the magical spot. "It's an exclusive party at Casa Del Grande Toro, a private mansion in Malibu. Very high end, very elite. They invited multiple hotwife couples."

His fingers work magic inside me as I try to imagine what a sex party would be like—with strangers. My pussy squeezes around his fingers as a wave of bliss threatens to overwhelm me. "And...and who am I fucking?"

"I don't know." He lifts his head from my pussy to meet my gaze, passion shining from his eyes. "They pick the bulls for the women. I get to watch from a camera or be in the room if I want. Watching you come undone with other men..." He trails off with a groan, grinding the hard bulge in his jeans against my thigh. "Fuck, it makes me so hot thinking about it."

I swallow the pool of saliva in my mouth as heat floods my cheeks. Lucas previously always knew who was going to fuck me, so this is different. The idea of strangers pawing at my body, shoving their cocks into whatever hole they want—it terrifies and thrills me all at once. I squirm under Lucas's touch, torn between pushing him away and pulling him closer.

He seems to sense my conflicted arousal and slows the motion of his fingers. "We don't have to go if you don't want to. Just say the word."

I stare up at the ceiling, chewing on my lower lip as I consider. My pussy gives a strong pulse and I almost laugh. Yeah, let's be honest here. I'm fine with fucking strangers, and I trust Lucas. He wouldn't have arranged this if he didn't think I was going to love it. And the way Lucas is looking at me, like I'm some prized possession he's willing to share with others...fuck, it's doing things to me.

"I want to go," I say finally.

Lucas's eyes gleam. "Good." He seals his approval with a deep kiss to my pussy. My fingers twist in his hair as his lips close over my clit. He flicks his tongue over the swollen bundle of nerves again and again, stoking the fire deep inside me until I'm writhing against his mouth. Just when an orgasm builds, he stops, leaving me empty and wanting.

"No fair," I whine, trying to pull him back between my legs.

He chuckles. "Patience, my love. That was just the beginning."

Lucas moves up to capture my mouth with a passionate kiss. I can taste myself on his lips, and it's intoxicating. His cock nudges at my entrance, the head slipping inside for a moment before retreating. I groan in frustration, rocking my hips to try to get him inside, but he denies me.

"Tell me what you want," he growls against my neck. His teeth graze the sensitive skin. "Tell me exactly what you need."

"I need your cock. I need you to fuck me. Please, Lucas!"

"As you wish." He sinks into me and I sigh from the bliss. My soft and loving husband is out tonight, and he plays with my body like only he knows how. I wrap my arms and legs around him as he fucks me leisurely with long, deep strokes.

It's loving and heavenly. The coil of heat in my core winds tighter and tighter. I'm so close, teetering on the edge of rapture. I close my eyes and hold on tight while he and I explode together. His warm cum fills me up, and I rock against him until we're both fully satisfied. Hell, do I even really need to go to the party? The sex beforehand is pretty fabulous.

The next morning, Lucas watches with amusement as I rifle through my closet, searching for my most seductive outfit to pack for the party. I try on several before deciding on a midnight blue V-neck dress that wraps around my body and ties at the hip. It's silky and clings to my curves, the hem reaching mid-thigh and showing off my toned legs. The deep neckline gives a tantalizing view of my cleavage. I choose a tiny, barely-there scrap of lace masquerading as panties and some strappy sandals. Yep, this will do.

"Trying to give the other men heart attacks?" Lucas asks, eyeing me appreciatively.

I smile, doing a slow spin to give him the full view. "Jealous?"

"Never," he says, though his gaze sharpens as he stares at me. I know he loves showing me off, his prize to be coveted and claimed.

"Though I may have to fight them off with a stick. You look delectable enough to eat."

"Promises, promises." My nipples harden under the thin dress as my pussy grows wet. His reaction tells me this is definitely the dress I want to bring on the trip.

Lucas steps closer, caging me against the wall. He cups my breast, squeezing gently before giving the nipple a pinch. I gasp, squirming as heat suffuses my body. "Before we go," he says, "there's something else you should know."

"What?" I ask breathlessly. My heart races in anticipation. What else could he possibly have planned?

"I invited someone else to go with us to the party. An old friend of yours, in fact."

My eyes widen. Oh no. After a high school reunion trip to the ocean last year, Lucas struck up a friendship with a guy I knew from high school—Zane. That's the only person it could be. A secret, passionate night with Zane from long ago flashes in my mind, and desire and panic swirl inside me.

"Zane," Lucas confirms with a wolfish grin. "This is going to be a fun party."

My heart nearly pounds out of my chest. Zane. I gape at Lucas, stunned into silence. He's bringing Zane for me to fuck? I never told him about my night with Zane. Oh God, this is a bad idea.

"Surprise," Lucas says, clearly delighted with himself.

"You should have told me," I say once I find my voice. I sound breathless, anxious. Guilty.

"And spoil the fun?" I wanted to see the look on your face. Priceless."

I smack his chest, annoyance warring with arousal. "This isn't funny! You can't just spring something like this on me."

"You're right, I apologize," Lucas says, though he doesn't sound sorry at all. "I should have given you time to prepare to go to a sex party with Zane."

My cheeks flame hot and Ms. Kitty buzzes. I'd like to pretend I'm not interested in fucking Zane, but I am...so damn much. He's muscular, fit, and an oh-so-yummy guy with tattoos and a bad boy vibe. If given the chance, I'd ride him to glory any day.

Lucas must not sense my inner distress. He reaches down and slides his hand under my dress to play with my pussy, one finger stroking my slit through the damp lace. I'm soaked, and it has everything to do with the thought of fucking Zane.

He rubs against me harder. "Seems like someone is getting worked up about the party."

My thoughts go fuzzy as he continues to stroke me. I've thought about Zane over the years, usually when Lucas talks dirty to me about old lovers and conquests. My pussy quivers at the memory of Zane's stubble against my inner thighs as he ate me out for hours.

"You're thinking about it right now, aren't you?" Lucas murmurs.

A whimper escapes me. Oh, I'm thinking about something all right, but probably not what he thinks I am. He's talking about the party while I'm imagining fucking Zane. I'm so fucking wet, and we don't leave for the party until tomorrow. "Lucas, please."

"Please what?" He grinds his hard cock against my hip. "Do you want me to fuck you and take care of your ache?"

I moan and close my eyes as an image flashes in my mind—Zane pinning my wrists above my head as he's pounding into me. Lucas sits in a chair across the room, stroking his cock as he takes in the show. I can almost feel the delicious stretch of Zane's cock as he slides into me.

"Is that what you want?" Lucas asks again. "Does Ms. Kitty need to come?"

I drag my eyes open to find Lucas watching me intently. I moan and crush my mouth to his in a searing kiss. Lucas groans in triumph and relief, grabbing my ass to keep me tight against him. By the time we break apart, we're both panting, and the ache between my legs has become nearly unbearable.

"Please," I gasp out. "Make me your fuck toy."

Lucas's eyes gleam. "Not now. You've got to wait for the party."

What? My eyes widen while my pussy practically vibrates with need.

He kisses me on the forehead. "It will be worth the wait. I promise."

Holy fuck. I married a sadist.

CHAPTER 3

I've been worked up and horny all day thanks to my annoyingly wonderful husband. Since we leave for the trip in the morning, I'm packing tonight. This also gives me something to distract myself with since I'm not getting sex.

It's not working.

As I stuff my luggage full of sexy lingerie–way more than is needed for our four-night trip–my mind races with thoughts of fucking Zane. My body tingles, but unease nips at me like an annoying little mosquito. Miri and Zane had a thing years ago, back in high school, and Zane was even her first hotwife experience last year. I don't want to upset Miri or ruin our friendship. I really need to talk to her about this.

I rub the silky fabric of a black satin teddy between my fingers and imagine Zane peeling it off of me. Caught up in my thoughts, I can almost feel Zane's powerful hands gripping my hips, his rough thrusts slamming into me from behind. I imagine him whispering all sorts of naughty things in my ear as he punishes my pussy with his rock-hard cock. Miri said he likes to fuck hard, and that's what I'm in the mood for after my husband edged me earlier.

I take a deep breath, trying to steady my racing heart. As much as the thought of Zane dominating me turns me on, I need to make sure I'm not crossing any lines with Miri. She's always been there for me, and as my best friend and employee, I don't want to fuck up our friendship over one night with Zane.

I flop down on the bed and quickly dial Miri's number before I can change my mind. As the phone rings in my ear, I can't help but think about how Zane's thick, veiny cock would fill me up, stretching my pussy to my limits. He had a thick cock when I saw it previously. I feel myself flush and my nipples harden beneath my thin shirt.

"Hey Jess, what's up?" Miri's voice snaps me back to reality.

A flush rises to my cheeks and I suddenly feel guilty. This is stupid. It's not like she's married to him. "Hey Miri, it's...uh, well, I need to talk to you about something," I stammer awkwardly. I quickly add, "It's about Zane."

"Zane?" Miri's tone shifts to one of curiosity. "What about him?"

"You know how Lucas is taking me on a trip?" Lucas said he cleared it with Miri, but I'm not sure what he told her.

She laughs. "Yes, and why aren't you packing? You don't sound happy."

Staring at the ceiling, I try to figure out the best way to ease into the conversation. "Did Lucas tell you what we're doing on the trip?"

"No, he said it was a secret, and he wasn't sure I wouldn't spill the beans to you," she grumbles. "I spoiled ONE surprise years ago and now he won't tell me anything."

I hold in my chuckle. Yeah, she got the date wrong on a surprise trip Lucas planned and thought I was calling her from the hotel. In hindsight, it's funny, but Lucas is still cranky about the mistake. That man has a long memory.

I quickly tell her all I know about the sex party—which isn't much—leaving the details about Zane for the end. I bite my lower lip and spit out the part I'm afraid she'll get upset about. "Ever since the reunion last year, Lucas and Zane became friends, and Lucas invited him to the party this weekend."

I wait for her to say something, but she's silent. "I just wanted to make sure that you're okay with it." Pausing, I take a deep breath before adding, "I mean, considering your history together and all that."

She laughs warmly, and the tension in my stomach eases. "Jess, you're my best friend, and you and Zane can fuck whoever you want—including each other. I only had that one night with him and I've got much *bigger* fish to fry now."

Miri's response makes me giggle. Last week she was describing the massive cock on a guy that she fucked in Cabo San Lucas. She's been having a fantastic time exploring being a hotwife, and she's definitely been catching some big fish.

"Jessica, I want you to promise me something." Miri's voice gets all serious, and I sit up to focus.

"Okay, what?"

"I want you to promise not to worry about me. Do whatever you want with Zane and have fun. I honestly don't care. He was fun to fuck, and it gave me some closure about my past, but that's it. I'm not pining over him, and I'm thrilled with how everything has turned out. So, promise?"

My heart warms. This is why she's my best friend. "I promise."

"We're best friends," Miri echoes my thought. "We've been through so much together, and this is just another adventure for us to share. Now go on this trip and get that magnificent cock if you can."

"Thanks, Miri," I say, laughing at her candid encouragement. "I also promise to give you all the dirty details later."

"Damn right you will. Have fun and make me proud."

"Will do." I'm feeling better about the trip as I hang up. I'm so glad I called her. With her blessing, I'm ready to take on Zane and whatever pleasure he has in store for me and Ms. Kitty.

I jolt awake the next morning with my alarm. The anticipation of today's trip has me eager to get started on our adventure. I throw the covers off and practically spring from the bed. Lucas stirs, and I can tell he's barely awake.

Today is the day! A grin spreads across my face and I don't waste any time getting ready. I race to the bathroom, feeling the cool tiles beneath my feet as I hurry through my morning routine.

I call out, "Lucas, you better get up," in between brushing my teeth and splashing water on my face.

"All right, all right. I'm awake," he groans from the bedroom.

I peer into the mirror, scrutinizing my reflection. My beachy waves frame my face and then cascade down my back. I'm flushed and looking gorgeous, if I do say so myself. I'm naked and I take a moment to appreciate my big breasts and trim figure. I'm going to be smoking hot at this party and make Lucas and a bunch of other men drool.

Ms. Kitty is definitely ready for action. I smile and run a finger between my legs and over my freshly shaved mound. I'm aching to be fucked and still worked up from Lucas edging me yesterday.

I quickly dress in something comfortable, yet sexy, for the flight—a pair of leggings that hug my ass, and a loose-fitting blouse. No need for anything fancy, but I still want to look good so I can torture Lucas for not fucking me yesterday.

Lucas appears in the doorway, his eyes lingering on my butt. "Ready to go?"

"Absolutely," I reply as I move into the bedroom and walk with an exaggerated swing to my hips in case he's watching. I toss my toiletry bag into my suitcase before zipping it shut. "Let's get this show on the road."

We make our way to the car, the thrill of the upcoming journey electrifying every cell in my body. As we load our luggage, my mind wanders to the party. What actually happens at a sex party? A pulse of pleasure from between my legs makes me rub my thighs together in anticipation. I don't think it matters what happens. I'm ready for action no matter what it is.

Lucas navigates our car through the bustling streets and informs me, "Zane's meeting us at the airport."

"Really?" The thought of seeing Zane again sends a tingling sensation straight to my pussy. I never wondered how Zane was getting to the party because I was too busy thinking about his cock inside me. A bubble of delight wells up in me and I sound happy when I say, "This is going to be fun. I can't wait."

Lucas grins knowingly, glancing over at me. "Neither can I."

When we park in the airport parking lot, I'm practically skipping in eagerness. We head to the gate, dragging our luggage behind us. As we round the corner, my eyes lock onto Zane's muscular figure leaning against a wall. Mmm, yummy. He's so damn sexy, I could eat him up right now.

"Hey there." Zane greets us with a devilish grin. His eyes take in every inch of my body. Thank God I wore something sexy today.

My nipples harden and I sound breathless when I say, "Zane." I'm aching to get his cock inside me, but I need to be patient.

Zane's voice is low and seductive. "Ready for some fun in Malibu?"

"Absolutely," I reply, trying to keep my composure as my mind runs wild with carnal thoughts of his cock buried deep inside me.

Lucas chimes in, breaking the sexual tension. "Great, let's get going."

I can't believe Lucas really arranged for Zane to come. This makes me love my husband even more.

We board the plane, relaxing into our seats for the quick flight from Oregon to Los Angeles. My body hums with happiness from the unknown adventure that awaits me. All I know is that Zane's cock is going to be inside me before this trip is done, but who else will I fuck at the party?

Lucas must sense my arousal, and he whispers in my ear. "Try to relax, baby. You'll need your energy."

"Trust me, I'm going to have all the energy I need," I assure him, my hand briefly sliding between my legs to brush over my throbbing pussy on top of the fabric of my pants. It's a good thing no one is paying attention to us on the flight. "Ms. Kitty is ready to play."

He squeezes my thigh. "Good, because I think you're going to be very satisfied by the time we get home."

Mmm, hell yeah. My mind fills with images of Zane's hard cock pounding into me as Lucas watches me on video.

The moment we step into the lavish hotel lobby, I'm struck by its opulence. Lucas and I have taken some very nice vacations, but this hotel is one of the nicest we've stayed at. My senses are overwhelmed —the scent of fresh flowers mingles with the rich aroma of leather. Soft jazz music fills my ears, accompanied by the gentle murmur of guests engaged in hushed conversations.

"Welcome to how the other half lives," Zane says with a grin, and Lucas nods approvingly as he takes in our surroundings.

I run my fingers over the cool marble surface of the check-in desk as I wait for the receptionist to give us the keycards to our rooms. "Wow, this place is gorgeous,"

Lucas and I plan on staying a few more days after the party, and I can already picture myself lounging by the pool, sunbathing while sipping on a cold cocktail.

"Room 512 and 513 for you." The receptionist hands us our keys with a polite smile. Lucas told me this trip is all expenses paid for us and Zane. I don't know who is footing the bill, and I don't care. I'm going to just enjoy it.

Lucas passes Zane a keycard. Shit, Zane is going to be right next door and I won't get his cock until tomorrow. This is not fair.

The receptionist offers to get someone to help us with our luggage, but we decline. Lucas takes my hand as we walk towards the elevators. Zane follows and as the doors slide shut, a dirty thrill runs through me. I have an entire day to wait until the party and I can hardly contain my exhilaration.

We part ways with Zane at the door to our hotel room. When we enter the lavish suite, Lucas sets his luggage down. "Are you ready for bed?"

The recessed lighting casts a soft glow over the plush furnishings, and I soak in the luxurious atmosphere of the room. Yeah, this trip was a good idea. I needed this.

I give him a suggestive smile. "Are you just going to mess with me again and not fuck me?" I already know the answer.

"Maybe," he grins, drawing me close and pressing his hardness against my stomach. "I want you so desperate for my cock that you won't be able to think straight at the party."

My panties are wet and if we were both naked, he could slide right in easily. His fingers trail down my body, slipping beneath the waistband of my pants and panties, rubbing my clit with expert precision. "Lucas, you're driving me crazy,

"Good," he breathes hotly into my ear, his teeth grazing my lobe. "That's exactly how I want you."

My legs tremble as pleasure courses through me and I whimper, "Fuck."

He continues his torture, bringing me to the brink of orgasm but not allowing me to tumble over. "Remember, tomorrow night, it's all about your enjoyment," he whispers, finally releasing me from his grasp. "Now, let's get some sleep. You'll need your energy."

Ugh. "Fine!"

I'm frustrated yet undeniably aroused by his relentless toying with me. I stick my tongue out at him and pretend to pout as we get ready for bed. As I drift off to sleep, thoughts of Zane's commanding presence and the promise of being fucked by him dance through my mind, fueling my desire. Just one more night and then his cock will be all mine.

CHAPTER 4

The next morning, a tingle runs through my body as I walk into the hotel's spa. I'm already turned on and desperate to get a cock inside me tonight at the party. It's going to be a long day.

The spa attendant has a warm smile. "Welcome, Jessica. We have a full day of pampering planned for you."

I murmur my thanks as I follow her to the massage room. Maybe if I can relax my body, my brain will follow.

I undress and lay down on the massage table, covering myself with a sheet. There's a small water fountain in the corner and the sound of a babbling brook plays low in the background. If anything is going to help me calm down before the party tonight, this should do the trick.

The masseuse enters the room, her hands coated in warm oil, and works her magic on my tense muscles. As she kneads my shoulders and back, my thoughts drift to the evening ahead. I imagine the taste of Zane's thick cock filling my mouth and the sensation of him pounding into me.

"Feeling relaxed?" the masseuse asks, breaking me out of my reverie.

I sigh, hoping I don't look flushed from arousal. "Very. Your hands are fantastic."

As the massage continues, the masseuse works her way down to my legs, her expert fingers finding knots I didn't even know I had. I groan in pleasure. This is the life. I need to book a massage more often.

I'm an odd mix of relaxed and horny. She isn't turning me on, but just having someone's hands massaging me while I have dirty thoughts about the party is more erotic than it should be. Great, I'm turning into a lusty slut from lack of sex. This is all Lucas's fault. I push my carnal thoughts aside and focus on enjoying the pampering.

"Your session is complete," the masseuse announces after some time. "I hope you enjoyed it."

I'm feeling more relaxed, yet still charged with erotic energy. If I were Catholic, I'd probably need to confess for all the images in my head during the last 90 minutes.

I thank her and head off for my next appointment–a soothing facial followed by a mani\pedi. As the pink polish on my nails dries, I glance at the clock. It's getting late, and I need to get ready for the party.

Back in our room, I slip into my midnight blue dress. The fabric clings to me, and I run my hands over my hips and down my thighs, imagining the hungry gazes of the guests at the party.

"Wow," Lucas says, looking me up and down as he buttons his shirt. He's dressed in black slacks and a white shirt that accentuates his broad shoulders and trim waist. I definitely have one sexy husband.

He gives me a long kiss. "You look absolutely stunning."

"You clean up pretty well yourself."

He saw me in this dress just the other day, but his appreciative gaze still turns me on. As we share an inviting smile, my body buzzes with anticipation. I can't wait to see what happens at a sex party.

Lucas extends his hand to me as we prepare to leave our hotel room. His eyes dance with desire. "Ready?"

I take his hand, feeling the familiar warmth of his touch. "More than ready,"

We make our way down to the lobby, where Zane is waiting for us. He's dressed casually, but with a sexy edge that makes my heart race. A black leather jacket hangs effortlessly over a crisp white shirt that clings to his muscular chest. His jeans fit him like a glove, emphasizing his powerful thighs. Completing his bad-boy ensemble are a pair of black boots that add an air of danger to his overall appearance.

"Hey, you two," Zane greets us, his blue eyes smoldering as he takes in my dress. "Looking good."

I try to keep my voice steady despite the butterflies in my stomach. "Thanks. You look great too."

"Shall we?" Lucas suggests, gesturing for us all to step outside.

A black limousine pulls up to the curb, its polished exterior gleaming under the setting sun. As we climb in, I admire the interior—leather seats, a fully stocked bar, and mood lighting set the stage for a night of indulgence. Whoever it is who invited us to this party, they sure know how to treat their guests right.

The drive to Casa Del Grande Toro is nothing short of breathtaking. The sun casts a warm glow across the sky, painting it in shades of orange and red before transitioning to a deep purple. I can already tell it's going to be a phenomenal night. The evening air is balmy, carrying with it the gentle scent of sea breeze and the distant hum of cicadas singing their nightly serenade.

As we approach the mansion, a cast iron gate swings open to reveal the sprawling property. We pass by a pristine tennis court on our left, nestled among lush greenery and towering palm trees that sway gently in the light wind.

"Wow." I take in the stunning view as our limousine comes to a stop in a spacious courtyard. The one-story, white mansion before us is a masterpiece of modern architecture. Its elegant lines and expansive windows complement the gardens and breathtaking ocean view.

Lucas grins at me and squeezes my hand. "Ready for a night you'll never forget?"

"God, yes." I can feel my pussy grow even more wet. I can't wait to explore the depths of pleasure with these two sexy men by my side.

"Let's go then," Zane says, leading the way as we step out of the limo.

"Welcome to Casa Del Grande Toro." A tall, handsome man in a sharp black and white tuxedo greets us as we step out of the limo. His warm smile reaches his eyes. "I'm called The Concierge. May I have your names, please?"

"Jessica, Lucas, and Zane," I reply.

The Concierge nods and checks our names off a list. "Ah, yes, welcome. The guests are gathering on the lawn through the house. Please, make yourselves comfortable and enjoy the evening."

"Thank you," Lucas murmurs, guiding me towards the entrance with his hand resting gently on the small of my back. Anticipation builds with each step, making my pussy throb with need.

As we make our way through the opulent interior of the mansion to the party outside, I catch glimpses of couples engaged in intimate conversations. Laughter and flirtatious banter echo through the air. My heart thunders, and there's a lightness in my step. Soon I'll be joining them in the hedonistic pursuits offered to all of us tonight.

"Hey, I'm going to grab some food and drinks. Would you like anything?" Zane asks. His sexy voice fuels a fire deep inside my core.

"No, thank you," I respond, my mind already wandering to the deliciously vulgar things I want him to do to me. As he walks away, I admire his ass as I think about his thick cock filling me up completely.

I exchange pleasantries with a nearby couple while trying to keep my lascivious thoughts at bay. They introduce themselves, two fellow first-time attendees who seem just as giddy as I am.

"Isn't this place amazing?" the wife gushes, her eyes wide with enthusiasm. "We've never been to anything like this before."

I feel a tingle of connection with her. "Neither have we. I can't wait to see what the night has in store for all of us."

As I mingle among the partygoers, my eyes suddenly fall upon a stunning woman who takes my breath away. She's a gorgeous blonde, her long locks cascading down her back like a golden waterfall. A green one-shoulder dress clings to her slender frame, leaving little to the imagination. The daring slit running up her thigh reveals tantalizing glimpses of her smooth skin each time she moves.

"Whoa," I mutter under my breath, unable to tear my eyes away from her. This place definitely has eye candy of all sexes.

"See something you like?" Lucas whispers into my ear, and I practically hum at him.

I don't want to admit that the sight of this beautiful woman makes me consider batting for the other team for a change. I've never slept with another woman, but that green dress on her makes me think twice about it.

I blow him a kiss and give him a mysterious, "Maybe."

My attention is drawn to a sexy guy standing across the lawn. He reminds me a little of Zane with a sexy bad-boy vibe. He's wearing a linen blazer, white Henley, and denim jeans, his chiseled features framed by tousled dark hair. Intricate tattoos snake up his muscular arms, hinting at a wildness beneath the surface. His intense gaze is locked on the blonde in the green dress, his hungry eyes filled with an unspoken yearning that makes my desire flare even hotter. Shit, I wish someone would look at me that way.

"You like the look of him?" Lucas nibbles on my neck playfully.

"It's always good to window shop," I shoot back, trying to keep my voice light despite the way my heart races at the thought of exploring what that guy could do to me.

Oooh, hell, or maybe he AND Zane could fuck me at the same time. I'd love to be the meat in that sandwich. Lucas said that I'd be fucking multiple people tonight. A girl can dream.

The party buzzes around me, guests mingling and laughing as they sip their cocktails and sample hors d'oeuvres. The air is thick with anticipation, the unspoken promise of carnal delights hanging heavy like an alluring perfume. As much as I try to focus on the lively atmosphere, my thoughts keep drifting back to Zane, his rough hands and dominating presence.

"Imagine how wet you're going to be by the time someone fucks you tonight," Lucas whispers in my ear, sending shivers down my spine. "I hope you get fucked so hard you won't be able to walk straight for days."

"Lucas!" Heat floods my cheeks. He's not usually this vulgar. I love it.

"Sorry, love," he smirks, clearly not sorry at all. "Just trying to help paint the picture for later tonight."

Before I can respond, a woman's voice rings out through a PA system, capturing everyone's attention. "Good evening," she begins warmly. "And welcome to our summer event. Please help yourself to food and drink and feel free to explore the gardens. The pool is open for any of you who might have brought swimwear. There are several sitting areas with their own mini-bars and at the end of the estate is a fire pit with ocean views."

I glance around, taking in the gorgeous surroundings, and wish I had thought to bring a swimsuit. Annoyance flares up, and I mentally chide Lucas for not mentioning the possibility of swimming. He knows how much I love the water.

I try to keep my tone light. "Kind of dropped the ball there, babe. I could have gone swimming."

He gives me a guilty grin. "Apologies, Jess. I guess you'll just have to find other ways to get wet tonight."

The woman's voice continues, "I am called The Manager, and you'll see me walking the grounds later today. But until then, if you need anything else at all, please don't hesitate to talk to any of the staff or The Concierge, who you will have met upon arrival."

"Speaking of getting wet," Lucas murmurs, his fingers slipping under the hem of my dress to fondle the edge of my panties. "How's Ms. Kitty feeling right now?"

"Behave, we're in public," I warn him, swatting his hand away while trying to suppress a moan.

He grins wickedly. "Exactly. Isn't that what makes it so thrilling?"

"Keep this up and maybe I won't let you fuck me tonight."

That gets me the hoped-for response. He growls, "Oh, you're going to let me," as he presses his lips against mine. Lust swirls in my stomach. Yeah, I'm going to let him do whatever he wants to me after bringing me to this party.

The Manager's voice interrupts us and fills the air. "You were all invited here because you're either involved in, or you've expressed an interest in, what we call The Lifestyle," she announces. I can't help but steal a glance at Zane across the lawn, wondering what he's going to do to me tonight.

The Manager continues. "But please, refrain from going to any of the rooms inside Casa Del Grande Toro just yet. The party will begin properly later when you meet your hosts, W and J. You'll all get a chance to…participate…when the moment is appropriate." The words make butterflies flutter in my chest, and my pussy throbs in response.

When the woman stops talking, my stomach rumbles, betraying the hunger that's been growing since we arrived. "God, I need something to eat."

Lucas chuckles and allows me to drag him toward the grill on the far side of the garden, where the tantalizing aroma of sizzling steak seems promising.

"Think you can handle a big, juicy piece of meat?" Lucas asks as we wait for our food.

"Only if it's served with a side of hard cock," I shoot back, giggling as his eyes widen in mock surprise.

As we mingle with other guests, the mysterious, sexy bad boy keeps catching my eye. He seems to be everywhere I turn. I bet he could do delightfully obscene things to me.

A commotion in the pool makes me smile. A woman jumps in wearing just her black bra and panties, and a guy joins her. I guess it's an option to go without a swimsuit, but I prefer to stay dry for now. Like Lucas pointed out, I've got plenty of ways to get wet tonight that don't involve chlorine.

Lucas leaves me briefly and talks to a guy who seems to be the husband of the blonde woman in the green dress. When Lucas also talks with the sexy bad boy, I'm intrigued.

"Who's that guy?" I ask Lucas when he returns.

He plays dumb. "Which one?"

"The hot guy over there you were talking to. The one with the tattoos."

Lucas grins. "Oh, just another guest. No one special."

Uh-huh. Right. My body buzzes with lust. Shit, maybe I'll get to be the meat of a bad boy sandwich after all. Wait, where is Zane?

Glancing around, I see him talking with some other guests. Hmm, for someone who's going to fuck me tonight, he sure isn't spending a lot of time with me.

Lucas notices I'm distracted and follows my gaze. "Jessica..."

Zane laughs at something a woman says to him, and I can tell he's flirting with her. "Hmmm?" I'm distracted by Zane's showing the woman the tattoos on his arm.

"Jess, love, I think you might have the wrong impression about something."

I take a sip of my drink and finally look at Lucas. "What's that?"

He gives me a deep kiss and I melt into him, enjoying his warmth. "Zane isn't at the party to fuck you. He's here for a different reason."

Wait, what? I'm stunned for a moment. Why in the hell did Lucas bring Zane with us if it wasn't to fuck me?

My heart sinks and I can't look at Lucas. Suddenly, the party loses a little bit of its sparkle. I've been daydreaming about fucking Zane for the last few days. It's hard to wrap my head around this change.

"Well," I say with a laugh that hopefully hides my confusion. "Zane should have a good time. It's not every day you get invited to a party like this."

Lucas is clearly oblivious to the turmoil churning inside me. He wraps an arm around my waist and gives me a side hug. "Oh, I think he will. Now, let's enjoy ourselves."

How am I supposed to enjoy myself after this bombshell? I don't have time to get even more worked up because the PA system crackles to life again, and The Manager's voice fills the air. "May I have your attention, please?"

A Black man appears at the top of the steps leading out of the villa—clearly not The Manager. He surveys our assembled crowd through a half-face mask. Stag's antlers rise above his short hair, adding an air of mystery to his already captivating presence.

"I hope you're enjoying Casa Del Grande Toro," The Manager continues as she emerges from the house. She's tall, blonde, and her willow-like body commands attention. She holds a microphone in one hand. "Let me introduce you to W & J, your gracious hosts for the evening."

"Wow," I murmur under my breath, my eyes taking in the masked man, before glancing at the beautiful Manager again. I try my best to focus on the present moment instead of my disappointment about not fucking Zane.

I whisper to Lucas, "Talk about making an entrance."

His grip on my waist tightens ever so slightly. "Indeed. I hope you enjoy tonight."

God, I hope so too. I swallow hard and force my attention back to our hosts. My mind races with thoughts of all the ways my pussy could be used tonight, but I can't help feeling a twinge of sadness knowing that Zane won't be the one to do it.

"Let's have some fun," I say, feigning enthusiasm as I plaster a smile on my face. I need to get over this mood real quick. There are plenty of other guys here who could give me the pleasure I crave...like the other bad boy I was checking out. I take a deep breath, determined to make the most of tonight.

As I look around at everyone at the party, the Black man in the stag mask leans into the microphone. "Hello. I hope you're having a good time. My home is yours until the morning." A quiet round of applause ripples through the assembled crowd as people move closer to the foot of the stairs where our hosts are standing.

"Hey, is that…" I begin to ask Lucas, recognizing the voice behind the mask, but he cuts me off abruptly.

"Don't name anyone," he warns, his mysterious smile making me feel both delighted and slightly apprehensive. Holy hell, we're at the house of someone famous.

A Black woman in a cloak steps out to join the man in the stag mask, her face also concealed by a mask that looks like some furry woodland creature. The Manager holds the microphone towards her and her seductive tone is another voice I recognize. "The food and wine will continue to be provided all evening. I am J, and together, we want to invite you to join tonight's main event. A very special game that we've planned for you all."

We're playing a game? I glance questioningly at Lucas, who smiles enigmatically at me. I think my dear husband knows something about this. Ms. Kitty purrs with anticipation, sensing that an erotic adventure is about to unfold.

"I hope you're ready to be used like a filthy slut," Lucas whispers into my ear, causing goosebumps to erupt on my skin. Suddenly, the thought of not fucking Zane doesn't matter as much. We've got a game to play!

I grin wickedly. "Absolutely." I'm ready to explore every dirty and depraved aspect of a mysterious game.

The Manager steps up, drawing my attention to her as W and J disappear for a moment. They return with a large glass bowl atop a wheeled pedestal. The Manager's voice is authoritative yet sultry. "The game works like this. In this bowl are room keys for each of the villa's bedrooms. We will invite each wife here to draw a key from the bowl."

I watch as The Manager dips her hand into the large glass container, plucking out a brass key. A small shiny disc swings from a ribbon attached to it. She continues to explain. "Then she will go to the room that matches the number on the key ring."

I watch her toss the disc back into the bowl. Ooooh, so this is why Lucas said he didn't know who I was going to fuck. Well, shit, he didn't arrange any of this. We're just participants in a kinky game. My pussy throbs. Yeah, I'm fine with this turn of events.

W takes over the explanation with a wide smile. "Once she's in the room, she'll wait to be joined by our special guests."

I rarely fuck random men, but I'm down for all of this. I try to remember all the hot guys I've seen at the party so far. Ms. Kitty quivers at the prospect of fucking any of them.

"You'll have met some of them earlier," W adds, grinning mischievously. "These guests are professionals. Some are exotic dancers. Some are just good friends of mine who are...shall we say, well-equipped for a party such as this."

Oh, hell yeah. A tingle runs up and down my body. I can't wait for this game to begin.

J, the masked woman, extends a slender hand, pointing inside the villa and I realize the mask is a fox—or more appropriately, a vixen. "The husbands can go to the room with their wives if they wish," she says, her voice dripping with seduction. "Or they can stay out here."

"Or they can join us in the media room," the man in the stag mask takes over, his voice smooth as silk. "Where we will have some excellent live entertainment for you." He pauses, and a collective gasp echoes from the guests.

I glance around, taking in their reactions. Most of them must not have known what the game was about. Some look surprised, some bemused. My curiosity is piqued, and I can't help but think this might make up for not fucking Zane. What a wild night this is turning out to be.

"If anyone doesn't want to participate," J says softly, her eyes scanning the crowd, "they don't have to. The reason you were invited here today was because of your interest in what we call 'The Lifestyle,' but if this sort of thing isn't for you, we respect that."

Her partner's head turns, gazing at all of us. "If you don't want to play, you're welcome to finish your food and drinks, and then your limo driver will return you to your hotel. We will start the draw in ten minutes."

The couple disappears back through the large glass doors into the villa, leaving The Manager watching the assembled guests.

My pussy throbs and I can feel myself getting wetter. "God, I want every hard dick in this place inside me," I whisper to Lucas. "I'm so fucking wet right now."

"Are you sure you're okay with this?" His concern barely masks the lust in his eyes.

"More than okay, babe. I need this." Especially after the letdown of knowing I'm not fucking Zane. But I don't add that.

He squeezes my hand. "All right. Just promise me one thing."

"Anything."

"Enjoy every single moment tonight." I can hear the raw desire in his voice.

Yep, this is my awesome husband.

"Trust me, I will." I kiss him on the cheek.

"Are we ready to begin?" The Manager's voice cuts through the chatter, drawing my attention back to the present. I glance around at the other guests; their anticipation is palpable, a delicious mixture of fear and desire.

"Excellent. The first to select is..."

My mind wanders as I watch the women's names called out. They step forward and pick their keys, one by one. Shit is about to get real here. I wonder how crazy it's going to get tonight? My mind conjures up images of hard cocks slamming into wet pussies in every corner of the villa.

"Jessica." The Manager finally calls my name, snapping me out of my lustful daydream. "Choose your key."

Well, here goes nothing. I step forward and plunge my hand into the bowl of brass keys. There are only a few left and I swirl them around, enjoying the feel of cold metal against my skin before picking one out.

"Room Five," W announces after checking the disc hanging from the key.

I search for Lucas and blow him a kiss before making my way towards the house, my heart pounding.

The villa is dimly lit and filled with a light floral scent. A staff member directs me to wait briefly before I'm escorted down the hall to Room Five. As we walk, my imagination runs wild once more. I picture firm hands gripping my waist, rough fingers sliding into my wet cunt, and thick cocks pushing into all my holes. I'm so ready to get fucked.

I finally reach my room and open the door. I'm ready to embrace my slutty side and get plowed by a bunch of men.

CHAPTER 5

The room is empty, and I'm momentarily disappointed despite being told the men would come in after me. I was hoping to be greeted by naked men stretched out on the bed and stroking themselves like Trey was last weekend.

The room is just as luxurious as the rest of the house, and decorated with light colors and modern furniture. There's a dresser across the room from the bed and I study the camera sitting on top. Lucas said he was going to watch me get fucked, and I blow a kiss at it in case he can see this already. I have no idea how this works for the husbands, and I don't care as long as I get a cock inside me soon.

My stomach muscles tighten the longer I wait, and I fiddle with the tie of my wrap dress. Should I be naked when the guy comes in? It might be more than one guy since Lucas said multiple men, but I don't think he actually knows for sure what's going to happen.

Knowing that Lucas will see everything that happens is erotic as all fuck. I want to bring out his beast and make him lose control with me later, so I need to put on a good show. Hell, I might as well start now.

Sitting on the bed, I lean over and run my hands down my legs. If someone is watching on the camera, they are getting a terrific view of my cleavage. I caress my legs and slowly unbuckle the straps of my sandals. Lucas loves how tiny my feet are, so I caress my hands over the tops of them and point my toes towards the camera to give him a glimpse of my pretty pink polish. He didn't have time to admire the color after my pedicure earlier today.

My heart rate increases when the door opens. Oooh, it's showtime!

Two guys walk in and Ms. Kitty buzzes and practically does a happy dance. I don't recognize the guys, but that doesn't matter. One is blonde, and the other is dark-haired. They're both wearing swim shorts, which makes for easy access to their cocks. I swallow a pool of saliva as I check out their defined abs and thick thighs. Yeah, this is going to be fun. It's a double stuffing tonight for me!

Wait, why didn't they close the door? I'm about to question them when a third guy walks in. It's the bad boy from earlier who kept catching my eye. Oh, fuck yes!

My pussy clenches and I feel wetness leaking onto my already damp panties. I give a broad smile to the third guy as he shuts the door. Looks like I'm getting mega stuffed tonight.

"Hey, I'm Alex." His voice is deep, and there is a hint of humor when he says, "Are you ready to be fucked hard, Jessica?"

A tremor runs through me at his words. He knows my name. This is turning out better than I expected. I cast a fleeting thought to Lucas, hoping he's watching this. He's going to laugh when he finds out one of the guys I'm fucking is the hottie from earlier—wait, unless he already knows.

The room is silent. Oh shit, they're waiting for me to respond. I bite my lip and nod. My voice shakes with anticipation. "Absolutely."

"Good," Alex grins wickedly, and I notice the other two men in the room smiling at me as well. They don't introduce themselves, but their lustful gazes make it clear they're just as excited as I am.

"Let's not waste any time then." Alex takes control and the other two guys seem to be fine with him directing everything. It's possible this was planned. I'll probably never know.

Alex looks me up and down. His eyes blaze with desire, and his deep voice is seductive. "I want you to give us a slow striptease. Show us what you've got."

My body feels like it's full of electricity as I rise from the bed gracefully. I pull on the tie of my wrap dress, letting it slip from my shoulders and pool on the floor. It's arousing to be removing my clothes in front of three men I don't know, and I revel in the sluttiness as three sets of eyes watch my every move.

When I unclasp my bra in the back, the straps slip slowly down my arms. I draw it out, making them wait to see my breasts in all their glory. The bra joins my dress on the floor, and I stand with my shoulders straight, letting them admire my tits. Yeah, I'm proud of my breasts and I enjoy showing them off. The hunger in the blonde guy's eyes makes my pussy tingle, and the dark-haired guy actually licks his lips.

The only thing left is my panties—if you could even really call the wisp of fabric that. I slide my hands down my hips and teasingly slip my finger beneath the fabric and pretend I'm going to peel them down, but I don't. With an inviting smile, I turn a circle so they can admire the curve of my backside.

Alex told me to go slow, so he asked for this. Bending over the bed, I feel my panties stretch over my ass and I wiggle my butt at them to tantalize them and Lucas. As I look over my shoulder, I focus on Alex. He's got gorgeous green eyes, and they're sparkling, so I can tell he's amused.

I keep my panties on and sway my hips as I watch Alex undress. Since the other two guys are wearing shorts, they only need to pull them down to be naked. Alex doesn't seem to be in any rush, and he's making me wait. The longer he takes, the more heat radiates from me, and I feel a pulse between my legs. Shit, I want this guy more than I've wanted anyone in a long time.

Alex removes his shirt and I can finally see his chest. He's lean and muscular, with broad shoulders that taper into a narrow waist. His skin is smooth and tanned, and I admire the full sleeve tattoos on both arms. His muscles flex as I imagine what it would feel like to have those powerful arms wrapped around me.

I'm barely paying attention to the other two guys, but when I glance at them, their eyes rake over every inch of my body hungrily. I jiggle my ass again, just for their benefit.

Alex removes his boots and undoes his pants. He lets them fall to the floor, standing in just a pair of boxer briefs that cling to his hips tantalizingly. Yeah, this guy presses all my buttons. I'm ready to do whatever he wants tonight.

He takes a step towards me and reaches out with one hand to caress my ass cheek lightly. His touch is electric and I gasp as he runs his fingers over the silk covering my pussy. Alex grins at me before removing his boxers to expose himself completely.

Ohhh, hell yes. There's the gigantic cock I was hoping for. His erection juts out, begging for attention. I almost ask if I can suck on him, but with one swift motion, he rips my panties off of me. Oh fuck. My entire body lights up and I moan as he drops the ruined scrap to the floor.

"Those were in my way," he jokes, and I give him a breathy, "They were."

Alex steps behind me and rubs his cock along my ass, tickling me but not getting close to my pussy. Shit, this is what I get for being a tease. Now it's his turn to torture me.

I give a brief thought to Lucas and almost giggle. I hope he enjoys seeing Alex's ass. From this position, the camera view will be this guy's backside as he's flexing and plowing me. Maybe it will make my dear husband reconsider being in the room more often.

Alex wraps my hair around his hand and pulls my head back so our eyes meet. His gaze is intense and passionate.

"Beg us to fuck you," he demands.

My mind blanks before I manage to form the word "Please." His grip tightens slightly as he waits for me to say more. My head is fuzzy from desire and I can't think. Jesus, this is so hot.

Finally, I'm able to moan out, "Fuck me, please. Fuck me hard."

Alex releases my hair and smiles at me before lifting me onto the bed as if I weigh nothing. He moves to one side. "Come over here and get on your hands and knees."

Why didn't he just fuck me here? Oh wait, this gives my husband a better view. If Alex is doing this on purpose, it's considerate of him.

I eagerly crawl over to the edge and position my ass towards Alex. He takes a firm hold of my hip with one hand and rubs the tip of his cock up and down my wet slit, not pressing in. I'm going crazy. I've been waiting all night for someone's cock inside me. He needs to shove it in and fuck me.

"Please," I moan. "Fuck me hard."

He doesn't give me what I want, and instead chuckles. "Are you sure you want it?"

He nudges the head of his cock against my entrance and I mewl out, "Yes!"

"I think you need to beg better than that."

Everything he says has an undertone of laughter. He's obviously enjoying me being a needy slut. "Please, fuck me," I plead. "I need to feel your cock inside me. I'll do anything you want. Just fuck me!"

"Mmmm, you do beg nicely, just like your husband said."

What? Oh fuck. Lucas did plan this. Alex eases inside me halfway, and I groan as his thick cock stretches me out. God, yes. This is exactly what I've needed all night. He pauses and doesn't push in all the way.

"Please," I moan. I'm about to beg and offer up any hole he wants to fuck when he plunges in all the way. I cry out and almost collapse forward, but his tight grasp of my hips keeps me right where he wants as he pounds into me.

He growls, "God, you're tight." His balls slap against my clit with each thrust, and it sends a shiver of pleasure through my body. I feel myself climbing higher and higher. I can tell Alex is enjoying the hell out of this, too. He's being vocal with each thrust, and the hands on my hips are gripping hard enough to leave a mark.

I hear a muffled noise and see the other two guys standing on the other side of the bed. They both are naked and stroking themselves while watching Alex fuck me. It makes my pussy tighten around Alex's cock even more.

"So here's how it's going to work," Alex huffs out as he whacks against me. "I'm going to fill you with my cum, and then these two guys are going to do whatever they want with you before I have another go at this sweet pussy of yours."

Oh god, I love it when a guy makes me feel like he is using me. Did Lucas tell him that, too?

Alex spanks me, and I cry out from the unexpected painful pleasure. "But first," he says, as he continues to drill into me, "you're going to come all over my cock like a good girl."

Calling me a good girl pings something in my brain, and I want to please him. I push back into him, trying to get his thick cock in as far as it will go while I watch the two guys stroking themselves. This is filthy and I love it.

Alex grabs my hair and tugs my head back. "God, you are a little slut. Do you like watching those two jerking off to me fucking you?"

It's almost like he's reading my mind. "Yes," I cry, as he lets go of my hair and holds on to my hips again. Alex continues to slam against me over and over, and I can feel my orgasm building. My legs quiver and my inner muscles contract as I close my eyes and welcome the bliss.

I come hard, screaming out and collapsing onto the bed. Alex follows me down and puts his hands on the mattress as he continues to fuck me. The aftershocks ripple through my body as I convulse under him. He growls out a loud, "Fuck," as his hot cum fills me.

He spasms a few times, unloading everything he's got before pulling out. I peek up and the other two guys are still jerking off. Their eyes are glazed, and if they don't stop soon, they won't last long once they're inside me.

"Good girl," Alex says as he smacks my ass lightly.

I yelp in surprise and then giggle. His cum leaks out of me, and Ms. Kitty throbs. I'm definitely going to need to take a shower when this is over.

"Have at her," Alex tells the other guys as he gets off the bed.

The dark-haired guy switches sides, and I roll over so I'm flat on my back. I want to see both guys at once. The blonde guy sits down at the head of the bed, and the dark-haired guy crawls between my legs.

"So beautiful," the dark-haired guy murmurs as he rubs my bare, wet pussy. "Did you enjoy what Alex did?"

I smile at him. "Yes."

He plays with me with both hands. One finger circling my clit while he finger fucks me with the other hand. I'm still sensitive from my orgasm, but I'm quickly getting turned on again.

The guy continues to stroke his fingers in and out of my pussy while the blonde guy moves closer to me, leans over, and kisses me passionately. His tongue swirls around mine and I moan. The dark-haired man pushes my legs up, and I bend my knees so he can spread me wide open.

His tongue circles my clit, and I cry out in pleasure. Oh shit, I didn't expect him to go down on me after Alex just filled me with cum. This is raunchy and marvelous. He keeps up the rhythm of his tongue until I'm writhing beneath him. I'm moaning and panting, and he pushes two fingers inside me. My entire body tenses. I'm about to come again. The blonde guy stops kissing me, and I turn to look at the camera across the room. I want Lucas to see how much of a slut he married.

"Fuck me," I beg. "I need your cock."

The dark-haired guy stands up, and I keep my face turned so Lucas can see my expression as the guy sinks into me. My face contorts with pleasure from how glorious his cock feels.

"Oh fuck, you *are* tight," he groans as he gives a few thrusts.

My eyelids flutter from the pleasure, and I imagine Lucas smiling as he watches. I moan and throw my head back. This is fucking awesome. The blonde guy kisses me again, and I get lost in the sensation of his tongue twisting with mine as the other guy fucks me steadily.

We rock together in harmony for several minutes. The only sound is our mingled moans and the squeak of the bed frame. The blonde man kisses my neck before sucking on my earlobe. "You like this, don't you?"

I gasp, "Yes, so much."

He smiles and reaches between my legs to rub my clit as the dark-haired guy picks up his pace. He coos in my ear. "Good girl. I bet you're going to come soon."

His fingers on my clit almost guarantee that, and I'm quickly careening towards ecstasy again. The dark-haired guy's thrusts become more erratic as I feel myself getting closer and closer. He groans and his body tenses as he spurts his cum inside me.

The blonde guy takes over for him, using his fingers to rub my clit furiously. "Come for me," he murmurs into my ear.

I'm there in seconds and I scream out, "Yessss," as the orgasm rolls over me. My body floods with bliss, and I don't want this to end.

The blonde man keeps rubbing me until I quiver from overstimulation. He eases his fingers away from my pussy and plays with my breasts. I whimper as he squeezes my nipples, sending more pleasure coursing through me.

He leans over me and kisses me again, his tongue probing between my lips as he plays with my nipples. My head is swimming with lust when he finally stops. He smiles at me. "I bet your pussy is going to feel amazing. It's my turn now."

I'm a mess and too far gone from the pleasure to do anything but whisper, "Fuck me, please," as he switches sides and kneels on the bed between my knees. He puts one of my ankles on his shoulder, and I wrap the other leg around his waist as he presses into me.

His cock isn't super thick, but he's long and hits a delightful spot deep inside me. I cry out in pleasure as he fucks me slowly. My head spins as the rapture builds with each thrust.

He's being gentle, so when he starts talking dirty, I'm surprised.

"I'm going to fuck you like a dirty whore until I come inside you."

My pussy clenches at his words, and I moan out, "Yes, please."

He keeps his pace steady while I writhe with each stroke. I'm not sure I can take much more of this. The pleasure is overwhelming and I can't think. When he moves his hand down to play with my clit, I come undone. I scream as the orgasm crashes through me.

He continues to fuck me, and I lose all sense of time. My body shivers from aftershocks as he focuses on his pleasure. He groans when he unloads his hot cum deep inside me, mixing it with the other two loads of cum I've already taken.

The blonde man pulls out of me and shifts on the bed until his cock is at my mouth. I part my lips as he eases the tip between them. I suck and lick my wetness off of him, getting the final few drops of his cum. He sighs when he's done using my mouth and lies beside me on the bed.

I'm a total mess. I can't help but smile. This was one of the best experiences I've ever had.

The dark-haired guy gets off the bed, puts his shorts on and heads for the door. Before he leaves, he turns and says, "Good night, Jessica."

Once he's gone, I turn my attention to the blonde man lying beside me. "That was incredible," I sigh.

"Glad you enjoyed it." He kisses me passionately. Yeah, this guy is a kisser, and I like that.

I almost forget that Alex said he was going to use me again until he sits on the bed next to me. He rolls me onto my side, facing away from him, toward the blonde guy, and lifts my leg up so he can slide his cock into my pussy from behind.

My eyes widen as his thick cock stretches me out again. He's bigger than the other two guys, and he pings every nerve ending along my cave walls. The blonde man kisses me deeply again, and I moan into his mouth as Alex pounds into me from behind.

Alex groans with each thrust, and I know he's going to come again quickly. The blonde guy stops kissing me and sucks on a nipple. I moan in pleasure as his mouth latches onto me.

Alex picks up his pace, and my body quickly responds to the delicious sensations. I didn't know if I'd be able to come again, but each pull of the guy's mouth on my nipple causes a ripple of pleasure in my pussy as Alex fucks me.

I'm chanting, "Fuck me," as I spiral higher and higher. My moans turn into a wail as the orgasm overtakes me. My pussy squeezes Alex's cock and he groans as he explodes. He keeps moving, fucking his cum back into me as he spasms with the last of his orgasm.

Alex withdraws, and I'm a quivering mess. I'm sticky with sweat and cum, and I couldn't be happier. The blonde guy moves away and I hear the door open and close. I'm too limp from pleasure to do anything but lie there.

Alex gets up, and a few seconds later, he hands me a bottle of water. "Drink this."

He already loosened the cap, so I'm able to take a long swig of it. My brain is too fuzzy to question where he got it from. He watches me take a few sips, and I can tell he's satisfied with how much I drank when I put the cap back on it.

I finally get the energy to push myself up on my elbows. "Wow. I don't even have words. That was wonderful."

"It was," he replies with a crooked smile. "Thank you for the fun night, Jessica."

I'm exhausted but exhilarated. I hope Lucas could see most of that. Rolling over, I watch Alex get dressed.

He smiles at me when he's fully clothed. "Have a good night. Your husband will be here in a minute."

I grin at him and give him a soft, "Bye," before closing my eyes and drifting in my bubble of happiness.

CHAPTER 6

I peek at the door when I hear it open again. Lucas enters the room, his eyes taking in my fucked-out state. I suddenly feel exposed and vulnerable.

"Lucas," I breathe, relief flooding through me at the sight of my husband.

"Hey there." He leans down and brushes his lips against mine. It's a stark contrast to the rough treatment I just received, and it makes my heart swell.

My voice is barely above a whisper. "Are you going to fuck me too?"

He chuckles, shaking his head. "Not yet, baby. Let's get some food and water in you first, and get back to the hotel."

The warmth and care in his words bring tears to my eyes. He helps me dress, his touch loving, and together we leave the villa and climb into the limo waiting outside.

"Here, drink some water." Lucas hands me a bottle. I'm curled up against him in the limo, still fuzzy from the multiple orgasms. My body is tingling and my mind is hazy as I take small sips of the cool liquid. He watches me with concern and affection in his eyes.

"Have some nuts too." He offers me a small bag and I nibble on them absentmindedly. He wraps his arm around me, and I rest my head on his shoulder, feeling content and safe in his embrace.

I nuzzle his neck. "Thank you."

Lucas kisses the top of my head, and I sigh happily. He's always so attentive after we've indulged in our wild fantasies together.

The limo comes to a stop outside our hotel, and Lucas helps me out, steadying me as I find my footing. My legs are still shaky from the night's activities, and I'm grateful for his support.

When we enter our hotel room, he leads me into the bathroom. He turns on the shower before helping me undress. As each inch of skin is revealed, he kisses my bare flesh and I shiver with delight. I feel treasured and loved.

"Your tits are so beautiful," he murmurs against my nipple as he sucks on one. I moan while Ms. Kitty throbs with need again. I've had a lot of men inside me tonight, but I still need the one man who matters the most.

"Let's get you cleaned up, baby."

He takes his clothes off and helps me into the shower. As the hot water cascades over us, Lucas takes his time washing my body, his touch making me needier. I really am lucky to be married to him. He enjoys me fucking other men, and then he thrills me even more afterwards.

His hands roam over my body, cupping my breasts and teasing my nipples into stiff peaks. I desperately need him to fuck me and tell me he loves me. When his hands cup my ass, I rub my soapy breasts against his chest to tempt him, and purr, "Fuck me, please. I need you."

I can tell my words flip a switch inside him. His hands become harder and more punishing as he kneads my ass.

"You're such a filthy little slut," Lucas growls in my ear. "But you're all mine, aren't you?"

He reaches between my legs, sliding his fingers along my slick folds, making me moan. I tremble with desire. "Always yours. Please, fuck me. I need you."

He pushes me against the shower wall and lifts me up. I wrap my legs around him as the head of his cock teases my entrance.

"Tell me how much you want me to fill you up," he demands as he reaches one hand between us and rubs my swollen clit.

My breath hitches, the sensation almost too much to bear. "God, I want it so bad. Fuck me, please."

He hums with pleasure as he slowly sinks into me. I gasp, my eyes rolling back in sheer bliss as I feel every inch of his cock. It's an exquisite torture, the way he takes his time, inch by agonizing inch. But knowing that he's enjoying every second of my desperation only makes me crave him more.

"Fuck, you're so wet," he groans as he bottoms out. I want to joke with him that we are in the shower, after all, but my head spins too much to form the words.

He's gentle at first, his strokes long and steady, but he gradually picks up the pace. Each thrust sends waves of pleasure coursing through me, and I can feel my climax building within moments.

"Harder, Lucas," I moan, clawing at his shoulders for support.

"Mine," he breathes into my ear as he fucks me harder. I'm gasping and moaning loudly, but the shower hides a lot of our noise. My leg muscles quiver and I close my eyes and let the pleasure overtake me.

I cry out that I'm coming as my orgasm crashes over me in a tidal wave of ecstasy. As my body convulses around him, I can feel him stiffen a moment before he comes with a final powerful thrust. He groans as he pushes deep, filling me with warmth. We cling to each other as the water beats down on us, panting and spent for a few moments.

When he pulls out of me and helps me find my footing, I giggle at how crazy tonight has been. He gives me a deep kiss and murmurs, "My filthy slut," before we help clean each other up. Afterward, Lucas carefully helps me out of the shower, drying me off with a fluffy towel.

Our arms wrapped around each other, we make our way to the bed, murmuring words of love and adoration. I snuggle against him, feeling his heartbeat steady as a wave of exhaustion hits me. Just before I drift off, I realize I haven't thought about Zane since the moment I saw Alex enter the room earlier. Guess I didn't need to fuck Zane that badly after all.

CHAPTER 7

When I wake up the next morning, I stretch languidly and try not to disturb Lucas, since he's sacked out on his stomach next to me with his leg hooked around mine. I'm feeling the delicious ache of last night's fuck fest in every muscle, and my pussy is already wet. I wonder if I can lure Lucas to stay in bed for a day of lazy sex.

A knock at the door breaks the peaceful quiet. Lucas untangles himself from our embrace and quickly puts on a robe before answering it. Ugh, who would come to our room this early?

"Room service," Lucas announces, pushing a cart laden with steaming plates into the room. The aroma of bacon and fresh coffee fills my nostrils, making my stomach grumble. Okay, so I approve of this interruption. I'll eat and then drag Lucas back to bed.

I slip out of bed, grabbing my robe from the chair. "Everything smells delicious. Did you order this?"

I tie the sash around my waist and take a seat at the small table near the window.

"Yep. I figured you'd need your strength this morning."

I hold in my snort. Little does he know I was ready to fuck him before breakfast. My strength is back already, and Ms. Kitty is ready for more action.

As we dig into our breakfast, we keep smiling at each other between bites. I'm practically floating from happiness this morning. I'm going to remember the key party for years to come.

Lucas's eyes sparkle with mischief. "Last night was incredible, but I have another surprise for you."

I'm curious what else he could have planned. I'm ready to fuck him silly, get another massage, and relax for a few more days before going home. "Oh, yeah. What is it?"

"Zane is waiting for us in his hotel room."

What's this? My mind blanks and I pause with a piece of bacon halfway to my mouth.

When I'm silent, he continues. "If you want, you can fuck him while I watch."

My heart skips a beat, and Ms. Kitty pulses involuntarily at the thought of Zane's hard cock inside me.

I repeat what he said, as if my brain needs to process this fully. "You want to watch me with Zane?"

The thought of fucking Zane while Lucas is in the room sends a thrill down my spine, and my nipples harden.

He grins and takes a bite of egg, chewing thoroughly before he continues. "Yep. I want to see how slutty you get with him."

A ripple of heat runs through me, and I fight the urge to wiggle in my chair to ease the growing ache between my legs. Oh, I can be the biggest slut in the world if he wants me to. I give him a coy smile to temper my eagerness. "I'm interested."

We finish our breakfast quickly, and I adjust the robe to cover as much of myself as possible. Lucas puts sweatpants on under his robe, and as we step out into the hallway, I hope no one comes this way. I don't need other people wondering why a man and woman, both in robes, are visiting the room next to theirs. Though who am I kidding? I'd probably love it if someone saw us and thought I was a slut visiting some dude's room to fuck two guys at once.

My heart races with a mix of excitement and nervousness. It's going to be odd to have Lucas in the room with Zane, but I can feel how wet I am, so I know I want it.

Lucas knocks on the door. "I hope he makes you scream."

My brain blips out right as Zane opens the door in nothing but a towel wrapped around his waist. My breath catches in my throat as I take in the sight of him—muscles taut, water droplets glistening on his skin from his recent shower. Oooh, I could lick him all over. This is my chance to fuck Zane and I'm taking it.

"Damn, Zane," Lucas jokes, "you're already half-naked and ready to go."

"Only for Jessica," Zane replies with a laugh and steps aside to let us in.

Lucas gestures towards a chair near the bed. "I'll be right here."

He sits down, looking completely at ease despite the situation.

Zane turns to me, his eyes searching mine. His voice is low and serious. "Are you sure you want this, Jessica?"

It's nice he's double checking, but he needs to know I'm 100 percent on board. "Oh yeah, bring it on,"

Ms. Kitty throbs at the thought of his cock sliding inside me. This trip can't possibly get any better than this. Lucas went all out for me.

His expression turns hard, like a mask drops over his features. "Okay. If you want to stop at any point, just say 'red,' and I'll stop immediately."

"Red," I echo to show I understand, and my pussy hums at the change in him. I'm finally going to get to fuck him.

Zane hauls me against him and he lifts me up effortlessly as I wrap my legs around his waist. Oooh, this is starting out nice. Our lips meet in a feverish kiss that leaves me breathless as his tongue caresses mine. I can feel his hardness through the towel and I try to rub against it.

He carries me over to the bed and drops me onto the mattress. I lie on my back as his towel falls away to reveal his hard cock, and moan, "god, Zane..."

It's been years since I saw his cock and it's as thick as I remember, with veins bulging along its length. An intense wave of desire washes over me. Shit, I'd do anything to feel that magnificent cock buried deep inside me.

He climbs onto the bed between my legs and grabs my ankles, lifting them towards the ceiling as he leans down to kiss me. His firm hands run down my legs, caressing my thighs, as he nips at my mouth.

He teases my lips before giving me another deep kiss. I moan, and my body trembles as my core aches for his cock.

When he sits back on his heels with my ankles on his shoulders, he runs his fingers along the edge of my robe. He looks at me with lust, and I try to wiggle closer to him, hoping he'll slide inside me. I'm not sure if this is going to be a soft and slow fuck, or a hard and fast one. Based on what I know about him, I'm hoping it's hard.

He unties my robe, and it falls open, exposing my breasts. He cups them in his hands, his thumbs rubbing over my nipples. "You have gorgeous tits," he murmurs as he massages them. I'm enraptured as his thumbs roll my nipples into hard peaks.

Zane shifts slightly, and the head of his cock slides against my wet slit. I moan as he teases me with his hardness.

I'm desperate for him to fill me up and I buck my hips. "Fuck me. Feel how wet I am for you?"

I look over at Lucas. He's keeping his eyes glued to my body. Lucas's robe is open, and I can see the outline of his hard cock against the fabric of his sweatpants. I want him to take it out and stroke while Zane fucks me, but knowing my husband, he'll just fondle himself through his pants.

"Yes," Zane growls, leaning over to kiss me fiercely as he finally slides his cock inside me. His girth makes me gasp. I'm still a little sore from last night, but it's a delicious pain and makes me crave more roughness.

Zane holds steady while I adjust around his size, and as soon as I wiggle my hips to show I want more, he pulls out and slams back into me.

"Oooh, fuck!" I cry out as my inner walls stretch with each thrust. I close my eyes and arch my back, offering more of myself to him.

"So damn tight," Zane murmurs as he pounds into me. I can hear the bed squeak with each hard thrust. The sound sends shivers through me and I claw at the bedding, unable to do anything but lie there while he fucks me hard.

I don't know how long this will go on, but I'm loving every minute. He grabs my hips and guides me with each thrust. It's so raw and primal and it's everything I hoped it would be.

"You're so fucking hot." He plows into me and I'm moaning with each thrust, unable to form words as the pleasure builds. My muscles tighten as I'm swept away on a wave of ecstasy.

I cry out, "I'm coming!" as I explode. My body convulses around him, my thighs quiver, but I can't catch my breath.

He fucks me through my orgasm before pulling out. I'm fuzzy and confused until he flips me over.

"Get on your hands and knees," he commands.

Ohhh, yes. I eagerly do what he wants.

He sinks his cock into me from behind. "You're going to take everything I give you."

"Yes!" I moan, rocking back into him. He reaches around to rub my clit in circles as he fucks me, sending shockwaves of pleasure through my body. He's fucking me so hard my tits are bouncing with each thrust.

Is Lucas enjoying this? I glance at him, and his cock is out while he's stroking it. Oh hell yes, I was thinking he'd keep it in his pants and just rub himself through the fabric, but this is better. I keep my eyes on Lucas's hand running up and down his length as Zane picks up his pace, thrusting deep into me. I can feel the familiar tingle of a second orgasm building.

He slams into me harder than before. "Jesus, Jess. You feel so fucking good."

"More," I moan, my body craving the intensity. He obliges, pounding me mercilessly as layers upon layers of pressure build. My breath is a ragged sigh as my body goes rigid. When I finally come apart, my pussy seizes around his cock in a soul-shaking orgasm I wasn't expecting. I scream his name as energy ripples through my body.

"Again," I gasp, barely able to catch my breath before Zane's relentless thrusts drive me over the edge once more. I quiver around him, blissed out and lost in the pleasure of my third orgasm as he comes with a roar. He whacks against my pussy, filling me with his hot cum as he continues to thrust into me, unloading every last drop.

My voice is harsh from moaning, and I collapse onto the bed when he pulls out of me. I feel empty, but the satisfaction of being used by Zane is more than I expected.

"You're a fucking goddess," Zane pants, crawling up the bed to lie beside me. His arm snakes around me and he tugs me against him. He kisses my cheek, and I'm surprised by the softness of his touch.

My vision is blurry from pleasure, and I try to focus on him. "Did you enjoy it?"

He smiles. "Yeah, that was amazing. Five-star rating from me."

I give him a dopey grin as he sits up. He directs his attention towards Lucas. "How about you, man? Did you enjoy the show?"

"Oh yeah," Lucas says, rising from his chair and strolling over to the bed. He kneels down and takes his cock out of his pants. He wraps his hand around his shaft and strokes it above my face. "I've never seen anything so fucking hot in my life."

Zane chuckles. "Mmm, that's good. I think Jessica needs to taste you."

My pussy throbs at the thought of Zane watching me suck on my husband, and I feel Zane's cum leaking out of me. Oh god, I want this. I look up at Lucas. "Yes, please,"

Lucas leans over me and kisses me.

"Do you want me to fuck your slutty wife again while she sucks on you?" Zane asks.

Lucas grins at Zane. "Let's do it."

I love the way these two are talking to each other about using me. Lucas kneels on the mattress and angles his cock towards my mouth. I open wide as he slides in, my tongue swirling around the head as he thrusts into my throat. I look up at Lucas's face whenever he pulls out of my mouth.

Zane positions himself between my legs again and I moan around Lucas's cock as Zane slams home. Everything I heard about Zane is true. He's a fucking god in the bedroom.

Wrapping my legs around Zane, I lean up on my elbows so that Lucas can fuck my throat deeper. I'm feeling gloriously used as I careen towards another orgasm. I don't even know how many I've had in the last two days, and my mind is hazy from so much pleasure.

Zane's cock stretches me out blissfully, and the room is filled with the wet sound of me slurping on Lucas's cock. Both men groan almost in unison and if I didn't have a cock deep in my throat, I would laugh. This is unbelievable. I wish I could make it last longer, but each thrust drives me closer and closer to the edge.

When another orgasm hits, I close my eyes and welcome the bliss. I explode in rapture as Zane drills into me, and I'm gasping around Lucas's cock as my entire body shakes from the strength of another orgasm. I cry out and my eyelids flutter as the orgasm recedes and then peaks again.

Lucas's breath is ragged as he warns, "Fuck, I'm going to come."

"Give it to me," I try to say, but it comes out garbled around his cock. Lucas groans right before he fills my mouth with his hot seed. I swallow every drop, savoring the taste of him.

As soon as Lucas is done, Zane growls as he climaxes. His eyes are closed as he whacks against my pussy several times before collapsing on the bed next to me again. Zane looks spent and I hold in a giggle. I don't know what he did last night, but I bet he's going to have some wild stories to tell his friends when he gets home.

"Thank you, Lucas," Zane says once he's caught his breath.

"You're welcome," Lucas replies, clearly pleased by our time with Zane.

Zane kisses my shoulder, and his voice is gentle. "Thank you, Jessica."

I smile at him. "Thank you for a spectacular morning."

I want to thank him for finally fucking me, but I still haven't talked to Lucas about what happened years ago with Zane.

Lucas helps me back to our hotel room, wrapping an arm around me as we stumble through the door. He eases me onto the bed and cuddles up beside me, our bodies pressed together.

"Are you ready to tell me about your history with Zane?" he whispers, his fingers tracing lazy patterns on my skin.

I give him an incredulous look. "You knew?"

Lucas smiles, a devilish gleam in his eyes. "I knew about it. Zane mentioned it when I offered him the chance to fuck you."

Huh, interesting. I snuggle against him and tell him the entire story. "After we graduated from high school, Zane was hurting because he liked Miri. She was with Joey by then and Zane knew he couldn't be with her."

"Did you comfort him?"

"We didn't have sex, but stuff happened." I admit, burying my face in his chest. "It was just one night. Nothing more."

I'm feeling vulnerable in the aftermath of our intense experience.

He lifts my chin so our eyes meet. "Hey, it doesn't change anything between us. I love you, and our adventures only bring us closer. What you did with other guys before me doesn't matter."

"Thank you," I whisper. "I love you too. More than anything."

He presses a kiss on my forehead. "I love how our lifestyle brings us closer, and I love seeing you let loose like that."

My cheeks burn with a mix of embarrassment and arousal. "Really? You enjoyed being there while Zane fucked me?"

He runs his hand down my body to rest on Ms. Kitty, still slick with Zane's cum. "Oh yeah, you were such a slut for him, and it turned me on more than I ever thought possible."

This vulgar side of Lucas needs to come out more often. I nuzzle against him. "Good, because I loved knowing you were there while I took his massive cock. Maybe you should watch more often..."

His fingers dip inside me briefly before he withdraws them, bringing them up to my lips. I eagerly suck my wetness off his fingers, moaning at the taste.

He gives a sexy growl. "Maybe, but only if you promise to keep being the insatiable little slut that you are."

"Deal," I whisper, sealing our pact with a passionate kiss. Even if he doesn't watch in the future, I love our lifestyle. I just need a few days of rest before he cooks up a new scheme. I want to spend the rest of this trip enjoying my wonderful husband and showing him how much I love him.

The End

Want more?

Join my newsletter and get a bundle of bonus erotic shorts of Jessica and Lucas exploring the hotwife lifestyle.

Find it at:

https://www.lacey-cross.net/jessica

GOING UP

A HOTWIFE STORY

PROLOGUE

The hotel check-in has a couple of people in line ahead of us, and my stomach flutters while I mentally run through the list of everything I brought to make sure our anniversary weekend at the swanky Oregon hotel is perfect: sexy dress — check; new skimpy bikini to drive my husband wild — check; special fertility lubrication that the doctor recommended we use — check.

Trent must have sensed my brain was running a mile a minute because he moves his luggage to his other hand and slides his palm into mine, giving me a gentle squeeze.

He leans over and murmurs in my ear, "Relax, Becky."

I can't stop my giggle when his breath tickles the sensitive hairs. "Yes, honey. I'll relax. I promise."

He's right, I need to stop worrying and enjoy our time together. I'm trying to not pin all my hopes on this weekend, but this is an important trip for us. We've been trying for a baby, and our anniversary this year is during my fertile time of the month...almost like it's fate. The dream is that we have a wonderful weekend and then find out in a few weeks that I'm pregnant.

Once we get to the counter, it doesn't take us long to get the keycards to our hotel room. It was a long drive, and I wouldn't mind stretching out for a while before we start our evening fun, whatever that is. We don't have a set plan this weekend, and the only goal is to rest up and enjoy each other.

And make a baby.

We're halfway to the elevator when Trent abruptly pauses. "Shit, I forgot the bag of snacks."

I stop pulling my wheeled suitcase and stand it upright. We always bring our own munchies to avoid the hotel minibar, but do we really need them right now? I really don't want to go back to the car.

"Why don't we get them later, after we settle in?"

Trent sighs. "No, I'd rather get them now. Go ahead to the room. I'll be just a minute."

Love for Trent spreads through me since he's going without me, and I know we're both tired from the trip. "Okay, honey. I'll see you up there."

He gives me a quick kiss on the cheek, and I watch him for a moment as he walks away. Dang, I really married a cutie, and he's so damn thoughtful.

Gripping the handle of the suitcase, I continue on to the elevator. If I'm lucky, I can get a couple of minutes on the bed before Trent gets back.

CHAPTER 1

I hit the button on the elevator, and the floor numbers tick down until the "1" lights up above the door. I'm still watching the numbers when the silver door opens.

I roll my suitcase into the opening but suddenly realize the elevator isn't empty. I look up and freeze while my brain blips out.

My lips part as I take in what is possibly the sexiest man I've ever encountered...one who looks exactly like the type of man that my younger self would have jumped into bed with and regretted. His clothes are fairly generic — blue jeans, a black t-shirt, and a leather jacket draped over his arm — but his bulging biceps and tattoos peeking out from under his shirt sleeves have my body singing.

His piercing blue eyes bore into mine, and heat floods my face. My mind still isn't working properly. What am I doing here?

The man takes a step back and moves over, as if he believes I'm hesitating because he's in my way, and the flush creeps all the way to the roots of my hair.

When I continue to stand there gawking at him, the corner of his mouth quirks up and his eyes sparkle. "Going up?"

His cool tone of voice doesn't match his facial expression, and my pussy throbs from the undercurrent of dominance in those two words. Holy fuck.

Coming back to my senses, I lurch forward and stagger but right myself before I fall flat on my face. "Um, yeah…going up."

I wheel my suitcase in, press the button for my floor, and stand next to Mr. Gorgeous as the elevator door closes. All the hairs on the side of my body closest to him stand at attention, and I swear I can feel warmth radiating from him. Wetness leaks into my panties, and I clench my thighs together.

Jesus, I need to calm the fuck down. I'm not the same person I was in college, but my body hasn't gotten the memo. There's been only one other person who I've ever responded to like this, and I'd rather not think of my asshole ex-boyfriend, Kurt, on my anniversary weekend. If he was even a boyfriend. We just fucked a lot…filthy, mind-blowing sex that I've tried to forget after all these years.

Why is this guy making me think of Kurt? I've been happily married to Trent for seven years now. I shouldn't be dripping wet for some rando in an elevator, and I definitely shouldn't be remembering Kurt's face above mine as I exploded around his cock multiple times in one night.

As the elevator ascends, the space inside feels smaller, as if the guy is sucking up all the oxygen. Don't look at the guy…don't look at the guy. I can't help myself and give him the side eye. Fuuuuuck, I want to skim my hands up those arms and check out what he's got under his shirt. If his arms are this buff, I bet he's got a six-pack.

His pose is relaxed, and he oozes self-confidence and serenity. I look at his face, and a jolt of lust heads straight to my pussy when I lock eyes with him. The blue depths harden with a speculative gleam as he scans the full length of my body. Oh shit, he's checking me out, as well. I guess it's only fair since he caught me doing the same thing.

I almost jump when the elevator dings that we've arrived at my floor, and I giggle nervously.

As I leave the elevator, his "Have a good night" is a deep rumble that stirs a longing inside me.

Since I'm probably never seeing this guy again, why not have some fun? Turning my head to look over my shoulder at him, I smile coyly and use my most seductive voice. "Oh, I always do."

His answering grin has me tingling all over as the door glides closed.

CHAPTER 2

My pulse is still thrumming as I let myself into our room, and I'm ready to jump Trent as soon as he walks in. The sexy stranger got me revved up, and I'm ready to start the weekend of baby-making. All traces of my desire to stretch out have faded, and I scan the room to figure out the best way to present myself for Trent, in the hopes he'll take the offering.

The room is elegant and the bed is tempting, but I don't want to risk falling asleep if he takes a while downstairs. There is a couch against the far wall that conveniently faces the door. Letting my luggage tip over onto the floor, I peel my clothes off as fast as I can. Everything gets tossed into a pile on the suitcase, and when I'm naked, I grab a fluffy towel from the bathroom and spread it out on the couch cushions before sitting down and opening my legs as wide as I can. If everything goes according to plan, this couch is about to get incredibly messy.

Leaning against the back of the couch, I cup my generous breasts and play with my nipples, imagining it's Trent's mouth creating the pleasurable sensation. My pussy needs attention too, so I slip a hand down between my slick folds, gathering moisture before focusing on my clit. Mmmm, now this is more like it.

Bliss builds in my core, and my soft moans fill the room. When I press a finger inside my pussy, I try to picture it's Trent making love to me, but the face of Mr. Gorgeous from the elevator shimmers behind my eyelids, and he's fucking me while Trent sucks on my nipple at the same time. Well, this is a hot fantasy. I push aside any doubts that I shouldn't be imagining another guy fucking me on my anniversary weekend and focus on the delight swirling in my body.

Mr. Gorgeous speeds up his fucking, and I work my pussy faster to match the naughty daydream. I arch my back and curl my toes against the carpet from an extra strong ping of pleasure. Fuuuck, if Trent doesn't get here soon, I'm going to come without him.

I'm so engrossed in playing with myself I don't notice Trent come in. The sound of bags hitting the floor alerts me to his presence, and I open my eyes and give him a saucy grin.

"Hey, you're just in time. Want to join me?"

He gives me a weary smile and starts unbuttoning his shirt as he strolls to the couch. "I expected to find you passed out on the bed by now. I thought you were tired."

Removing my finger from my pussy, I spread the moisture around my clit and enjoy watching Trent strip. "I was, but once I got up here, all I could think about was your cock."

Technically it was the handsome stranger's cock, but he doesn't need to know that part. He doesn't take his shirt off once it's unbuttoned, and his bare chest peeks out while he works on removing his pants and boxers. Yeah, Trent is far from having a six-pack, but he still turns me on after seven years together. Sure, a nice, sculpted body is fun to touch, but after all the bad boys I dated in college, finding a stable guy was exactly what I needed.

Once his pants and boxers are off, I beckon him over to me with the hand that was on my breast. "Come here, you. I'll help you relax, and we can start our vacation off with a bang."

He chuckles. "A bang, eh? I like the sound of that, but if you want all this sexiness, you're going to have to ride me."

I'm fairly certain it's his turn to be on top, but I don't remind him. No way in hell am I ruining my chance of getting his cock inside me, and he looks tired so he might say no otherwise. I stop playing with my clit and haul myself off the couch. My legs are wobbly from being so close to coming, and I take a moment to steady myself before moving to him and tugging on his neck to make him lean down for a deep kiss.

I pour all my pent-up desire into him and glide my hands along his chest as I devour his mouth. After so many years, we've lost a bit of the heat in the bedroom. Sex is fun, but more of a comfortable sameness after you've explored every part of the other person's body and you know exactly how to get them off. There are rarely any surprises anymore, and it's been a long time since I've wanted him this badly. I'm not sure what's gotten into me tonight, but I need it rough and hot. Breaking off the kiss, I push him onto the couch.

"Whoa!" Trent laughs as I climb on top.

Wasting no time, I grab his cock and guide him to the entrance of my wet pussy. One swift downward press, and I impale myself on his shaft. His groan mingles with mine as bliss ripples down to my toes. God, this is exactly what I needed, and with me on top, I'm going to take everything I want and not stop until I orgasm.

Grabbing his hands, I shove them against my tits as I ride his cock. I hold his shoulders as he plays with my nipples, and pleasure flickers through me with each downward stroke along his full length. I set a punishing pace and rotate my hips, rocking back and forth as the ecstasy builds.

"I want you so bad, honey," I whimper as I chase my orgasm.

His cock is average sized and isn't as big as a lot of my past boyfriends', but he's still able to reach that magical spot deep inside me. Sometimes I miss the fullness of a massive cock, but most of the time it doesn't matter. If Trent doesn't get me off with his cock, he knows how to work his tongue to finish the job.

My body is on fire, and I need to come so desperately that I'm focused only on my goal, and grind the base of his shaft. The room spins as I get closer and closer to the tipping point, and I slam into him so hard the couch creaks. I don't give a flying fuck if we break the couch, and if we do, I'll make Trent explain at checkout.

Trent grabs my hips, and my breasts bounce close to his face while he attempts to thrust up to meet me. I'm almost lost in a sexual haze, but I can tell by his moans that he's getting close to coming so I speed up. I need to beat him there.

"I'm going to come," he moans. "Fuck!"

Oh, no he doesn't. I ride him with wild abandon, not caring about anything but my need as the electricity builds in my core. Clasping his shoulders tightly, I slam down on him while he groans in what sounds like pain.

His cock throbs right before he comes, and the warmth of his seed spurs me on. I hammer against him, so close to my orgasm that I don't care when he grunts in pain. Shit, I might not come!

I close my eyes and picture that I'm riding Mr. Gorgeous with a gigantic cock. When Mr. Gorgeous flips me over and takes control in my fantasy, imagining his cock drilling into me shoots me over the edge. Crying out, I quiver around Trent's cock as waves of rapture wash over me. I slow down as the orgasm turns into soft tremors of bliss, and I mash my wet pussy against Trent's softening cock a few more times before finally stopping. I'm shaking uncontrollably from the intensity of my need, and my breath is ragged as I lean my forehead against his.

We're both addlebrained from the euphoria and stay silent. When my head clears, my chest tightens and I try to avoid thinking about how I orgasmed to the fantasy of another man. The wetness leaking out of me snaps me out of my stupor.

Fuck!

Scrambling off Trent, I beeline for the bed, lie on my back and raise my feet above my head. I'm sure Trent has a graphic view of my dripping pussy from his position on the couch. Oh well, we've been married long enough. He's seen it all at this point.

My doctor told me it's an old wives' tale that putting my feet up helps, but I'm so desperate to get pregnant, I'd try anything at this point. I better not have lost too much of his cum. I close my eyes and will his seed to make its way to my fertile womb. Please, God, make it happen this weekend.

Trent removes his shirt and stretches out on the bed next to me. "Wow, that was hot. You were right about starting with a bang!"

"Uh huh," I murmur as I continue to concentrate on willing his swimmers to get to their destination. Shit, I should have applied the special lubricant before he got to the room. We've been trying for a baby for over a year with no success, and we found out that Trent's sperm count is our problem. The doctors said we should still try because it might happen naturally, but they recommended we consider fertility treatment. I don't want the pain and expense of IVF treatment, but if I don't get pregnant this weekend, Trent and I are going to have a heart-to-heart about trying IVF.

My body tenses as I contemplate how uncomfortable the talk with Trent will be. He's been optimistic, and I don't want him to feel inadequate. Shit, I need to stop worrying about something that might never happen. The doctor says the more we stress about getting pregnant, the less likely it will happen.

I giggle when Trent strokes the side of my exposed ass. "What got into you tonight?"

"Maybe I just needed you," I joke.

He and I both know I'm not normally like this, but no way in hell am I telling him I got horny for another guy and took out my aggression on him.

He beams. "I knew you wanted all this sexiness. I'm so hot you can't keep your hands off me."

I snort. Yeah, I did all the heavy lifting, and all he did was lie there. He's soooo going to be on top next time so I don't risk losing any of his cum. He snuggles against me, and I lower my legs slowly and relax and roll onto my side so we can spoon.

Contentment spreads through me. I love Trent so much, and he makes me feel safe. The guy in the elevator would not be safe, and I dislike my body's response since it reminds me too much of my old boyfriend's hold over me. I put up with way too much for amazing sex back then, but I'm a different woman now. I'm not the naive girl in college who will spread her legs for any guy promising a thrill.

Trent nuzzles my neck. "Stop thinking so much, and relax."

Shit, he's right. I snuggle closer to him. "I'm relaxing, I swear."

His, "Mmm hmm," doesn't sound like he's convinced.

Wiggling my ass against him, I force myself to unwind.

"Stop that," he growls playfully when my ass brushes against his cock.

I give him my cutest, "Oops, sorry," before settling down.

We're both silent for a moment, and he yawns. "Did you want to go down to the restaurant for dinner?"

I'm drained, and his yawn triggers one from me. "Um, how about we nap first?"

His drowsy, "Sounds good," means he's already halfway there, so I close my eyes and snooze with him.

CHAPTER 3

The room is dark when I wake up, but a streetlight shining through a crack in the curtains illuminates Trent's shadowy form next to me. He's fast asleep with his head buried into the pillow. I should be nice and let him sleep so I get up as quietly as I can. I gingerly creep my way to the bathroom.

I'm almost there when my toe slams into my suitcase in the middle of the floor.

"Motherfucker!" I screech, and Trent jolts up.

"What happened?"

I didn't hit my toe hard enough to do any actual damage, but I'm a weakling and can't handle much pain. I limp back to the bed while Trent turns the lamp on.

"I stubbed my goddamn toe. I'll be fine," I gripe at him and flop on the bed.

He knows I always get pissed and cranky when I hurt myself, but the mood dissipates quickly.

He examines my toe. "Yeah, it looks fine. No broken skin."

The sting is already easing, and he plants a kiss on my knee. I smile as he nibbles his way up my thigh, and my pussy hums to life once more. Waking him up might not have been so bad. We can go for round two and then order room service.

My stomach growls loud enough that we can both hear it.

Trent sits up and stretches. "Why don't we take a quick shower and hit the restaurant downstairs for dinner?"

Wiggling my eyebrows suggestively at him, I try to convince him otherwise. "You sure you don't want to order room service?"

"Hah, get your lazy butt out of bed. I'm taking my wife out for a nice dinner."

He's relaxed and smiling as he razzes me. Yeah, this trip is good for us. We needed to get away from the daily monotony at home.

"Fine, but I'm taking the first shower because I take longer to get ready!"

Skirting around my suitcase, I make it safely to the bathroom and speed through my shower. I avoid getting my hair too wet since it's getting late and we need to hurry. I don't want to get all dolled up just to get downstairs and be told they stopped serving dinner.

When I come back out to the bedroom, Trent puts my suitcase up on the luggage rack for me, and I blow him a kiss. I bought a dress for this trip, and it's sexier than I normally wear, but I wanted this weekend to be special. I shimmy into the form-fitting red number, and it molds to my curves, accentuating my round breasts and ass. A bit of see-through lace at the bottom creates the illusion that the dress is shorter than it actually is. I exercise regularly and stay fit, but since I don't flaunt it often, I want to make sure he doesn't forget he has a desirable wife. Hopefully it will put him in the mood to ravish me.

I'm smoothing it down my hips when he comes out of the bathroom, and he stops in the doorway. His mouth drops open, and a tingle of lust zips through me at his reaction.

When he doesn't speak for a few moments, I don't want to admit that I'm beginning to feel embarrassed. Is the dress too short, after all? I shift my weight to my other foot and fiddle with the lace on the dress. "Cat got your tongue?"

He laughs at my quip. "No, you're gorgeous. I'm a lucky man."

Oh, that's more like it. Yeah, he likes it. I wiggle my ass at him with a sassy, "Yes, you are," and finish getting ready.

Either the dress befuddles his brain or he wants to treat me right, because once we leave the room, he becomes a perfect gentleman, holding my hand and opening doors for me. He's cleaned up nicely too, in his dress slacks and button-down shirt, and several people give us double-takes as we cross the hotel lobby.

Peeking out of the corner of my eye, I notice the older men are the ones staring the longest, and the admiration in their gaze boosts my self-confidence. By the time we get to the restaurant, I'm swaying my hips sensually and relishing all the attention. Shit, I should dress like this more often. I don't want to sleep with any of these guys, but knowing so many people find me attractive gets me wet. If this keeps up, my panties are going to be shot by the time we're finished with dinner. I didn't know I was going to get turned on by so much attention. Thank God I wore panties, otherwise my thighs would be a slick mess.

They are still serving dinner and as we wait to be seated, I scan the visible tables in the dining room. A guy facing me at one of the far tables makes me glance back at him. My brain freezes…wait, is that Kurt Brock? I shake my head. No, I'm being silly. That can't be Kurt. Narrowing my eyes, I study him closer. The guy is obviously rich. He's wearing a finely cut gray suit with a white shirt. His perfectly tousled blonde hair looks as if he recently walked off a movie set. But when he grins at his approaching server, I know without a doubt it's him. I would recognize that knowing smile from anywhere since it still occasionally haunts my dreams — or rather, my nightmares.

Adrenaline shoots through my veins, and my vision sharpens while I go on high alert. When Kurt scans the room in our direction, I quickly swivel to face Trent. I'm not sure if Kurt would remember me, but I'm not taking any chances.

I lean into Trent, give him a soft kiss, and use the sultry tone of voice I know he loves. "Honey, can we sit in the bar instead? I know you wanted to eat in the restaurant, but don't you think the men in the bar would appreciate this dress and think you're lucky?"

Trent had mentioned in the past that he likes other guys finding me hot because it strokes his ego to know I chose him. I'm banking on him wanting to see men drool over me.

He grins. "Oh, yeah...I've noticed people checking you out. Let's go give them some excitement."

Halle-fucking-lujah. I hook my arm with his as he leads me to the bar. It's not too busy, and we grab empty bar stools as the bartender comes over.

"What can I get you two?"

I open my mouth to order some wine, but Trent speaks first. "Do you serve food in the bar?"

"Sure do!" The bartender gives us menus and asks, "Do you want me to get you a drink while you decide?"

This time, I get my order in before Trent. "May I get a glass of sparkling rosé?"

Trent gives me the side eye while requesting a scotch and soda, and I can't decipher the look.

When the bartender leaves, Trent skims his hand up my thigh, leans over, and whispers in my ear, "You planning on getting tipsy and flirty?"

When he gently squeezes my thigh, a flush runs through me. Does he want me to get flirty?

I tease him a little, and give him my most seductive smile. "That depends. Who do you want me to flirt with?"

Trent sits up straighter and his, "Hmm," as he scans down the bar makes my pussy throb. Wait, does he think I was serious?

I playfully swat his arm. "Hey, look at me!"

"Yes?" His grin leads me to assume he really was joking.

I blow him a kiss. "Honey, I've only got eyes for you. You know that."

He practically twinkles, and I can tell he likes my response. "Damn straight, because I'm one sexy mofo."

I laugh as the bartender brings us our drinks. After he sets them down in front of us and leaves, I mimic Trent and slide my hand up his thigh, but this time moving up even higher until his quickly stiffening cock surges against me.

Giving his hardness a squeeze, I purr, "Now don't get all cocky on me."

The double entendre wasn't missed. "But I thought you liked it when I got cocky?"

I give his cock a firm tug before letting go. "Yeah, well…maybe."

Even in the dim lighting of the bar, I can see the blush creep up his face. I take a sip of my wine, pleased with myself. By the time I'm done with him, he's going to be begging to fuck me when we get back to the room.

The bartender comes by and we order fish and chips, and continue to joke around while we wait. I'm already on my second glass of wine when the food arrives. We dig in, and I let one of my high heels fall off so I can play footsie with Trent. When I wiggle my toes up the cuff of his pants, he grins at me.

"Behave, Becky."

I take another sip and giggle. "Oh yeah, or what?"

He munches a piece of fish before replying. "Or else I'll really get you to use that sexual energy on someone else and see if you can get them hot and bothered."

I'm tipsy enough to find the idea hilarious. Trent is such a big talker. No way is he going to have me flirt with someone, but I try to push his buttons anyway. "Oh yeah, my stud? Who would you choose?"

He tips his head towards the other end of the bar with no hesitation, as if he already had the person chosen. "See that guy in the leather jacket? Him."

I scan down the bar, and a thrill runs through me when my gaze locks onto the guy from the elevator. Ohhh, fuck. How did I not see him down there? I guess I really was only paying attention to Trent tonight.

The dude's eyes bore into mine, and I imagine I can see the steely blue even from this distance. He still looks like the bad boy of my youthful fantasies, and my pussy clenches in agreement. Oh yeah, we would both enjoy flirting with him.

The guy bobs his glass towards me, acknowledging that I noticed him. He's got a hungry look that makes me think he'd ravish me and give it to me as rough as I want. God, one night with him would be fucking incredible. He drains his drink, sets it on the bar, and slides off of his stool. Both Trent and I watch him head towards the exit, but before he leaves, he peers over at me and smiles suggestively.

The answering buzz from my pussy makes my mouth crack open as the nerve endings along my exposed skin hum. Holy fuck, if that's what he can do to me with a smile, what would he do to me if he touched me? I might combust.

I shoot a guilty look towards Trent, but the glazed passion in his eyes says he liked the subtle flirting.

Trent wipes his mouth with his napkin and puts it on his dirty plate. His voice is husky with need. "Becky, let's get out of here."

Ohhh, hell yes. I toss my napkin on the bar as well and slip my shoe back on while Trent makes sure the charges go to our room.

CHAPTER 4

Trent clutches my hand, practically pulling me along with him as he strides across the hotel lobby to the elevator. Jesus, this is awesome. What's got into him?

As soon as the elevator doors close, he presses me against the wall and grinds his hardness into my stomach and kisses my neck.

"Mmmm," I moan as wetness leaks from my pussy. I'm starting to think hot guys should smile at me more often.

"Tell me, Becky. Was that guy hot enough that you'd want to fuck him?"

Um, what? "Nooooo," I groan as he grasps one of my breasts and squeezes.

Trent hauls up my dress and shoves his hand between my thighs, fondling my pussy through my damp panties. Holy fuck! Anticipation floods through me and he bites at my neck.

"No? You sure? Your dripping pussy says otherwise."

This type of talk coming from anyone else but Trent would be a huge *Hell no*, but it's my loving, adorable husband. He's never said anything like this before…and it's so fucking hot.

I pant, "Trent–" and almost squeal as he rubs my pussy harder. "You know I only want you!"

He laughs. "Oh, I don't know about that. Do you think that guy has a massive cock?"

What is going on? I don't have a chance to answer because the elevator stops on our floor. Trent releases me, and I struggle to pull my dress down as the doors open. Oh thank God, no one is in the hallway. I totter after Trent as he speed-walks to our room.

Trent doesn't turn the lights on before dragging me to the bed, shoving me onto it. The streetlight still illuminates enough of the room that I can see that he's stripping. Hell yeah, I might be getting the rough fucking I've been craving. I kick my shoes off and scoot to the end of the bed, intending to get up and remove my dress.

Trent has his pants unbuckled, and when he realizes what I'm doing, he presses me back onto the bed and crawls over me. "Where do you think you're going?"

"I was going to take my dress off." Mmm, oh yeah, I need to bring this side of him out more often.

He laughs, harsher than I've ever heard from him, and yanks up the hem of the red fabric until it bunches at my waist. "No need, I can get what I want with it still on."

His eyes flash in the darkness with a hunger I've never seen before, and he fumbles with his pants to free his cock. He holds his shaft as he grazes the tip against my panty-covered pussy, and I squirm from neediness. Jesus, I'm going crazy without him inside me!

"Is this what you want, Becky?"

"Yes," I whimper, hoping he'll push my panties aside and slam into me.

"Then answer my question. Do you think that guy has a massive cock?"

Fuck, why is this so hot? I moan as Trent presses against the fabric right at my opening, stretching it and digging the tip into me just enough to drive me wild.

"Yes, he probably has a huge cock." I buck up against him, torturing myself as I cry out, "Now please fuck me!"

"Soon," he growls. "Get on your hands and knees."

Excitement zings through me. I love it when he fucks me from behind. He rolls to the side, and I scramble up on all fours. Heat climbs up my body and into my face as he rubs his cock against my panties. He toys with me by sliding a finger underneath the edge of the fabric to caress the sensitive skin, but doesn't move his fingers any further. I'm panting as a delicious ache between my legs consumes me.

"Do you want to fuck him?" he asks in a low voice.

A vision of the sexy stranger plowing into me has my heart racing. Why is he asking this? I'm not going to admit I want to fuck someone else. Instead of answering, I wiggle my ass at him, hoping he'll tear my panties off and pound into me.

His hand delivers a ringing slap to my ass, and I jerk from the pain. "Hey!"

"Answer me!" he demands, and I moan loudly when he spanks me again.

"Yes…okay? Is that what you want to hear?"

He groans in response and massages where he spanked me, shooting sparks through my body from the pleasure. When he inches his hand beneath my panties and slips between my wet folds, I moan louder and lower my head to the bed, opening myself up for him. He plunges a digit inside me, and I rock against him as spikes of bliss swirl in my core. Mmm, now this is more like it.

He finger fucks me for a moment, and I close my eyes, letting the rapture almost overtake me. Tension coils in my belly, and I press back, urging him to fuck me faster. When is he going to give me his cock?

"Becks?" His voice is intense and insistent.

Peeking over my shoulder, I'm startled by the raw hunger emanating from him. "Yes, Trent?"

"Would you let me watch you fuck him?"

Ohhh, he wants to imagine me fucking someone else? I can get into this fantasy. My pussy throbs, and I undulate against him as the ecstasy builds.

"Yes," I moan. "You can watch him pound his thick, meaty cock into me."

He moves his attention to my clit and caresses me gently. The change from the rough finger fucking to this softness confuses my body. Ripples of bliss start from my toes and travel up my legs, and my pussy pulses in response.

"Would you come harder for him than you would for me?"

"No!" Oh god, why is he asking me this stuff? Imagining Mr. Gorgeous fucking me seven ways to Sunday is hot as all fuck, but it's Trent I want, not some nameless dude from the elevator.

He moves from my clit and plunges into my pussy roughly and smacks my ass at the same time. I yelp from the unexpected pain.

"No, Becks? You don't think a massive cock is going to please you enough to make you come harder than you do when I fuck you?"

When he delivers several more ringing slaps, I'm half out of my mind from the dark thrill. I can't take it anymore, I need his cock.

"Please, fuck me," I beg. "Please?"

He works his fingers into my pussy again, and my body shudders at the invasion. "Becks, I need to hear you say it."

The rising tidal wave of bliss threatens to consume me, and I cry out, "Yes! He's fucking huge, and I'd come all over his cock all night long — stronger than I ever came for you!"

He wrenches on my panties, shredding them and exposing my pussy right before he slams his cock into me. I cry, "Yes, fuck yes," as he hammers against me.

He holds onto my hips and growls as he fucks me roughly. Pings of delight swirl inside me, and I lean on one arm so I can run a hand between my legs and reach my clit. Ohhh, god. As soon as my fingers brush against my bundle of nerves, I spasm and my pussy clenches around his cock. I'm going to come any second now, and it's going to be a good one.

I reach my orgasm right before he does, and I scream his name as his cock pulses, filling me with his warm cum. I ride the bliss as he shudders and slumps against me. We're both panting when he pulls out, and I collapse onto my stomach as he crawls up on the bed beside me.

"That was so good," he sighs as he flops next to me.

I dutifully roll over, lift my legs, and giggle at him. "I've never seen you like that before."

"Yeah," he snorts. "You know I like it when men check you out."

I hold in my smile. My dear husband's fantasy went beyond other guys checking me out, but I found it hot as well. I wonder if that's what he wanks to when he's alone? Did he just reveal a dirty little secret of his? Most people fantasize about stuff they'd never do in real life, and Trent is probably no different from anyone else.

I give him air kisses. "Well, don't worry. You're the only one I want to fuck."

I don't add that it was freaking hot to imagine Mr. Gorgeous fucking me. Trent's content, "Mmm hmm," gives me a warm glow of happiness as he rolls over. Within a few minutes, his deep breathing tells me he's asleep.

Lowering my legs, I sit up and remove my dress so I can join him. I spend some time focusing on his sperm and urging it to find my egg. It's dumb, but I hope with enough positive thinking it will really happen.

CHAPTER 5

We don't talk about his fantasy from the night before as we eat our room service breakfast. Since I was tipsy, everything after the bar is hazy and feels like a dream.

We're almost finished with breakfast when Trent clears his throat and speaks. "I want to ask you something."

I lick the last of my eggs from the tines of my fork. "Hmm?"

He's matter-of-fact when he continues. "Becks, if you don't get pregnant this weekend, would you consider using someone else as a stand-in for me instead of fertility treatment?"

I freeze with the fork midair, and my eyes widen. What is he saying?

He shifts in his chair, and his face reddens. "Don't look at me like I'm crazy. You know we can't really afford IVF."

"But…" I lay my fork down and turn my body to face him squarely. This is a serious conversation and not one I expected to be having this morning. "Honey, I thought we'd try IVF with your sperm."

He lowers his gaze to the table, toys with his utensils, and shrugs. "You know they said we should consider using a sperm bank. I'm okay with the baby not being mine genetically." He looks up at me and reaches over to squeeze my hand. "I wouldn't love our child any less."

My stomach tightens. I don't want to think about this…not now…not on our anniversary weekend. I'm not ready to give up hope. He might not believe in signs, but I still think there's a reason I'm fertile right now. I *have* to believe it.

Smiling tenderly at him, I bring his hand up to my mouth and kiss the back of it. "Trent…honey, if we don't get pregnant this weekend, I'll be open to the idea."

His shoulders relax at my words. Dang, he must have been concerned how I would respond. I need to get us back in a lighthearted mood.

I take a gulp of water and swallow before joking, "Next you'll be demanding to watch me fuck the stand-in."

His eyes smolder. "Oh yeah, I'll want to watch."

I think of Mr. Gorgeous fucking me in Trent's fantasy last night. I was feeling quite satisfied this morning, but my pussy zings alive again. Shit.

When a tingle ripples over my body, I try to hide how turned on he's making me, so I get up from the table. "Well, we'll see," I murmur and head into the bathroom.

I stand in front of the sink and stare at myself in the mirror. Could I really fuck someone else while Trent watched? I never in a million years would have considered anything like this, but after last night, the idea intrigues me. My pussy throbs, and I run my hand between my legs to rub my clit. I think about being on the hotel bed, spread out for Mr. Gorgeous while Trent watches from a chair. When I picture Trent stroking himself, a burst of longing makes me gasp. Oh, yeah, I think I could do it.

Since I don't want to come without my husband this weekend, I stop touching myself and prep for my shower. I have a new bikini, and I plan on wearing it at the pool today. Now if I could just stop thinking about fucking someone other than my husband.

When I leave the bathroom, Trent is already wearing his swimming shorts, and I toss a pair of huge sunglasses in my beach bag in case Kurt is lurking around the pool. He's probably slept with plenty of women in the last seven years, so I'm confident he won't recognize the older, curvier me unless we make eye contact.

We hold hands as we head to the lobby, and being close to Trent helps calm any apprehension that I'll run into Kurt. Nothing bad will happen to me if Trent is by my side. The plan is to take it easy this afternoon and possibly eat in the dining room restaurant tonight. I brought one more fancy dress for the trip, so maybe I can get Trent worked up again later and get another wild fucking. I half feared we wouldn't have a lot of sex this trip and we'd waste the chance to get pregnant, but Trent is rising to the occasion quite nicely.

The rest of the hotel is nice, sure, but the pictures I saw online of the hotel pool are what sold me on coming here. The ocean on the Oregon Coast is never warm, so the hotel built a gorgeous heated pool, with broad palms surrounding it and a beautiful waterfall at one end. A lazy river decorated with faux volcanic rock weaves around and connects to both ends. I could relax there all day. But the best thing about it is the cove. There's a secluded nook there that is perfect for canoodling in private.

As soon as we're in the water, I lead Trent into the cove and attack him, crushing my lips against his and wrapping my legs around his waist.

He pulls back from the kiss and laughs. "I see someone is still frisky from last night."

"Shut up and kiss me."

When he complies with my demand, I ravish his mouth while our tongues dance. I'm consumed with desire, but there's no way in hell I'm telling him it wasn't last night creating this inferno of need in my belly, it was our discussion this morning about him watching someone else knock me up. I grind against him, desperate for his cock, but we both freeze when we hear another couple laughing and heading towards us.

Unhooking my legs from his waist, I float next to him and by the time the couple enters the cove, we're innocently snuggling. They smile at us and we exchange hellos, but when it's obvious they're sticking around, Trent and I venture back out to frolic in the main pool area. Dangit, I wanted to slip his cock out of his shorts and have my way with him. Oh well, we have all day.

After swimming and lounging for a couple of hours, Trent wants to go back up to the room to rest. I send him on his merry way without me. I'm not leaving this pool until I need food. If I could live here, I would. This is almost my idea of heaven.

I camp out on a poolside lounge chair and get my e-reader out and scan through the erotica titles I've picked up. I'm in the mood to read something dirty where the woman fucks someone other than the hubby, but nothing I currently own fits my requirements. A quick internet search on my phone tells me I'm looking for hotwife erotica, and I'm not disappointed when I search for a book. I pick the first one that looks like it's a woman getting railed by some hot dude and settle back to enjoy the dirty story.

At one point I take a sip of water and notice Kurt on the other side of the pool. Oh fuck! My heart pounds as I dig in my bag, trying to seem casual so any frantic movement doesn't catch his eye. Once my oversized sunglasses are firmly on my face, I relax and bury my head in my e-book.

I get absorbed in the story again but occasionally check what Kurt is doing. He swims for a bit, but when he's done, he takes his towel and leaves. Oh thank God. What are the fucking chances he would be here? I don't even want to contemplate those types of odds. I thought of him and it's almost like I manifested him. The power of the mind right there.

When my stomach growls, I'm not ready to leave yet, so I eat a granola bar I brought with me and keep reading. When the staff fire up tiki torches around the pool, I check the clock on my phone. Jesus, how did it get so late?

I'm shoving my water bottle and e-reader into my beach bag when Mr. Gorgeous strolls by wearing only swimming trunks. He's lightly tanned and his narrow waist, well-defined chest, and broad shoulders make my mouth go dry. Reading erotica all afternoon about a woman fucking a guy while her husband watches, and then having this eye candy stroll right in front of me after all my dirty fantasies last night, is more than my body can take. My pussy clenches, and I squirm in my seat, wishing I was in Trent's lap so I could dry hump him.

My gaze lowers, and Mr. Gorgeous's shorts aren't tight enough to tell me too much, but whatever he's got in there looks to be fairly large.

Fuck, where is Trent? I would have pointed out the size of the guy's package to see how Trent would react. When I focus on Mr. Gorgeous's thick muscled thighs, my brain turns to mush as I imagine it's now me dry humping HIS leg and not Trent's.

My husband's voice calls over my shoulder. "Hey, Becky, there you are. Aren't you hungry yet?"

I tear my eyes off the real-life Adonis as my husband sits down in the chair next to me. I'm practically vibrating with need, and I know I'm glowing and dazed when I look at Trent.

He raises an eyebrow. "Wow, what's got you all worked up?"

I speak fast, stumbling over my words. "Oh, I was reading erotica all afternoon, and it got me thinking about you."

Mr. Gorgeous chooses that moment to dive into the pool, and when he surfaces, he's facing us, and Trent finally notices him.

"Uh huh, were you thinking *only* of me?"

He sounds amused so I know he isn't angry, and I use the opportunity to distract him. Getting out of my chair, I climb into his lap and sit with my ass snug against his growing hardness. Interesting...which part of this is turning him on?

I wiggle around, pretending to get comfortable as an excuse to rub against him.

Trent growls, "Behave, Becks. We're in public."

Maybe I can lure Trent into the cove again. "Do you want to take one last swim before we get ready for dinner?"

The pool is way less crowded now since people cleared out as it got closer to dinnertime--plus Mr. Gorgeous. I don't see him anywhere right now, so I'm not sure where he went.

"Hmm..." Trent pauses like he's debating. "I have a better idea."

"Oh?" As long as his 'better idea' gets his cock inside me, I don't care what it is.

"Becks, I want you to flirt with the guy from the bar. If you can get him to kiss you, I'll do anything you want after dinner."

Ohhh, do I still remember how to flirt well enough to get a guy to kiss me?

I push my bottom lip out. "I don't see where he went. That's not fair."

Trent holds onto my cheek and turns my head for a passionate kiss. Yearning swirls in my core, and I moan into his mouth while I contemplate dragging him to the hotel room and having my way with him. Why do I need to kiss Mr. Gorgeous when I can have my husband's cock instead?

When he pulls his mouth from mine, he smiles at me. "He's in the cove right now. You better hurry. I expect all the details."

Trent is fully erect now, and knowing he's turned on works me up even more. I'll have a little fun and get my reward. "Okay honey, one kiss and then I'm coming back to you. If I get to choose what we do, you better be prepared to eat me for dessert."

I stand up while he laughs, and a swift smack on my ass makes me squeal from the sharp pleasure. I toss his words back at him. "Hey! Behave. We're in public."

He only chuckles again as I lower myself into the warm water and swim towards the cove. Why am I doing this? Do I want to play this sort of sexual game? My breasts ache to be sucked, and my pussy desperately needs a cock. Who am I kidding? I'm 100 percent on board with this little game of Trent's.

Swimming into the cove, I bump into Mr. Gorgeous just as he's leaving.

He steadies me with his massive hands on my shoulders while I sputter, "Oh, sorry!"

His deep blue eyes twinkle at me as he lets me go. "No need to apologize. I ran into you."

My skin burns where he touched me, and I'm curious what magic those enormous paws of his could do if he was playing with my nipples. Sexual energy courses through me from being this close to him and reminds me of how I felt when I was a teenager. What is it about this guy that turns me on so much?

"Where's your husband?"

What's this? His eyes bore into mine, and I tremble from desire.

"He's… around." I practically stumble on my words. God, he's going to think I'm an idiot.

Mr. Gorgeous contemplates me for a moment and I want to squirm. "What?" I blurt out defensively.

"Did your husband send you in here?"

His voice is smooth as butter, and a thrill runs through me. How did he know?

I bite my lip before answering with a soft, "Yes."

"Why did your husband send you in here alone?"

Shit, I was supposed to come in here, flirt with him, and get him to kiss me, but I feel like he's playing cat and mouse with me. Fuck, it's time to take control of the situation.

The water only comes up to my waist and I stand as straight as I can. "I'm supposed to get you to kiss me so I can tell him about it."

His voice is low and seductive with a hint of humor. "Only kiss?"

I part my lips to tell him just one kiss, but his chuckle stops me. He holds out his hand. "I'm Zane. It's nice to meet you."

When I take his hand, I almost moan from the skin-on-skin contact as pleasure spikes down my arm and heads straight between my legs. I'm sure it's because I'm so damn horny, and has nothing to do with him in particular. If I keep telling myself that, maybe it will be true.

"I'm Becky."

"Well, Becky, do you want that kiss so you can thrill your husband?"

Ohhhh. I peep out a tiny, "Yes," and he wraps his arm around my waist and drags me towards him. His lips are firm and warm, and they taste like chlorine, but as he deepens the kiss, my toes curl against the bottom of the pool as he masterfully takes control of my body with his mouth.

Our tongues duel as passion rips through me, and I try to plaster myself to him. His enormous cock is hard, and I can feel the outline of his length as I rub my body against him. How amazing would it feel to have that monster pressing inside me for the first time?

Trent's passion-roughened voice breaks through my frenzy. "More."

My head spins as Zane eases his lips from mine. "Becky, do you want more?"

I search for Trent, and he's in the cove with us, sitting on the edge of the pool and stroking his cock through his shorts. Knowing he's enjoying this is all I needed to see.

Kissing someone other than my husband feels dirty in such a delicious way. I tip my head up towards Zane, and my resolve is firm. "Yes, more."

Zane studies me and doesn't make a move, and my pussy buzzes angrily that she doesn't have a cock inside her.

"I need to know how much more you want."

The tone of his voice sends shivers down my spine, and I know without a doubt that I'd give him anything.

I don't know what to ask for, and I hesitate. When Trent replies, it startles me. "I want to watch you fuck her."

My nipples harden, and I gasp as I whip my head towards Trent. He nods at me. "It's okay, Becks. If you want this, take the chance."

If the last 24 hours hadn't happened, there is no way in hell I would have said yes. But Trent got so crazy turned on last night, and I've been a wet mess most of the day reading hotwife erotica. This is my shot at doing something wild.

Zane gently holds my chin and turns my head towards him. "Becky, say it and you can have it."

What DO I want? I'm mesmerized by his blue eyes, and my stomach flutters as desire ripples through me. If I'm going to do this, I want something I can't get from Trent, otherwise there is no point.

"I want to be a slut that you use for your pleasure, and I want you to fuck me hard enough to make me scream."

All traces of humor leave him, and his face hardens, leaving behind a man who knows delicious ways to give me exactly what I asked for.

He flips me around and presses my stomach against the edge of the pool. His, "As you wish," is spoken in a calm, firm tone, and he shoves my shoulders down until I'm bent over the side.

He makes quick work of shoving my bikini bottoms down, and since I expect him to slam into my pussy, I reach behind me and grip the edge of the pool. Instead he probes my depths with his hand, and I moan as he explores every inch of my folds. When he threads his fingers in my hair and forces my head up, I arch my back.

"For as long as it takes for me to come, you're my slut. You got that?" he bites out.

My brain blips for a split second and a gush of wetness leaks from me. "Yes, I'm your slut."

Oh hell yeah, this is exactly the type of dirty talk that Trent can't do.

"Good slut. Now we have a few simple rules."

He pulls on my hair again, and I cry out from the painful pleasure as he works his finger in my dripping cunt.

"The first rule is that if you want to stop, say 'red light'. Got it?"

Whoa, did we find an actual dom guy? Shit, I never even thought of needing a safeword when I asked him to fuck me and make me scream.

He removes his hand from my pussy and smacks my ass harder than Trent did last night.

I yelp. "Got it! Red light."

As he caresses the spot he spanked, I melt and relax against him. Mmmm, yeah this is nice.

He's still gripping my hair, and he runs his free hand around to my front and up my stomach until he reaches my bikini top. Pushing it up, he frees my breasts to the cold air and my nipples harden even more.

When he plays with my nipple, rolling it between his thumb and index finger, I can't hold back my moan. Fuck, this is hot.

"Next rule." He pinches my nipple, and I mewl in discomfort from the jolt of pain while my pussy clenches in need like the slut she is. "You said to use you for my pleasure."

"Yeah…"

He presses my chest down on the side of the pool again and forces my head to face towards Trent. "You aren't allowed to close your eyes. You're going to watch your husband enjoying you being used because that would please me."

Ohhhh, shit. I lock eyes with Trent, and he's stroking his cock faster, clearly loving the show.

"Yesssss," I groan when he grabs my hips to steady me as the head of his cock probes my slick entrance.

With me bent over the edge of the pool, my pussy is out of the water, and he's getting a graphic view of how much of a wet mess I am for him. Anticipation lights my blood, and I fight the urge to close my eyes.

With a swift thrust, he impales me, and I cry out, "Ohhhh, fuck."

I knew he was massive, but this is bigger than I expected, and he stretches my pussy walls further than I've been in years. He pauses for a moment, and I barely have time to adjust to his size before he withdraws and slams back into me.

"Oh, my god," I groan and lock eyes with Trent, who is still stroking, but now his cock is outside his swim trunks.

Zane lights into me, slamming against my ass and almost bringing tears to my eyes and driving me towards my orgasm. My nipples scrape against the rough pavement, and it's a glorious pain that shoots bolts of delight straight to my clit.

He's fucking me vigorously while each plunge of his thickness hits a perfect spot inside me. I start chanting, "Fuck me," not caring if anyone outside the cove can hear us.

Zane pounds into me and grits out, "You're just a filthy slut who wants to be used. Aren't you?"

"God, yes…a filthy slut."

He smacks my ass harshly, and I buck my hips as my breasts and nipples smash into the pavement.

"Is this what you want, Becky, to be fucked and filled with my cum?"

Wait, his cum? Lights flicker at the sides of my vision, and my eyes grow round as I stare at Trent. He's got a pained look on his face, as if he's trying not to orgasm. When he gives me a tiny nod of his head, I almost come undone.

I cry, "Ohhhh god, yes, fill me with your cum."

He digs his fingers into my hips, forcing me to move with him as he thrusts at an unrelenting pace. He speeds up and his heavy balls whack against my clit, and I bring a hand up to my mouth, trying to stifle my moans. I'm racing towards ecstasy, and yet I don't want this to end. I'm not sure I'll ever get fucked with this much abandon again, and seeing the lust radiating from Trent adds to my gratification.

When Zane's forceful jackhammering picks up speed, my eyes roll into the back of my head and I sense a movement at my side. Trent is on his knees next to my face as he jerks on his cock, and I can tell he's getting ready to come all over me.

Zane laughs harshly in what sounds like perverse delight at the turn of events as he savagely drills into my pussy.

"Becks…" my dear husband groans, and I'm watching his cock, enthralled and getting ready to close my eyes when he comes. He's panting, and I wish he was in my mouth. "Becks… tell me you're enjoying this."

A sense of calmness invades my mind as my thighs quiver and my body tightens. I'm on the brink of coming, but I want to watch him come first.

I smile at my husband and answer the best I can between Zane's rough thrusts. "Trent…my love…his cock feels soooo amazing. I love you….now come for me."

Trent groans louder, and I close my eyes right as his watery cum hits my face. Having my husband jizz on me while another guy is fucking me is more than I can take, and it pushes me over the edge. Nothing muffles the cries of my pleasure, and I scream nonsense as my orgasm rips through me. My body convulses with the strength of my climax, and rapture engulfs me as Zane continues to pound into me, seeking his own release.

He's so thick, I feel the exact moment he comes. His cock pulses, and my pussy squeezes around him as he growls and unloads load after load of his hot sticky cum as deep as he can inside me. He thrusts into me a few more times before pulling out.

I'm not sure if I black out from the ecstasy, but I'm roused when wet fingers wipe the cum from my face. I swipe the wetness away from my eyes before daring to open them, and Trent is sitting next to me, dazed, with love for me written all over his face.

Zane draws up my bikini panties and adjusts them as Trent caresses my cheek and whispers, "Are you okay, Becks?"

I'm floating in a happy place and give him a dopey grin. "Oh yeah…it's all good. I love you, honey."

He smiles, and I close my eyes again for a moment and drift. I vaguely hear the guys discussing aftercare for me, and Zane is instructing Trent to make sure I eat and drink as soon as possible. I hear mention of our anniversary, but I can't follow the conversation.

A firm hand on my back has me cracking my eyes open, and I turn my head to look over my shoulder at Zane.

"Becky, thank you. This was unexpected. Enjoy your anniversary."

I give him a soft, "Thanks! Bye," as Trent helps me up onto the ledge.

I wobble to my feet and notice Zane has already left. There is enough room to walk the edge and leave the cove. Trent holds on to my hand and starts walking, but I pull on him to make him stop.

"Trent, shouldn't I get in the water to wash off?"

I'm filthy, does he really want me to walk out in public with cum on my face and dripping from another man?

He stares at me seriously before answering. "No, Becks. We don't want to wash away his cum, do we?"

Ohhhh, shit. What did I do? My stomach tightens, and I feel sick.

He squeezes my hand, and he can obviously tell I'm close to panic. "Becky, listen to me…" He tugs again to get my attention. "We both wanted this, and it was fabulous. Let's get to the room and order food. You need food."

"Okay, honey," I murmur, numbly.

Trent helps me adjust my bikini top, and I follow him around the pool to the chair with my stuff. He grabs my beach bag and dries me off with the towel in the bag while I stand there, too tired to think, before leading me up to our room.

CHAPTER 6

Trent zips up my luggage and sets it on the floor before giving me the handle. It was time to leave our little paradise vacation.

After sex at the pool with Zane, Trent got food in me and we snuggled in bed and reassured each other, whispering words of love until we both fell asleep. The rest of the trip was relaxing and wonderful. We talked for hours about the experience and what it meant for us, and I'm not sure yet what this weekend means for our marriage, but I feel more connected to Trent than I have in over a year. The experience with Zane is the jolt our marriage needed, and we both have a spring in our step as we head to the elevator.

We saw Zane a couple more times over the weekend, but we only briefly talked to him and it was pleasant, like meeting an old friend. We found out he owns a couple of bars in Montana and was touring the Oregon Coast while on his first real vacation in years.

As we wait for the elevator, Zane's deep, "Why hello," makes us look at him, and we all laugh. He's got a bag on his shoulder, and he's clearly checking out as well. I slide my arm in Trent's and he smiles down at me.

Another voice joins us. "Going up?"

Oh fuck, it's Kurt. I lean against Trent and hide my head in his shoulder while Zane replies, "No."

Kurt sighs. "I'll wait. The ice machine broke on my floor so I had to come down here." The sound of ice cubes rattle together, like he is shaking his container to prove he needed ice.

The doors open, and Trent and I get in while Zane follows behind and presses the button for the lobby. "Ah yeah, sorry. We're going down. Good luck with that."

I keep my head hidden until the door closes and we all go down together.

The End

SHARED IN THE OFFICE AND BEYOND

If you haven't read my Miranda hotwife stories yet, check out my big bundle of her first 10 stories.

Enjoy the first 10 stories of Miranda's hotwife journey.

The first 5 books are Miranda with her bosses, and then she moves on to being a birthday gift.

When opportunity knocks, does Miranda take it?

Miranda works for four hot lawyers but never considered herself more than just an employee. Her husband suggests they change the boundaries of their relationship and encourages her to hook up with her bosses. This suggestion turns Miranda's world upside down as her bosses bend her over their desks and introduce her to bondage and multiple partners.

The freedom is liberating, and Miranda loves being a hotwife. She's been busy banging her four bosses at work, but then she keeps agreeing to be a birthday gift for various people.

The boss at work who likes to tie her up has her craving domination and she's able to get small samples of it with each birthday adventure. Every new encounter leads up to her own birthday celebration where she finally gets what she's secretly always wanted--a night with her boss outside of the office.

A collection of erotic short stories featuring Miranda and her bosses.

Includes:

Servicing the Senior Partner

Delighting the Boss

Bonding with the Boss

Breaking in the Junior Partner

Miranda's Reward

Harold's Hotwife Birthday

Alec's Hotwife Birthday

Jon's Hotwife Birthday

Chloe's Hotwife Birthday

Miranda's Hotwife Birthday

These stories contain graphic depictions of sex between consenting adults and features elements of hotwife, infidelity, BDSM, bondage, pet play, older men, and office kinkiness. Reader discretion advised.

Find it at your favorite online retailer in paperback or in ebook.

ABOUT LACEY CROSS

I was a bored part-time housewife that turned to erotica writing during the pandemic and found I loved the challenge of writing short and hot. I focus mainly on wife sharing stories with elements of hotwife, freeuse, and BDSM.

My alter ego, **April Cross,** is home for my super filthy erotic romances. I write ghost pepper spicy romances that are really just an excuse to write a ton of sex—preferably with a hint of BDSM—and a happily ever after.

goodreads.com/laceycross
bookbub.com/authors/lacey-cross

www.ingramcontent.com/pod-product-compliance
Lightning Source LLC
Chambersburg PA
CBHW031836310726
48972CB00005B/1300